FAKE

ALSO BY ERICA KATZ

The Boys' Club

FAKE

A Novel

ERICA KATZ

HARPER

An Imprint of HarperCollins*Publishers*

FAKE. Copyright © 2022 by Erica Katz. All rights reserved. Printed in the United States of America. No part of this book may be used or reproduced in any manner whatsoever without written permission except in the case of brief quotations embodied in critical articles and reviews. For information, address HarperCollins Publishers, 195 Broadway, New York, NY 10007.

HarperCollins books may be purchased for educational, business, or sales promotional use. For information, please email the Special Markets Department at SPsales@harpercollins.com.

FIRST EDITION

Designed by Bonni Leon-Berman

Library of Congress Cataloging-in-Publication Data has been applied for.

ISBN 978-0-06-308258-8

22 23 24 25 26   LSC   10 9 8 7 6 5 4 3 2 1

For Daniel, for leaving me locked in the basement
(at my own request) to finish this book and for your
bottomless reservoir of support during a writing process
you didn't always understand but always respected.

Also, you sort of have to read this book now
since it's dedicated to you, right?

(Daniel hates when I tell people that he never read my first
book. I'm just going to leave that right here.)

We have art in order not to die of the truth.

—Friedrich Nietzsche

UNITED STATES DEPARTMENT OF JUSTICE
FEDERAL BUREAU OF INVESTIGATION

June 26, 2021—Federal Bureau of Investigation—26
Federal Plaza, 23rd floor, New York, NY 10278
Unclassified/For Official Use Only

VERBATIM TRANSCRIPTION

Participants:

Special Agent Trevor Garritt
Special Agent Benjamin Tillwell
Emma Caan

AGENT TILLWELL:	Thanks so much for coming in.
EMMA CAAN:	No problem at all.
AGENT GARRITT:	We'll be recording this, so please try to answer all the questions verbally—no headshakes or what have you.
EMMA CAAN:	Sure. Do you always record these conversations? You said I wasn't in trouble.
AGENT GARRITT:	Are you concerned that you're in trouble?
EMMA CAAN:	You guys are the FBI. Has anybody ever not been concerned they're in trouble when you show up?
AGENT TILLWELL:	Fair enough. There's no reason for us to believe you are in trouble with the law.

EMMA CAAN:	That's less than comforting.
AGENT TILLWELL:	Well, we know you're busy, so we'll get right to it. Can you tell us a bit about Gemini Reproductions? What the company is and what exactly you did there?
EMMA CAAN:	I don't understand. You know what Gemini is, Agent Garritt. Intimately. You probably know more about the company than I do.
AGENT GARRITT:	We'd like to hear it from you. Indulge us.
EMMA CAAN:	Okay . . . It's a company that produces handmade copies of high-end artworks.
AGENT TILLWELL:	How exactly is that different from forgery?
EMMA CAAN:	In that we're not forging art. We're copying it. Like how you buy a print of the *Mona Lisa* in a museum gift shop—but higher-end. It is common practice among serious art collectors and museums to have a company like Gemini copy a very expensive painting they own. Then they can place the original in a vault for insurance purposes, or a museum or freeport for tax purposes, and hang a high-quality replica on their wall so they can still enjoy it and impress their guests. If something happens to the copy, a guest spills on it or smokes toward it or there is a fire in the house or museum, the owner is out somewhere between five and fifty grand. If something were to happen to the original, they'd be out millions. Copying is not forging. I have always signed the back of every single copy I've done, with my name, and indicated it was a copy.
AGENT GARRITT:	How did you go about obtaining your clients at Gemini?
EMMA CAAN:	I didn't really have my own clients at Gemini. The clients were clients of the company. I assume Jeremy Jacobsen, the CEO, did a fair amount of business development, but the artists never had to. They were just assigned to us as the work came in.
AGENT GARRITT:	Is that how you met Leonard Sobetsky?
EMMA CAAN:	Yes. He was a client at Gemini.
AGENT TILLWELL:	Do you always meet all your clients?
EMMA CAAN:	No, he's the only one I've ever met. He just came into the office one day and asked to meet me.

AGENT TILLWELL: And that's not typical?

EMMA CAAN: No, it isn't. But nothing about Lenny Sobetsky is
                     typical.

I took a step back to broaden my view and found that the vibrant greens and verdant bursts of purple and blue in my Tahitian country-side mimicked those in his perfectly. I had gotten the shape of the women's curves just right, and they waited expectantly on the porch and in the yard, and my colors shared his exact balance between dazzling and muted, evoking a sense of hedonism and humidity. Still, I wasn't satisfied. I shuffled to my right, so that I was now standing in front of the original. I leaned in closer, my nose almost touching the green and pink impasto, as I narrowed my eyes in an attempt to channel the artist.

I came up empty.

I straightened my back and allowed my cheeks to puff out as I exhaled, acutely aware of a tingle of dissatisfaction at the nape of my neck. My painting was good. To an untrained eye, it would appear an exact replica of Gauguin's rich, confident *Te Fare*, which depicted two women working in a yard and a house with an older woman on the porch, while the mountains of Tahiti stretched skyward in the background. I had used the same unprimed fabric for the canvas that he had, the same paint, the same brushes, the same, the same, the same. I nodded resolutely in an attempt to convince myself I was content with my work, but the tingling endured.

It would be simply too tragic to be mediocre at copying somebody else's work, even if I had already resigned myself to the fact that my own paintings were unexceptional. *Technically superior. Emotionally detached.* That's what my college professor had said about my work. I felt a familiar self-loathing begin to choke me, so

I quickly closed my eyes and steadied my breath. When I opened them, my focus settled on the woman on the porch. I put down my brush and picked a white cotton glove out of the box sitting on the shelf behind me, then pulled it over my palm, so as not to damage the painting with the oils from my hand. I gently placed my covered index finger to the woman's head in the original, attempting to touch whatever inconsistency I couldn't quite find.

The painting I was copying had just sold at Sotheby's for $137 million, and its buyer, Leonard Sobetsky, had given it to my company for us to produce an exact replica. Other clients rarely gave me an original to copy from, but Mr. Sobetsky was particular, demanded I use the same materials the artist had, and often insisted I paint from the original to get the textural intricacies and borders correct. He also always paid his thirty-thousand-dollar fee in advance.

"It's annoyingly perfect." Sienna's voice punctured my thoughts, and with that the noises of the busy studio around me did, too. I turned and looked past her at the large room blanketed in paint-splattered drop cloths, speckled with pairs of easels and my twenty-five coworkers diligently copying priceless works of art. The clock on the wall indicated it was noon, though it seemed like only a few moments had passed since I'd arrived at seven o'clock that morning.

"Not quite perfect," I said. I slipped off the cotton glove and threw it in the trash before grabbing the orange brush and slathering the woman's sturdy legs with an extra coat of paint. I waited a couple of minutes for it to dry, then allowed myself a satisfied smile before turning my attention back to Sienna.

My only work friend was just shy of six feet tall and rail thin. The thick dark hair she tied up in a messy ponytail further accentuated her large almond-shaped brown eyes. Today she wore a gray V-neck sweater over tight black jeans with ripped knees, and not a stitch of makeup, but despite her best efforts to make herself appear average, she was striking in a high-fashion-model sort of way. Her entire personality was almost an apology for her superior genetics—she was kind and funny and took particular care to befriend me when she saw me eating lunch alone during my first week at Gemini.

"There." I motioned to my easel.

"*That* made it perfect?" Sienna gestured at my replica. "You make the rest of us look bad. You shouldn't even *be* copying, with your talent." I inhaled sharply, and she took her cue to change the subject. "Make sure you sign your copies with the new signature pens!" she warned, wagging a finger at me sarcastically.

We had gotten no fewer than three emails and two announcements from Jeremy, our stressed-out, micromanaging CEO, delineating the need to use the new felt-tip markers when we signed the back of our replica canvases. Supposedly, the new markers were "more permanent" than the old ones, as though permanence were something that had gradations. It was an absurd detail for him to harp on while the company's finances were almost certainly in the red and 3D printers threatened our very livelihood, but attention to ridiculous details was par for the course for Jeremy.

"What new signature pens?" I joked, but I felt a tightness in my stomach as I thought of all the new security protocols being implemented and wondered what other changes the consultants would suggest—a leaner employee base, perhaps. "By the way, I left after ten last night, and the consultants were still here."

Consultants had been buzzing around the offices for going on three weeks, and chatter was sprouting up at the Nespresso station in the kitchenette that it was only a matter of months before the experts advised Jeremy to replace all of us with artificial intelligence.

"Was the hot one there?" Sienna raised her eyebrows and giggled. I nodded, wishing that I, too, had a rich boyfriend who paid the lion's share of the rent on our apartment and therefore the luxury of greeting impending unemployment with humor. "You should just ask him out!"

I shook my head. "I feel like there's a conflict of interest somewhere in there. He's about to tell Jeremy to lay me off." What I didn't add was that I preferred the perfect creature I had made him out to be over whatever disappointment of a human he would undoubtedly prove to be.

Sienna had already moved on, though, and I traced her line of vision through the air to Jeremy as he entered the studio, a room he rarely graced with his presence. My coworkers stopped painting, popping up for a view and ducking back down below their easels in a high-stakes game of Whac-A-Mole. I imagined Jeremy's mallet lingering over my workstation as he looked directly at me, then walked directly toward me.

Jeremy usually engaged with his artists only to scream at us or fire us. *I'm one of his best performers*, I reassured myself. None of us liked Jeremy because he was objectively unlikable, but I resented him as well. He had given me a job that lulled me into complacency, sucked out my inspiration, and made me a parasite to the host creativity of others. But still—it was a job I needed.

Sienna quickly returned to her own easel so as not to get caught in the cross fire.

"Emma," Jeremy said, stopping a few feet from me, his musky cologne intruding on my airspace. His well-tailored gray suit made his five-feet-seven-inch frame appear stockier than it actually was, and he had coated his dark hair in a thick layer of product that reflected the fluorescent studio lights back at me. He was probably fifty years old, with what everybody knew to be a hefty trust fund from his father and a textbook Napoleon complex.

"Hello." The word came out feebly and seemed to linger in the still studio air. I cleared my throat and tried again. "Hi, Jeremy."

"Leonard Sobetsky is here. He just showed up," he said, looking annoyed by the interruption. "He's in my office and wants to see you."

I felt suddenly off balance. "Why?" I blurted out before remembering I was speaking to the CEO of my company and the question rang slightly paranoid. "I mean . . ." There was no reason I could imagine for a client visiting the studio besides a massive defect in my work, and I certainly would have noticed a massive defect in my work. "Why?" I repeated, unable to help myself.

"He wouldn't say," Jeremy said shortly, obviously peeved that Sobetsky hadn't given him a reason, either. He shrugged before turning on his heel and heading toward the exit, and I understood that I was supposed to follow.

Sienna, who stood in front of her easel a few yards away, pointed at me and then to her right cheek. I wiped my palm down the side of my face and looked at my fingers, which were covered in white paint. I pulled my sleeve down over my hand, spat on it, and wiped again at my cheek before looking back to Sienna. She gave me a thumbs-up and I hurried to catch up to Jeremy.

I undid my messy bun as I fell into stride beside him, letting down my long hair, and struggled to braid it neatly, knowing I would find dry clumps of the white paint in it later. I dropped my hand and opened and clenched my fist to steady my nerves. As much as I'd been dreading the idea of being laid off for cost-cutting reasons, I was truly panicked at the prospect of being fired due to a mistake I'd made.

My thoughts swirled as I attempted to calculate how long I could live off my most recent paycheck. *A thousand dollars in rent each month, ten dollars a day in food if I stop drinking coffee and eat half a wrap for lunch and the other half for dinner, five dollars in daily subway tolls.* In between paychecks, I almost always paid an overdraft fee for my checking account, and I had zero dollars in my savings account, so the answer was . . . not very long. My mind barreled through worst-case scenarios, lingering on the idea of asking my mother for money for the first time since I had left for college.

"After you." Jeremy held the door open to his office when we reached it, and ushered me in ahead of him. I had never been in Jeremy's office—my awkward interview had taken place in the studio, where he'd watched me paint for three hours straight.

The office was small and flashy, like Jeremy. I scanned the glossy white desk and the painting on the wall and the framed picture of Jeremy and his much taller, much younger wife before doubling back to the painting. *Original Chagall. And I'm making sixty thousand dollars a year while he . . .*

Jeremy saw me notice it. "Isn't it extraordinary? It was a gift from Leonard after the first few copies we did for him," he said proudly. *The first few copies* I *did for him,* I thought.

"Emma Caan, I presume," Leonard Sobetsky said with a mild Russian accent as he rose from the guest chair, where he'd been sitting with his back to me. As we shook hands, he covered my hand with his other large palm. He was well over six feet tall, with a full head of thick gray hair and a clean-shaven square jaw, and even though his large, firm stomach protruded slightly under his camel-colored cashmere turtleneck, he was handsome in a manly way rarely spotted within the confines of New York City. A feeling that we had already met tugged at the corners of my attention. "What a pleasure, my dear!" he boomed.

I noted with relief that he looked happy, even jubilant, which was surprising given his strictly business emails that our staffing director always forwarded to me.

"The pleasure is mine, Mr. Sobetsky," I finally managed, and prayed that when he released my palm, I wouldn't leave paint or sweat residue in his hands.

"Lenny. Call me Lenny," he insisted as he dropped my hand and thankfully made no motion to wipe it clean. I nodded politely, though I had no intention of ever doing so. The three of us stood in uncomfortable proximity in the small office, wondering how we should proceed, as there were only two chairs—Jeremy's and the one our client had just risen from.

Jeremy cleared his throat. "Lenny asked if he could meet you, though I admit I don't completely understand why. But I'm glad we're all here," he said, as if inviting Leonard—I couldn't think of him as Lenny—to explain.

But he simply stood there, giving me an assessing look with eyes so light blue they were almost clear. I wondered how my cargo pants, Hanes T-shirt, plaid flannel, and clogs looked to somebody who clearly took as much pride in his appearance as Leonard Sobetsky did.

"Jeremy doesn't like to let me out of my cage for unscheduled visits," I said dryly, trying to dispel the tension in the room.

Leonard let out an approving snort of amusement, and though I didn't look to see Jeremy's reaction, I expected he was trying his best to hide blind rage that I would dare to undermine him in front of a client.

"Here. Please, sit," Leonard said as he gestured for me to take Jeremy's leather chair on the other side of the desk.

The vein down the middle of Jeremy's forehead bulged, like it had just before he threw a can of paint at my colleague Wade last week for reasons that remain unclear, but before he could erupt, he coolly said, "Let's head to the conference room instead," in an unprecedented display of emotional control. I should have known Jeremy would never risk jeopardizing an account the size of Leonard's with one of his meltdowns.

We exited the office and walked a few yards down the hall to the glass-walled conference room, which was sleek and modern, with impractically delicate chrome-legged leather chairs and a long double-paned glass table. It was where we put clients when they visited, because if they were to see our studio, littered with paint-smeared drop cloths and lined with shelves sagging under the weight of books on Vermeer and Rothko, they might never entrust us with their masterpieces.

When we were seated, Jeremy and I on one side of the rectangular table and Leonard on the other, Jeremy opened his mouth to speak, but Leonard went first.

"I wanted to meet the artist who does such good work. To thank you," Leonard said, leaning back in his chair, which wasn't engineered to recline but yielded to his weight nonetheless.

"My pleasure. It's an honor to work with the originals you've sent me over the years." I straightened my spine, the occasion eliciting my best manners. I found the recognition intoxicating, as it was the first time a client had exhibited a modicum of appreciation for my work.

"Did you study formally?" he asked, leaning forward.

"I was an art major at Yale," I told him, imagining that an undergraduate degree didn't count as "formally" to somebody with Leonard Sobetsky's exposure to artists. I had always regretted not getting an MFA, but with the grades I'd received in my senior studio, it had hardly seemed worth the student loans I'd need to take out for two more years in school.

"Emma is one of our most skilled technicians," Jeremy announced, injecting himself into the conversation.

"Do you create art of your own? I mean, your replicas *are* art. But do you ever paint anything that isn't a copy?" Leonard asked, holding my gaze.

I hated the question, which came up almost every time I told anybody what I did for work.

"Not in a long time." I smiled politely to combat the sinking feeling as I heard the same benign but demeaning tone my father always used. *I think it's brave to shift gears and go into copying. So few artists actually make it. You gave it your best shot.* Leonard watched me intently, his eyes flickering with interest. "I used to, but not since my college studio," I continued. "These days, if it's not a light installation or multimedia . . ." I waved my hand in the air as I trailed off. "Nobody is interested in traditional paintings anymore, which is what I really love and what I'm really good at."

I was aware that people obviously still bought paintings, just not mine, but I still found comfort in blaming market forces rather than my own lack of talent for my failure. Leonard watched me for a moment, more comfortable with silence than anyone I had ever encountered, while I picked at my cuticles under the table.

"Born in the wrong era, perhaps," he finally said, his voice soft. I wondered if I had imagined his response, as I had thought that very same thing almost every day since my senior spring. I watched Leonard carefully, realizing it was my first time speaking to a man with the kind of power he wielded—not the kind my father pretended to have in our small town, where he'd use every waiter's first name and tip more than necessary, or buddy up with the mailman and ask how his kids were doing. Leonard was *actually* important, and when he did speak, his words were unhurried and carried weight, the kind I feared mine so rarely did.

"Perhaps," I agreed lightly, confirming my fear. As a welcome distraction from the topic of my failed career, we both turned slightly to watch the cleaning woman passing by in the hallway beyond the glass wall of the conference room. She wore a purple uniform, long dark hair pulled up in a ponytail, a slight limp to her gait. I turned further, struck by her beauty. She must have been new—she was somebody I would have noticed—but my focus on her was cut short as Leonard slapped his palm to the glass table and rose from his seat.

"Miss Caan, I won't take any more of your time, since I know you must be busy finishing my *Te Fare*. But thank you for the beautiful work. Do you have a card?"

"Not on me," I said, suddenly embarrassed that I didn't have one off me, either. "But you have the office number, and I basically live here." I gave an apologetic laugh as Leonard stared at me blankly.

"Here," Jeremy said, offering him an eggshell-colored business card from a thin metal case hidden in his breast pocket.

Leonard took it reluctantly, as though he didn't understand why he wasn't being given what he had asked for. He glanced at it for a moment then handed it to me. "Could you write your cell or email on the back? I sometimes think of new projects on weekends, and by Monday I've forgotten entirely. It's like robbing you of money when I lose track of what I need copied." He smiled as though there was nothing remotely imposing about what he was asking. Until then, I had felt no flirtatious undertones to our encounter, but I wondered if I'd missed something.

I looked at Jeremy, who just gave me a small nod, sending a reflexive pulse of resistance down my spine.

I turned back to Leonard. "You give us so much business. I could never think of you as robbing us," I said, and smiled obsequiously. "But we have digital voicemail, so if you leave me a message in the office, I get it on my cell right away." I returned the card to him, and he placed it in his pocket, watching me with a seemingly amused half-grin.

"*My* cell is on there. Call me any time at all," Jeremy said quickly. I met Leonard's eyes, and while his expression remained neutral, I was certain he shared my delight at Jeremy's fawning. He broke our eye contact by pushing his palms together in front of his chest, bowing his head slightly, turning, and walking out the door without another word. I noted that the back of his chair was still reclining more than the others, permanently warped into submission to his form.

Jeremy and I sat in silence for a moment as I watched him wrestle with how to ream me out. "Did you finish the *Te Fare*?" he finally asked.

I nodded. "It's drying."

"Have you started on the new assignment from the Met?" He moved his palm lightly across his gelled hair.

"I didn't know a new one came in. I'll talk to Daniella now." Daniella was our staffing director, in charge of assigning the work that came in from clients to Gemini artists.

"Fine," he said tersely, and tapped the nail of his index finger on the glass table twice to indicate I was dismissed.

I returned to the studio and stood in front of my two easels, pretending to focus on them, as Sienna appeared at my side.

"What the eff was that about?" she whispered.

"Leonard Sobetsky was in Jeremy's office," I began. Her eyes widened. "Apparently, he just wanted to thank me for the replicas I've done for him," I added, and she breathed a sigh of relief. "How weird is that?"

"So weird," she agreed. "Why now? Haven't you done like ten assignments for him in the past few years?"

I shrugged. "I did manage to piss Jeremy off, but he couldn't yell at me because we were in front of a client."

Sienna conspiratorially fist-bumped me. "Good job. But back to Lenny—can you even imagine being worth *so* much money?" Her eyes brightened. "*Forbes* has him at fourteen billion last time I googled."

"Um, excuse me." A disdain-laced voice came from off to my left. We both turned to see Wade put a finger to his lips to shush us. Our lanky, skittish, postmodern art specialist maintained a highly inflated opinion of his artistic capabilities despite the fact that he, like the rest of us, couldn't hack it as a real artist. But unlike the rest of us, who struggled daily with the complex brushstrokes of Vermeer and Monet, Wade mindlessly painted Campbell's soup cans on autopilot and silkscreened Marilyn Monroe on a loop.

I started to apologize, but Sienna stopped me. "Wade!" she said, exasperated. "Just use headphones, like everybody else!" She gestured out over the studio at the other painters, all of whom were wearing noise-canceling headphones. "This is a *shared* workspace. Deal with it!"

Chastened, he ducked back behind his easel without another word.

"What's Sobetsky *like*?" Sienna said, speaking more quietly this time.

"He's actually kind of . . ." I began as Sienna watched me intently. A burst of laughter escaped my lips. "There's something . . ."

"A je ne sais quoi." Sienna nodded. "That's how he dates all those models in their twenties."

"Or however you say that in Russian," I said with a small smile. "But no, not that. More that I feel like I know him from somewhere."

"Did you grow up in the Russian mafia?" Sienna asked before taking a quick glance at the round clock above the studio entrance. "I have to get back to work, but if you do have a checkered past replete with KGB hit men, I expect a full report later." She winked and turned to walk back toward her easel.

"You can get offed for saying such things in public," I warned her. She gave me a wave over her head and continued toward her workstation as I grabbed my phone and headed toward the ladies' room for a break before I checked in for my next assignment.

I sat in the last stall and opened Instagram to see what my favorite art world personality, @JustJules, was doing with her day. Art influencers ran rampant on social media, even more so since the impossibly Instagrammable world of art fairs like Art Basel and Frieze—with their drug-drenched, vodka-soaked, billionaire-populated poolside parties—had become increasingly popular with young Americans who had no real interest in actual art. For the most part, Jules and her ilk, who shared their day-to-day doings with the entire world to engage viewers and made money from sponsorships of the brands they used and places they visited, seemed phony and unknowledgeable to me. But not Jules herself—she had grown up in New York City, studied modern art at the Sorbonne, was fluent in French and English, and had a keen eye for talent. She also had two and a half million followers and could make or break an artist's entire career with a single post. Her content seemed genuine and positive, and those private moments I spent in the bathroom, watching beautiful Jules Braun interview a buzzworthy Peruvian muralist, were the closest thing to therapy I could afford since I could no longer take advantage of the Yale Health Center's free student counseling.

I watched the next story, about her heading to the airport, her chic rolling Louis Vuitton carry-on in tow, and boarding a flight to São Paulo to attend her friend's gallery opening. She pulled her *Breakfast at Tiffany's*–inspired eye mask down from atop her thick caramel-colored waves and reclined in her first-class seat, saying goodbye with the blow of a kiss from her palm. The caption read: *Does anybody else sleep better on planes? Or is that just me? Xx, Just-Jules.* I breathed in deeply, enjoying the familiar envy, the covetous quickening of my heartbeat, as I peered into a life so far from my grasp that I felt lucky to have an inside view.

I exited the bathroom into the studio and made my way over to Daniella.

"Hey, hon," she said, never breaking from typing furiously on her computer keyboard. "I have a new one from the Met for you. And we just got a new client in who's transferring the original to a freeport and wants a copy . . ."

"Cool," I said, waiting for the printouts so I could get to work, but she stopped typing and looked up at me.

"It's called *Philosopher in Meditation*," she said carefully, looking back at her computer, still not typing. I hadn't heard of the work, but I had been getting my assignments from Daniella long enough to be able to guess why her eyes avoided mine.

"Rembrandt?" I asked skeptically. She nodded, and I knew from her expression that we'd need to have the same embarrassing conversation we'd had more than once. Obviously, Rembrandt couldn't help that he was born before the advent of the lightbulb, but he did choose to paint the firelight that illuminated his subjects, and as a result I often refused to copy his works.

"Is there a hearth in the painting?" I asked. Daniella nodded and forced her eyes up to me.

"Is there a fire in the hearth?" I asked, and the apologetic downward turn of her eyes answered my question before she nodded.

"Jeremy told me to ask you because it's a new client. But it's no problem if you're not comfortable! I'll give it to Sienna," she said, handing me a printed email from the Met with a falsely casual smile—the kind I, too, would likely give to a person I thought was unstable. "Hang on, I have photos," she said, and headed off toward the printers.

I hadn't expected my fear of fire to be an issue when I joined Gemini. But in my third month here, a full-blown panic attack while copying a torchlight, resulting in a call to 911 and an ambulance carting me away, alerted me and every single one of my coworkers to it. My pyrophobia was no longer relegated to actual fires, and even their two-dimensional representation induced shortness of breath, sweating, and uncontrollable trembling.

Daniella returned and extended the large high-def pictures to me, rolled up and secured with a rubber band.

I scanned the email as I walked back to the studio. The Met

needed a replica of Monet's *Garden at Sainte-Adresse* to hang for a week while they cleaned the original, and they had asked for me specifically. I hoped that personal requests like these might help me keep my job a bit longer.

I placed the two easels supporting the *Te Fares* off to the side to dry further, and set up two new easels, one with a blank canvas and one with the printouts I'd unrolled. I contemplated the pictures for several minutes before kissing the tip of my pencil to the canvas. I lightly sketched the fashionable couple, the blossoming garden surrounding them, the calm sea behind them, and when I couldn't deny the cramp in my hand any longer, I stood up straight, arched my back, and shook out my hand. The clock on the wall indicated it was already eight-thirty.

I could no longer tell if I was always last to leave the studio because I had no social life or because I was so scared of losing my job, but either reason was depressing enough to encourage me to throw in the towel for the day. I pushed the Monet sketch to the side and looked at the two easels of *Te Fare* from a few feet away, unable to keep a small smile from spreading.

The few hours away from the Gauguin and focused on the Met project had proved my suspicion correct: My copy was good—maybe even good enough to pass as the original on professional inspection. I couldn't see that any of my strokes needed editing or revising, so I decided to take the original *Te Fare* to the vault and head home for the night. I stared at the two paintings again, my eyes bouncing from one to the other. What might happen if I marked the original as a copy—would Leonard even notice? Would anyone else? Of course, my code of ethics would keep me from doing so—that and the knowledge that Jeremy had security cameras positioned in the uppermost corners of the room.

I stole a glance overhead. "I wouldn't dare!" I yelled at whomever was watching or listening.

Do you create art of your own? I heard Leonard's words in the air around me as my fingertips pulsed with anticipation. I stared at my perfect replica of somebody else's creative genius and had the uncomfortable sensation that I was disappearing—that I was being swallowed whole by the world around me. I grabbed the green brush and jabbed it into the lower-right-hand corner a few times, feeling as if my hand were possessed. Then I took the brown paint-brush around the exterior, dabbing the canvas feverishly, my heart thudding so intensely that I felt the *lub-dud* rhythm vibrate my rib cage. I dropped the brush to the floor and stared at the small shrub I had just added to my version.

I immediately wanted to take it back, to paint over it and make it disappear. But I'd have to wait for it to dry first, and then wait for the paint-over to dry, and a delay in delivering a painting that I'd already said was done would only draw attention—something I definitely didn't want. I willed myself not to glance up at the security camera again, reminding myself that nothing I had done *looked* suspicious.

"Shit," I whispered, suddenly feeling sick with regret over my impulsive action. I shoved it down in my gut with a hard swallow, reminded myself that my version was only a copy and didn't have to be perfect, and walked a few paces over to the table of supplies. I grabbed one of the new felt-tipped pens from the canister marked *For Signature* and made my way around the back of the easels.

I stared at the raw side of the two canvases and felt my breath catch. I rubbed my eyes with the backs of my hands, still holding the marker. The letters remained, very much real, in black ink: *Copied after P. Gauguin's Te Fare by Emma Caan.*

I didn't remember writing the words, and though they were in my handwriting, they didn't *feel* like words I'd written. *Of course I signed the painting. I must have just forgotten . . .* I managed to partially convince myself, though the plausible alternative explanation that I was losing my mind gnawed at the base of my skull. I shook my head to shake out the thought and replaced the unused marker in its canister. I returned the original to the vault and headed out to grab the 1 train up to Washington Heights.

AGENT TILLWELL: Where were you living when you met Lenny?

EMMA CAAN: Up in Washington Heights.

AGENT TILLWELL: And you commuted down to work every day?

EMMA CAAN: Yes.

AGENT GARRITT: Did you ever replicate works outside of Gemini?

EMMA CAAN: No.

AGENT TILLWELL: You never freelanced on the side for anybody while working there?

EMMA CAAN: No. When I worked at Gemini, I had no other source of income. Every reproduction I did came in through the company. I wish I had been savvy enough to freelance.

AGENT GARRITT: Why do you say that?

EMMA CAAN: No, I just mean, living in a tiny studio in Washington Heights and working twelve-hour days was less than ideal. It would have been nice to make more money. But no, I never freelanced while working at Gemini.

AGENT GARRITT: When you met Leonard Sobetsky, did you think he might be able to help you supplement your income?

EMMA CAAN: No. I didn't. I was thinking that I hoped I wouldn't get fired.

AGENT GARRITT: Were you aware he's one of the richest men in the world when you met him?

EMMA CAAN: Yes. I had read that.

AGENT GARRITT: Let me be more direct—did anything in your life change as a result of meeting your client Leonard Sobetsky while working at Gemini? [pause] Ms. Caan? Could you please answer the question? We're just trying to determine the nature of your relationship with a man facing serious allegations.

I saw my father that night for the first time in months. We just stared at each other with wide, frightened eyes as the fire raged behind him. His mouth was closed, but I could hear a high-pitched wail ring out in the darkness. I finally yanked myself from my nightmare and stopped the screaming in my head by slamming down my alarm. I touched my neck, slippery with perspiration, and peeled myself out from under the covers.

Why?

Why did I still have those nightmares? Why couldn't I get over my fear of flames despite all those years of therapy? I had no answers, and the dead air weighed on me until the drilling mercifully began, as it always did at six-thirty sharp. I was certain the drilling was intended to create a nuisance, to make my apartment unlivable so that I'd relinquish my rent-stabilized studio so the management company could complete the building's conversion into a luxury low-rise like the one next door. What the new management did not know was that the early-morning racket was far preferable to the nightmares it tore me from and the pounding thoughts it interrupted, and so my landlord and I found ourselves in a stalemate.

I popped a set of foam earplugs in my ears, as I did each morning before heading out the door.

"Morning," I said with a nod to the two men drilling yet another hole into the hallway wall just outside my door. They nodded back at me, a mutual understanding of the futility of their work passing between us. The hole would be covered by the time I came home and redrilled tomorrow at six-thirty.

By the time Sienna arrived at Gemini, I had already been working on the Met assignment for the better part of an hour. She raised her coffee cup in greeting as she headed to her station, then paused and veered toward me, an empathetic frown weighing down the corners of her lips. I knew she was contemplating the bags under my eyes.

"You know what your landlord is doing is illegal, right?" she asked. I nodded but said nothing further. She set her coffee down on my stool. "You need this more than I do," she said, walking away before I could refuse it. I took a long sip, allowing it to rouse my senses, and dove back into work, where I stayed focused for the rest of the day with only a couple of short breaks.

The painting was more difficult to replicate than I had anticipated, and I stayed late in the studio, dabbing colors on the canvas in an attempt to match the calm patrician mood of the original. Finally, I looked up at the clock, which mercifully informed me it was just past nine; the runway of lonely evening stretching out before me was comfortably short. I cleaned my brushes and zipped my coat, swiveling my head to peer into the conference room as I headed toward the exit, though I never broke my stride.

As I passed, I counted five men in suits and Jeremy, sitting around the table, which was speckled with iPads, cell phones, and take-out cartons. The thirtysomething sandy-haired consultant whom Sienna and I liked to gossip about had rolled his cuffs to his elbows, exposing tanned and toned forearms. His eyes lifted to meet mine, but I kept going without holding the contact, worried he'd noticed me checking him out.

My cell phone vibrated in my purse and I shoved my hand into my bag, quickly sifting through wallet, keys, Purell container, granola bar wrappers, expired MetroCards, and losing lottery tickets to find the smooth screen of my iPhone. I grasped the sleek rectangle in my hands and freed it, my heart sinking as I stared at the caller ID.

I exhaled and picked up. "Hey, Mom!" I tried for glad-to-hear-from-her, but the words came out an octave below convincing.

"Hi, honey." She sounded low—lower than usual.

"How are you?" I asked as I shoved my shoulder into the revolving lobby door and exited into the biting wind and blaring horns on the corner of Sixth Avenue and Twenty-Fourth Street.

"Good . . . okay. I'm okay," she said, barely above a whisper.

I plugged my left ear with my finger as I pressed the phone to my right. "How was your day? What did you do?" I said, then instantly regretted the questions because I knew what she had done that day, and I felt a pang of guilt that I hadn't called her first.

"I met with the lawyer." She paused. "I'd love to come into the city to discuss some things. Can we have dinner next week?"

I stopped short on the Chelsea sidewalk, dimly registering a grumbled expletive from the man on my heels as he narrowly avoided crashing into me. I had made it clear since the day I'd graduated from college that I would not be taking a penny from my parents. Money was the only thing my father ever provided for me. No stability. No honesty. No affection. Money was all he was capable of giving, but I resented that he thought it replaced those other paternal duties. I knew my mother probably wanted to talk about my inheritance and tell me how much he'd left me, but given my precarious situation, I worried that necessity would win out over integrity if I were to engage with her on the topic.

After the consultants at Gemini wrapped up their review, I guessed that at best, I could get a gallery job that would undoubtedly pay less than Gemini, and at worst, I'd be unemployed. If I got a gallery job, I could bartend or waitress on the side. Anticipatory exhaustion overtook me as I began to push my feet forward along the pavement, New Yorkers not weighed down by financial burdens whizzing past me, and I started down the stairs to the subway and through the turnstile to the 1 train platform.

"Next week is really busy for me, but I will find a time and let you know," I assured my mother as I saw lights burning just down the dark tunnel. "But my train just got here, so I'll call you soon. Love you!"

I hung up just as the brakes screamed on the steel tracks. My brain flashed with the image of my father in the hospital bed, and

I could smell the smoke on his faded blue gown as he pulled me close to ask if I would be "okay" with money after he was gone. The doctor had been in the day before to warn us for the fifth time how harmful it was to continue smoking while undergoing chemo, and I had answered his question by saying that he "couldn't take care of himself, let alone me!" before storming out of the hospital. It was the last thing I had said to my father, and I rarely allowed my brain to access the memory.

The train doors opened, and I wormed my way through people into the cool steel of the subway car and to a free seat in the corner. A broad-chested, bearded man took the seat next to me, his knees spread far apart and his arms hanging casually at his sides. I crossed my legs and curved my shoulders forward, trying to make myself smaller, while he made no such concession. Normally, I would have been annoyed, but today I felt that my insides might have spilled out sideways were it not for the burly stranger and the cold wall sealing me in myself.

That was always how it was for me when I thought of my father. I'd be able to avoid thinking about him for weeks at a time, and then suddenly, I'd be drowning in dreams and memories of him. I wiggled my toes in my shoes as I recalled craning my neck to watch him through the window of the toolshed while my mother was inside in front of the TV; my toes ached from pushing down on them so hard. I stopped there, unable to look directly at those parts of my past that made me feel so heavy, I feared I'd plummet through the subway car floor and onto the tracks. I watched blankly as the doors opened at Forty-second Street, but I didn't switch to the express train, in no rush to be home alone.

I closed my eyes to stop my head from spinning, but flashes of the funeral, the flowers, the heavy makeup on his hollowed-out face, rushed in on me. I peeled my lids open and looked around the train at the dozens of people packed in, wondering how many were playing mindless games on their phones because they were bored and how many were doing it to quash their more painful thoughts and emotions. I opened my Solitaire app and played until the train pulled into the 168th Street station, where I climbed out into the overworld and made my way to my five-story walk-up. My building's lobby featured a tastefully tiled foyer floor, now dulled with grime between the inlays, with small slopes of muck in the corners that no amount of scrubbing could remove. It wasn't luxurious, but it was the first place I was able to call mine—no roommate, no parents—and because of that, it had felt like a haven at first.

I climbed the three flights to my apartment, peeled off my coat, and flopped onto my bed with phone in hand, prepared to see what @JustJules was up to. Instead, I noticed an email indicating that I had a Gemini voicemail. I dialed my extension, entered my passcode, and pressed my phone to my ear.

"Emma. Hello." The "h" came from the back of his throat as a "ch," with a wet crackle. "It's Lenny Sobetsky. It was a pleasure meeting you yesterday. I'd like to invite you to a charity event at my home. We always receive a great turnout from the art community, and I think you would really enjoy it. Please call me back and I'll tell you more." He recited his number once, then hung up. I listened to the message again, not quite sure I had heard correctly. I called Sienna, but it rang once and went straight to voicemail. A text from her popped up before I had a change to leave a message.

> At dinner with Michael. First time I've had dinner with my boyfriend this month! Never date an investment banker! All good?

I stared at her text for a moment. I couldn't quite figure out how the entire city was constantly going on dates and falling in and out of love, or why people had so much success on dating apps that only reinforced the sense I had that my life was not one that was appealing to share. I didn't have tons of friends or travel to exotic places or dine in trendy restaurants. I looked around my small studio, an ache in the pit of my stomach forming, and composed a text back.

All good! And roger that! Enjoy. We'll talk tomorrow. X

I opened Instagram and watched as Jules filmed herself lying in her hotel bed, telling me she would soon be heading to California for the inaugural edition of the Frieze Art Fair in L.A., the West Coast version of the New York standby. Her green eyes shone despite no makeup, and her honey-brown hair spilled out over her white pillow. *I am so lucky to live this life, but sometimes the planes and the hotel rooms get old, and I miss my apartment and my friends. Feeling lucky. And lonely. And tired. Anybody else? Or is it just me? Love you all. Xx, JustJules.* I nodded against my own pillow and sent her a bunch of floating hearts in a reply, one of thousands she was probably receiving. I then clicked through to the feeds of the artists and friends she'd tagged in the picture, and when I had been through them all, I turned to watching her live feed until sleep overtook my eyes.

In the kitchenette at Gemini the next morning, Sienna hunched up her shoulder to hold the phone to her ear as she listened to Leonard's message. She handed the phone back to me as her eyes narrowed over the lip of her mug and she sipped her coffee.

"It's so weird," she said, and paused for another sip. "If you told me that a rich male client asked you for your number and, when you wouldn't give it to him, he called you at work and invited you over, I'd absolutely say he was hitting on you." She cocked her head. "But it doesn't *feel* like he is . . . Plus"—she took out her phone and moved her thumbs rapidly across the screen's keyboard—"he has a girlfriend." She handed it to me, revealing a picture of Leonard with a leggy brunette on a red carpet. "So why not call him back and tell him you'll go?"

"I know, I know." I shook my head, though I was agreeing with her. "I will. I just can't shake the feeling that he wants something from me. Why else would he be doing all this?"

"Maybe he just wants you at the event." She bit her lower lip. "You can't really *not* go. He's a client. And he's well connected, and . . ."

"We're going to be out of work soon," I finished her sentence for her.

"Bingo," she said with a definitive nod. "Think of all the gallerists who might be at a Leonard Sobetsky party! I bet you Florence Wake will be there. Who knows, you could get a job from her. Or you could slip somebody your portfolio and get your big break!" I felt a pang of guilt as I passed on yet another opportunity to tell Sienna that I already had submitted my portfolio to Florence Wake and fourteen other galleries, after graduation, in the hope that my professors had been wrong about me. After fifteen submissions and, in an almost impossibly cruel turn of events, sixteen rejections when two different people at the Petzel Gallery reviewed my work separately and both passed, I had resigned myself to copying the masterworks of others.

"I'll call him," I assured her. "I can't afford not to."

Resolving to do it before I lost my nerve, I made my way over to the row of black phones on the back wall of the studio, selected my extension, and called the number he'd given me, expecting a secretary or assistant or whomever typically answered rich people's phones to answer.

"Emma!" he bellowed into my ear. "I'm so glad you called."

I paused for a moment, taken aback by how casual he sounded.

"Hi. Hello. Mr. Sobetsky. Hello." I inhaled sharply and checked over my shoulder to confirm that I was out of earshot of my co-workers.

"Lenny," he corrected me. "I know you're busy, so I'll get right to the point. I'm on the board of a charity, Young Picasso, that offers college art scholarships to high school students each year. I host an event at my home to honor the five winners and raise funds, and it's on Thursday. I would love for you to come." He stopped speaking and I knew that I was supposed to respond, but nothing came out. I had never been to a charity event. *What's the dress code? Where is your home? Who will I talk to? Is it a sit-down dinner? Who will I sit with? Am I coming as your date?*

"It'll be quite a collection of people in the art world. Gallerists, artists, auction houses," he continued.

"I'd love to come," I said before I could chicken out.

"Wonderful! My assistant, Micaela, will be in touch with details." He paused. "Should I have her email you at Gemini?"

I thought for a moment. "I can send you my personal contact information. It's probably easiest that way," I said, knowing Jeremy monitored our emails and definitely would have something to say about the invite. There was a beat on the other end at the phone, and I realized that I was giving Lenny what I had denied him just days before. I wondered if he was the type of man who always got exactly what he wanted eventually.

Even before Micaela emailed me the invitation to the party, I couldn't stop myself from envisioning the evening ahead. I thought of which gallerists I might meet and tried to keep my brain in check, but still I saw my art hanging in their sleek West Chelsea spaces. I thought of the men who might flirt with me, and how I'd say something impossibly clever and charming about the new craze for NFTs despite not fully understanding the purpose of owning something others could replicate for free with a screenshot or by saving a JPEG file. I imagined one of them would ask if I'd come work for him after I explained the benefits of the market for underpaid digital artists. But first I had to figure out what to wear, and I realized I'd need to enlist Sienna's help on that front if I didn't want to stick out like a sore thumb.

"I think I like this one best!" I yelled from a Gemini women's bathroom stall on Wednesday as I looked down at the hunter-green silk slip dress that clung to every inch of my body.

"Come out of there already! How can you tell what you like best if you don't look at yourself in the mirror?" Sienna shouted back at me.

I exited the stall. Sienna was perched on the small piece of countertop between the bathroom sinks, her feet dangling. She looked me up and down and nodded resolutely. "You look beautiful," she stated, as though it were an indisputable fact. "It looks way better on you than it does on me, honestly." She dispensed compliments the way only people who were constantly receiving them were comfortable doing.

I backed away from the mirror so I could see as much of the dress as possible, twisting from side to side to view all the angles.

"It's too tight," I finally decided, shaking my head.

"You're crazy! You look amazing," she said, laughing. "And it's longer on you than on me but, annoyingly, I like it better this length!"

I turned to the side and twisted my head to look at myself. The color was captivating—deep and dark and seemingly alive, like moss.

"Are you sure this is cocktail attire?" I asked.

"Positive."

"Are you sure you're comfortable lending it to me? I'll dry-clean it after," I promised.

"Emma! Positive!" She thrust herself off the countertop and slid up behind me, pushing my long blond hair out over my shoulders so it cascaded down the green straps. "Shoes?"

"I have," I promised her, trying to recall the last time I had worn the black strappy sandals my mother had bought me before Yale and hoping they were still somewhere in my closet. Sienna looked skeptical that my shoes would suffice but opted not to press the issue.

"I have a feeling the night is going to be awesome. And you'll look great. First-Instagram-post-worthy," she joked, making fun of the fact that I had never posted a single photo.

"You just want me to take pictures so you can see the inside of his house," I teased.

"Yeah—Zillow has it estimated at thirty-nine million! Obviously, I'm only dressing you in return for pictures. Was that not clear?" She turned and began to pack up the three other options that she had brought for me to try on. "Oh!" she said, approaching my side and taking my cell phone. "Unlock it," she commanded. I did and watched her fiddle around on it. "If I'm wrong and Leonard Sobetsky is about to sell you into sex slavery or something, you're now sharing your location with me."

"You better come rescue me," I said.

"I promise I will," Sienna said. "But now I gotta get back to work." She slipped the extra dresses into her tote and headed for the door.

"Thank you again!" I shouted after her as she exited. I stole one final look in the mirror before changing back into my paint-spattered clothes and returning to the studio for another long evening of work.

CHAPTER

3

AGENT TILLWELL: Did you ever see Leonard Sobetsky outside the office?

EMMA CAAN: Yes.

AGENT GARRITT: And what did—

EMMA CAAN: Sorry to interrupt, but just to be clear, all of our encounters were focused on art, even the ones outside the office. All of them.

AGENT TILLWELL: All? So you spent a good deal of time with him? Would you say you got to know him well?

EMMA CAAN: I don't know. I don't know how well anybody really knows Lenny Sobetsky.

AGENT GARRITT: What was the first time you saw him outside of the Gemini offices?

EMMA CAAN: He invited me to a charity event at his home for an organization called Young Picasso.

AGENT TILLWELL: Could you describe for us the art in his home? To the best of your recollection.

EMMA CAAN: The art in his home was incredible. All modern, lots of pop art. Hockneys, Kusamas. It was mind-blowing.

AGENT TILLWELL: Did you meet anybody else at the party?

EMMA CAAN: Yes. It was a party. I met a lot of people.

AGENT GARRITT: Anybody in Leonard Sobetsky's inner circle, so to speak? People close to him?

EMMA CAAN: He hosted the party. Practically everybody was in his inner circle. But he introduced me to Florence Wake, the gallerist. And his best friend, Sergey Bartenev. Is that interesting? What are you writing?

AGENT TILLWELL: Just taking notes. To help us when we look back.

---

* * *

I twisted the ends of my hair around my finger as my Uber turned off the FDR Drive onto East Seventy-First Street and headed west, the streets growing more sterile as we got closer to the park. Not wanting my hair to curl, I occupied my fingers by running them over the black leather seat beside me, marveling at how much nicer an Uber was than a subway car. It was worth the three meals of ramen noodles I'd be eating that weekend to balance my weekly budget. I pulled my foot backward in the strappy sandals I had found smushed under the bed after a frantic search, releasing the pressure the front strap placed over my toes and remarking at the red indentation it had already formed. How did women do this every single day? I looked at my watch, noting it was already thirty minutes past the party's start time. I'd had a little mishap while trying to apply the lessons of the smoky-eye tutorial I'd watched on YouTube and had to start over, but I thought I looked okay. I opened my mouth as wide as possible and shut it, convinced I could feel the foundation on my face crack into tiny pieces.

Finally, the car slowed to a stop across from the incredible limestone-and-brick facade of 4 East Seventy-Fourth Street. The doorway was flanked by impressive columns, and my gaze drifted up to a carved stone balcony. A man stood just inside the wrought-iron gate wearing a coat with a fur-lined hood, consulting a clipboard before ushering in two women, one of whom wore an elegant flowing white cape, and the other, a floor-length chocolate-brown fur coat. I hadn't realized capes were in fashion or that people still wore real fur, and a rush of fear that I was completely out of my element made my breath quicken. I continued to stare from the backseat of the car, wondering if I should simply turn around and head home, as I ran my finger over the green silk blanketing my thigh, the dress I had thought elegant just moments before now seeming gauche.

The man—was he a butler? Did people still have butlers?—held the door open for the ladies and turned to a man in line behind them who was wearing dark jeans, white sneakers, a white shirt, and a blue tie hanging loosely around his neck. My sense of dread that I was underdressed was replaced by confusion—I had no idea what appropriate attire for the evening was, given the sample size of guests I'd just seen.

"Have a good night, miss," the driver said, politely encouraging me to exit. I thanked him and stepped out of the car. Suddenly embarrassed to be wearing a bulky brown winter coat, I hastily removed it and shoved it amid the flowerpots outside the town house across the street from Leonard's, saying a silent prayer that it would still be there when I returned. I shivered in the February air, wearing only the silk slip dress, and did my best to hurry gracefully across the street, feeling that my ankles might betray me at any moment as they wobbled in my high heels.

I made my way up three of the stairs, now feeling invigorated by the frigid temperature, but tripped up the last one. I stumbled forward in two clumsy steps before I felt strong arms on mine, catching me before my face met the concrete landing. My cheeks reddened as the embarrassment settled in, and I met the butler's concerned eyes, cursing the fact that I had worn Crocs every day since college because they were the only thing that supported my back for the long hours standing and could be run under a sink to wash the paint off.

"Are you okay?" he asked kindly in a Russian accent, not letting go. Two men in suits approached from the street and watched me with slightly stupefied expressions, clearly having watched my near-faceplant from the steps below, before continuing their ascent.

"Mortified," I whispered, my cheeks growing hotter. "But fine. Thank you."

"Name?" he asked, releasing his grip and picking up his clipboard from where he had dropped it to catch me.

"Emma Caan?" I asked my name as though it were a favor and immediately began to justify my presence. "I should be on there. Mr. Sobetsky is a client—"

"Here you are," he interrupted me, but continued to read something off his clipboard. "Oh, yes." He looked up at me and smiled broadly. "Micaela asked that you wait just inside for Mr. Sobetsky. I'll let him know you're here." He opened the door and leaned in toward me. "I think you dropped your coat on your way in. I'll have it waiting for you on the way out," he said quietly, then stood up straight and winked as I blushed yet again. "Enjoy!" he said as he opened the door for me, already turning his attention to the men behind me.

I stood inside with my jaw slackened, stuck in place by the lavish room before me. Manhattan town houses look perfectly elegant from the street, but I realized that it was impossible to fathom their grandeur from the outside. The heavy door (black wood with a brass tiger knocker) had opened into a gaping foyer of white marble swirled with soft gray. My eyes drifted to the people dotting the space, but my attention continued up over their heads. The walls were a deep, dreamy blue-gray bordered with white molding, and a modern chandelier of blown golden-colored glass hung in the center of the ceiling. The dark wood staircase, with a plush runner, seemed to stretch on for at least five stories. The house was elegant and modern and absolutely nothing like what I had expected, given Leonard's traditional taste in art. The security guard touched my arm, reminding me that I still hadn't taken a step through the door, as he attempted to close the door behind me.

Spanning the length of the foyer was a gigantic, richly colored David Hockney painting of a swimming pool; my brain struggled to fathom what it must have cost. People dotted every corner of the foyer, and beyond them stretched a great room of black hardwood floors and white furniture. Guests plucked drinks and canapés from passing silver trays and held them calmly in their fingers before leisurely sipping or nibbling at them, as though they were accustomed to an unlimited supply of both. To my relief, some women wore gowns, while others wore pants and loafers. One tall woman with purple hair wore an oversize men's dress shirt and high-top sneakers, while one man wore full makeup and fake eyelashes and a well-tailored conservative navy suit. There was no discernible dress code, so while I might not have fit in, I was pretty sure I didn't stand out.

As the people swirled around me, I sniffed the air and was immediately transported to my parents' country club, where we would have dinner every Sunday when I was growing up. The scent was clean and unbothered—good French soap that had never mingled with the rancid odor of the subway or sour, anxious perspiration. The people drifting throughout the $39 million town home smelled not of perfume but of privilege, a scent that could not be bottled or bought, and I wondered if they'd notice I smelled like Pert Plus two-in-one shampoo and conditioner.

"Emma, my dear! So glad you could make it. You look wonderful!" Leonard appeared a few paces from me, and I watched the people around me clear room for his path. He held his arms open as he approached, and I thought he might hug me, but he took both my hands in his and leaned in to kiss me on my right cheek. I straightened before realizing he was then about to kiss me on my left and recovered quickly to do the same.

"Thank you. Thank you for having me," I said, flustered. "I didn't know what to wear . . ."

Leonard made a *pfft* sound with his lips. "Anything goes at an art party. I don't even know why I bother to put a guideline on the invitation." His eyes drifted left to a man in a perfectly tailored charcoal-gray suit, crisp white shirt with no tie, and a black leather dog muzzle over his mouth. Leonard touched his temple as though the man's outfit pained him, then smiled and leaned in close. "The more absurd you look at an art party, the more talented people think you are. Because people are fools," he said, and winked.

I let out a small laugh and relaxed my shoulders just as a petite blonde approached, wearing enormous black sunglasses though it was eight o'clock at night and we were indoors.

"You've outdone yourself, Lenny!" she exclaimed as she kissed him on both cheeks.

"Cassandra Taylor, Emma Caan. She's a budding artist I discovered," Leonard said, and I wondered if I had ever seen Cassandra's art. "Emma, Cassandra is the manager of the Barnes Foundation in Philadelphia."

I should have been completely consumed by being in the presence of somebody who managed one of the most impressive collections in America, but instead I was fixated on the fact that, if I had understood correctly, Leonard had just referred to me as a "budding artist."

Cassandra leaned in close to kiss my right cheek, then my left. "I look forward to seeing your work!" she said with a polite wave before she was absorbed back into the sea of people.

"Friendly!" I commented to Leonard.

"Took me a while to get the hang of the double kiss as well. In Russia, we shake hands," he said with a shrug.

I suddenly remembered that he was playing host to throngs of people. "I'm sure you have tons of people to—"

"I do," he said, but he made no motion to leave my side.

A beautiful young woman dressed in a tea-length black dress offered me a glass of red or white wine as Leonard turned to greet a tall, suited man. I smiled politely and extended my hand toward a glass filled with golden liquid.

"No," Leonard said, holding out his hand to stop me from taking it, and his friend shook his head as he noted my outstretched arm.

I retracted my hand, embarrassed that I had somehow overstepped and misunderstood my place at the party. Had I not been invited as a guest? Was I there to work? *I shouldn't have taken a drink, should have waited for him to tell me what my role is* . . . I clasped my hands together in front of my midsection and squeezed, wanting to punish them for embarrassing me.

"We'll get the good stuff." His friend cocked his head toward the expansive living room, speckled with mingling guests, and clicked his tongue as though coaxing a horse forward.

"Have it if you like, of course!" Lenny clarified. I smiled broadly and shook my head at the waitress to decline the drink as politely as I could, curious to see what these two men considered "the good stuff."

"Sergey Bartenev," the man said with a thick Russian accent, extending his hand to me. He had wavy brown hair and pock-marked skin evidencing a battle with teenage acne. "Lenny and I know each other from back in Russia," he said, the accent completely evaporating when he spoke English, then added with a smile, "Before it was Russia."

Lenny gestured for me to follow them, and I trailed behind as they forged a path in the crowd. Progress was slow; Lenny continually stopped to play host. As he did, I scanned the living room to see if any of my work was hanging, though the walls were covered not with impressionist works but with neon Warhols, and the floor was punctuated with pedestals displaying Yayoi Kusama's yellow-and-purple-spotted pumpkins. We finally arrived at a bar set up along the far wall, with a bartender standing at the ready.

"What can I get you?" Lenny asked me.

I worried that any drink I could think of would be considered somehow bourgeois. "I'll have whatever you're having," I finally said.

"We drink vodka," he warned me, and Sergey nodded.

I smiled with a confidence I didn't feel. "Vodka it is."

Lenny leaned over the bar, speaking Russian to the bartender, who then crouched out of view for a moment. As he did so, Lenny's attention was taken by the gray-haired woman next to him.

"You're a painter," Sergey said, studying me as we waited for our drinks.

"How did you know that?" I adjusted my posture and self-consciously wondered how I'd revealed that I was not part of the art-patron demographic, but he just smirked and pointed to my right hand. I followed his direction to my cuticles, still green from the day's work. "Ahh, I get it. No, I just work for a company that replicates high-end art," I explained, not sure if Leonard would want it divulged that he had his works copied.

Sergey's eyes lit up. "Oh! I know you! Lenny tells me you're the artist responsible for all his impressionist replicas."

"That's right." I allowed the word "artist" to linger sweetly in my ears for the second time that night, though as I scanned the room, I wondered again: Where were all the priceless paintings I had copied for Lenny? Even if they didn't quite fit with the decor of the room before me, why would anyone spend that kind of money on famous paintings and then hide them away?

Sergey seemed to read my mind. "The more," he started, then paused as if choosing his next words carefully, "timeless pieces are displayed in his homes in Switzerland and Monaco, mostly. And the originals are in Delaware, of course."

"Delaware?" I asked, then quickly realized why it might be there. "Oh, freeport?"

Sergey nodded and leaned over the bar to see what the bartender was doing, while I recoiled in embarrassment. Asking if somebody was making use of a freeport was tacky, and I winced at the thought that I had offended Sergey and my host.

I had never even heard of a freeport before working at Gemini, but every so often I was assigned to copy some magnificent master-work for an unnamed client with the instructions to hand the finished product to a bonded courier sent by the client, so we'd never know its destination address. Sienna had explained once that these were almost always copies of works stored in freeports, one of the primary benefits of which was secrecy—mostly a benefit to the owner, who would never need to declare ownership and there-fore would never be taxed on the purchase of the paintings. I had read a good deal on the topic over the years, but the best I could figure was that I didn't have enough experience with money to re-ally get how they worked—aside from keeping paintings safe. From what I understood, most paintings were bought by completely legitimate means and stored there with the sole purpose of main-taining the integrity of the work, but they inevitably were stored beside pieces paid for with drug money or pieces that hadn't been paid for at all. Years ago, the Geneva Freeport had been investi-gated when a piece by Modigliani looted from a private collection by the Nazis during World War II and valued at $63 million was found there. Since then, a shocking number of international art collections had been moved to Delaware, whose veil of secrecy had never been breached.

Thankfully, the bartender had reappeared with a clear, frost-coated bottle of vodka, decorated with the etching of a stag where the frost hadn't accumulated, and proceeded to pour it into what looked like three tiny wineglasses. Leonard had extricated himself from the gray-haired woman and signaled a waitress with a platter of miniature pancakes topped with tiny, glistening black beads.

"Blini with caviar?" she offered.

Leonard and Sergey each popped one in their mouths, and I fol-lowed suit. I had never had caviar, and I nearly gagged as the dark orbs of seawater burst on my tongue before my taste buds leaned into the delicate, briny flavor.

"Always eat with vodka," Sergey instructed me. "Actually, every time food is offered while drinking, eat it." He gave me a sideways grin and I nodded, relieved that he seemed totally unbothered by my faux pas.

We held up our glasses, and Sergey declared some Russian word with authority as we clinked our crystal rims together. "To your health," Lenny translated. I was about to shoot the vodka, like I'd done at college parties, before I noticed him taking just a sip. Grateful that I hadn't yet gone full American sorority girl, I sipped it as well. The vodka was so cold that I tasted it only at the very back of my throat, when my tongue had warmed it enough to register the sharpness of the alcohol.

"Tell us what you're working on right now," Sergey said, turning to me eagerly.

I swallowed, finding their attention confusing, as we were in a roomful of far more interesting people, but relishing it nonetheless. I was suddenly transported back to my childhood home when my father would call me down to meet his friends after golf and they'd ask me questions about school and my art classes that I'd answer as politely as I could.

"I'm about to begin on a Renoir for the National Gallery," I said, hoping that exercising discretion in not naming the title was enough. I never quite knew if my clients would want their use of my services made public.

"Do you enjoy your work?" Leonard asked. "I couldn't ask you that in front of your boss."

I thought for a moment longer and shrugged, still slightly self-conscious. "I don't love it. But I don't think I'll be doing it much longer, so it doesn't matter."

"Why is that?" Sergey inquired, taking another blini off a passing tray. Leonard and I did the same. I was uncertain whether it was the vodka or the energy in the room giving me a buzz, but either way, it seemed prudent to put more food in my stomach.

"The company isn't doing very well. Consultants have been analyzing our office procedures for a few weeks now. It's just a matter of time before they suggest that AI take over for us." I took another drink of the clear liquid, which had warmed in my hand and now burned my throat on the way down. I felt a shift in the energy of the men that I couldn't quite describe.

"What firm are they with?" Leonard asked.

"Actually, I don't know," I said, furrowing my brow. "I've never met any of them. They only meet with our CEO. Things seem a bit . . . tense around the office since they got there. New security guards, new security measures . . ." I heard myself babbling as a waiter holding a tray of shrimp and oysters nestled in a bed of ice magically appeared. I reached for one, following Sergey's earlier advice and welcoming the opportunity to plug my lips.

"It doesn't sound like leaving would be such a tragedy, then. What do you want to do next? If it's anything in the art world, there is somebody here who can help," Leonard said, and gestured around the room.

"Actually, I have been applying to galleries," I told him, looking out over the crowd. "It would be great experience, but I'd probably need a second job if I did that. Gallery jobs are great stepping-stones, but the pay is—"

"Florence is here, isn't she?" Sergey asked Leonard before I could finish.

"Florence Wake?" I was almost afraid to ask, knowing the entire rest of my evening would be consumed by the thought of talking to her.

Not only was her gallery esteemed, but Florence herself was a celebrity in the art world—known not only for her uncanny ability to connect artists and collectors but also for her aptitude with predicting and generating trends in contemporary art through her work with emerging artists. She was rarely photographed and seldom interviewed, a puppeteer of sorts pulling strings from out of sight. I wasn't even certain I knew what she looked like; I wouldn't have been able to pick her out of the crowd.

"She's a dear friend. I'll introduce you," Leonard offered.

"That would be incredible," I said, my jaw slackening slightly.

"Sergey and I just need to do a bit of handshaking and then . . . are you okay if . . ."

"Please! I'm fine. Thank you so much." I waved them off and looked around the room as though I had other people who were keen to speak with me. "Thank you for having me!" I said. "Did I say that already? I meant to."

Leonard gave me a slow downward nod, and Sergey turned to him and said, "You're right. She is charming," before they disappeared into the crowd.

I felt off-balance though standing perfectly still as the room swirled around me in an intimidating display of talent, wealth, and bizarre outfits. Mercifully, the vodka began to unwind the knots in my body, and I felt my arms and legs relax, the petite glass growing heavy in my hand and my ankles wobbling slightly above my high heels. I cursed passing up all the country-club parties my parents attempted to drag me to in high school, thinking perhaps I wouldn't feel quite so out of place now if I'd gotten that practice, but this wasn't upper-middle-class pseudo-intellectual suburban Philadelphia, this was a roomful of the most established and promising members of the elite art community and wealthy philanthropists. I took a longer drink from my glass, tipping my head back to get the last drop before placing it on the bar.

"Would you like another?" the bartender asked. A faint voice in my head advised against a second glass of straight vodka at a party where first impressions mattered, but I nodded. "Of . . . um . . . of the same?" he asked, as though mentally debating whether he'd be allowed to refill my glass from what I assumed was his boss's personal reserve. I didn't have a chance to respond before he retrieved the stag bottle, giving me a wink as he poured.

"Cheers," a deep voice next to me said. I turned as a tall man extended his stout glass filled with brown liquid to my delicate small one; I watched his glass clink gently against mine, sending vibrations up through my arm. I raised my glass to my lips and took him in: his tanned skin offset by greenish-hazel eyes, his tall and slender frame, his dark gray suit with no tie. I studied his face while searching for something clever and sexy to say to the most attractive man I had ever encountered in person. He finished the sip of his drink and placed the glass back on the bar, his movements elegant.

"Ryan Parker," he said, focusing on me for only a moment before turning to look at something over my shoulder. I followed his eyes to a woman whose long, silky brunette waves covered her bare shoulders. She wore a snug canary-yellow cocktail dress that hugged her hips in a way that commanded the focus of the people she weaved between. I turned back to Ryan Parker, prepared to recapture his attention, but before I could introduce myself, he said, "Excuse me," touched my arm with his free hand, and started off into the crowd after the dazzling brunette.

I stared as the crowd swallowed them both. "And I'm Emma Caan," I said quietly to myself, internally rolling my eyes at my own social ineptitude.

I wandered along the perimeter of the room in the hope of spotting him again and took the opportunity to study the paintings that Leonard had chosen to display. After two laps, I swallowed the rest of my drink and began to give up hope of meeting Florence Wake or seeing Ryan Parker again. I didn't know for sure why I had been invited in the first place, but I was certain Leonard had already forgotten I was there.

"There you are!" He appeared at my side. "I've just told Florence about you. Come!" He held his elbow forward for me to link arms and pulled me toward the front door. "Florence!" he yelled at a woman standing in the foyer, talking to a man wearing an entirely white tuxedo, carrying a white cane, and sporting a white scarf that covered the portion of his face below his eyes. Florence was small and slender, with the smooth porcelain skin of a young woman, though I knew she'd owned her gallery for at least twenty years and had started it at the age of forty. Her brown hair was cropped in a pixie cut, revealing petite diamond studs that sparkled brilliantly despite the dim overhead lighting. She wore a crisp white button-down tucked into a pair of tailored black tuxedo pants and black patent pumps. I would have looked like a waiter in her outfit, but she looked like Audrey Hepburn.

When she saw Leonard, she smiled pleasantly and excused herself from her conversation with the masked man with a touch to his arm. The world slowed to match her pace as she drifted toward us with an ease and control that rivaled Leonard's, and when she finally stood before us, she kissed the air next to each of Leonard's cheeks.

"Florence, this is Emma Caan," he said as he placed his hand on the small of my back and pushed me forward slightly. I braced myself for embarrassment, as I worried she'd recognize my name from when she'd rejected my art, but her expression remained placid, sprouting only a polite smile as she extended her delicate hand toward mine.

"Pleasure," she said, her voice almost entirely drowned out by the conversation and music swirling around us.

I leaned in even closer. "It's an honor," I said, then shook her hand too eagerly.

"Emma is a dear friend, and she's in the market for a gallery job," Leonard declared.

"Well, any friend of Lenny's . . ." she began, then looked at me. "Why don't you come by to interview next week?" I watched her lips continue to move and dimly registered something about her assistant contacting me. Then the two of them laughed at something he had said, and she waved politely and left my side. *Was that it? Did I just get an interview at Florence Wake?*

"Thank you so much, Leonard," I said, then corrected myself. "Lenny." He was right, the nickname suited him far better. But in all my excitement, I'd forgotten the depressing reality of my financial situation. I could barely make ends meet on my Gemini salary, and giving it up before I was forced to seemed foolish. "I'm sorry. I don't think . . . I can't take a position at a gallery," I said as I stared at the tips of my shoes sheepishly, realizing that I stood under a chandelier that likely cost more than I stood to earn in my life. "I don't want to waste her time if—"

"It's perfect!" Lenny grabbed two glasses of champagne off a passing tray and handed one to me. "You told me Gemini is in trouble. And I still need replications done, because Lord knows I'm not going to *stop* acquiring art any time soon. You can work at Florence's and freelance for me! It's perfect!" I tried to catch my brain up to his. "I must admit, my intentions behind inviting you here tonight weren't entirely selfless. Did you know I paid Gemini sixteen grand for the last Monet you did for me? I bet you saw pennies on the dollar for that. It's to my benefit to have you work for me directly and cut out the middleman. But of course, I understand somebody with your talent won't want to copy full-time. Between freelance and Florence's gallery, I'd guess . . ." He trailed off. "You know what, I'll make certain you don't regret the move. In fact, I have a project I need soon. You can start immediately."

I imagined what it would be like to live without the constant dread of defaulting on credit card payments and bartering for any luxury with instant ramen, how nice it would feel to check the mail without worrying about the bold red print on my ConEd bill. I nodded slowly, allowing my brain to cautiously approach the idea that for the first time in my adult life, I could be financially stable. I nodded more definitively, and I surrendered to whatever he had planned for me.

The next time Lenny left my side, I was drunk enough to confidently entrench myself in a conversation with the white-tuxedoed man about Julian Schnabel's latest exhibit and how it related to his upcoming and much anticipated film. Halfway through my blathering about the symbolism of a butterfly as I sipped my drink, a little boy yanked on the side of my dress.

"Do you want to see a magic trick?" he asked. I looked around, wondering just how drunk I was, what time it was, and where the boy's parents were. "I'm going to make you disappear!" he said, his blue eyes widening for dramatic effect. He took out a small pad and drew a smiley face with a black marker. He added three large strands of hair, then declared, "That's you!"

"I could tell. Looks just like me," I said, bending low and reminding myself to remain balanced. He turned around, fiddled with something in his pocket, and spun back around. The piece of paper was now entirely blank. I opened my mouth as wide as I possibly could. "How did you do that?" I gasped.

He giggled in delight. "A magician never—" he began.

"Alexei, I said it was time to go!" A tall woman in chic jeans burst through the crowd, grabbing him by the arm and hauling him off without so much as a word to me. I looked around for the tuxedoed man, hoping to continue our conversation, but he was already gone.

"Everyone's disappearing," I smirked to myself as I wobbled off to get one last drink.

AGENT GARRITT:	Can I ask—how old are you, Ms. Caan?
EMMA CAAN:	Twenty-six.
AGENT TILLWELL:	How old is Leonard Sobetsky?
EMMA CAAN:	I have no idea.
AGENT TILLWELL:	He's sixty-one. Don't you think that age difference makes yours an unlikely friendship?
EMMA CAAN:	Why did you ask me his age if you know already? [pause] What do you want me to say here? I guess. Maybe?
AGENT GARRITT:	Why do you think he took such an interest in you?
EMMA CAAN:	I think Lenny and I shared a common interest and it bonded us. I viewed him more as a . . . parental figure in my life. I had never really had one of those.

My hangover the next day was tempered by the excitement of the night on the town, and I suffered only a hint of motion sickness as I rode the 1 train from Washington Heights to Chelsea, reliving the hazy memories and grateful I had gotten my coat back, though I couldn't recall the man at the door giving it to me. Flashes of the outfits at the party and the silk of my dress on my skin, the sting of vodka in my throat and the salinity of the caviar on my tongue, Florence's delicate hand in mine and Lenny's easy words in my ears. My Uber app indicated I had taken a car home just past midnight. I felt deliciously alive for the first time in far too long.

Sienna picked up a salad for lunch, while I attributed my instant

ramen to hangover cravings rather than the uncomfortable truth of
my budget having been tapped out by two Ubers in a single night.
It was the kind of day that tricked New Yorkers into thinking we
had put the bite of winter behind us for the season, so we took our
food to Madison Square Park and found a bench in a thick beam
of direct sunlight. I swept the park with my eyes, watching faces
tilt toward the sun, invisible solar panels on foreheads recharging.
I knew I'd emerge overconfident the following day in a sweater
instead of a down jacket and sneakers instead of boots, because
despite all evidence to the contrary, I always fooled myself into
thinking fair weather was permanent.

I told Sienna about Lenny's home, the sheen of the marble and
the colors of the Hockney, as I pulled the not-soft-enough noodles
through my lips. We leaned in close to each other, and she giggled
as I described the man with the white scarf covering his face and
the one in the dog muzzle.

"And . . ." I said, trailing off to increase the suspense. "You're
never going to believe who I met."

"Who?" Sienna stopped chewing and waited.

"Florence Wake!"

"What? No way. I heard she never goes to art events. How
did you meet her?" She put her salad down and squeezed my
forearm.

"She's a friend of Lenny's."

Sienna raised an eyebrow. "Lenny? Is that what we're calling him
now?"

"Anyway, Florence said her assistant would set me up with an
interview, but who knows if that will actually happen." I shrugged,
trying not to get my hopes up.

Sienna let go of my arm and leaned back on the bench. "Wow,

that's . . . amazing," she said, her tone flat as her eyes searched the treetops.

"What?" I asked, studying her face.

"Nothing." She shook her head. "I'm happy for you. It sounds like an amazing evening. What I would have given to be there . . ."

"Shit," I said. "I forgot you applied for a job there." I inwardly cursed my insensitivity.

"That's okay. That's how gallery jobs work—you don't get one without a personal connection. Screw my dad for being an accountant, right?" She forced a laugh, but it came out as more of a snort. "I'm happy for you," she said softly. "Give me a sec—I will be happy for you. Right now I'm jealous."

"Can I change the subject?" I asked.

"Begging you to."

"I met the hottest guy at the party." I knew I was stretching the truth a bit, but I so rarely had fun news to share, and I couldn't pass up the opportunity.

"OMG. Tell me everything! Did you make out? Did he take your number?"

I resisted the urge to stretch the story past reality and shook my head. "But I felt this really intense connection to him. It was so strange," I said.

"Ughhh, I miss that feeling. I've been with Michael so long, I'm pretty sure I've forgotten how to flirt." She frowned. "I don't think he has, though. I think he flirts at work. I guess that's the trade-off for him paying for the apartment."

"I'm sure he doesn't," I assured her as my phone vibrated in my pocket. I picked it up to see a text from my mother reminding me to set a date for dinner, and a new email that almost made me drop my phone.

From: leah.moniker@florencewake.com
To: Emma Caan
cc: Leonard Sobetsky, florence.wake@florencewake.com
Subject: Interview Scheduling

Hi Emma—
Florence would like you to come in to interview for the Assistant
Director position of our New York gallery. Please let me know
your availability over the next few business days, as Florence
leaves for Art Basel Hong Kong in a few weeks and would like to
meet with you before then.

Best,
Leah
Leah Moniker
Executive Assistant to Florence Wake

I read the email twice, blinking hard in between reads to keep
my eyes honest. Leapfrogging intern and assistant positions and
going right to assistant director would bypass the mundane grunt
work, the fetching of coffee, the feeling of being underappreciated.
But most important, it might mean the salary could be enough to
live on even if Lenny didn't come through with his freelance work.
Lenny. I stared at the cc: line of the email, understanding exactly
why I was being offered an interview for that position.

"All good?" Sienna asked, watching my face carefully. I wrote
back that I was available at Florence's convenience on Tuesday and
locked my phone quickly.

"I'm supposed to have dinner with my mother at some point," I
said, which of course was part of the truth. I started to imagine the
conversation with my mom about the will, and I placed the Styro-
foam ramen cup on a wooden slat of the bench beside me, the

artificial chicken smell suddenly making my stomach lurch. I had an idea. "Do you want to come to dinner? Maybe Monday? You'll love my mother." That much was true. Barbara Caan was excellent at first impressions. "Please?"

"Would love to," she said, and smiled.

On Monday at five o'clock, my mother texted me that she was outside Gemini an hour earlier than she'd said. She assured me there was "no need to rush," as though that made her timing less invasive. I closed my eyes and took a breath to curb my irritation before walking over to Sienna's workstation. "My mom is early," I said, still annoyed. Sienna pulled off her headphones and let them hang around her neck. "My mom is early," I repeated with an eye roll toward the ceiling. "You're still working." I pointed at her easel. "You don't have to come."

"I'll just clean up a bit and come right down," she said cheerily, overcompensating for what she could tell was my foul mood.

I exited Gemini and saw my mother's pristinely kept older-model Lexus, once the nicest car in my car-pool line but now one of the oldest on the street, illegally parked with the hazards on. She claimed she didn't want to get a new one because it had all the memories of carting me around as a child, but I suspected she'd also never leased or bought a car without my father to negotiate for her, and she didn't want to start now. I made my way to the car to see that she was staring straight ahead, hands frozen at ten and two on the wheel despite the fact that she was parked. As I opened the passenger door, the click of the handle seemed to jolt her back to the present.

"Hey, Mom!" I said brightly, hoping that if I pretended I didn't know what kind of mood she was in, she'd in turn pretend to be in a better one. "I have good news! My friend Sienna is going to join us for dinner." As my mother turned her whole upper body toward me, I registered the difference in her appearance since I had last seen her. Her thick dark hair fell messily over her shoulders, and I could tell from how it was slightly slicked back that she had been running her hand through it, the way she always did when she was anxious. She had lost weight since I'd seen her over the holidays, and the impossibly high cheekbones that always inspired strangers to ask her if anybody had ever told her she looked like Ingrid Bergman (she always pretended it was the first time anybody had ever told her that) looked as though they might pierce through her translucent skin.

She pursed her lips. "I was planning on keeping it casual. I thought we could even order in at your apartment because we have things to discuss," she said, pulling down the flap above her head and flipping the plastic rectangle up to expose a mirror. *Exactly what I'm trying to avoid.* She studied herself for a moment before snapping it shut. "I really wish you had told me she was coming. We don't have a reservation." Her eyes darted up and down the street as though a *suitable* restaurant would reveal itself to her.

"Mom, Sienna is fine with ordering in. She doesn't care. She just wants to meet you," I said, but my mother's phone was already to her ear.

"Hi, this is Barbara Caan," she announced, as though that meant something to whoever was on the other end. "Could you possibly squeeze three of us in for dinner . . . nowish? I know it's late notice, but I'd consider it a personal favor." There was a hint of desperation in her tone. "Thank you!" She glanced over at me with a self-satisfied grin and a thumb in the air as she hung up. I opted not to mention that a five thirty dinner was not a difficult reservation to snag. "That's settled," she said quietly, her lips tightening as though resisting a frown.

"Are you okay, Mom?" I asked. She raised her large eyes to mine as though preparing to divulge a secret, but then looked out the passenger window and straightened her spine. I turned to see Sienna waving eagerly.

"Hi, I'm Sienna," my friend said as she climbed into the backseat.

"I'm so glad to finally meet you. Thank you for joining us," my mother said, rising to the occasion.

"I wanted to say that I'm so sorry for your loss, Mrs. Caan," Sienna said, cocking her head to the side the way everybody did when referencing my father's death.

"Call me Barbara," my mother insisted, ignoring the condolences. "If it's okay with you, we're going to head to Giorgio's, just a few blocks away."

There were only two occupied tables between the scarlet walls and thick burgundy velvet curtains in the dimly lit dining room. I saw a small flame on each table, and I resisted the urge to extinguish them all as we passed. I leaned over the small votive candle in the middle of our table and blew it out quickly when Sienna wasn't looking. She knew the vague details of my pyrophobia, the nightmares and anxiety, and she'd always been supportive, but having me practically tachycardic at the sight of a romantically set table probably wouldn't make for a relaxed dinner.

"Emma's father and I used to come here all the time," my mother explained to Sienna as we perused the menu. Provided with an audience who didn't know that he drank too much, cheated on her constantly, and smoked himself to death, my mother slipped into recounting old, whitewashed stories of my father with a well-rehearsed, nostalgic smile. We ordered and Sienna nodded politely in response. When the food came, I savored each bite of my veal Milanese, wondering if I'd have the willpower to stop eating and wrap up the rest for lunch tomorrow, checking back in only when my mother told her the story of how I wandered out of the hotel lobby during a vacation in the Bahamas when I was six years old, and they found me in the middle of the dance floor at a stranger's wedding.

"Emma must have been the funniest kid," Sienna said.

"And the cutest," I heard my mother say as I zoned back out, wondering what the assistant director position at Florence Wake would pay and whether I might be able to come back to Giorgio's on my own dime soon.

"Oh my God!" Sienna exclaimed. "So cute!"

Shit! I whipped my head around to see Sienna fanning out the accordion of school pictures that my mother carried in her wallet.

"Oh my God, no!" I tried to lighten my emphatic objection with a smile as I grabbed at the photos, but Sienna pulled them out of my reach.

"I'm dying!" she said, and pointed to my eighth-grade photo, holding it up for me to see. "What the heck happened to you between seventh and eighth grade?" she asked before dissolving into giggles.

I settled back down in my chair, my brain sparking with flashes of flames and screams and my father's horrified eyes. I stared at the beaming seventh-grader in the baby-blue sweater, perched above the photo of the solemn eighth-grader wearing too much black eyeliner. My mother shifted in her chair, and I realized the silence was bordering on awkward. I plastered a smile on my face and touched my temple in feigned light embarrassment, but in reality I was teetering on the edge of a panic attack.

"I saw *The Addams Family* on Broadway. Twice!" I said with a shrug, retreating to emotionally solid ground.

While Sienna started to tell me about her own "Goth phase," I stole another glance at my eighth-grade self and wondered how the sadness in her eyes could have eluded Sienna.

"I have an announcement," my mother said, tapping the teeth of her serrated knife to the rim of her water glass. I didn't know if it was intentional, but I was grateful to her for changing the subject. "I'm selling our house." She sat up proudly as Sienna looked to me to gauge the appropriate reaction. "Emma's childhood home," she clarified to my friend.

I stared at her. "But . . . you love that house!" I said, while Sienna politely focused on her Bolognese.

The house I grew up in was a stone structure of almost seven thousand square feet in Ardmore, Pennsylvania, perched atop a rolling front lawn and abutting a nature preserve in the back. A house of that size always came with expensive and time-consuming projects—to address cracks in the roof, floods in the cellar, termites in the attic, dated decor. Every ounce of upkeep came with a dramatic groan from my mother and the comment "*This* is why I can't go back to work." I suspected it was the work of maintaining the house and the status my mother thought it granted her in the community that kept her above the sadness always lingering just below the surface, even before my father got sick.

"It's just *too much* house," she said, and I knew making such a statement was a particular source of pride for her. "I'll downsize, move closer to town. Simplify." She gave us a resolute nod.

"Well, I think it's great," I said, but I felt my heart begin to pound in my chest, and my breaths started to come more quickly, each shallower than the one before. I took a long sip of water to break the cycle of nerves I could feel spinning out of control, the red dining room that had been cozy moments before now seeming bloody and tyrannical. I excused myself to the ladies' room and leaned in close to the mirror, staring at my reflection.

I blinked, but she was still there, in my eyes, the girl from my eighth-grade photo. I wondered if she had reappeared or if she had never left. I saw the flames then, devouring the toolshed. I remembered my breaths escaping in tiny puffs of vapor in the chilly October night. Finally, my eyes watered, obscuring my adult reflection as well as my childhood memory. I blinked again, ran my hands under cold water, tapped my cheeks to bring me back to the present, and returned to the table in time to convincingly participate in the discussion about what to order for dessert, though my mind remained engulfed in flames.

It was still early when we finished our tiramisu, and Sienna went to surprise Michael at his office to steal him away for a drink before he settled in for a long night of work. I walked my mother to her car in silence, Sienna's absence relieving us of the need to fake joviality or even speak at all. I wanted to ask why she was selling the house but couldn't figure out how to without sounding as though I was opposed to the idea, which I was not.

My mother broke the silence. "That dinner was more expensive than I planned on," she said as we reached the car. I'd never heard her comment on the price of anything, unless she felt it was her duty to warn somebody in a dressing room that "cheap is cheap" in order to "save her" from an ill-advised purchase.

I opened my mouth to apologize for the choice of restaurant before remembering I hadn't chosen it. "I'm sorry," I said anyway, because I didn't know what else to say. "Thank you for dinner. Text me when you're home, okay?"

She nodded and slid into the driver's seat, closing the door behind her and rolling down her window to lean out and kiss my cheek as I bent toward her. I watched her car turn west toward the Lincoln Tunnel and asked Siri to set an alarm in two hours so I could make sure she had gotten home safely.

I walked back toward the West Side and descended underground to take the train uptown. When I got home, I opened my computer and clicked through the Florence Wake website—losing myself in the incredible photos of the current art on display in the galleries in New York, Rome, London, and Berlin. I was just googling the latest artist to sign with Florence Wake in London when my alarm went off, reminding me to check on my mother.

EMMA: Home?

MOM: Home! I loved tonight. Thank you for the most wonderful evening I've had in a while.

I reread the word "wonderful" and felt my brow furrow. I hadn't thought she'd enjoyed herself, but she had always operated under the assumption that she could revise the past by using adjectives in the present. *We adored each other. We were happy.* I shrugged and turned back to my computer.

The next day, I ducked out of Gemini a bit before my usual lunch break and grabbed the N train down to SoHo, making it to Florence Wake one minute before my interview was scheduled to start. The brushed concrete floors were punctuated with white pillars holding up the impossibly high ceiling. The walls were covered with massive paintings that basked in the glow of thoughtfully placed overhead lighting. There was a desk a few paces in from the entrance.

"She's not here right now, but she'll be back any moment. Have a seat," the glamorous auburn-haired young woman at the front desk said politely. "I'm Leah, Florence's assistant." Leah Moniker, I recalled from the email signature.

She fetched me a sparkling water, and I sat in a white leather chair, tapping my fingers anxiously on its arm, just across from the sleek reception desk, where Leah filed her nails behind the glowing apple of her silver MacBook Air. I watched her hold her hand up to the fluorescent light and examine it before lowering it and continuing to file. The smooth concrete floor gave off a chill, the vents pumped delicate floral notes into the air.

I attempted to calm my nerves by placing my hands on my torso, and occupied my eyes with the pieces gracing the gallery walls, skimming over the cursive neon writing instructing me to "Kiss me and tell me you love me," and pausing on the oil painting of a topless pregnant woman with shockingly large nipples. I lost myself in her flushed cheeks and peaceful eyes and felt my heart rate slow. As I reached for the glass of sparkling water Leah had given me and spotted my wristwatch, my pulse quickened yet again. Florence was already running twenty minutes late, and I had only forty-five left before people at Gemini would start to wonder why I hadn't yet returned from my break.

I felt a draft as the door opened, and I whipped my head around, hoping it was Florence. Instead, I saw a beautiful young woman wearing a caramel-colored cashmere trench over a white sweater and jeans, perfect long brown waves framing her face. Even if I were to spend hours every morning primping and pruning, I would never look as chic as she did.

Leah looked up from her nails for only a moment, her eyebrows arching curiously before she returned to her cuticles. The other woman lingered at the wall just past my chair, taking in the painting, and I could smell her rich sandalwood perfume. I turned to see a large contemporary painting of a small crowd sitting in the tiered stands around a boxing ring. Some of them pointed with their mouths agape, others held up their iPhones to film the ring with their lips twisted in horror, and a few others smirked sadistically. The viewer experienced the painting from the vantage point of a fighter in the center of the ring, able to see only the ropes while staring up at the crowd, no opponent in view. I studied the expressions of the crowd and could hear their jeers, their cheers. Reflexively, I searched for the painting's flaws. It was admittedly brilliant in concept, making me feel as though I were involved in a fight that I could have been either winning or losing, but there was something painfully elementary about the brushstrokes.

The woman in white took a large black camera out of her bag and attached a square flash to the top, then removed the lens cap and took a step back. She twisted the black barrel to adjust the focus, and I heard a series of mechanical clicks as she began to snap photos. I turned away until the clicking stopped, then looked back to see her standing just a few feet from the wall, head cocked to one side, considering the painting carefully.

"What do you think of this?" she asked. I looked up to confirm she was speaking to me. For the first time since she had walked in, I noticed her face under her thick hair. I felt my eyes widen despite my brain's command not to react as I tried to formulate an appropriate response to the woman I had stared at on my phone for years. Any social nicety or artistic insight I'd ever used eluded me as I was faced with the sight of @JustJules in the flesh, even more beautiful in person.

"What?" I asked to buy time, my eyes darting quickly around the room. I registered the scene before me. How was I standing in Florence Wake Gallery, waiting to interview with Florence Wake herself for assistant director, and meeting the woman whose life I'd been coveting for years? Lenny Sobetsky's face popped into my head. I understood that meeting him might have changed the trajectory of my entire life, and for the first time in a very long while, I felt supremely lucky.

CHAPTER

5

AGENT TILLWELL: When you went to interview at Florence Wake, did she seem skeptical that you were qualified for the position, given that you were coming from Gemini?

EMMA CAAN: Isn't the concept of an interview predicated on the idea that all employers are skeptical that applicants are qualified?

AGENT TILLWELL: Fair enough. But you had never worked in a gallery. Did you ever doubt you were qualified?

EMMA CAAN: Sure. I think that's just my personality, though. I also think that is a perfectly appropriate concern to have at some point when interviewing for a large promotion or a new job entirely. Were you unequivocally positive you were prepared to be an FBI agent when you began at the Bureau?

AGENT TILLWELL: Hmm. Did you ever contemplate not taking the job? Did you feel you could have said no to it?

EMMA CAAN: I don't think I understand. I certainly had the free will to say no to the job or not interview, if that's what you're asking. But as soon as I entered the gallery and saw all the art on the walls, I knew Florence Wake was the place I wanted to work. Plus, Gemini was tightening security and establishing all these protocols, and Jeremy was more stressed out than usual, and I just thought the company was becoming a less than desirable place to work. A job at Florence Wake is a dream.

"What do you think of this?" Jules repeated.

I sprang out of my chair too eagerly and walked over to stand beside her. As I got closer, I could see that the colors were slightly

muddled, and technically, the faces in the crowd were nothing spectacular. I looked at the name on the small plaque beside the work:
Fighter, Fredrick Thomas, New York, 2018. There was no price posted,
though I knew he was selling well from the research I had done over
the weekend. The sour taste of jealousy that my technically superior
paintings had never made it onto the wall of any gallery coated the
back of my throat, blocking my words until I swallowed.

"Well, he's already drawing crowds," I said, giving her a half-
smile. She watched me curiously for a moment and then looked
me up and down. I felt a rush of wind as the gallery door opened
again, but I was too busy regretting my stupid joke to see who had
entered.

"That's really good. Jesus. That's good," she said, her voice
deeper and less polished than it was in her videos. "I pay somebody
to caption my posts, and she's never come up with anything that
clever. Can I use that?"

"It's all yours," I said proudly, too flattered to feel aggrieved that
she didn't write her own content.

"Emma," a voice to my left said loudly, and I turned to see Florence. "Shall we?" she asked, then turned on her heel and headed
toward the back of the gallery.

Jules's eyes flashed toward me, and her lips pursed slightly as she
extended a hand to me. "Emma, is it? I'm Jules."

"I know. I follow you," I said, and it somehow sounded far less
creepy than I feared.

"Thank you! I have the absolute best followers!" she said at a
higher octave, sounding much more like the Jules I knew online.
"What's your handle?" she asked.

I instantly regretted my admission. I had only twenty-two followers, and I had never posted anything, which made me look like
an Instagram parasite, or nobody, or both. What would Jules think
of that?

"I'm at ecaanart," I said quickly, hoping she wouldn't know how to spell it. "I really have to go. Nice meeting you!" I turned and ran after Florence without giving Jules a chance to respond.

Florence was just taking a seat behind her tinted gray glass desk when I peeked in. There was no art on the walls of her office nor any clutter, not even any paper around her small silver laptop. The wall on the left side of her desk was taken up entirely by a massive whiteboard calendar for March and April, with every weekday and most weekends neatly packed with appointments written down in perfect penmanship. I continued to stare, realizing that somebody as busy as she was surely didn't review every submission that came across her desk, and hoping that mine was one of those that hadn't made it to her.

"You brought a friend to your interview?" she asked. Though her tone was completely neutral, I saw a hint of disapproval in her eyes.

It took me a beat to understand what she meant. "Oh! No, I've never met her before. I mean, I *know* who she is. But she just came into your gallery a few minutes before you did."

"Who *is* she?" Florence asked dryly.

"She's an art influencer," I ventured carefully, not knowing what Florence would think. "On Instagram."

"I don't have Instagram," she said in a way that made me embarrassed I did. She looked at me carefully. "I'm thinking of banning photography in the gallery so nobody can post about the art. Do you think that would be prudent?"

I could tell that it wasn't small talk but an interview question, though it wasn't one I'd prepared for. My mind raced forward through possible answers and how they would be received.

"No, I don't," I finally said. "Galleries are meant to be social experiences, a place for the meeting of art minds and a way to experience art as it *should* be experienced. But not everybody is lucky enough to live in New York, or in the vicinity of great art, and not everybody can travel to it. Instagram is an excellent way to reach the masses and a powerful marketing tool to sculpt an artist's career. That being said, people think it *is* a substitute, which is misguided. I think galleries need to work even harder to create experiences people want to attend so they can realize the benefits of viewing art in person." Florence bent down and rummaged around in her tote, pulling out a manila folder. I paused, slightly thrown by her lack of attention, but forced myself to conclude my argument. "I suppose the extra effort is a burden for galleries. But still, Instagram is a useful tool for them, in my opinion."

"What about NFTs? And virtual galleries for buying them?" she asked. I wiped my brow as inconspicuously as possible. Another question I hadn't prepared for, on another hotly debated topic in the art world. I cursed the hours I'd spent researching new artists Florence might want to sign and debating the economics of a larger supply of work despite the risk of diluting demand for any given piece. *Stupid.*

I knew NFTs stood for "non-fungible tokens," like a one-of-a-kind bitcoin made unique with the imprint of the creator, and that digital art was the poster child for commonly traded NFTs. I knew they traded on a blockchain like bitcoin, although in truth, I didn't know exactly what a bitcoin was. I did know that I had just made the argument that Instagram was a useful tool, and my best bet was to remain consistently pro–technology and innovation.

"I haven't really educated myself on the intricacies, but I do think that a virtual showroom would provide a market for digital art that never existed before and would allow digital creators to support themselves. I also think, regardless of my personal opinion, it's a huge market. I have no idea whether it's a bubble, but there is a lot of money to be made in that space right now."

Florence studied me carefully. "Why would somebody spend money to own an NFT when the entire world can download them for free?"

"You could say the same about copies of tangible art," I said.

She pursed her lips. "Copies are never as good as the originals," she said plainly as she pulled my résumé out of the manila folder and gazed down at it. I couldn't help but feel stung, though I reminded myself I had no pride in copying the works of others, and I was sitting here in an attempt to stop.

"You only studied at Yale?" she asked. I winced at the use of the word "only" and swallowed, a knot of panic tied in my stomach. I inhaled and told her about my formal training at Yale, my experience at Gemini, my passion for modern art (a stretch of the truth), and my own paintings. I searched for any recognition in her eyes when I mentioned my own art, but she just nodded slowly and asked about the replicas I did for the Met.

We chatted a bit more before Florence looked at her watch and then at the calendar on the wall beside her, searching for something amid the hundreds of appointments meticulously penned into March's squares. I didn't know if I had lost her interest, if she had to run to another appointment, or if she had a reservoir of tough questions that she was about to tap into.

"We'll start you at eighty-five thousand a year and full benefits. That's nonnegotiable," she added, leveling me with her eyes, though I couldn't imagine trying to negotiate up from a raise of twenty-five thousand dollars. "I'll need you at Art Basel in Hong Kong the third week of March to man our exhibit," she continued. I felt myself staring at her. "Emma?"

"Yes! Yes. I can be there," I managed to get out.

"Wonderful, we're so happy to have you on board," she said without a hint of a smile. She stood and straightened her blouse, extending her hand, and I rose and pushed my palm to hers.

"Sorry, just to clarify . . . I have the job?"

"It's yours to lose," she said. I realized I was still holding her hand, and I let go. "We create the modern art market here at Florence Wake. We don't drop prices. We don't lose artists to other galleries. We get everything right the first time. Mistakes are not tolerated. Do you understand?"

"Yes." I nodded, my eyes wide. "Thank you! I will give Gemini my two weeks' notice today." I pushed my palms together and bowed my head to her in gratitude, something I had never done before, but it seemed an entirely appropriate gesture to give somebody who had just dramatically improved my life.

"You might want to see if they'll let you start sooner so you have some time here before Hong Kong," she said. I could tell it wasn't really a suggestion. Even if I could have started that minute, I would have been wildly unprepared to represent a gallery at an art fair. I had been to only one art fair, at the Armory in New York, and that was because Jeremy had gotten a few free tickets that he'd handed out to us. I didn't know even the basics of what representing an international art gallery entailed, where to be, how to act, how to sell.

"You'll fly over with Lenny," she stated. My heart sank as I realized I'd need to explain to my impossibly successful new boss that I couldn't afford to fly first class with Lenny Sobetsky—that I couldn't afford to fly to Asia at all. "On his plane," she added, as though it were a matter of course.

My breath caught as I understood that she and Lenny had already agreed upon this plan and that my performance in the interview was a formality. The job had been mine the moment Lenny introduced me to Florence.

"I can't thank you enough," I said, forcing up the corners of my lips. I was aware how lucky I was to have landed a job at Florence Wake, to have no unpaid days between leaving Gemini and beginning there, to be offered a private flight to Hong Kong, but I heard my father's voice in that moment: *A favor is just a socially acceptable way to make people feel indebted to you.*

"Is something wrong?" Florence asked.

"Nothing!" I assured her, dismissing him from my mind. "I'm just so happy!"

For an instant, knowing this cheapened the thrill, but in its place grew a cautious bud of hope that the "unlucky" label I had branded myself with my entire life might be fading, and I reminded myself that I was overdue for a lucky break.

I returned to Gemini from my interview not too long after I would normally have from lunch. Given that nobody except Sienna even glanced up from their work when I entered, it didn't seem like anybody else had noticed I was gone. I rushed back to my workstation, meeting Sienna's quizzical gaze from across the room with a smile. I looked out from behind the easel at the studio sprinkled with canvases and the brushes that slid across them, the stools supporting paint palettes and coffee mugs, my coworkers rushing to create works that weren't theirs for people who didn't know their names. The room felt smaller, less important, than it had that morning. I didn't *need* it the way I had six hours before.

When the vast majority of my twenty-five coworkers had left for the evening, I ventured toward Jeremy's office, both dreading and looking forward to sharing my news. When I had finished my "this experience has been invaluable, but it's time for me to take the next step" speech, he leaned back in his chair and inhaled sharply.

"Congratulations," he said. "Do me a favor and try to finish up your current projects before you leave? Whatever you can't finish, we can assign to somebody else." If Jeremy was remotely upset that I was leaving, he was hiding it well, which I found insulting. I had given him five years of my life, after all. "And if I can give you some advice, stop copying—even freelance. Try to paint something original," he concluded. "Just a suggestion. You have the talent."

I nodded. "Thank you for saying that."

"If you want to start at Wake sooner rather than later, you have my blessing, as long as you complete or hand off any current projects."

I ignored the bruise to my ego at the idea that I was so disposable and chose to focus on being able to get in more training for the fair. "It would be great to start next week. I can finish everything by then," I said. As I stood and shook his hand, I wondered if I had misjudged him entirely.

On the subway home, I analyzed the day's interactions—with Jules, with Florence, with Jeremy—until I found myself standing on the street in front of my apartment. I ran my forefinger over the teeth of the key, then promptly tossed it back in my purse and turned on my heel.

The bar across the street from my apartment—not the gastropub where all the young surgeons from the hospital down the block went, which served duck confit fries, the other one—was the kind of place people went to drink alone in public. It was dark and narrow and smelled of stale beer. There were three men perched on stools around the L-shaped bar in the back, all of whom appeared to be over sixty, with their eyes glued to the hockey game on the television mounted above the rows of liquor. All the tufted green leather booths were empty. I took a seat at the far end of the bar, ordered a vodka soda from the young female bartender, and took out my phone so I didn't need to pretend to watch hockey.

I sipped my drink mindlessly through my straw, trying not to feel pathetic for celebrating my new job in a dingy sports bar by myself, the mild flavor of alcohol percolating up through the fizz so I could taste it as I scrolled through Instagram. Jules had posted a series of photos from the gallery, including one of *Fighter* with my caption: *@FThomas is an artist to watch! He's already drawing crowds*

#punnystuff *@ecaanart*. I felt a delicious tingling sensation when I saw sixty-two new follow requests and a text from Sienna telling me to check @JustJules's latest post.

SIENNA: Somebody didn't properly fill me in on her day!!
EMMA: Honestly, it was one for the books. ☺ Tell you all about it tomorrow.
SIENNA: <3

I clicked on @FThomas's profile to see a man wearing outfits of all one color in every picture—blue jeans with a blue shirt, a black suit with a black collared shirt—plus a scarf over his mouth the same color as his clothes. *That guy!* I googled his name, and the first hit was a *Wall Street Journal* article with the headline: "New Artist Thomas Sells First Piece for $1 Million."

Just then, a follow request from @JustJules popped up on my screen. I sucked in through the straw and heard the last bit of liquor being pulled away from the ice, so I shook it to redistribute the cubes and sucked again. *What would Jules think if she saw me sitting alone in this dive bar? What about how few followers I have? I should just delete Instagram right now. But where would I get all my information? How would I know who the hot young artists are or what transpires after hours at art fairs? I would need to sift through online art publications for weeks to get the same information Jules provides me with in a few hours.* I shuddered at the thought.

"Could I have another, please?" I asked the bartender. She shot me a smile and flipped the bottle of Absolut upside down over a glass as I wondered what Leonard would think of the liquor brand.

"I'm celebrating," I explained to her.

"Cool," she said flatly, before heading toward the man flagging her at the far end of the bar. I turned to my phone and hungrily accepted all the requests from my new followers.

After I finished that drink and paid the bill, I pushed outside the bar onto the sidewalk, where a teenage girl was lighting up a cigarette as she passed.

"Jesus!" I yelled. "You almost burned me with that!" I shook my head in disgust and continued across the street, pretending I hadn't heard the girl mutter, "Psycho." I fell asleep to thoughts of good vodka, the walls of Florence's gallery, and Jules. For the first time in as long as I could remember, I awoke slowly and before the drilling. My breath was calm and even, my shirt was dry. I sat up in bed and took a moment to look around my small studio, thinking that maybe I'd freed myself from the life I had been running from since the night of the fire.

AGENT TILLWELL: What were your last few days at Gemini like? Did anybody react oddly to the news of you leaving?

EMMA CAAN: Hmm. No, not really. Everybody was extremely professional, especially Jeremy. They were all happy for me. Honestly, it made me second-guess my decision to go for a split second.

AGENT GARRITT: But you did go in the end.

EMMA CAAN: I did. I wanted a change. I wanted to do something more than copy others' art. And I thought the increased security at Gemini and consultants everywhere meant the company was in trouble.

AGENT GARRITT: How exactly was security increased?

EMMA CAAN: I guess "increased" is the wrong word. Reinforced, maybe. We always signed the back of every copy, but our pens were changed, and we were constantly reminded to sign. Things like that.

AGENT GARRITT: What pens?

EMMA CAAN: Signature pens. They're common across the industry. It looks like paint, but it's a pen.

AGENT TILLWELL: You just took the pen and signed the back of a canvas when you were done?

EMMA CAAN: We were all instructed to sign as "Copied after 'name of artist' by 'name of copier.'" That is also industry standard.

AGENT TILLWELL: Did you always sign every copy?

EMMA CAAN: Yes.

AGENT TILLWELL: What? You were just about to say something.

EMMA CAAN: Nope. I wasn't. I signed every copy.

I spent my final days at Gemini finishing my last painting, transferring all my good projects to Sienna, and asking Daniella to assign someone else to complete the others. When everybody gathered around pastel-frosted cupcakes in the conference room on Friday, I had to blot genuine tears from the corners of my eyes so I could properly read the notes they had all penned in the beautiful deckle-edged card, whose hand-painted flowers I could tell Sienna had done. At four o'clock, I was just checking that I had my few personal belongings in my canvas tote before heading into my exit interview when Sienna made her way over to me, looking nervous.

"I messed up," she said. "I'm going to get fired." I rolled my eyes, having heard this kind of thing more than once from her. "No, seriously. I messed up this painting for the Met a few years ago. Well, I forgot to sign the back. And I was afraid if I said anything, Jeremy would fire me. I had nightmares about it for so long after. But I'd finally forgotten . . . And now somebody from the Met is in there, and she's *not* happy, and I heard my name coming through Jeremy's office door."

I put my hand on her upper arm. "I'm sure it's not—" But before I could finish, the door to the studio swung open, and Jeremy stood at the front of the room, scanning his employees, a glimmer of perspiration on his reddened brow. His eyes settled on Sienna, and he started off swiftly toward us.

"What year?" I whispered. She gave me a quizzical look, and I squeezed her upper arm between my fingers. "When did you do the painting?"

"Um, must have been the fall of 2016," she stammered, looking confused.

"Sienna," Jeremy said from a few feet away. "The new head of restoration at the Met is in my office, and do you know what he told me?" A vein in his forehead was visibly pulsing.

Sienna shook her head.

The whole studio was listening, but only Wade stuck his head out from behind his easel. I gave him a look and he ducked back behind it.

"That they cleaned one of the paintings you did for them, and the back wasn't signed, and it caused them a huge fucking head-ache. Obviously, it wasn't good enough to be confused with the original," Jeremy continued. I winced at his unnecessary dig at her skills. "But that is a mistake we CANNOT MAKE!" For the final two words, he clapped his hands on each syllable. "You are—"

"I did that painting," I announced, stepping forward.

"What?" he said.

"I'd just joined the company, and Sienna had been so wonderful helping train me that I asked if I could repay her by taking over one of her projects. I'm so sorry," I said, clasping my hands in front of my chest for effect.

Jeremy looked even more enraged. "You can't just *switch* proj-ects!" he said, and ran his palms roughly over his shiny hair. "You're fired!" he said, immediately noting the futility of the statement and turning on his heel to head back to his office.

Sienna turned to me with a look of immense relief. "I'd have never gotten another job if that got out," she whispered. "Thank you."

"My pleasure. I just made Jeremy fire a person who"—I checked my watch—"officially no longer works for him." We gave each other a big hug, then I made my way to Jeremy's office for my exit interview, which I knew would be a rough one. But when I walked in, he just looked at me calmly.

"Somebody's head had to roll for a mistake of that size, and I honestly didn't feel like losing two of you in a day, so thanks," he said. I stared at him, wondering how he knew I'd lied. "You'd never be so sloppy. Plus, that copy was done in June. You didn't join us until September of that year." I opened my mouth to protest, but he held up a palm, then pointed back out into the hallway. I turned, and he followed me out of his office. Was it possible that I had enjoyed the exercise of disliking Jeremy, the distraction from my life that it provided, more than I actually disliked him?

"Your exit interview will be in the conference room," he explained. Even before Jeremy peeled open the thick glass door, I saw the handsome sandy-haired consultant sitting alone at the opposite end of the long table. He stood and shook my hand, introducing himself, though I was too flustered to catch his name, and he gestured to the seat across the table from him. As he did so, Jeremy left the room. I turned back to the consultant, feeling as though I had just been called to the principal's office. I pulled down my long sleeves over my hands until only the tips of my fingers were exposed.

"I heard you're joining Florence Wake. Congratulations!" He smiled warmly as I eased myself down into the leather chair.

"Thank you," I said, still confused about why I was meeting with him instead of Jeremy.

"Doing anything fun before you start there?" he asked, attempting small talk as he opened his laptop. "Any vacation plans?"

I didn't think he wanted to hear that travel was a luxury reserved for people who were not reliant on Gemini salaries, or that there was no way I could go two weeks without a paycheck. "They need me in Hong Kong for Art Basel, so I need to start right away," I said instead.

"That's fast," he commented. I now wasn't sure why I had been so afraid to approach him. He was objectively attractive—fit and tall, with a square jaw—but there was something a bit awkward about his demeanor. "Before you leave, we wanted to get your take on a few things. We figure you're perhaps the only person in the building who would answer totally honestly."

"Who is 'we'?" I asked.

He gave a short laugh, then typed briefly into his computer and waited a moment before speaking. "Mr. Jacobsen provided us a list of all copies you've been formally assigned to paint here, but have you ever freelanced outside of Gemini?"

I shook my head, but he was staring at his screen, poised to type, so I said "no" aloud.

"Did you ever copy *Where Do We Come From? What Are We? Where Are We Going?* by Paul Gauguin?"

"I've never worked for the MFA," I said. He looked up at me blankly. "No, I've never copied that. It's in the collection of the Museum of Fine Arts in Boston," I explained. He nodded and continued to type. I'd never done an exit interview, but I couldn't imagine a less relevant question to ask a departing employee of a struggling company.

He took a black binder from his briefcase and flipped through it, stopping and pulling letter-size sheets out of protective plastic sleeves and placing two of them before me. "Can you tell which is the original and which is the copy?"

They were two versions of one of Monet's water lilies, a painting I had seen Sienna replicate. I studied the brushstrokes, the way the ones in the picture on the right were careful and loving, whereas the ones on the left were carefree and created a feeling of the water and sky mingling.

"This is the original," I said, pointing to the one on the left. He took the photos back, giving no indication of whether I was correct, and handed me two more, these of the banks of the Seine, almost certainly by Alfred Sisley. I pointed at the one on the right, said, "Original," and again he put two more in front of me. I lost count of how many sets of pictures he showed me. My eyes glazed over, but the best I could hope was that if I got the answers correct, they wouldn't be so quick to assume we could be replaced by computers and my colleagues could keep their jobs just a bit longer.

"Okay, last one," he finally said as he placed two different images in front of me. One painting was of a pale woman with a white bird on her shoulder and a small smile on her lips; the other was of an older man in what looked to be a military uniform. I imagined both had been done by the same artist, and I might have guessed it was Frans Hals, whom we'd covered briefly in my senior seminar "Journey Through Dutch Art."

"Um, these are of two *different* paintings," I said.

He nodded but said nothing else as he watched me intently.

"Are they Frans Hals?" I asked. I felt like I was on a game show, but one where the rules had never been explained to me and there was no prize to be won.

"You tell me."

"I'm sorry, I don't understand. You realize I'm *quitting* my job, right? This feels like an interview." I gestured at his binder of artwork.

"Sorry, I should have explained. We're trying to figure out whom to suggest for Jeremy to hire as your replacement. The company will feel your absence, and a replacement will be hard to find; we're just trying to figure out *how* hard," he said, and finally cracked a smile. I softened at the compliment. "I know you must want to get out of here. But I promise, this is the last one."

I nodded and looked back down at the woman, studying her artificial pose, her playful eyes, and the confident brushstrokes. I turned to the man and leaned down close to the table. There was something *off*. I didn't know how long I studied the pictures, but I noticed my tongue starting to hang out one corner of my mouth, and I yanked it back in and lifted my head.

"What do you think?" the consultant asked.

"I have no idea. You stumped me. I lose," I said, sliding the papers back toward him.

"Take a guess," he said flatly, no warmth in his voice now.

"They're both fake," I said.

His eyebrow arched curiously, which I took as an indication that I was correct. "What about the paintings makes you say that?"

"Just a gut feeling. Same as all of the others," I said, and leaned back in my chair and folded my arms over my chest to indicate that I was done.

"Okay," he said, gathering the papers into a stack and bouncing it against the glass table to align the edges. I didn't want to seem needy by asking whether I was right.

"Now . . ." he began, turning back to his computer. "Have you noticed any new staff here at Gemini?"

"Nope," I said, and then paused. "Well, we rotate security guards now. So one of them is always a fresh face." Rotating them was part of the enhanced security protocol, along with the improved pens. "And there's that new cleaning lady, but she's not a Gemini employee. No new artists."

The consultant had stopped typing and was looking at me. "What new cleaning lady?"

"I don't know her name." I tried to picture seeing her through the glass of the conference room when I'd met with Lenny. "She's new. I would have noticed her earlier if I had seen her before."

"Why do you say that?"

"Because she's really pretty. Long black hair, bright blue eyes. I only saw her once."

He typed something. "Oh, one last thing—I see you've done a lot of work for Leonard Sobetsky, is that correct?" he asked. I nodded. "And you know him personally?"

It occurred to me then that Jeremy was probably being so nice to me because he was afraid I'd try to take business with me when

I left, not because he was a good guy. I couldn't imagine he knew about the charity event at Lenny's house, though, because Sienna never would have told anybody, and nobody else knew.

"I've met him," I answered, making direct eye contact. "He came into the office just a couple weeks ago."

"Has he ever approached you to copy a painting for him outside of Gemini?" the consultant asked, confirming my suspicion.

"Nope." The word escaped my lips even as I wondered whether Lenny's suggestion that I freelance for him would be some violation of the Gemini employment contract I skimmed my first day on the job and hadn't looked at since. I wondered how the company could possibly find out if I continued to work for Lenny. Tax returns, maybe? What was the punishment for violating a noncompete provision? I felt my heart rate spiking. "So, how'd I do in the game of Spot the Original?" I asked.

"You batted a thousand," he said, raising an eyebrow as though trying to figure out how I had cheated.

"It's a gift," I said with a smile. He stood reluctantly, seeming to want to ask me something more, and shook my hand. My shoulders finally relaxed as I realized I was being dismissed, and I exited the conference room at Gemini for the last time, then ducked back into the studio to give Sienna one final hug before taking the stairs and pushing the revolving door out onto Sixth Avenue.

It was a quiet dusk in the city, with the sky between the buildings tinted a dusty rose, and because I had been a New Yorker long enough to know such moments were fleeting, I stopped and took it in. Daylight saving had robbed me of experiencing my favorite time of day for the past three months, and the presence of light after a day of work was something to savor. When I exhaled and began to walk, though, I felt oddly hollow. There was an urgency to my steps when I should have been strolling.

It was often like that with me, having the wrong reactions to things. Debilitating anxiety that I'd break it when my parents got me the exact bicycle I had wanted for my sixth birthday, crippling fear that I wouldn't make friends when I got into Yale early, relief when my father passed away, and now a weird sense of sadness as I made a long-awaited career move. I turned east to the park to try to capture the calm evening light and convince myself that my irreconcilable emotions didn't somehow make me a lemon of a human.

I won't be back here every weekday, I reminded myself as I took time to look over the grass and trees and strollers. I watched a father chasing after his daughter as she screamed with delight, blond pigtails slapping at her shoulders as she stumbled fearlessly ahead of him. I suddenly remembered my manners and grabbed for my cell phone.

"Emma! I was *just* about to call you," Lenny sang into the phone even before the first ring was through.

"I should have called sooner," I apologized. "I've been meaning to thank you for the introduction to Florence. I start there Monday!"

"Please, it was nothing. I heard you'll be representing the gallery next week. The art at the fair promises to be very exciting this year. We'll all head over together—Sergey, whom you met at my party, and his wife will fly with us. It will be good fun."

Questions ping-ponged around my brain. *What airport do private planes fly out of? What flight do I say I'm on? Do I get a boarding pass? What do I wear?*

"Well, thank you again. I've never been to Art Basel before," I said instead. "Or Hong Kong. I've actually never been to Asia!" As I spoke, I smiled. Even my parents had ventured only as far as Europe—this opportunity was an incredible one.

"You're in for a treat!" he said warmly, without any hint of snobbery or judgment. "And by the way, I was going to call you for a favor."

I swallowed, preparing myself for the rub. My brain began to calculate what I would be willing to give him, and how few options I had now that I had quit Gemini, when he cut my thought spiral short. "I have a Pissarro I plan to vault, but I'd like a copy for my home in London. I have a studio in Soho with great light that you can use to paint if you like. I'll give you ten grand cash for the Pissarro, but I'll need it before we leave for Hong Kong. Or fifty grand to be on retainer for the year."

I waited for something to happen—a laugh to indicate that he'd been joking. Instead, he went on, all business. "And, of course, we'd supply all the materials. You can give my assistant a list of anything else you need—food, drinks, anything. Emma?" My jaw hung open as I tried to calculate which one was the better offer. I'd never done more than three paintings a year for Leonard at Gemini, but I balked at the idea of being on retainer, committing to something this big just as I was starting a new job.

"Yes." I managed to force the word out, needing to speak before the offer was rescinded.

"Yes to what? The retainer or the single project?"

As good as it would feel to deposit fifty thousand dollars into my bank account at once, I said, "The single project."

"I'll take it. When are you free?"

"Um, this weekend?" I asked, pacing in a small circle, drawing stares from an older man seated on a nearby wooden bench.

"This weekend is great. Micaela will send you the address of the studio, and we'll have the original waiting there for you. You can tell her what else you need. I'm so glad we can cut out the middleman now that you're leaving Gemini. Thank you!"

I switched my phone to the other ear, sweat cooling on the cheek where the sleek rectangle had been. Had he just offered me ten thousand dollars in cash to paint a single painting and then thanked *me*?

"You're welcome," I said, blinking twice. Still holding the phone to my ear after he hung up but yanking it away with a start as it rang. The screen flashed a New York City area code, a number I didn't know. "Hello?"

"Hey, it's Micaela, Lenny's assistant," a woman said quickly, seemingly in a rush. Had she and Lenny been sitting in a room together? "I'll email you details, but Lenny wanted me to remind you that banks report any deposit of ten thousand dollars or more to the IRS. So . . . thanks!" she said, clearly about to hang up.

"Wait!" I interrupted. "What does that mean?"

"I'm not sure I can be more clear," she said sharply, and I could hear a man's voice in the background. "If I were you, I'd either pay for things in cash for a while or break up the deposits across a couple of banks. Or you can deposit it in one account and give forty percent to the IRS. Your call."

I heard the click of the call ending and furrowed my brow. I decidedly did not wish to give away almost half to the government. I reluctantly arrived at the conclusion that I'd use the cash as I needed it instead. Nerves gnawed at my exhilaration until they devoured it entirely. Was Micaela really trying to save me from a big tax hit? What interest could she possibly have in doing so? Or was she trying to obscure a record of where the money came from? To pay me under the radar for Lenny's benefit? And if it was to his benefit, what was he hiding?

My feet stopped short to avoid the man sitting on the third step down into the subway, and I realized I had been gliding across town the entire time my brain was tripping over itself. The man's head hung low, and he let out a soft groan.

"Are you okay?" I asked, taking four more steps down so I was standing in front of him. No response. "Sir?"

"Fuck off!" he yelled as he picked up his head angrily for a moment, just before it dropped yet again.

I straightened my back and sighed, looking back down into the dark concrete tunnel and picturing the cash I would be holding in my hand after completing the copy. Leonard Sobetsky was a billionaire. He had more money than some small countries. He didn't *need* to do anything illegal. Hanging on to money you made was simply good business. I nodded at my conclusion and backtracked up the subway steps, a tingle of satisfaction shooting up my outstretched arm as I hailed a yellow cab. I had the sense that I had just been offered admittance to the elite group of New Yorkers who did not need to but who could opt to use the subway system if and when they pleased. I slipped into the backseat, rolled down the window, and breathed out.

AGENT TILLWELL:	After you left Gemini, was Florence Wake your only source of income?
EMMA CAAN:	No.
AGENT GARRITT:	What alternate sources of income did you have?
EMMA CAAN:	I freelanced for Leonard Sobetsky a few times.
AGENT GARRITT:	Define "freelance."
EMMA CAAN:	[pause]
AGENT GARRITT:	What did you paint? Where did you paint? What did he pay you?
EMMA CAAN:	I painted whatever he asked me to. It was mostly impressionist works. And I painted in his studio—he provided the materials. I think I only did two jobs for him in total. Nowhere in my contract at Florence Wake did it say I couldn't freelance!
AGENT GARRITT:	Ms. Caan, there's no need to get defensive here. We're just information-gathering.
EMMA CAAN:	I'm trying to be helpful, but this feels like an interrogation. You keep saying I'm not in trouble, but I feel like I'm in trouble.
AGENT TILLWELL:	Let's just take a step back. Can you describe Mr. Sobetsky's studio that he had you paint in? Was there art on the walls?
EMMA CAAN:	Actually, no. There was nothing on the walls. There was really nothing in there at all. It was just a blank canvas.

That Saturday morning, I looked at a rather shoddy-looking metal door in the middle of a white-pillared industrial building on Greene Street, slightly confused. Directly to my right was the entrance of

Louis Vuitton, which seemed to indicate that the building was fancier than it seemed. I looked again at the door, graffitied with faded initials, a bit disappointed by this real estate holding of Lenny's. I'd secretly been hoping for something as grand as his town house to paint in.

I confirmed that the building number, 115, etched into the glass panel above the door was in the right spot, then took the fob that Micaela had messengered to my apartment the night before and touched it to the credit card–size black pad on the right side of the door, half expecting it not to work. But the light turned green, and a soft mechanical buzzing beckoned me inside to a small entryway with a scuffed wood floor. There, a set of steel elevator doors opened into a metal-floored industrial elevator with only one button: "PH." The mystery of it all made it one of the more exiting Saturdays I could recall.

I hesitated for a moment, worrying about walking into such an unfamiliar place, but I pushed the button and was propelled upward in the rickety elevator. When the doors parted, I was let out into another small, unremarkable chamber, with only a black door and keypad on the wall. I took out my phone and launched the app Micaela's email had instructed me to download, placing my thumbprint where I was told, watching as it glowed green and blinked "9–0–0–1–3–4" on the screen, a code I then entered into the keypad. A check mark appeared and I heard a click in the door, which I accepted as an invitation to open it.

"Woah," I whispered to myself as I stepped across the threshold. My lower lip dropped at the sight of wide-plank hardwood floors pouring out like streams of honey and rays of warm sunlight barreling in from the wall of floor-to-ceiling windows. I tried to imagine how many times my tiny studio could fit into the space and guessed more than ten, meaning I was looking at about five thousand square feet of pristine open space.

An all-white chef's kitchen, warmed with brass cabinet knobs and a gray marble island, was nestled in one corner of the loft. The other side was made even brighter by a square of light beaming down from a skylight, soaking the cream-colored drop cloth and two easels below. I drifted toward the easels first, and only when I was a couple of feet away did I realize they were in a room of their own—surrounded by perfectly Windexed glass with no dust or streaks to make it stand out from the rest of the room. I had spent a summer in college working at the Yale University Art Gallery in a room very much like this one, so I knew it was pressurized, temperature-stabilized, humidity-controlled—all the bells and whistles for the priceless works it must have seen.

One of the easels had a blank canvas resting on it, and the other had a cloth draped over it. Against the wall were all the paints I had asked for and more, as well as palettes, brushes, brush cleaners, and white gloves. There was also a mini-fridge with a clear door, through which I could see water bottles and some type of green juice, and a Nespresso machine. I stared at the setup a moment longer, then looked across the massive open space to the kitchen and laughed out loud. Whoever had the idea for the mini-fridge was correct—the kitchen *was* too far away.

I spotted a note perched on the shelf of the easel in front of the blank canvas, almost blending in.

Emma,
Let me know if I've forgotten anything you need. The linens on the bed are fresh if you need a rest. The easel that the original is on has a sensor alarm, so if you need to move the painting for any reason, move the whole easel, but never out of the room. Shoot me a text when you finish up and we'll come collect your piece.
—Micaela

There's a bed here? I noticed five doorknobs jutting out of the doors on the same wall from which I had entered, and I headed over, feeling like I was in a fairy tale. The first one led to a beautiful half-bathroom that was triple the size of my full one at home; the second was a coat closet with no coats but fifteen or so blank canvases stacked against a wall; and the third was the front door to the space. The fourth was another half-bath, which seemed redundant, and the fifth opened to a metal staircase. I paused at the bottom, then climbed up to find myself standing in a picturesque bedroom. An unbelievably inviting queen-size bed was positioned in the middle, draped in white linens that smelled ever so faintly of lilac when I fell into them face-first. Besides a faded blue Persian rug, there was nothing else in the room, which made me feel that it had been designed purely for rest, and it sedated me almost immediately. The bedroom windows faced southeast, looking out over downtown and showing the Manhattan Bridge, dotted with cars making their way to Brooklyn. The other door in the bedroom led to a gray marble bathroom with a large white soaking tub, and within the bathroom, I found a large walk-in closet with satin padded hangers hanging bare on every rod and a small safe perched in the far corner.

I resisted the urge to strip down and spend the afternoon in the tub or under the covers, and pushed myself toward the stairs, allowing gravity to do the rest. As I walked the length of the brightly lit apartment, I noted that none of the overhead lighting was switched on, nor was it needed. Once at the two easels, I pulled back the sheet covering the original and took in the magnificent Pissarro—the bits of bright green fields revealing themselves as workers cleared the dry hay, stacking it into impossibly tall golden hills.

I painted until the sun dipped below the building tops and then turned on the apartment lights, which were almost as good as natural light. I kept going, feeling the rush of Pissarro himself in my fingertips as I directed the brush, something I hadn't experienced in quite some time. Something about the grandeur of the apartment and the unadulterated view of the city awoke creative urges in me that had hibernated away at Gemini. A few times I felt the urge to break free from the confines of the Pissarro and paint my own. But the idea of ten thousand dollars in my pocket kept me on track.

At some point before dawn, I stumbled upstairs into the bedroom and closed my eyes. I had feverish, sweaty dreams and awoke atop the covers to find a blaze of sunlight filtering through the window and directly onto my face. I sat up and breathed in, then took a long sip of water to soothe my scratchy throat, and I knew I had been screaming. I should have known better than to think the nightmares were gone, but I hadn't had a bad dream since I'd landed the new job. I was tempted to draw the blinds and duck back under the covers, but the sun was that brilliant, yolky color that lasts only an hour or so after the sun rises, and the beautiful apartment made the memory of the nightmare fade more quickly than usual.

Two coffees and three green juices later, I finished the Pissarro copy just as the sun was setting. I looked back at the two easels and waited. I felt nothing. No dissatisfied tingling in my extremities, no frustration in my chest. I took a moment to relish a job well done before I moved over to the supply wall for a signature pen. I grabbed a felt-tip marker, the good kind whose white lettering read *Phosphos Chemical Corp.* and which we used at Gemini before Jeremy made us switch, and signed the back of my copy. They really were the most amazing pens—thick black ink came out smoothly from the smallest felt tip in the sleek exterior. I threw a pen in my purse, certain Lenny wouldn't miss one out of the box, and emailed Micaela to tell her that the copy was complete. *If okay with you, we'll deliver payment to Florence Wake tomorrow,* she emailed back almost immediately. *Okay with me!* I responded.

The half-bath closest to the easels was prepped for paint cleanup. There were black hand towels instead of white, and plastic squirt bottles of mineral oil and dish soap, plus lotion for the red and raw skin the scrubbing would leave in its wake. I poured a bit of mineral oil on my palm, added a dollop of dish soap, and kneaded the flesh of one hand into the other, watching as the dried, caked oil paint sloughed off, melted into blue and green ribbons, and swirled down the drain. I scrubbed at the residue of paint clinging stubbornly to my cuticles for a full minute, but my nails were still outlined in a sickly green. I knew that however hard I tried, and even if I couldn't see it, the paint would be with me for weeks—leaving grass-colored stains on any white shirt I wore and on my cheeks when I woke up in the morning. That's how it always was with stubborn stains. They always reappeared long after I was certain I had scrubbed them clean.

Downstairs, I pushed the door open onto Greene Street and paused at the "1" encased in a red circle leading down to the subway, unable to bear the thought of going underground after the weekend I'd spent looking out over the city from above. Instead, I walked west and turned right at the West Side Highway. It would be a long walk to my apartment, and despite the facts that I had barely slept and was starting a new job the next morning, it seemed exactly what I wanted to do in that moment. I took out my phone and dialed my mother.

"Hi!" she said, but her voice sounded pained. I could hear the evening news in the background and imagined her all alone in that huge house in front of the television.

"Hi!" I sang, trying to cheer her up.

"How's your week been?" my mother asked.

"Great," I said, unable to recall the last time I had been able to say that and mean it. "I actually just got this great new job at one of the best art galleries in New York. They have branches all over the world. I'm really excited. I start Monday. *And* they're sending me to Hong Kong soon."

"Wow! Honey! Congrats. I didn't even know you were interviewing," she said, and I knew she was insulted that I hadn't told her.

"I was thinking I could come home before I leave for Hong Kong, to help with packing up the house or at least Dad's stuff. You shouldn't have to do that by yourself. Maybe next weekend?"

I paused and waited for what I thought would be an easy yes, but my mother's breath grew heavier, and I thought she might be crying.

"I'd really like that," she said in a way that made my heart ache slightly. I resolved to be more attentive to her. The freedom of having cash to spend made it so easy to be a better daughter—the train ticket home was suddenly affordable. I breathed in contentedly, realizing how hard it would be to return to the anxious, constricted life I had been living since college.

"And hey, good luck tomorrow! First day at a new job. That's very exciting," my mother said. "You're going to be great."

The next morning, my mother's words of assurance seemed far away as I stared at my closet with my arms at my sides, trying to pick out an outfit for my first day as assistant director at Florence Wake. I was firmly aware that I'd never look as fashionable as the redheaded receptionist I'd seen during my interview or as chic as gallery patrons like Jules, so I aimed for unremarkable: black pants, a black turtleneck, and black patent pumps. I listened to a centering meditation on the subway down to SoHo and entered the gallery at nine o'clock sharp, feeling confident that I could handle whatever Florence threw at me after I'd let my stress "wash out like a wave and retreat back to sea."

I spotted Florence standing in the middle of the gallery, wearing black ballet flats, black leggings, and a white button-down shirt, staring at the wall with her arms folded over her chest. Everything the calming voice on the meditation had said suddenly left my brain as I began to panic that I was officially the new assistant director of Florence Wake Gallery and I had absolutely zero experience. My feet already throbbed from wearing heels, and the stress lodged in my chest was making no motion to retreat.

"Emma," she said quietly, her brow wrinkling slightly when she saw me approaching. "I hadn't realized you were starting today." She turned back to the painting, leaving me to grapple with my own expendability. "Remind me how you know Lenny," she said, which I took to indicate regret that she had hired me—as though, if I didn't know him well enough, she would fire me on the spot.

"I did replicas for him while I was at Gemini," I said, my throat dry.

Florence seemed to think and then cocked her head to one side. "Tell me, how would you price this?"

I felt a trickle of sweat on the back of my neck as her warning that the job was mine to lose rang in my ears. I hadn't even put my bag down, and already I was being tested. I forced my focus on the painting, noting the similarity of the men around the racetrack to the ones surrounding the ring in the Fredrick Thomas painting I had seen when I interviewed, and stole a glance at the plaques of the pieces on either side. Both were by Fredrick Thomas, but neither had prices listed.

"It's not entirely fresh. The faces are similar to the ones in *Fighter*," I said, and gestured to the fight scene two paintings down on the same wall. "And the colors are a bit muddled. But it's . . . captivating."

"And?" she asked. I couldn't hear any annoyance in her tone. It took a moment to realize that she was telling me I hadn't answered her question.

My brain jumped ahead as I tried to articulate some clearer thoughts. "I think you'd want to price above a million, even though it's not his best, to maintain the popular market. He's new, so you don't want to lose momentum. I'd say one point two million. But that's partially an exercise in anchoring the buyer's mind. I think you could take nine hundred thousand," I said. What I didn't say was *I could have done this painting with my eyes closed*, but I was thinking it.

"Correct," she said, as though there were a scientifically validated answer, and I felt myself exhale. She turned back to me and stared at me for a prolonged moment, as though seeing me for the first time. "Correct," she repeated, and then walked toward the back of the gallery. It took me a moment to realize she was still speaking to me, assuming I had followed.

"Leah gets in at nine-thirty, but I tend to arrive before eight . . ." she was saying as I fell into stride just behind her.

We entered her office, and Florence took a seat behind her desk as I stood next to her guest chair, my toes squishing ever farther into the tiny points of my shoes. Increasingly certain I was doing permanent damage to the balls of my feet, I cautiously lowered myself into her guest chair, half expecting her to instruct me to remain standing.

"This year I am focusing on being more present in our foreign offices. So you will be doing everything I usually do here while I'm out making sure the brand is consistent worldwide."

I nodded, wondering why I'd left the comfort of a job I knew I was good at for one I was woefully underqualified for.

"You'll be going to Basel Hong Kong, and I'll be there before you, but we won't overlap. And I'll be in L.A. a few days next month." She pointed to the calendar wall as though I could memorize her whereabouts for the next few months in that very moment.

"You . . . aren't staying in Hong Kong for Basel?" I asked. I had been nervous about representing the gallery at one of the world's biggest fairs, and doing so under her watchful eye, but I was downright panicked at the idea of doing it alone.

"Unfortunately, I need to be in London," she said, then leaned forward and rested her elbows on her desk, touching her fingertips together gently. "I only go to pre-Basel. They let the VIPs buy extortionately expensive tickets to preview art a few days before the fair starts, and that's where any serious buyer is. The rest isn't about art—it's parties for art influencers like your friend. Luckily for you, Lenny can't make it out before the nineteenth, anyway."

"I just . . ." I fumbled. "I am so grateful for this opportunity. But I've never worked at a gallery before and . . ."

"You'll be fine," she assured me, picking up a piece of paper on her desk as though it were urgent, and I understood it was more to dismiss me than to read it. "We have all week to prep you."

"Yes," I said, despite finding it very difficult to breathe. I slipped a finger into my turtleneck and pulled to try to free my throat from the fabric that seemed to be tightening around it.

"Are you warm?" Florence asked, her eyes widening. She rose quickly from her chair and made her way to the thermostat by the door to her office. "We keep the gallery at sixty-nine," she called over her shoulder. "It's good for the art. And supposedly, it's the best temperature to encourage spending money."

As she confirmed the temperature was just right for the art, making it clear my comfort was secondary, she looked out into the gallery and seemed to decide that while she was vertical, she might as well continue training me. She beckoned to me and headed into the main gallery, and I followed. The fear that I was unqualified was replaced with a far more immediate concern that I was about to fall on my face in my heels.

"When Leah gets here, she'll show you the art intake and accounting system," she said, pointing to the reception desk. "I don't know how to do any of that," she added proudly. "You'll sit at the front desk with Leah. I've added a chair for you."

I looked over to see two white leather chairs in uncomfortably close proximity behind the desk built for one person.

"Now let's talk about pricing. You said you'd price this at one point two million," Florence said as she stopped in front of the painting that we were looking at earlier. "That's right. But that's also wrong. That is exactly the right price for your average person walking in off the street. But if an A-list celebrity walks in, and I mean *A-list*, not like your little Instagram friend, we knock twenty percent off." She turned to me. "Do you know why?"

I forced myself to imagine why somebody with more money to spend than your average customer would be given a discount. "Because a celebrity owning the piece would do tens of thousands of dollars in marketing if we could publicize the sale? And the word of mouth that a celebrity telling friends would afford us, as well as any other press the celebrity gives us?" I guessed.

Her eyes brightened. "Yes. And then we add a twenty percent markup and every trick in the book to discourage somebody off-brand from buying."

"How do I know if somebody is on- or off-brand?" I asked.

She looked disappointed, as though she had overestimated me, and I made a mental note to be more judicious with asking *how* I should know things.

"It will depend on the celebrity. And the artist. And your instincts," she told me. "Even if they're 'famous,'" she said, using air quotes, "no reality television stars, no social media influencers, nobody suspected of domestic abuse, being anti-Semitic, homophobic, or racist. For reference, I've dropped the price three times in the past decade, and once was for Brad Pitt, so . . . the term 'A-list' is to be used judiciously."

"What percentage of each sale does the gallery keep?" I asked.

"We keep fifty. Every artist's contract stipulates our ability to use discretion in dropping the price up to twenty percent, so all of that is kosher."

I bit my lower lip as I contemplated my next question. "Aren't galleries supposed to list all prices? Like . . . display them?" I said sheepishly, having noticed not a single painting had a price listed beside it.

"Legally, yes," she said, seemingly amused, as she continued to move past the painting toward the front of the studio. "I put the artists I want to really push here," she said, pointing to the wall where Fredrick Thomas's paintings were hung. "The established artists who will always sell go on that wall," she said, making a sweeping gesture with her palm toward the far wall, covered in exposed brick. "Something about the Starbucks on the other side throws off the whole energy over there. It's bad for new artists."

She continued to drift toward the front of the gallery. "As for where we hang everything else—that's just instinct. I never let the previous assistant director have any say in placement, so I'm really hoping you have an eye for it." She glanced around the gallery, looking satisfied with her own choices, and I wondered who the previous assistant director was and where they were now. "For now, take a seat at the front desk. As I said, Leah will train you on the intake and accounting systems, as well as customer relations. You should accompany her as she approaches everyone who walks in the door. We have a distinct and highly professional style here at Florence Wake," she said, looking me up and down but keeping her face stoic.

As soon as Florence retreated into her office to take the first of the dozen pre-noon calls listed on her calendar, I sat down at the reception desk and finally took a breath. I heard the door to the gallery open, and Leah walked in wearing an army-green jumpsuit with impossibly high-heeled tan combat boots. Her hair was tied up in a messy bun, and her face was almost entirely obscured by enormous black sunglasses that made it impossible to tell where she was looking. I smiled at her nonetheless, but she didn't acknowledge my presence as she sipped her venti coffee, plunked herself down at the desk next to me, then unlaced her boots, removed furry black slippers from the drawer below the desk, and slipped her feet into them with a sigh of relief. I almost salivated with envy at the thought of comfortable footwear.

"I'm Emma, I'm not sure if you—" I began, but she never looked at me, so I trailed off.

She logged onto her computer, still without a word to me, and all at once the idea of leaving a job where I saw one of my best friends every day for a job where I knew nobody seemed like a terrible mistake. Florence seemed entirely indifferent to my presence, and Leah seemed acutely displeased to be sitting beside me. I gripped my thighs to try to stop my mind from spinning with the feeling that I had made the wrong decision and now I had to live with it.

AGENT TILLWELL:	In addition to freelancing, did you have any other sources of income?
EMMA CAAN:	No. Florence Wake was a pretty consuming job. I didn't have a ton of free time after starting there.
AGENT GARRITT:	What was your job title at Florence Wake Gallery?
EMMA CAAN:	Is. What is my job. I am the assistant director.
AGENT GARRITT:	Is that an entry-level position?
EMMA CAAN:	No.
AGENT TILLWELL:	But you had never worked in a gallery before, is that correct?
EMMA CAAN:	Yes. That's correct.
AGENT TILLWELL:	That must have been stressful, to come in at such a high level.
EMMA CAAN:	It was. But I got up to speed pretty quickly. I had a good teacher.

Leah finally turned to me, still wearing her sunglasses.

"I'm incredibly hungover," she stated, as though it pained her to speak. "And I know I'm supposed to train you on the system or whatever"—she waved her hand toward the sleeping computer screen as though it were an inconvenience—"but can we do that tomorrow, please?"

Perhaps she wasn't the nightmare of a human that my anxiety had made her out to be. "Of course," I said.

"Wonderful," she said flatly. "I assume her highness is in already?" I nodded as Leah put down her coffee and touched her temples.

"She's a machine. I've never been in before her. But I'm also a terrible assistant, so don't follow my lead." She gave a small laugh, one that brightened her entire face.

"I'm sure that's not true!" I protested. She had one of the most coveted entry-level jobs in the entire art world, one that people didn't get by being terrible at their jobs.

"It's true. Florence tells me so all the time!" We both laughed this time. "In a rare display of productivity, I did manage to create your Florence Wake email address yesterday before I drank myself into oblivion. And I ordered you your own computer, but for now you can log into mine." She nodded to her MacBook Air. I pulled it toward me, brought the screen to life, and saw that "EmmaCaan" was already a registered user next to "LeahMoniker," so I created a password and logged on.

Leah finally removed her sunglasses, revealing striking green eyes highlighted only with minimal mascara, and began to show me how to navigate the system we'd agreed she wasn't training me on until tomorrow. I got the sense that she was far more competent than she made herself out to be. She clicked a few buttons and pulled up an example of how to photograph new works while they were still in packaging and then again after they were hung, so the artist couldn't accuse us of any mishandling.

"You can mess up basically anything for Florence and not get fired, except something involving an actual work of art. She'd blow a gasket," Leah warned. "And no matter who calls, take a message. Never put them through to Florence. Anybody she actually wants to talk to has her cell." Leah paused and put her hand on my forearm to make certain she had my attention. "Except Jane Kantrowitz. When she calls, pretend you're taking a message, but never give it to Florence. It just upsets her."

"Who is Jane Kantrowitz?" I asked, trying to keep my voice low.

"Florence's former best friend. She got caught selling forged

Degas at the Whiteshall Gallery. Florence cut her out of her life entirely."

"She knowingly sold forged art?" I asked, feeling my eyes widen.

"Not knowingly. Or so she claims. Whatever, it's under investigation. I personally believe she had no idea. But she probably had a fair amount of willful blindness when it came to holes in the provenance. Regardless, she's dead to Florence."

"Harsh," I said.

Leah shrugged. "Maybe. But all anybody has in the gallery world is their reputation. If that gets muddied, it's over. I mean, Florence *is* harsh, but I sort of agree with her on this one."

While we were waiting for a photo file to upload, I felt her looking at me and turned to meet her bright green eyes. Her skin was a dewy alabaster. I could see the small veins underneath it and knew it would be covered in tiny freckles if it ever saw the sun.

"So, what's your deal?" she asked, narrowing her eyes playfully as though I were about to tell her a secret.

"Oh, um . . ." I stammered and looked back to the computer, hoping the picture had loaded and would save me from talking about myself, but I still saw three dots bulging and shrinking in order.

"We have the Internet guy coming today. Something's wrong with our connection," she said.

"I grew up outside Philly. And I studied art at Yale, and I just left this company called—" I began.

Leah held up a palm to me and shook her head. "I read your résumé when you sent it in," she said, as though her hangover had drained patience from her body. "How do you know Lenny? And *how* do you know JustJules?" She asked the last question in a mocking tone, but one that made me feel like I was in on the joke.

I hadn't realized that she knew I had gotten the job through a personal connection, and I wondered if it made her think less of me. "Lenny was a client at my old job. And when I mentioned I needed a change . . ."

"He got you a job where you *wouldn't* be copying anymore?" Leah looked at me skeptically as I nodded. "I find that hard to believe."

"Well, I freelance for him now," I added.

"That makes more sense," she said dryly, before taking another sip of coffee. I didn't know what she meant, but I didn't have time to dwell before her next question: "And Jules?"

"I just met her in the gallery that day I interviewed," I said, looking at the screen, where the image had finally loaded.

"Hm," Leah said, leaning in toward the computer, her cheek inches from mine.

"Those bloggers make friends fast. She already mentioned you in a post. The online art world is *abuzz* about her new friend, the one who's never even posted to Instagram." She snorted, then wiggled her fingertips at me for dramatic effect. I shook my head in protest, which I could barely believe I was doing, because I had spent the past few years fantasizing about being friends with Jules. "Even if you barely know her, perception is reality these days. So you're friends now!"

Before I could respond, Leah straightened her back and pointed a silver-polished fingernail at the computer screen. "Finally!" she said. "Okay, so here's where you take and save the photo. And you insert the link to the picture in the notes section of the accounting spreadsheet here." She took the mouse from my hand and opened an Excel file. "Are you seeing anybody?" she asked, delving back into my personal life.

I thought for a moment, wanting to be somebody worthy of the curiosity of Jules's followers, the interest of this captivating new coworker. I nodded as I thought of the man at Lenny's party, my heart picking up speed as I struggled to figure out why my head wasn't shaking instead. "Sort of," I said, so the lie wasn't quite so boldfaced. "It's super-new, I don't want to jinx it by talking about it." All of a sudden, I was aware of how I'd longed to answer this question in the affirmative.

"Oh, I totally get that!" She turned her whole body away from the computer and toward me. "'Sort of' is way better than what I have going on. I went on a date last night with a guy who told me he was a restaurateur, but it turns out he only had an *idea* for a restaurant. A bad one—involving very long utensils so you could eat off each other's plates. He is currently unemployed." Leah pressed on her temples. "Hence the hangover."

I giggled, both entertained by the story and relieved that she wasn't asking me questions about my completely fabricated sort-of boyfriend.

"How'd you meet?" Leah asked.

Shit. I guess I have to tell her. "At this charity event at Lenny's. I had just finished my drink, and we were both at the bar. He raised his glass to mine and said, 'Ryan Parker,' very James Bond–like. And that was it," I answered.

"Ryan Parker? Shut up!" Leah gasped, and I felt the color drain out of my face.

"You know him?" I said, dreading the answer.

"Not personally, but I know he's impossibly attractive," she said.

"Anyway, it's nothing yet," I reiterated, breathing a sigh of relief and vowing to never again underestimate just how small New York was.

"Well, yeah. It never is with him. That's sort of his MO, isn't it?" She snorted again.

I laughed, pretending to know just what she meant, but her words felt both disappointing and like a challenge. Searching for a change of topic, I scanned the top bar of the file: *Artist, Date Painted, Date Displayed, Date Sold, Title, Sale Price, Artist's Cut, Profit.* "We don't mark here if we sold it at a discount or a premium?" I asked, wondering how we could possibly track our success if we didn't.

"Nope." Leah leaned back in her chair and announced, "I have to pee," then slipped into her boots and headed toward the back of the gallery.

I was leaning in closer to the spreadsheet, trying to familiarize myself with the intake program, when I heard a shriek from the back of the gallery. I froze, wondering if it was more polite to check on Leah or ignore her cry entirely. I finally got up and raced toward the back of the room, trying to keep an eye on the front door, paranoid I'd be the new girl who let the gallery be ransacked in broad daylight. As I neared the bathroom, I heard more expletives and banging.

I knocked lightly. "Leah?" I had barely finished her name when the door swung open. She was buttoning the top of her jumpsuit, but her green pants legs were darker toward her ankles and dripping wet. The bathroom floor was soaked, and the toilet seat was on the floor.

"I fucking *hate* Instagram!" she seethed.

I didn't understand how a toilet overflowing was logically connected to the social media platform, but the scene was so ridiculous that I had to stifle a laugh. "Did you fall in?"

"Yes! I absolutely fell in!" Leah said, still yelling but now working hard to keep from laughing as well.

"Walk me through why Instagram is to blame for you falling in a toilet?"

"Florence had some social media viewing party on Saturday. Apparently, she was inspired by something *you* said in *your* interview. So I also hate you, by the way," Leah said.

"I'm so lost." I shook my head and ducked my head back into the gallery to make certain I didn't miss any customers.

"Wannabe influencers like to pretend they're on private planes," she said, then picked the wet, hollow white porcelain toilet seat up off the floor and held it against the wall, standing in front of it and then turning to me. "Take a picture," she said. "With your phone. Hurry up. This is disgusting."

I took my phone out of my bag, noting that I had two missed calls from my mother, and snapped a shot. Leah placed the toilet seat back and extended her hand to me to grab my phone.

"Ew! No. Wash your hands first!" I laughed.

When she was done washing, she took my phone and zoomed in, then colored the wall behind the toilet seat blue with an app I didn't know I had and showed me the picture. The outline of the porcelain toilet seat looked exactly like the frame of a plane window around my head.

"With a glass of champagne and an eye mask, nobody would ever know you're in a bathroom and not on a plane," she said, and rolled her eyes. "Now, what the fuck did they do with the screws they removed?"

"That's wild," I said, still marveling at the picture of her as she located the screws in the cabinet with the extra toilet paper.

"That's nothing," Leah assured me, starting to screw the seat back on. "You better learn these tricks, because for some reason Florence is under the impression that you can help build the FW global brand on social media."

I swallowed hard. "You're probably much better suited for that than I am. You know the tricks . . ."

"I restrict my Instagram. That shit is a rabbit hole for me. I download the app for one hour every Sunday night and give myself a little treat. After sixty minutes, I delete it from my phone," Leah said. I waited for her to tell me she was joking, but she clearly wasn't as she turned back to the toilet. Deleting Instagram weekly seemed such an unnecessarily dramatic move. I had never tried to cut back on my screen time, but I was certain I could look at the app only once a week if I wanted to.

"We'll take some pictures later of the art so you can document your first day here. People will want to see that," Leah said as she rotated her wrist to tighten the bolt around the screw. "The glamorous part of it, anyway."

"Emma?" Florence stuck her head in the bathroom. "What in God's name are you doing," she said, more of a judgment than a question, and turned on her heel before either of us could respond. We both giggled, and I jumped up to follow her into her office.

Florence sat down at her desk, reached into her purse, and pulled out a manila envelope, filled with enough paper to make it thick on only one end, and extended it to me. I took a step forward and felt the weight of it in my hand, and I knew, though this knowledge was based on watching too many movies, that it was filled with cash.

"Micaela dropped this off for you early this morning," Florence said with no apparent curiosity. I thanked her, suddenly feeling that what I had done was illicit, and tried to hold the envelope as casually as possible. I felt like screaming that I was holding ten thousand dollars in my hands, wanted to fan it out and touch it, but I restrained myself.

"Thank you," I said, tucking it awkwardly under my arm the way I would have a clutch, recalling what Micaela had mentioned about the ten-thousand-dollar trigger to alert the IRS, and wondering what to do with the stack of bills if I wasn't going to deposit it.

"Your mother just called the gallery. You probably didn't hear it because you were using the restroom with Leah," Florence said, snapping me out of my reverie. My heart sank. Most people I knew stopped feeling self-conscious about their moms after middle school, but mine was constantly finding new ways to embarrass me.

"I wasn't using the restroom *with* Leah," I mumbled. "I'm so sorry she called here, though. I'll tell her not to from now on."

"Why? She seemed lovely. She was worried because she couldn't get in touch with you. And she's in the market for some contemporary art, which I assume you know, so I was glad to speak with her."

That was a new one. My mother knew nothing about art, almost to the point where I found it insulting that she refused to become conversant in the language of the world I was so passionate about. I was certain she had only pretended she was interested in order to have an in with Florence.

"I'll call her back. Thank you," I said. I pushed the envelope farther under my arm and turned to leave Florence's office, willing out of my mind the image of my mother yapping loudly to soft-spoken Florence Wake.

I sat down next to Leah and texted my mother that I was great and I'd call her later, adding that the Florence Wake phone was really for customers only, hoping she'd get the hint. I sat stiffly and ran my finger over the corner of the envelope, immediately anxious that somebody might rob the studio and me. The image of the safe in Lenny's studio popped into my head. During my lunch break, which I took after Leah returned from her break with a large order of french fries and a fountain Diet Coke from McDonald's, claiming they worked "way better than Advil," I went to Lenny's. I ran upstairs to the safe and read the directions on how to program it, then peeled a few bills out for use before clicking it shut and relaxing my shoulders for the first time since Florence had handed me the envelope.

I headed back to the office, and when I entered, Leah rose immediately, grabbing my cell phone off the desk, and beckoned for me to follow. She began taking pictures of me in front of our newest works as I pretended to contemplate the art while wondering how my plain outfit would photograph. Apparently wondering the same, Leah looked down at the scuffed black pumps on my feet. "What size are you?" she asked.

"Seven and a half," I said.

She turned on her heel and headed to our desk, where she opened her bottom drawer, pulled out a pair of red pumps and handed them to me. "Bought these a half size too small," she said as I removed my shoes and wiggled my way into hers. "How do they fit?"

"Perfectly."

"They're yours," she said, raising her phone to eye level again and continuing to snap. Though the heels were the same height as my pumps, their superior quality made me feel taller, thinner, and sturdier. I felt my chest protrude slightly, and I imagined how long my legs would look in photos. Leah handed me my phone.

"I can post for you if you unlock it," she offered casually. I unlocked my phone and gave it back to her. I watched her fingers swipe and zoom in and then her thumbs type furiously. "Good?" she asked, handing me my phone with a draft post of five pictures of me before the art, ready for my review. I looked tall and slender, and she had adjusted the lighting to make the art pop even more than it did in reality, and she had somehow edited out the shiny spot on my forehead that I hated. The caption read, *If you don't know, now you know. @FlorenceWakeGalleryNYC.*

"If you don't know what?" I asked.

"Who cares? People like to know secrets, so they'll scroll. Trust me on this one," Leah said.

"I'm posting it," I said as I clicked the button, feeling the rush of being a presence on the platform where I had been only a voyeur.

"Now the trick is putting your phone away for a while and not constantly checking your likes. It's a drug," she warned me, taking my phone and shoving it in my bag.

I forced myself to wait until I was home to check the post. Leah had reposted it from @FlorenceWakeGalleryNYC, and I had 137 new followers, more than two hundred likes, and several comments, one from Jules informing the world, *Oh, I know. <3.* I was still confused about what I knew, let alone what she knew, but I couldn't argue with Leah—it was a good post. I had scrolled through Instagram thousands of times before getting into bed, but tonight was the first night I had ever looked at my own post before getting under the covers. I put my phone away and rested my head on my pillow, thinking of the people I had never met who were viewing my life, and feeling somehow more relevant in the universe than I had that morning. I allowed myself a satisfied sigh and closed my eyes to reality.

AGENT TILLWELL:	Do you know Jane Kantrowitz?
EMMA CAAN:	I know the name. She and Florence were close. Not anymore.
AGENT GARRITT:	Did you speak to Florence about Jane? Or why they lost touch?
EMMA CAAN:	No, I wasn't given any information from Florence.
AGENT TILLWELL:	But you know about Jane's trial?
EMMA CAAN:	At this point, even people outside the art world know about Jane's trial. It was on the front page of the Sunday *Times* a few weeks ago, you know?

The next morning, I beat Leah to work and sat down to log onto the system. The gallery was still, with only the clicks of my keyboard echoing against the concrete floors.

"Emma!" Florence's voice came from the back of the gallery, just loud enough to hear but startling me so that I spilled the coffee I had picked up from the cart outside. I wiped at the drip on my chin and checked my blouse, noting gratefully that most had missed me and fallen right to the floor, before I looked up to see Florence poking her head into the main room from her office. "Call us a car to Sotheby's at six this evening, please. We're going to an auction," she said before ducking back in.

Just then Leah sauntered through the front door and looked at the coffee on the floor. She smirked. "Is there anything scarier than when she appears out of nowhere with a request?" She grabbed a roll of paper towels from a desk drawer and handed it to me.

We busied ourselves cataloging the new pieces from an artist Florence had signed a few weeks before and opted to eat lunch at our desk, rather than take separate breaks, so we could chat. Passive browsers drifted in and out all afternoon, and I finally glanced at my watch and saw that it was already six o'clock. I grabbed for my phone.

"Emma?" Florence asked from her office doorway.

"The car's on its way!" I called back to her, ordering an Uber as quickly as my fingers could type. Thankfully, a man named Keiran was only one minute away in a Suburban. I stood and straightened my blouse, waiting for Florence to walk past me before I joined her in stride. We headed out of the gallery and onto the street, and it was only a moment before the car pulled up. We sat silently, stuck in gridlock, horns blaring all around us.

"Are you new to the city?" Florence asked Keiran, without looking up from her phone, in what I thought was an uncharacteristic display of interest in another person.

"No, ma'am," the driver said. "Born and raised in Staten Island."

"Then you should have known to take First Avenue at this hour," she said.

Through the rearview mirror, I watched his eyes narrow, and I knew my Uber rating was about to take a hit. "Here we are," he finally announced, pulling up to the Sotheby's building on York Avenue. When we stepped out of the car, cameras immediately flashed, and I noted a small pack of reporters. I had never been to an auction, but from what I saw on Jules's Instagram, press wasn't common. I buzzed with the anticipation at the level of art we were about to see, if the media had decided to show up for it.

"Florence!" "Florence!" A chorus erupted as they recognized her.

My boss drifted easily toward a smartly dressed blond woman in horn-rimmed glasses, ignoring the others. "Avery, how are you?" Florence greeted her.

The reporter smiled and leaned in close, clicking a red button on her recording device. "Thanks for taking a moment, Florence. Can you tell us what you expect to see here today at the Chinese contemporary art auction?"

"I'm interested to see how the market values the later works of Liu Xiaodong," she answered. "I don't get to interact with his work nearly as much as I'd like in my gallery. I expect the market to show strong support in value of his pieces. After all, auction houses are perhaps the cleanest, most unbiased way to value art. Here, demand always speaks for itself, and I'm predicting large numbers."

"That would be exciting. Let's hope you're right," Avery said, jotting down a note. "I'd also love to hear your thoughts on NFTs. Sotheby's is having their second NFT auction next week, and I have a source who confirms that Belcussi Gallery will be rolling out their first virtual gallery next month for NFTs, accepting crypto payment."

I turned to study Florence, hoping to detect regret that she hadn't listened to my advice to take advantage of the burgeoning NFT market, but there was none.

"I'm so pleased other galleries have volunteered to work out the kinks in the virtual gallery and NFT space," Florence said confidently. "But with every new art medium there is a surge of fraud, a resulting breach of confidence in authenticity, and a resulting dip in valuation. As soon as I feel that I can protect our gallery's artists and their intellectual property, we will be moving into this arena, too."

I watched her tuck an escaped tuft of hair back behind an ear and was reminded of the first time I saw her, at Lenny's party—of the quiet power she exuded, the sense of integrity she conveyed.

"Speaking of fraud," Avery continued, "any comment on the Jane Kantrowitz trial?"

"Avery . . ." Florence said, shaking her head with a perfectly shame-inducing blend of admonishment and disappointment, then moved past her and the row of other reporters. Her expression was placid, but I could feel hot annoyance radiating from her as I hurried to catch up, and I was glad Leah had warned me how sensitive the topic of Jane Kantrowitz was. There was a "No Photos Outside of the Press Area" sign, so I quickly snapped a shot of the Sotheby's facade before entering. I followed Florence through the glass doors of the auction house into a lobby where a line of people showed their IDs and received paddles with numbers in return. I looked down at my work attire and then at the long silk skirt of the woman trailing ahead of me.

"I didn't know I was supposed to dress up for this," I said as I leaned in to Florence.

"You're fine," she said quickly, and I took it as an indication that she didn't think it was her job to make me feel better about my fashion choices.

"Do we get paddles?" I asked, looking ahead in the line.

"Sure. But I'm not here to buy. You're welcome to," she said as she extended her hand toward the woman checking identification, then added, "but my source said the lowest reserve price is half a million."

"Well, then, apparently *I* am not here to buy, either!" I said with a laugh, trying unsuccessfully to lighten the mood, though I didn't even know exactly what a reserve price was. Whatever it was, it was more money than I had.

"Florence!" the slender woman checking IDs in a classic long-sleeve black dress with an iPad said happily as we reached the front of the line. "Plus one," she said, thinking aloud and handing us two paddles. Florence looked at the number on hers and nodded as though she understood where our seats would be based on the paddle number, which I found difficult to believe. She continued down the marble foyer and through the wood double doors leading to the auction room. There were only a few clusters of empty seats and we peeled right off the strip of aisle into one of the openings and sat in uncomfortable silence. *I can do this. I can sit quietly and not speak.*

"That was a great quote you gave the reporter. I never thought about auction houses being the most honest valuation of a work. Makes total sense," I said, then immediately wished I hadn't.

"Oh, please," Florence said, studying my face as though I couldn't possibly be serious, then looking annoyed that she needed to explain herself. "Auctions are just an elaborate ruse to either legitimize a shady seller, or to make the highest bidder feel warm and fuzzy about his purchase. Of course, sometimes the highest bidder is savvy enough to be wise to the game, but most often he's some schmuck off the street who doesn't know that Adam Schwartzwald called all his fellow Fanzhi collectors to make sure his pieces sell for a certain amount today, an instruction they will eagerly oblige in order to maintain the value of their own collections." She looked around the room and cocked her head in the direction of an older woman in a Chanel suit with a young man at her side. "Sotheby's guarantees a minimum price to the sellers, so there's no real risk there. Then they spend weeks rounding up buyers who guarantee a floor price. I'm guessing the Youngs from L.A. will place the opening bid, but they don't like to be seen, so they're probably in an auxiliary room. The Huismans will call in from Switzerland," she continued, pointing out a white box to our left containing twenty or so people with phones to their ears. "The Parks always send Gabriel, their wealth manager. Except I don't see—" She looked toward the front of the room just as a man walking down the aisle tapped her shoulder. "Ah, Gabriel! I was just wondering where you were," she said, standing to kiss him on either cheek before sitting back down with a smug grin. "They'll seat the Petrowskis right across the aisle from Gabriel because the Petrowskis and the Parks hate each other."

I furrowed my brow. "Then why would they seat them nearby?"

"Because they're hoping they hate each other enough to stupidly outbid each other just to keep the other from getting the work," Florence said, as though it were the most obvious thing in the world.

I scanned the room, processing what Florence was saying. If she was right, the price fetched by each piece wasn't based on whether people felt moved by the art; it was all a charade—an investment not in art but in the art market as a whole. Suddenly, copying paintings didn't feel quite so bottom-feeding, if this was what went on at the top. Florence nudged my shoulder and nodded in the direction of two gentlemen, who I assumed were Petrowskis, stiffly greeting Gabriel before taking their seats across the aisle from him.

A slender woman in a fitted white dress stepped up to the podium and welcomed everybody briefly, pointed to the image on the wall behind her, and calmly stated, "This is the Zeng Fanzhi, and let's open the bidding here at five million." She barely took a breath before she announced, "Five point five. Six. Seven." I looked around the room, hoping to catch sight of who was bidding.

"Seven and a half, please!" announced a man who obviously didn't think she saw him.

"Seven point five. Eight to Donald. Nine. Nine and a half. Ten. Eleven. Twelve million to Samuel. Still with Samuel. Thirteen to Donald. Fourteen to Samuel. Fifteen to Samuel. Still with Samuel. Fifteen it is, to you, Samuel. Sold for fifteen million." My attention bounced around the room as the auction for the first piece concluded mere moments after it began, attempting to process what I had just witnessed. It had all happened too quickly to understand, but I assumed Florence's prediction had just come to fruition.

I opened my phone and posted the photo of the building facade to Instagram with the caption *What happens in Sotheby's* . . . The auction progressed precisely as Florence predicted, and she was asked to pose with the Petrowskis and their new piece for an on-line publication. She ignored Avery as we exited through the glass doors, me struggling to catch up with her.

"Good night, Emma," Florence said with a small smile and wave as she quickened her pace toward the street and hailed a cab.

I hadn't expected us to get a drink and chat about the auction, but it was still early in the evening, and I was left alone in midtown east. So I strolled west, knowing I'd eventually reach a subway to take uptown. In the meantime, I took out my phone and checked to see the reaction to my post, which had already received more than a hundred likes and one direct message from Sienna.

> @SSHAW212: This is 🔥! Can I see you this weekend and hear all about it?
>
> @ECAANART: I'm going home to PA on Saturday to help my mom pack up some stuff at the house ☹
>
> @SSHAW212: Can I come?

Sienna and I spotted each other across the waiting area below the screen announcing the platforms. I'd known the appropriate response to her offer was that it wasn't necessary and I would be fine, but both were lies. I'd gratefully accepted, and we'd arranged to meet at Penn Station early Saturday morning.

She frowned slightly when she saw me. "Nightmares or drill-ing?" she asked, presumably noting the bags under my eyes.

I shrugged. "Both. And trying to get up to speed at work. What about you? Your eyes are red," I said just as we looked up to see our train announced for track 3.

"Late night with Michael," she said, and smiled, heading toward the platform.

I rolled my eyes. "Jealous," I said as we boarded, the air between us quieter than usual.

My chest tightened with every mile the train barreled closer to my hometown while Sienna slept peacefully beside me, her mouth slightly agape. The abandoned gas station where my friends and I used to skip class to smoke pot whipped by the window, and I felt my anxious, angry, tearful former self creeping back into me, as though she were a product of location rather than time. When the train finally slowed to a stop at the station, I felt the thick layers of myself that I had worked so hard to make permanent at Yale sloughing off easily, and memories of my father seeped in through my pores.

"This town is so cute!" Sienna cooed, stretching her arms up and rotating her wrists as we stepped off the train onto the platform. "Look at that farmers' market!" She craned her neck.

"That place is actually really good. We'll get food there for the ride home. I want to get out of here before dinner," I said, then looked right at her so that she knew I meant what I was about to say. "Thank you for coming." I wondered if I'd have gotten on the train at all, or had the strength to get off, if she weren't with me.

"No thanks needed. I want to be here," she said with a small shrug, and I could tell she really didn't want me to feel indebted to her.

Ardmore was a clean and neat suburb, with Lilly Pulitzer and Soul Cycle outposts nestled between artisanal bakeries and trendy clothing boutiques—the kind of place called home by people afraid to live messy lives. I had always felt out of place here, knowing that my family wasn't automatically a happy one because we lived in a town filled with manicured lawns and responsible citizens who dragged their recycling bin to the bottom of their long driveway every Wednesday.

I spotted my mother parked illegally directly across the street, standing outside her car in her winter coat, her hair blow-dried and her makeup fresh. She proudly held a Starbucks cup in each hand, and I knew that if I'd come alone, she'd have been parked in the lot across the square, waiting catatonically in the car in pajamas. One major benefit of Sienna coming was that my mother was far too proud to be a mess in front of a stranger. She set the cups on the hood of the car and pulled me in for a hug. "Hey, Mom," I said as I leaned in to her.

"Sienna, I'm *so* glad you made the trip out here. I brought coffee!" My mother hugged her and beamed with her own generosity as she took the coffees from the hood and handed them to us, basking in our thank-yous with a broad smile. "It's the least I could do, considering you woke up early on a Saturday to do manual labor. Come in out of the cold."

I gave Sienna the front seat because I knew she was about to get "the tour" from my mother. As we drove, I heard my mother in the periphery of my consciousness, telling Sienna about the town— Kobe Bryant went to high school just up the road, Meredith from *The Office* was our neighbor, my father saved a child on these very tracks from getting hit by a train. I forced calm breaths. *In and out. In and out.*

"He sounds like an incredible man," Sienna said as we crossed over the tracks. I couldn't argue with that. The story did *sound* incredible, far more incredible than the truth—that he and I had spotted a young boy sitting on a bench at the train station and we had stayed with him for the full thirty seconds it took his mother to sprint there to yell at him for running ahead of her. Arguing with my father's version of things was like wrestling with a bedsheet—it only tired *me* out, made *me* look ridiculous. His was the version that survived him.

We finally pulled into the driveway of my childhood home, and I sat in the car for a moment after my mother and Sienna had exited, looking at the glossy black shutters and the pristine white facade, dreading stepping inside.

"Your home is gorgeous," Sienna said as we entered. She stared up at the vaulted entryway ceiling.

"We like it," my mother said, and smiled with false modesty. I studied her, fighting the urge to ask her who "we" was. As my mother paraded Sienna from room to room, walking backward like a campus tour guide most of the time, my cheeks grew hot, and I began to wonder whether she had any intention of selling the house or this had just been her way of guilting me back.

"Mom!" I interrupted midway through her story of how they'd kept the original fireplace stones when they restored the house. "You should take a few hours to yourself while we do Dad's closet. Go run errands. Pamper yourself. Whatever! We can finish the tour when you're back."

Sienna nodded encouragingly, and my mother acquiesced and headed out in her car after a few more compliments on the portion of the house she had already shown off.

"I'm so sorry," Sienna said, staring into my father's closet upstairs. "I know I said I'd help, but I have no idea what to keep and what to toss. What if I throw out something important, something with big sentimental value?"

"Don't worry, we're donating it all. We just need to make it look like we sorted everything so my mother doesn't freak out," I said, turning to her, knowing that I sounded harsh. "It's too painful for my mother to have this stuff around." What I didn't add was that he was barely living there toward the end, and my mother should have tossed him and his stuff out decades ago.

Sienna nodded empathetically at the story I had fed her, and we started on the right side of the walk-in closet, where his two remaining suits hung alongside the rest of his clothes. He'd been buried in the third. I reached out and touched the navy sleeve of one and immediately felt him around me, smelled his cigarettes on the dark fabric though it had been dry-cleaned since he'd worn it last. I saw my father's prominent nose, and then the rest of his face, and suddenly I found myself back at the funeral, seeing him resting peacefully in a bed of cushioned white satin. He looked handsome in his full face of makeup—far better than he had in the hospital. Then I spotted *her* in the back pew, looking more beautiful than anybody had any right to look at a funeral, wearing a turtleneck so nobody could see the ugly scars on her chest. I angled myself so my mother couldn't see her, before stealing one final glance back.

I blinked, and I was back in the closet, tears streaming down my cheeks. Sienna moved her hand gently over my back and rested her head on my shoulder.

"You must miss him," she said gently.

I nodded, wishing the emotion felt that simple. Almost reluctantly, I did miss his jokes, his loud, boisterous laughter, the way he pulled my mother up off the couch to dance when she was sad, and the way he sang off-key ballads while scrambling eggs on weekends. But it was impossible to disentangle these memories from the recollection of how he always smelled of cigarettes and gin and sometimes the sickly saccharine floral smell of a woman's perfume. I remembered playing under his secretary's desk, my hair still in pigtails, and asking him on the way home why he sometimes smelled just the way she did. He'd scooped me up in his arms and surprised me with a trip to Toys "R" Us and let me pick out whatever I wanted, allaying his guilt and buying my silence.

Snapping myself into the present again, I unclenched my fists, wiping the mucus from under my nose with the back of my hand. How could I begin to explain all this to Sienna?

"Okay, let's try this again," I said, taking one suit off its hanger and shoving it into a trash bag, finding comfort in the action.

We worked side by side in silence, interrupted only by a few questions from Sienna about things she thought I might want to save—twelve years' worth of the T-shirts my father's whole office was made to wear on annual off-sites (toss), the Lucite paperweight on his dresser honoring his 2005 country club golf championship (toss), the Cornell T-shirt that was so full of holes you could barely tell what it said (keep), all my report cards from pre-K through senior year (toss, though I cried that he'd kept them), his St. Thomas hooded sweatshirt (keep), his beige cable-knit sweater (keep). When we finished, I wiped the small tear from the corner of my eye, noting the "keep" pile was much larger than I had planned—almost an entire garbage bag's worth. I had a bad habit of holding on to things I knew I should let go of.

An hour in, we found a jar of THC gummies and a canister of joints tucked into his sock drawer. "For the chemo," I explained.

Sienna nodded, and we looked at each other and giggled. "Should we smoke?" she asked.

"I'd rather eat a gummy . . ." I said almost apologetically; just the idea of my face being so close to a burning ember made me sweat. She whacked her forehead with her palm, realizing she had forgotten my fear of fire, and twisted open the jar of gummies.

We each took one and sat at the kitchen counter, acknowledging twenty minutes later through nervous giggles that they were incredibly potent and there was a chance we should have split one.

"I need air!" Sienna declared, and we slipped out the back door into the yard, laughing at absolutely nothing and agreeing that the entire scenario—the high and the house and the suburbs—reeked of our respective high school days. The remaining patches of snow in the backyard dotted the dead grass with white heaps, and the world slowed to a sluggish pace as we strolled across the thawing earth. I winced as Sienna commented on how "naturally beautiful" the land was, because I knew others might call it "overgrown" or "unkempt."

"What happened *there*?" Sienna asked, and I followed her gaze to the patch of charred earth along the side fence. It was usually covered by the shrubs, but they were now bare. I stared for what I knew was too long as my brain retreated to the memory of peering through the window of the toolshed, seeing *her* up on the work-bench and my father's pants around his ankles. I turned to the trill of a bird from off in the woods abutting the yard, using it as an excuse to take a beat and gather my thoughts, and exhaled a thin stream of visible breath into the cold air.

"There was a fire in the toolshed when I was little. My dad and his friend were stuck inside. I saw the whole thing. It was crazy!" I added, giving a careless snort of laughter so she wouldn't suspect how often I thought of that night, of those flames. "They both got out." Her eyes widened, and I felt encouraged to continue. "It was a total accident. Probably from one of my father's cigarette butts. It was an accident," I repeated.

"Do you think that's where your fire nightmares come from?" she asked, still looking at the patch.

Absolutely, 100 percent. "Maybe. I should be over it," I thought aloud.

"I don't know. I think seeing your father escape a fire is pretty traumatic!" Sienna stared at the charred earth, and I knew she had more questions, but I was high and wanted desperately to get back inside, so I turned and headed toward the house.

On the way back upstairs, Sienna stopped and stared at the mantel in the living room. "Is *that* your dad?" she said, pointing at the picture of the three of us at my cousin's christening when I was in elementary school.

I nodded, noting her furrowed brow as she leaned in closer to the picture. "Why?" I asked.

"He reminds me of Leonard Sobetsky!" she breathed.

I inched closer to the picture and cocked my head to the side. "A little," I agreed, seeing a slight resemblance.

"A lot! The height. The hair. The broad chest. Jeez!" Sienna gasped incredulously. I laughed in casual agreement and dragged her by the hand back to my father's closet.

By the time my mother came home a few hours later, Sienna and I were still very high, had finished off an entire sleeve of Double Stuf Oreos we had found in the pantry, and were just tying off the floppy red plastic handle loops of the large black garbage bags we had filled with the contents of my father's life. I had neatly folded up a couple of sweaters and T-shirts that I thought my mother might like to cozy up in one day and placed them on her bed. The closet looked somehow smaller with less in it—a room of empty hangers with a few black bags in the middle.

"What did you do all afternoon?" I asked my mother.

She fanned out her cherry-red fingertips with a broad smile.

"Love the color!" Sienna said excitedly.

"We have time, do you need us to do the office?" I asked my mother, whose expression immediately darkened as she caught sight of the garbage bags.

"Oh, no, the firm took care of it," she said absently.

"What do you mean?" I asked.

"I told you, didn't I? Some man from your dad's office came a few weeks ago and took most of what the company needed, and I sent the rest to our accountant because I don't know what any of that stuff means." She was still staring at the bags. I opened my mouth to explain that my father had been technically "retired" for years, which simply meant his partner had shoved him out and stopped paying medical leave, so it made no sense that they'd need anything at all, but I decided to avoid the discussion.

Sienna followed my lead and joined me as I refused multiple offers from my mother to have us sleep over, which she gave up on and asked us to stay for dinner, which she gave up on and begged to make us a late lunch, until she acquiesced to our "need" to get back, which was really my desire to get away from all the memories, and drove us to Goodwill. We threw the bags in the curbside drop-off receptacle as she watched us from the car, then said goodbye to her outside the farmers' market with thirty minutes to spare before our train home. I looked back at her just before we entered the station's automatic sliding door—she was sitting in the driver's seat, staring at nothing, until the car behind her honked her back to reality and she drove away.

I tried to ignore the guilt of leaving her, knowing the visit had probably made her more depressed. Tomorrow's phone call would be somber, about how she missed me, and how everything seemed even more lonely now that I was gone, the house emptier without my father's clothes, and so on.

"This place is incredible!" Sienna pulled at my arm, distracting me.

The Ardmore Farmers' Market was less of a farmers' market and more of a specialty food store, with French cheeses, prepared foods, fresh local produce from Amish farms, and anything else a yuppie picnicker might need. I watched Sienna drift happily from stand to stand, trying samples of hummus and asking about the process for making the fresh sourdough, buying everything she liked, while I only browsed. At our last stop, the Bake Shoppe, a heavyset woman with a white apron and kind eyes threw in a black-and-white cookie with our caramel apple crumb cake and was ringing us up when my eyes drifted across the aisle. I froze in place, unable to look away and pretend I didn't see her. I blinked twice, begging her to disappear back into my imagination, but she remained in front of me.

"Hellooooo?" Sienna waved her hand in front of my face. "Who's making us late now? Seriously, we have to . . ."

I hadn't seen her since the funeral, though I thought of her more often than I cared to admit. She was admittedly still gorgeous, though I could see the skin below her right ear didn't look real—as though it had been melted down and smoothed over with a spatula, like pinkish-yellow frosting on a cake. My stomach flipped as the world slowed around me with an amniotic swooshing noise, leaving only us. I placed my hands on the glass counter filled with cookies, afraid I might lose my balance.

"Miss, you can't lean on that, it's not stable," I heard somebody say from behind the counter. But I was suddenly back in my yard, pushing up on my toes to see them in the window. Her head, leaning back, and my father's, buried in her chest.

"Who is that?" Sienna asked, calling me back to the present as she followed my gaze. "Do you know her?" she tried again.

"My father's secretary. I don't know her well," I muttered.

My mind unlatched from the world around me, drifted somewhere more pleasant, and returned to my body just in time to refuse the half of the black-and-white cookie Sienna was offering me as she sat beside me. I didn't know how I had arrived at my seat on the Keystone back to Penn Station.

"You sure you're okay?" Sienna asked. "You seem . . . off."

"Just tired," I lied.

"Long day," she agreed. "Want to just sleep? Or . . ." From her bag, she pulled a bottle of Malbec she'd bought at the farmers' market and raised her eyebrows twice to entice me. "Got a twist-off," she said with a wink, making a fist around the bottle neck.

"Smart," I said as I exhaled.

My memories faded into one another as we drank, the borders of the flames, affair, anger, and resentment corroded by alcohol until they were just one fiery mess. When Sienna excused herself to the bathroom, I stared out the window and took comfort in the trees whizzing by, reminding myself that I was leaving the young girl in all those pictures farther behind with every revolution of the train wheels. Sienna returned just as the trees gave way to lawns, and then the sprawling lawns contracted into small strips of green between houses, and then they disappeared entirely into slabs of pavement between apartment buildings. As the train dipped below ground, the scream of the wheels on the tracks grew louder in my ears, making it difficult to breathe. I forced small talk about Jeremy and Gemini until the train slowed and pulled into Penn Station. I walked Sienna out of the station, hugged her close while extending my hand over her shoulder to hail her a cab, then descended the escalator to catch the subway uptown. Once home, I burrowed my head into the pillow and allowed my barely open eyes to close for the night, dreading the flames I knew would come before I opened them again.

AGENT TILLWELL:	Did you travel with Leonard Sobetsky for work?
EMMA CAAN:	I'm sorry, I'm glad to help, but why are you asking me questions you know the answer to?
AGENT GARRITT:	What was the first time you traveled with him for work?
EMMA CAAN:	When I saw you. We went to Art Basel Hong Kong.
AGENT GARRITT:	How did you get there?
EMMA CAAN:	On Leonard's plane.
AGENT TILLWELL:	How many times had you met Leonard prior to him inviting you on his private plane to Hong Kong?
EMMA CAAN:	A few. Two or three. But offering somebody a ride is nothing to Leonard. He was going anyway.
AGENT TILLWELL:	Who else was on the plane?
EMMA CAAN:	Sergey and his wife and their child and his nanny. Lenny's assistant. And some security. On the way home, there were a few more people.
AGENT GARRITT:	Wow. That must have been quite an experience.
EMMA CAAN:	It was. It really was.
AGENT TILLWELL:	I bet it was hard to go back to regular life after a taste of the good life.
EMMA CAAN:	Not really. It was the good life, but it wasn't mine. I never fooled myself into thinking it was.

I spent the majority of Sunday in bed, but I was still exhausted as I headed to Florence Wake on Monday. My body was tired from having slept so much, and my mind was drained of energy by bad dreams. As the subway tunneled downtown, I gave myself a silent pep talk, preparing to throw myself into my last week of work before heading to Hong Kong. *Ask every question out loud. Write everything down.* I burst through the door of the gallery and sat down, looking over the electronic ledger of sales before Leah arrived.

"Do we *have* to do this today?" Leah whined after she adequately caffeinated herself, gesturing to the spreadsheet open on my computer screen.

"Not really. I think I'm fine with this program," I said.

"Good, you'll never do it anyway, but it's good for you to know. Data entry is in my wheelhouse, unfortunately," she said as she rolled her eyes.

In contrast to Leah's laissez-faire attitude toward my computer literacy, she took teaching me how to sell quite seriously. In my short time at the gallery, I had noted that the morning hours were usually sparsely punctuated with customers who oozed New York City downtown cool, while the afternoon was filled with younger people who were out early from work. Leah explained that the rules for judging serious purchasers by their covers were different below Twenty-Sixth Street—I was to look for horn-rimmed Warby Parkers and alpaca teddy coats instead of the Oliver Peoples and mink you'd keep an eye out for uptown. Leah also knew precisely how to approach customers, easing them into pleasant, intelligent conversation about themselves rather than the art. More often than not, the personal conversations ended with the exchange of money for a piece of art (or, rather, a sales receipt promising its delivery). I wrote down in a small notebook everything I heard her say and saw her do.

The next day, Leah instructed me to let a tall blond woman in Chanel boots browse on her own but perked up when two informally dressed men entered just before noon. One was Black and one white, and both wore tapered Lululemon joggers and Allbirds, looking as though they had just worked out.

"You got this one," Leah instructed me, giving a nod toward them.

"Can't I watch you handle one more buyer first?" I protested.

"Start by offering them a drink," she said, ignoring me. "Look, if you blow it and they leave, nobody except me will ever know. But if you sell on your first try . . . you're employee of the century. There's only upside," Leah reasoned, waiting for me to move. "Come on!" she said, snapping me out of my trance. I inhaled and rose from my seat to approach the men.

"Hello," I greeted them as they stood looking at Fredrick Thomas's *Bombshell*, featuring a bunch of men on a stoop gawking at whoever was passing by. As was typical of Thomas's pieces, the interesting part was the point of view, which was that of the person being gawked at.

"We're just browsing," the Black man warned me, but the white guy shook his head ever so slightly and winked at me.

"You have a good eye. Even if you're just browsing," I said, holding my hands up in peace. "There's something about this one, isn't there?"

"Is this the artist who always covers his face?" one of them asked. I nodded and told them more about Fredrick Thomas and some of his recent projects. When they asked the price, I spotted Leah out of the corner of my eye, raising her hand high above her head, faking a stretch, and extending a single pointer finger: *$1 million.*

"One point one million," I responded calmly, building in a cushion to negotiate and forcing my eyes to remain steady. It was worth an eighth of that, in my opinion, and it was a poor investment because I couldn't really imagine the work appreciating. To my shock, they nodded and began asking logistical questions about delivery to East Hampton.

"We'll take it," the Black man announced casually once I'd as-sured them that we routinely delivered to East Hampton. "Happy birthday," he said, and kissed his partner.

"Wonderful!" I said cheerily, trying not to allow my astonish-ment to register on my face. "Florence's assistant, Leah, will be out in just a moment with the paperwork. Please, enjoy the view of your new piece while I get everything in order." I turned from them and met Leah's gaze, peeling back my eyelids to indicate I could barely believe what had just happened. I deliberately walked slowly and calmly back to the desk and sat beside her. "Sold."

"I don't get it," she said under her breath. "I wish somebody had told me while I was still in art school that I could paint shitty pieces and sell them for millions if I dressed like a freak show. I'd be laughing all the way to the bank, too. How much?"

"One point one," I said softly.

"Shut the fuck up! You're a natural!" Leah whispered, trying not to giggle. "You didn't even offer them a drink!"

I winced. "Shit, I forgot!"

"Sale for one hundred thousand over list price on your first day. You're officially the best one Lenny has ever sent us!" she exclaimed, playfully checking me with her shoulder as she gathered the sale paperwork and headed over to the men. I barely had a moment to harp on how many of me there had been before the next question came. "Where are they taking delivery?"

"East Hampton, I think."

"Classic," Leah said with a smirk, and we finished the paperwork for the sale and presented it to them.

When we sat back down, Leah picked up the phone. "Hey, Eve-lyn, we just sold Fredrick Thomas to a couple from East Hampton on a whim. They might be buying up in the space . . . sure . . . sure . . . no problem . . . well, we owe you one . . . I'll send their info over to your assistant now." She hung up the phone. "We try to keep our friends at the auction houses apprised of the market—this way they can pack auctions with very interested buyers. And they send buyers our way in return," Leah said, leaving me to assume she had just called an auction house.

Florence burst through the front door as our newest customers were departing, and she breezed back to her office without so much as a look in our direction. I drifted toward the back of the studio, determined to try for Hong Kong preparation time with her. I knocked lightly on the doorframe to announce myself, and she looked up from her computer, seemingly confused by my presence.

"Hi. Um," I stammered as I stepped in without being invited, "I was hoping we could discuss Hong Kong. I'm leaving in just a few days, and I want to make sure I'm representing this gallery and you in the best li—"

"You'll be fine," she assured me.

"Thank you," I replied to her completely unfounded vote of confidence. "But maybe we could discuss the pieces and prices—"

Her cell phone buzzed on the table, and her eyes lit up at the name on the caller ID. "Hello there," she answered, a subtle levity in her usually stoic demeanor. "You know what, let me call you right back," she added, indicating that she didn't intend to spend any appreciable amount of time explaining to me how to handle one of the most prestigious booths at one of the largest art fairs in the world.

"So, when I get to Basel, will the booth be—"

"Emma," Florence interrupted, pointing to her free chair and contemplating me for a moment. Her cell phone buzzed again, and she looked down at the screen and then back at me. "You'll be *fine*."

I opened my mouth to argue with her, but she cut me off. "Look, I usually let the new girl figure this out on her own, but I am going to be traveling a lot in the next year, and I need you to run this place while I do, so I'm going to save us some time." She leaned back and smoothed her shirt over her torso. "A good portion of this world is a show, Emma. You realize that, right? Real artists, real geniuses, are few and far between. When they create a piece that moves people or changes the way people see the world, it's not worth millions—it is priceless. If I waited around to sell those pieces, I'd be bankrupt." She smiled at me softly but not warmly, in a way that made me feel like a tiny toddler in an adult chair dangling her feet above the ground.

"You don't think the art you sell is good?" I asked, not sure whether to judge her for being a sellout or feel relieved to hear a critique of the world that had rejected my own work.

"What is *good* art?" she asked, throwing her hands up in the air. "It's art people *want*. And I know what people want—how to package it to make them want it. Others make money in far less scrupulous ways. Somebody makes hundreds of thousands supplying cocaine to partygoers at each art fair. Hotels jack up their prices . . ." She paused and cocked her head to one side. "You know, a few years back somebody was stabbed at Art Basel Miami, and people just stood by photographing it. They thought it was performance art." Before I could respond, she went on, "Last year a slice of an apple, an actual apple that would be brown in an hour, sold for one hundred and twenty thousand dollars. The art market is an elaborate show, and we are the best showmen. With postwar contemporary galleries, it's feast or famine. There is no in between. You either play the game or you shutter your gallery. So I pay the equivalent of a year's New York rent for the gallery to have twenty square feet at Art Basel Hong Kong, and *you* will sell every single piece you can to make it worthwhile. I don't care how you do it. I'm not going to pretend to train you, because everybody has their own style. You will figure yours out, and given the alert I just received about this morning's sale, you're already on your way. So, I say again, you will be fine. You only need to show up and go to a few parties."

Her phone buzzed with a new call, and she picked it up. "What does that mean?" she calmly said, finishing her conversation with me by beginning another.

We were slated to leave for Hong Kong on Monday evening. I allowed my cheap black rolling suitcase to thud down the subway steps behind me on the way to work Monday morning while saying a silent prayer that it wouldn't escape my grip and bulldoze anybody below me.

After work, I did a quick change in the bathroom, breaking into a slight sweat under the strain of dressing in a confined space, exited the gallery, hurled my suitcase into the trunk of the cab that pulled up next to me, and loosened my jacket collar to release the heat sealed in against my chest. I glanced down at my watch, noting that it was almost five p.m. and the flight was taking off in three hours, then removed it from my wrist because the people I'd be with would most certainly judge me for wearing a Casio.

"Teterboro Airport, please," I said, meeting the driver's eyes in the rearview mirror.

"Teterboro?" he asked skeptically. I was sure he'd looked at my navy leggings and wondered why someone like me was going there, but I nodded confidently.

I hadn't flown since the ninth grade, when I had spent Christmas in Aruba with my parents, who spent the entire time arguing, apparently having given up on the idea of an enjoyable family vacation. Now I was flying private with a bunch of Russian billionaires. I should have been excited, but I felt a sense of impending doom that I'd embarrass myself. Attempting to steady my nerves,

I rummaged around in my purse to touch my phone, my wallet, and my passport one last time. *I'm flying private to Art Basel Hong Kong with a bunch of billionaires*, I repeated to myself. My heart slowed and I began to feel what I had been wanting to for weeks: the unbridled thrill of living a life I had only ever imagined.

As we exited the Lincoln Tunnel and I recovered all four bars of reception, I took out my phone and opened Instagram, noting four new follow requests, then changed my username to *CaanArtist* and my profile to read, *My friends call me Emma. Assistant Director @FlorenceWakeGalleryNYC*. I took a look at the changes and pressed a button to make my profile public, then clicked my phone off before tossing it in my purse, craning my neck to watch the city disappear in the rearview mirror.

There was a small security station at the entrance to the airport, where a guard asked both me and the driver for our IDs, checked a list, and allowed us through. When we pulled up to the terminal, there were no other cars around.

"Enjoy!" my driver said as he yanked my luggage free from the trunk, apparently having decided, based on my destination, that I was now somebody worth helping with her luggage.

"Thanks." I beamed, realizing it was quite a change from the "Have a safe flight" I'd heard when flying commercial.

The airport was more like a hotel lobby, draped in calming beige tones and muted greens. There were no porters or security lines, not a single other person to be seen except the woman seated behind a large rounded desk.

"Hi. Um . . ." I said to her as I glanced around the empty room, realizing that I had no boarding pass or confirmation number. "I'm flying with Leonard Sobetsky to Hong Kong?"

"Welcome!" she said cheerily. "I have your flight leaving at eight, is that still correct?" She knew our schedule off the top of her head, as she hadn't looked away from me. I nodded. "Oh, you're early.

That's great! Could I just see your ID?" I grabbed my wallet and handed it to her, painfully aware of my awful license photo as I imagined all the beautiful faces she usually saw. "Do you have a passport? I don't need it. Just a heads-up that they'll ask for it in Hong Kong. Have you been here before?" she asked politely, handing my license back to me with a smile. I shook my head as she secured a plastic band around my wrist with a snap. "Well, we have a theater and a gym that you're welcome to use. I'd be happy to give you a tour . . ."

"Oh, no, that's fine. I'll just wait for everybody here," I said, gesturing to the leather armchairs by the large windows.

"Great," she said, looking me up and down. "You're in for a real treat. You're taking the new Boeing BBJ. And with the way the wind is blowing, I think you'll be there in less than fifteen hours!" She delivered the news as though it were positive. I'd been prepared for a long flight, but hearing the actual duration I'd be trapped in a small space with strangers made a nerve between my shoulder blades tingle.

"Great!" I said, and rotated my neck slightly to try to release the tension. I pulled my fraying luggage behind me, positive the woman was looking at it and judging me, and took a seat, flipping through an *InStyle* that had been placed on the coffee table, unable to think about anything but that I looked nothing like the people in the pages of it.

At seven-thirty, the terminal was still empty, and I'd seen only one family—with four kids and a tiny yapping dog—deplane from their jet. I watched as they tornadoed their way through the waiting area, leaving in their wake Go-Gurt tubes, RXBAR wrappers, a plastic Peppa Pig figurine with one arm missing, and a special gift from the poorly trained Pomeranian. As the airport staff descended to clean up after them, and I refreshed my email for the sixteenth time to see if Leonard's assistant had sent an updated itinerary, the doors to the terminal opened and a beautiful mass of three men and four women entered. The men wore skinny black jeans and white sneakers, while the women wore dresses short enough and heels high enough to make their long legs appear anatomically impossible.

I blinked twice, focusing my attention on the man in the white V-neck. He was there, in Teterboro Airport, looking even more handsome than I remembered from Lenny's party. *Ryan Parker.* I watched him, certain my mind was playing tricks on me, unable to move or speak but willing him to notice me, to see me existing in his world.

And then he was gone, having exited the building onto the tarmac and into a hangar. *Nothing would have happened if I'd said hello. He'd never have remembered me.* But just beneath those practical words was a nervous voice that told me I'd missed my one opportunity with Ryan Parker, and just below that was a harsher one that told me I was the type of person who always missed the opportunities life presented me.

"Hi," an approaching voice said loudly, yanking me from my whirlpool of thoughts. A beautiful woman in a gray cashmere ensemble held up one hand in a wave and pulled a rolling suitcase with the other. Her dark hair was pulled back neatly into a silky ponytail, and her blue eyes pierced the distance between us. I squinted, knowing I had seen her before, but I was far more intimidated by her beauty than curious about where we had met.

"Micaela Anderson," she said as she shook my hand. I recalled the name from my email correspondence. "Lenny's assistant," she reminded me, her demeanor cold.

"Oh! Right! So nice to put a face to the name." I smiled broadly, hoping my own affability would encourage hers. "Did we meet at Lenny's party?" She shook her head and said nothing. "I keep having this bizarre sensation that I've already met people."

"Maybe you should see a doctor," she said flatly, turning to the window and pointing out at the tarmac. My back reflexively straightened at her stiff response. "This is us."

I followed her pointer finger to an enormous white plane with a gold anchor decal on the tail. It rolled slowly to a halt, and a set of stairs burst from its belly and dipped toward the concrete. It didn't look different from a commercial plane in any discernible way, and I began to wonder if I had misunderstood our travel plans and we had simply reserved a section of a large flight. Would I need to pay Lenny back for my seat?

My phone buzzed in my purse, distracting me from my momentary panic, and I fished it out. "Lenny says we should board," I said, looking at the screen. "He'll be here in a few."

Micaela looked at me suspiciously. "He just texted *you*?"

I nodded as I clenched my jaw, and she began to walk toward the sliding doors to the runway without another word, leaving her massive hard-shelled luggage in its spot beside me. I could think of nothing I wanted to do less than spend fifteen hours in a confined space with her. Looking from her luggage to my own, I wondered if she intended for me to take both.

"We'll take care of that for you, Ms. Caan," the concierge called to me from her desk, shooting a look at a man in the corner who ran over to assist me with the bags. I smiled politely, took my purse over my own shoulder, and followed him as he wheeled the two suitcases through the sliding glass doors and out to the tarmac. I climbed the steps of the plane but stopped a few shy of the top as the interior came into view.

A beautiful foyer with a lacquered wood entryway table and charcoal carpeting with shiny blue swirls revealed itself. Two men in crisp navy uniforms and a woman about my age in a navy pencil skirt and white silk blouse stood at the entrance. I continued to climb, confused as to how this massive mansion was supposed to soar halfway around the world.

"Welcome," the pilot with four yellow stripes on his uniform greeted me, while the one with three stripes smiled. "I'm Captain Lucas. This is my copilot, Captain Arnold, and Liza will be your flight attendant, along with Samantha, who will be back in just a moment."

"Emma," I said, nodding politely to all of them.

"Can I offer you a vodka?" Liza asked, presenting me with a silver tray of dainty glasses filled with clear liquid. I stepped forward onto the plush carpet and looked beyond the pilots to a sitting area with four coffee tables, three soft tan leather chairs around each, all four with a different offering: cheese and crackers on one, fruit on another, crudités, and pretzels and nuts on the one closest to me. "Or any other refreshment? We have a full bar." She nodded over her shoulder at another lounge area containing white leather reclining chairs, a poker table, and a deep mahogany bar along the far wall. "We can't display the liquors because they'd go flying away on takeoff. But we have everything," she assured me. "We'll give you the tour in just a moment."

I reminded myself this was a business trip and that Leonard was a very important potential source of income for me. "Oh, no, thank you," I said, holding up my palm, also realizing that a night of sober sleep would help me not to completely screw up representing Florence Wake at one of the most important art fairs of the year. Liza nodded politely and lowered the tray a bit as I looked around once more, realizing there must be more rooms, as Micaela was nowhere in sight. "Holy shit," I said, my voice low. "Excuse my language."

"I know, right?" Captain Lucas said with a smirk, his formal demeanor fading for just a moment before he straightened his shoulders yet again.

"Samantha will be back in just a moment from getting your friend settled," the young woman said. "She'll show you the plane, or feel free to explore on your own. It goes straight back for quite a ways."

I took her words at face value and drifted away from them with a thanks. I passed through the bar room and into a narrower hallway. I saw a bathroom and a lounge area with couches and a huge television across from them. Next, I entered a media room with a mixture of plush couches and soft leather chairs all facing a sizable movie screen. Micaela was lying on one of the couches, her shoes on the floor next to her, and though I was certain she heard me come in, she didn't look up from her phone, so I continued on.

A woman wearing a maroon skirt and black blouse greeted me from the other end of the hallway: "Hi! I'm Samantha. Let me finish up the grand tour for you." She beckoned for me to follow; she pointed out two more bathrooms and led me through a guest bedroom, an en suite bathroom complete with a shower, a formal dining room, a master bedroom and bath, all compact but pristinely appointed. I was trying to take it all in when Samantha announced, "And here you have another bathroom."

"Oh, good. I was just going to say this plane could really use another bathroom," I said, giggling. Samantha smiled, but it quickly disappeared from her face as she touched her finger to her left ear.

"You have Samantha," she said, and I noticed a small black earbud. "Great, on our way. The rest of the guests have just arrived," she told me, her eyes meeting mine. I suddenly felt nauseated at the prospect of being introduced to anyone else like Micaela, and I hoped Lenny was among the guests. I needed a friendly face. "That door is just a small office, and"—Samantha pointed at the end of the corridor and then winked—"another bathroom. We'll meet everybody in the lounge. Right this way." She turned and walked slightly ahead of me, chatting away with no awkward pauses. I marveled that she was in the correct line of work.

"Here we are," Samantha announced, gesturing for me to enter the lounge with the large bar. Micaela was already there, standing with Lenny and two other terrifyingly muscular men I had never seen before, and Sergey, who had his arm around the waist of an impossibly tall, incredibly thin blond woman whose perfect posture made me straighten my own spine. A young woman struggling to carry a sleeping child shuffled up the last step to the plane, passed us without a word, and disappeared down the hallway.

"Emma! My dear!" Lenny bellowed as he made his way to me, the hand holding his vodka remaining outstretched and the other pulling me in close.

"Thank you so much for giving me a ride," I said, glancing around the plane, though the expression felt woefully inadequate.

"What do you think of the plane?" he asked. "It's brand-new!"

"It's, um . . ." I wondered if I should subdue my reaction, *Act like you've been here before*, but my smile spread out toward my earlobes. "I'm trying so hard to say something blasé right now, but honestly, this is the most insane thing I've ever seen!"

Micaela snorted contemptuously, and I felt my cheeks flush in shame.

"Don't pay attention to Micaela. She's blasé about everything," Sergey said, and flashed a look at Micaela, who rolled her eyes and drained her small glass of vodka, then extended it toward Samantha for a refill.

"I'm so glad to have you aboard," Lenny said with childish exuberance, as though showing me his new tree house on a playdate. He then yelled, "The briefcases go in the office!" I furrowed my brow at the last part and turned to see the man who'd been loading luggage onto the plane holding a rather large briefcase. He gave Lenny a quick nod and headed toward the back of the plane.

"Leonard Sobetsky is the only person on earth to travel with a briefcase, or actually many briefcases, after the advent of the laptop," the tall blonde joked in a Russian accent thicker than the men's.

"You will all be stumbling around blind in a few years from staring at those screens, while I won't even need glasses. Mark my words!" Lenny said, looking at me. "Right?"

"I'm the new kid! Don't involve me," I begged, showing both my palms in a display of neutrality. Sergey and Lenny laughed.

"You were right, she is charming," the blond woman said, loud enough for me to hear as she leaned affectionately in to Sergey, taking a sip of her vodka.

"Emma, this is my wife, Yelena," Sergey said to me with a warm smile. "And Hank and Steve are here just to ensure our safety," he explained, gesturing to the two muscular men, then nodded to the back of the plane. "And that was our son, Alexei, and his nanny, Sophie."

"It's lovely to meet you, Yelena," I said, then turned to the guards. "Which of you is Hank?" I asked, squinting at what I thought was a red coil leading to an earpiece up the taller one's neck. As I realized it was the tongue of a tattooed snake head, I thought about how painful getting a tattoo there must have been.

"Steve," the tattooed guard said, smiling brightly at me, instantly changing my impression of him. "And that's Hank," Steve said, pointing to his friend, who was looking over my head and off to the entrance of the plane with a frown.

"Oi! The art stays with me, mate!" Hank yelled to the porter carrying the luggage, startling me and revealing a Cockney accent. The man immediately released the handle of the large flat box he was holding, eyes wide as he took in Hank's stature.

"You're not drinking, Emma?" Yelena exclaimed, a playfully accusatory tone in her voice, calling my attention back to the people before me.

"I really want to try to sleep, and I never sleep well when I drink," I explained.

"Nonsense!" Lenny said, motioning Liza to bring the tray.

"Are we waiting for Lori?" Yelena asked, holding her glass reluctantly, as though we should wait to take a drink.

"My girlfriend," Lenny clarified to me, and I recalled the blond woman who often popped up on his arm when I did my Google Images searches. He turned to Yelena. "She is in London for work now. She's meeting us there."

He pointed again at the tray being thrust into my line of vision, and I shrugged. *When in Rome, I guess* . . . I took a glass off the tray and joined them in a "*Na zdorovye!*," which I was starting to get the hang of. I clinked my glass last with Micaela's, and must have done it harder than I intended, as she dropped it on the floor between her feet.

"The glass didn't even break," the flight attendant announced triumphantly, already on her knees cleaning it up before we even had a chance to step back. Lenny whispered something to Micaela in Russian, and she brushed past me, checking my shoulder, and exited the room.

"She's going to get into pajamas and finish her movie during takeoff," Lenny explained as I cringed at yet another faux pas before the plane had even taxied out of the gate.

We took seats in the lounge next to a dish of meaty green olives, a fortuitous snack because I found the gesture of holding the olive with two fingers and spitting out pits to be a great equalizer between me and my exorbitantly wealthy hosts. Our chatter about the fair was interrupted by Liza asking us to fasten our seat belts, which I hadn't noticed were attached to the soft leather chairs, before she apologetically collected our snacks and drinks, promising they'd be returned as soon as we were in the air.

True to her word, she refreshed our drinks a few minutes after our smooth takeoff, and platters of caviar and shrimp cocktail were brought out, along with more vodka, after which Lenny decided we should remain in the lounge rather than moving to the formal dining room for dinner. Though the four of us maintained the conversation, I noticed that Lenny and Sergey were checking their phones regularly, and when I sneaked a glance at mine, I saw I had full service as well, making me wonder if the no-phones-during-flight rule was just the FCC gratuitously pulling rank. Micaela didn't return, nor did anybody acknowledge her absence, and dinner of roast chicken and root vegetables was served, along with more vodka.

Despite eating an embarrassing amount of the delicacies on offer to absorb the liquor, I heard myself pontificating to the three of them about the merits and downsides of glorifying the artist rather than the art, and explaining that I thought NFTs were a bubble but one worth riding, because soon the environmental costs of blockchain would make the investment unfashionable (something I had read in a *Wall Street Journal* op-ed over a year ago and barely taken in). As I finished my spiel, I realized I was quite drunk, but was confused as to how I had quickly taken the lead as the most inebriated person at the table when everybody else had drunk more than I had.

After dessert and coffee, I made my way to the sitting area with plush couches and found myself reclining next to Yelena, who I was now convinced was wearing a corset under her clothing to keep her spine so straight. She'd taken off her shoes, and her spindly legs were crossed at the knee and again toward the ankle.

"Ah, it feels so good to relax," she said, her words dripping out slowly after a few vodkas, from what appeared to me to be a very unrelaxed position. "My feet are killing me. They're always killing me. Ballet gave me a great life, but it destroyed my body."

"You're a ballerina? I should have known. You have the perfect ballerina body," I said, allowing myself another sip of the drink I hadn't touched since halfway through dinner.

"I was always lucky with weight. Always ate whatever I wanted. That's the worst part for some girls. I struggled more with technique."

"Where did you dance?" I asked, sitting up straighter to mimic her.

"I was the prima ballerina at the Bolshoi in the eighties," she said, giving a small, indifferent shrug.

I'd heard of the Bolshoi only because my exceptionally proper freshman-year roommate at Yale was always taking trips with her mother to various far-off places to watch them perform, but I knew that it was a big deal.

"Oh my God! That's incredible! Your technique couldn't have been too bad!" I joked, realizing I was speaking to one of the best ballerinas in the world.

Yelena stared into her glass for a moment. "No," she said softly, still looking at the clear liquid. "My father ensured I corrected it quickly. The alternative wasn't pretty. His method worked, I guess." I watched a darkness descend over her as she drained her drink and signaled to Samantha for a refill.

I sighed in understanding. "Fathers . . ."

"Everybody's got a sad story, yes?" she asked, and then her eyes brightened, as though she had dismissed the thought. I glanced around the beautiful room hurling us through space to the other side of the world and thought that perhaps having a present like this one made the past easier to forget.

"You must be a beautiful dancer," I said, trying to change the subject away from families.

"I was. And it was my ticket to this beautiful life," she said, looking around the plane along with me. "Speaking of beautiful, how do you like the apartment?"

"What apartment?" I asked, thinking that I would have known the answer if I hadn't been so drunk.

"The studio!" she said. "Lenny's place."

"Oh! It's amazing. I was there this past weekend for the first time," I said.

She looked slightly confused. "I didn't realize you hadn't moved in yet. But never mind. Should we watch a movie?" I opted not to correct Yelena and tell her I was only painting in the studio.

"I think Micaela is still in the theater," I said, the thought of my last interaction with her making me cringe.

"Oh, don't mind Micaela. She's just jealous that you're the new her," she said, and patted my leg.

"Sorry?" I leaned forward, making sure I would hear this part correctly and avoid further confusion.

"She used to paint for Lenny. Poor girl. The MS is getting worse and now, with the tremors, she can't hold a brush like she used to. So she does anything else he needs. I give her a lot of credit for figuring out how to stay useful. But I hated how she decorated the studio, not that I blame her. Poor girl had a tough childhood, in and out of orphanages. How could she possibly have learned good taste, you know? Can't wait to see what you do with the place. *You* have good taste, I can tell," she said with a wink.

I felt my chest swell despite telling myself she must be mistaken, that there was no way Lenny would ever offer me his studio to live in. Still, my mind flashed forward to morning coffee on the balcony and painting by moonlight late into the evening. I shook my head, determined to stop salivating at the possibility of a different life at just the whiff of one.

"It's a shame. She's really not getting around as well these days," Yelena continued as she finished her refilled glass. I had a hazy vision that I couldn't quite hold on to, and it felt like a memory, but it could have been my imagination.

"What?" Yelena asked, staring at what must have been a very odd look on my face. "Emma?"

"Jesus," I said, remembering the glass Micaela had dropped and how she'd stormed off. I held up my glass. "I think I've had one too many of these."

Yelena laughed. "That's four too few!"

"I'd love to take a rain check for the movie—I might try to get some sleep," I said apologetically.

"Take the guest bedroom!" she said warmly. "Nobody ever uses it. Lenny sometimes sleeps in the master, but Alexei and Sophie are in there. Sergey always passes out in the bar, and I curl up in the media room with Micaela. Lenny usually works all the way."

"Really?" I asked, imagining being so accustomed to life on a private plane that you'd have routines and regular spots. I leaned forward to look down the long corridor and saw Lenny's feet up in the air on the reclining chair, allowing me a bit of comfort that Yelena was right and he wouldn't take a guest bedroom.

"Really," she promised as she shooed me toward the back of the plane.

I made my way to the gorgeous guest bedroom and had just plopped down on the pristine white bed when I heard a knock on the door.

"Miss," Samantha said. "So sorry to disturb, but I'm about to fetch your bags. I wondered if you'd like a pair of pajamas, too?"

"Um . . ."

"If you decide you do, they are right in that cupboard," she said, and pointed to the drawer below the TV.

In my real life, if I waited too long to make a decision, my options disappeared, but here in this alternate universe, waiting a beat opened even more doors. I suddenly understood Lenny's comfort with silence.

I went to the drawer and looked at the six sets of pajamas: three in heather gray, small, medium, and large; and three sizes in eggplant. I opted for the small in the deliciously soft, deep purple. As

I pulled the top over my head, I tried to remember the last time I'd worn actual pajamas, rather than sweats and a T-shirt, to bed.

I washed my face in the compact bathroom, which was the most well-appointed one I had ever used, and when I emerged, my luggage was waiting for me. I picked up the navy silk eye mask off the nightstand and ran my finger over it, wanting to sleep but dreading leaving this spectacular present for what always seemed to be the grip of the past. I put the mask down over my forehead but above my eyes and grabbed my phone to make a more permanent imprint of the plane than the one in my memory.

I took a few pictures of the bedroom and bathroom, then a few selfies in the eye mask with the backdrop of my plush pillow. I breathed in and filtered a picture of myself, so the light was softer, and captioned it: *Not the worst way to cross the world. Art Basel Hong Kong here we come #ArtBasel #isthisreallife #FlorenceWakeGallery.* At first, nobody liked my photo. I gnawed the skin on my thumb knuckle as I contemplated taking it down, wondering if it came off as entitled and vapid, or if the time change meant that none of my followers were awake, or maybe—hopefully—service was slow and I simply couldn't see the responses yet. But finally, @JustJules commented, *Can't wait to see you there, beautiful!* After that, the likes began rolling in, followed quickly by another flood of follow requests.

I refreshed obsessively until I was at over one hundred likes. I blinked and rubbed my eyes, which were drying out in the cabin air. As much as I needed rest, the adrenaline of connecting with new people propelled me out of bed. Even though I wouldn't post more of Lenny's plane, feeling he might not like it, I still wanted to document my experience—maybe just to show Sienna and my mother when I got back. I grabbed my phone to capture footage of other parts of the plane, extending my arm and turning my phone toward me as I led a tour through the bathroom and bedroom and out into the hallway. I turned into the office, commentating the entire way: ". . . and here we have Lenny's office, complete with a desk that is nothing short of a piece of modern art," I said, looking at the camera as I ran my hand over the top of the smooth white desk with tile inlay—until I knocked something off, and it crashed to the floor with a bang. "Shit!" I swore and stopped the video. "Shit," I repeated, staring at Lenny's briefcase on the floor and its contents spilling out in all directions. I dropped to my knees to return his papers to their rightful place, knowing I'd never get the order right and hoping he wouldn't notice.

The papers were mostly Excel spreadsheets, a few pictures of paintings with cataloging numbers beneath them, and printed-out emails. Lenny was just as low-tech as Yelena had promised. I tried not to look at any of them, knowing none of it was my business, and was almost done when a word in an email leaped out at me. I stopped, staring at the word: "ARDMORE."

From: DonPattnerPI@platinumintelligence.com
To: Leonard Sobetsky
Subject: EC

2/15/2021

Mr. Sobetsky—
I don't have much to report. No criminal record. Juvenile records are difficult to ascertain, though I can't find any evidence of a sealed file, so I'm inclined to think there is none. Perhaps the only two subjects of interest are: 1) a newspaper article discussing the fire on the family's property; and 2) her family's finances.
    In 2005, the local paper, *The Daily Ardmoreite*, covered a story of a fire that consumed the toolshed at the back of the Caan

property in Ardmore, PA. The fire department was called and put
the fire out before it reached the main house. The notable part
of the article is that Emma's father, Frank Caan, was reported to
have been treated for minor burns, and his then-secretary, Karen
Simmons, was rushed to the hospital and placed in a medically
induced coma for three weeks while being treated for third-
degree burns and carbon monoxide poisoning.

The fire was put out at eleven p.m. on a Tuesday (query what
work Frank was doing with his secretary in a toolshed at that
hour), and arson was suspected but not proven. Barbara Caan was
on the phone with Comcast customer service on a recorded line
when she noticed the flames and so was dismissed as a suspect.
Karen Simmons's then-husband, Phillip Simmons, was thoroughly
investigated and found to have been in California at the time of the
fire, and the fire was declared an accident for insurance purposes,
even though Frank denied smoking that night.

Frank Caan passed on April 2, 2020, and left the family with
over $100K in unpaid medical bills—surprising for a successful
lawyer, though he seemed to be less active in his firm's cases in
recent years. What piqued my interest is his will. Emma's mother,
Barbara Caan, recently contested it in probate, but the ruling went
in Karen Simmons's favor. The will was formally filed and is now
public, so I included a copy here, but in brief, after debts are paid,
all remaining proceeds from his estate will go to Karen Simmons,
while Barbara Caan will retain rights to the family home. My
forensic accountant believes she will need to sell the property, as
we cannot find any further assets in Barbara's name.

Note, this seemingly does not affect Emma directly, as she
apparently lives well within her means in her Washington Heights
studio, but it might be a pressure point.

The family home is worth an estimated . . .

I attempted to read more, but the words on the page blurred as my hands shook. I placed the paper on the desk, stepping away from it as though it were radioactive. My father had actually done it. He had left everything to *her*. Since I was a young child, I had been trying to understand the concept of a loveless, unfaithful marriage. Once it had sunk in, I'd fought with my mother to get her to see that she was married to a lying, manipulating addict. He couldn't stop smoking, drinking, screwing his assistant—and we were always left to clean up his messes, to show up with him to work and civic events and look like a happy family. But my mother never listened to me, just getting sadder and sadder as the years went on, and she stayed with him until the day he died. *For what? She didn't even get anything in the end!* She had been left with nothing but the home she loved. That was why she had to sell it. She couldn't afford not to. And I wasn't even mentioned in the will.

The bile in my stomach crept into my throat, and I fought hard to swallow it down. I wanted to be angry at Lenny for prying into my personal life, and irate at my father for leaving everything to *her*. But I wasn't. I was simply unfathomably, irrationally, endlessly hurt that my father hadn't even tried to apologize to me at the end of his life in the only way he ever had been able to express love— with money. He had left nothing to me. Nothing to my mother for my future. Nothing.

I felt the tears I had promised never to shed for him spill out of the corners of my eyes with such force that they hit my chest. It was as though my body had been flipped inside out and I was wearing all the awful memories of my father on the outside. The exposure was painful. I wiped frantically at my face, trying desperately to absorb the hot tears with my palms. I shook my head and breathed in.

When my heartbeat slowed, I turned back to the letter. I thought of my mother, recalling her comment on dinner being expensive, her suggestion that we order takeout, her refusal to upgrade to a new car. Regret nipped at my right side as I understood what had been going on beneath the surface. I couldn't believe I hadn't checked in with her more after the funeral, visited her more often in the past six months, wondered why she had so many meetings with the lawyers and accountants, or asked any questions when she said she was going to sell the house.

All remaining proceeds . . . will go to Karen Simmons.

All I could hear was my mother's repeated, hushed pleas to my father that he not take Karen out in public; all I could see was the image of him with her in the toolshed, then the flames, my father running out of the shed with *her* behind him, tripping over his undone pants, his panicked expression as he saw me standing there in my pajamas, my mouth open and my throat burning with smoke, and her screams as she writhed on the grass, trying to put out the flames that had licked at her clothes. I forced my eyes open and lifted my right palm up to a vent of the pressurized plane cabin, feeling the slight gust swirl around my fingers. *There's nothing in my hand*, I assured myself. *I did nothing wrong.*

My stomach relaxed for only a moment before lurching up into my throat, and I ran to the bathroom off the office just as my entire dinner came back up, the vodka burning my nostrils as it did. I heard myself making awful sick noises—the kind I hadn't made since I was a child with a stomach virus. I breathed heavily after the first rush, worried that it would start all over. Once it seemed finished, I spat a few times and rinsed my mouth with water before flushing the toilet.

I stared at myself in the mirror. *Plenty of kids find out that their fathers are unfaithful pieces of shit and turn out totally fine. Get over it. Just . . . get over it!* I gagged again and put my fist to my lips, waiting until my stomach stopped churning. I found a travel-size mouthwash in the mirrored cabinet and distracted myself by trying to find the invisible dotted line in the plastic seal so I could open it.

Unable to locate it, I twisted off the top, the seal ripping off with it, and tipped the bottle back into my mouth, relishing the cathartic sting on my cheeks.

When I emerged from the bathroom, my eyes teary and my face hot, Micaela was standing in the middle of the office, wearing an identical pair of eggplant-colored pajamas, reading the report, which I had left on the desk in my rush. The room focused and blurred synchronously with my heartbeat.

Micaela raised her head to me slowly, and I searched her expression. I didn't know if I felt worse about the idea of her telling Lenny I'd been snooping or what she would think of me and my family when she learned the truth.

Her hand shook slightly, and she pushed her lower lip out over her upper one, as though wondering what to do with me.

"That belongs to me," I said through a clenched jaw as I extended my hand, possessive of my family secrets.

She placed the paper carefully back in Lenny's briefcase. "Leave it alone," she said gently as she closed the case with a faint click. "We all have pasts. He just wants to make sure there's nothing about us that would mean he can't trust us."

I recalled what Yelena had said earlier about Micaela having a rough childhood, about her continuing to remain useful to Lenny. I pressed my lips together, not wanting to disturb the memory bubbling at the back of my consciousness, and a couple of puzzle pieces floating around my brain fit together for a moment.

Seeing the purple pajamas offsetting her piercing blue eyes, I knew where I'd seen Micaela before.

"Why were you in a cleaning woman's uniform at Gemini a couple of months ago?" I asked cautiously.

Micaela's face remained completely placid. "Leave it alone," she repeated, and dug into her purse. "Here," she said, placing a small white pill in my palm. "Get some rest. This is like . . . the Russian

Ambien. It'll help you sleep," she promised, before brushing past me and out of the office.

I stood alone, my legs rubbery, with only the echo of her "Leave it alone" around me. I went back to the bathroom and stood over the toilet, but nothing came up. I watched the pill in my palm stretch and straighten and morph into a small red matchbook as my mind delighted in playing tricks on me. I closed my eyes and tossed it down my throat quickly with a sip of water. I was certain I was past the point of pharmaceutical calming, but it was worth a try. I slunk out of the office and into the bedroom, still hearing her screams and seeing those awful flames, and lay down on the bed, praying the pill would kick in.

AGENT GARRITT:	And did you meet any of Leonard's other friends while in Hong Kong?
EMMA CAAN:	Yes. I did. I met Curtis Tremblay, a friend of his.
AGENT GARRITT:	Where?
EMMA CAAN:	We went to his house for dinner.
AGENT GARRITT:	Okay, so you go to Hong Kong on Lenny's private plane. And he takes you to Curtis Tremblay's house for dinner?
EMMA CAAN:	That's correct.
AGENT GARRITT:	Do you know anything about Curtis Tremblay?
EMMA CAAN:	I know that he is a very serious art investor. And that he lives in a very expensive home.
AGENT TILLWELL:	But you know nothing else? Nothing about the business he's in?

The light seeped in slowly through my lids, and it took me a few moments to realize where I was. I closed my eyes again, easing myself into the world, and wiped the drool from the side of my mouth with the back of my hand. I was flat on my back on top of the covers, a down pillow beneath my head. I'd barely wrinkled the sheets, but my brain still felt foggy. I closed one eye and grabbed for my phone on the nightstand, uncoupling it from its charger and pulling it toward me. I opened my other lid, blinked twice, and stared at the time again. 8:32 p.m. I sat up in bed, wondering if I was still dreaming. I must have been on the plane longer than half an hour, right?

I dropped my feet to the floor and touched my temple as I winced at the recollection of my file in Lenny's briefcase. I wished that it was a dream for a few moments before giving in to reality and opening the last video I'd taken on my phone.

I watched myself give a tour of the office to my imaginary viewer; I heard the childish excitement in my tone. I froze the frame and zoomed in on the background, scanning the ceiling and walls of the office for any video camera that would have captured my snooping. Though I didn't find any, I was positive they were there, and I was sure there would be repercussions. What did a man like Lenny do when he felt his trust was betrayed? My nerves fired at the thought, and I pressed play. I saw the papers spill out onto the floor. My hurt about my dad felt muted and far off now, and I thought instead of my mother and how it must have crushed her when their lawyer read her the will. She had tended toward sadness my entire life, and for the first time, I wondered whether she would have been more balanced without him—perhaps the life my father had saddled her with had worn her down into a dulled, darkened version of herself.

I heard the faintest tap on the door, so gentle that I doubted it was Lenny. I knew I could have ignored it entirely, but I didn't want to be alone with my thoughts any longer. I cleared my throat, still raw from throwing up, and called, "Come in!"

"Oh, good, you're up!" Liza stood in the doorway, a stack of fluffy white towels in her hands. "Do you need fresh towels?" I shook my head, wondering just how many showers she thought I was taking on this flight. She went on, "We should begin our initial descent into Hong Kong in just about an hour."

"What time is it? My phone says—"

"Don't pay attention to your phone. Whenever we lose Wi-Fi, phones get stuck on whatever time zone we were in when it stopped. We're only about two hours away—we're over Russia now, and we'll be landing at five p.m. Hong Kong time, but it's the day after when we took off." She laughed, studying my face. "I know! I don't even try to keep track anymore while flying, it's too confusing."

I nodded and forced a smile while I calculated that I must have been sleeping for almost ten hours.

"Anyway, Mr. Sobetsky requested just a light lunch because I understand you have dinner plans when you land. It will be served in the dining room in about twenty minutes."

The idea of having to sit at a table with the man who'd hired a private detective to investigate me and learn my family's secrets erased any trace of an appetite I might have had, but I managed to keep my face placid until she had closed the door behind her. Feeling exposed all over again, I pulled my pajama collar up around my neck, then reached for my phone and unlocked it.

I had a number of new emails, but one caught my attention:

From: leah.moniker@florencewake.com
To: Emma Caan
Subject: HK

Hey! I'm just emailing to let you know I'm not jealous of you at all, and that I think it makes perfect sense that you are being sent on a private plane to my favorite city in the world even though you've been working at FW for thirty seconds when I've been grinding away here for three years.;) KIDDING—emailing because I suck at my job and wanted to send through your hotel confirmation because I forgot to before. You're at the Hyatt Renaissance right in the convention center, which is totally passable and MUCH better than the Airbnb we used last year. Confirmation attached.

Also, just some advice that you can take or leave: I overheard Florence thank Leonard for getting you invited to dinner at Curtis

Tremblay's. Figured I'd shout it out that Curtis is a huge name in the art world but doesn't play much in the modern art space. He is in the art market for profit, not for love of the work, and there's no reason he shouldn't be a client of ours. Also, amazing job on Instagram, the reaction to your post was incredible. Florence would never say it because she thinks she's above social media— but it's great for the gallery!

Enjoy Hong Kong!! It's amazing. I was there with my dad a few years ago and I absolutely cannot wait to go back. Let me know if you need anything at all while you're there. I'm also reattaching the exhibition map for Basel just so you have it handy.

xx,
Leah
Leah Moniker
Executive Assistant to Florence Wake

I looked at the fresh towels the flight attendant had brought in and decided a shower might help. I stripped down and dipped my head low under the stream of water, feeling it slough off the lethargy on my brain walls and wash the film of anxious perspiration from my skin. I squeezed a dollop of body wash into my palm and worked it into a creamy lather, allowing the earthy vetiver scent to rouse and soothe me at the same time. I closed my eyes and was transported back to the charity event at Lenny's house, the Barnes curator surprising me with a kiss on both cheeks, her scent wafting toward me. When I was finished, I toweled myself off and opened the cabinet under the sink to look for a hair dryer, instead finding a dozen containers of travel-size toiletries with brand names I had never heard of. I sniffed the Byredo body wash and Philip B. shampoo and conditioner, and recognized the calm, clean aroma of the

people in Lenny's home at his party. I grabbed a couple of each and
shoved them in my suitcase, along with a few samples of La Mer
face cream from the medicine cabinet for good measure. The absolute best-case scenario if Lenny knew I had gone poking around
his office was that he wouldn't give me a ride back home. I didn't
want to think about the worst. Regardless of outcome, I didn't have
much to lose by pocketing a few toiletries.

As much as I was dreading seeing Lenny, it occurred to me as I
looked at my bag of loot that he had been right to do a background
check on me. He'd invited me into his home, trusted me with
his art, locked himself in a plane with me and his dear friends. I
couldn't afford any of what he had, and if there were any indication
in my past that I'd try to steal it, he was wise to find out. I applied
a bit of makeup in the hope that it would make me look less like
someone who'd thrown up violently then slipped into a veritable
coma, threw on the same black pants and blouse that I had worn on
my first day at Florence Wake, and slipped into Leah's red pumps.
I checked myself out in the full-length mirror, feeling slightly more
confident and clearheaded, and opened the door.

I passed through the den, where Hank and Steve looked up from
a soccer game with curt nods in my direction, before continuing
on to the lounge. I heard their voices first—the boisterous laughter
that came from Lenny's belly, the sass in Yelena's retort to something Sergey said. I entered to see them seated around the table,
Yelena in a flowing floral maxi-dress and leather jacket, Sergey and
Lenny in cashmere sweaters, and Micaela still in pajamas, though
undeniably beautiful. I chose the seat farthest from Lenny and next
to Yelena. Nearby, Alexei and Sophie lay sprawled on the floor with
a pack of markers and a book of construction paper. Alexei looked
up at me with huge blue eyes from below a mop of thick blond hair
and gave me a small wave with a marker still in his hand, and I

recognized him as the little boy who'd done the magic trick for me at Lenny's charity event.

Lenny smiled broadly. "Look who has decided to join us! We were starting to worry about you!" Either Micaela hadn't ratted on me yet, or she had and he didn't care, but whatever the case, he didn't seem upset.

"That pill worked like a dream," I said, turning to Micaela. She smiled awkwardly, as though I had said something I shouldn't have.

"Micaela! What did you give her?" Lenny asked, some accusation in his tone.

She rolled her eyes. "Relax. Just a Corvalol."

"Oof. You must feel awful," Yelena said, passing me the platter of herring and smoked salmon. "Eat up."

"Actually, I've never slept so well," I said, realizing that I had logged ten hours' sleep without a single nightmare. I stared at the platter, fighting the urge to gag. "Maybe I could have just some coffee and toast for now?" I asked Samantha, who nodded and turned to leave as Liza mercifully moved the fish platters away from me.

"I want toast, too!" Alexei cried out as though the matter was urgent, making everybody laugh.

"Oh, Emma, I wanted to invite you to a dear friend's home tonight for dinner when we land, if you don't have other plans. He's a big player in the art world. Curtis Tremblay," Lenny said. "Heard of him?"

"Just did, and I'd love to," I said, giving him a grateful smile.

Micaela let out a snort. "Curtis's house is the happiest place on earth," she said, her tone disapproving.

Lenny ignored Micaela and picked up whatever conversation he'd been having with Sergey before I joined them. Yelena found whatever she was looking for on her phone and handed it across the table for Micaela to inspect, and I filled my stomach with toast and jam, exchanging funny faces with Alexei.

"You're wonderful with him," Sophie, Alexei's nanny, whispered from over my shoulder as I put my thumbs to my temples, making moose ears, and crossing my eyes as Alexei shrieked in delight. "Do you have little brothers and sisters?" she asked. I shook my head. *Just a lifetime of wishing somebody played with me this way.*

"Do you want to see a magic trick?" Alexei asked me, taking out his marker.

I was sure it was the one I'd already seen, but I nodded anyway. He drew a stick figure with two thick lines of hair down either side. "That's you!" he declared.

"Looks just like me!" I said, widening my eyes for effect.

"Now close your eyes!" he commanded, and I obliged. When I opened them, the paper was entirely blank, and the whole table applauded as Alexei glowed. "For my next trick . . ."

"We're almost there. No more magic right now, Zaychik," Sergey said.

Alexei pouted but obliged, and our plates were eventually cleared with promises of a smooth landing and beautiful spring weather awaiting us.

"We will begin our initial descent shortly, so please fasten your seat belts," Samantha announced. "And I'm sorry to say that we'll need to go through public customs, as the private one is currently closed."

I felt the mood in the room tighten for a beat, but Lenny said, "That's fine," and conversation quickly resumed, leaving me to wonder whether I had imagined it.

Moments later, the wheels gently met the runway in Hong Kong, and the notion of stepping off the plane onto a new continent made my legs bounce with excitement. We deplaned into a private hangar with shiny cement floors where the luggage crew allowed Sergey to smoke, sucking hungrily at his cigarette, even though there were "No Smoking" signs everywhere. I looked at him for a moment, struggling to breathe as I imagined the glowing embers traveling too quickly toward his face and hot flames swallowing him. I averted my eyes and walked ahead, focusing on the glossy floor below my feet.

Though a porter wheeled our luggage on a cart, Lenny carried one of the large rectangular boxes under one arm as we wound our way through the modern airport, whose soaring ceilings of glazed white triangles formed a dome that reminded me of Epcot Center. Throngs of fashionable people moved economically, stepping briskly onto the moving walkway, efficiently continuing their migration to gates or exits. Conversations were spoken quickly into cell phones in various languages, and most of the English I heard snippets of was spoken with a British accent. Besides the Chinese lettering on the signs, it felt like we were still in an international terminal in the U.S., though cleaner and more high-tech—the U.S. of the future, maybe.

We went through customs individually, and though I had absolutely no reason to be nervous, when a broad-shouldered Asian man beckoned for me to step forward, I suddenly feared I wouldn't be allowed in the country. He studied my blank passport pages with intentional disinterest. He held up my passport and looked from my face to my picture twice, finally landing back on my face.

"Are you here for business or pleasure?" he asked in British-tinged English.

"Business. I'm here for Art Basel."

He nodded and slammed a stamp down on a previously blank page, giving me a rush, before handing it back to me and letting me know he hoped I had time to enjoy the city a bit, too. When I came out to the other side, I saw my travel companions waiting in a row of black leather chairs—all of them except Lenny.

"He's in there with an agent," Yelena said, cocking her head to indicate a small private room. I could see her slouching into a hang-over as the traces of her last glass of vodka faded from her blood-stream, while Sergey's foot wobbled anxiously, crossed over his opposite knee, as he stared at the closed door. When he caught me watching him, he smiled and uncrossed his legs, and as I pretended not to notice his nerves, I wondered what customs was going to find in that rectangular box. Alexei was perched on Sophie's lap next to a dozing Micaela, and he giggled with delight and slipped his tiny finger in and out of Micaela's parted lips as she slept. Hank and Steve stood with their hands clasped behind their backs, their knees locked in place. I thought I sensed tension in their muscles, but perhaps that was always their demeanor.

"Let's go!" we finally heard Lenny command brightly, emerg-ing with the box under his arm and handing it to Hank, and we rose to follow him. Just outside sliding glass doors, three men in suits stood, one with a sign reading "Sobetsky." They shook Lenny's hand and took our luggage. I watched for any judgment in their eyes when they saw my ancient carry-on, but I couldn't detect any.

"I'll ride with Emma," Lenny announced as we approached two black Mercedes sedans and an Escalade. My heart sank, wondering if he was looking for a quiet moment to fire me for snooping, but before I could form a cogent protest, Sergey, Yelena, Micaela, and Steve were getting into the Escalade with the art; Alexei and So-phie were stepping into the first Mercedes; and Lenny was sliding into the backseat of the other sedan as the driver held the door open for me. I had no choice but to obey.

Hank took the front seat of our Mercedes, which was on the left side of the car while our driver was on the right, and we took off on the left side of the road, which made me feel for the first time that I was really in a foreign country. I closed my eyes and my face burned with embarrassment about what was in the file and having been caught with it. I peeled them open and forced myself to look out the window, anywhere but at Lenny.

Our car glided along a road adjacent to a smooth bay, with lush mountains sprouting up in the distance and large ships pulling in and out of a port up ahead. Street signs and billboards were in Chinese and English, reiterating to me that I had climbed a staircase onto a plane in New Jersey and stepped off on the other side of the world. We crossed onto a bridge and then lurched forward as the city came into view, skyscrapers springing up in the fading evening light.

"It's a remarkable city," Lenny said softly. I nodded, though I wasn't sure if he was looking at me. "Mark, let's stop at the lookout point on the way. It's almost eight," he called to the driver.

"Of course, sir," he responded.

I turned to Lenny, wanting to remind him about dinner, but he had just flown me halfway around the world, so I thought better of questioning his judgment. I sat back quietly, acutely aware of his presence, as the car wound its way up a well-paved road in the green mountainside.

"This one won't have too many tourists," Mark assured us as he put the car in park and opened my door.

Lenny and I joined fifteen or so other people on the concrete slab overlooking the city, and I turned back quickly to see Hank trailing a few paces behind us, keeping a watchful eye. The last streaks of pink and purple were just disappearing into the horizon as the city darkened, the skyscrapers now only dark shadows in the distance.

"So, you saw your file," Lenny said. It wasn't a question but a statement.

I closed my eyes for a prolonged moment, realizing it was foolish to think that Micaela wouldn't have told him. "It's dark," I managed, my heart racing as I peered over the railing and down the cliff, feeling vulnerable as a soft wind picked up behind me, as though the universe were conspiring to throw me off the ledge. Lenny didn't budge, though, and I could feel his eyes on me. "It was an accident," I explained, turning to him for the first time since the plane.

"I know," he said calmly. "There are cameras."

Of course. I wondered if he had watched me while I stole his toiletries, while I showered, while I slept.

"It's necessary for me to know a lot about my employees. I have to be careful in a way that others do not," he said, a hint of apology in his tone.

He was only saying what I had already told myself. "I understand," I said.

"Do you? Sometimes when people learn that I need to know a lot about the people I surround myself with, they begin to have questions about what I do. Do you have any questions?" he asked, looking at his watch.

I wanted to ask how he made his money, whether he was involved in anything illegal, what Micaela was doing dressed as part of the cleaning crew at Gemini the day he'd come to the office. Instead, I asked, "How did the PI find all that stuff out?"

"Wills are public. The fire was in news archives. And . . . the PI posed as an employee of your father's firm and offered to clean out his home office," Lenny stated matter-of-factly. I recalled my mother telling me somebody had come from my father's office, and I felt somehow violated and exposed all over again as I understood Lenny had sent a stranger to wriggle his way into my childhood home.

"Why did you choose me? Out of all the artists at Gemini, why me?" I asked, meeting his gaze for the first time since I had read my file. *Because I'm struggling to pay bills? Because I need a father figure and you thought that would make me loyal to you?*

"Because you're a brilliant painter," he said gently.

"You knew I needed the money," I said.

Lenny shrugged. "Everybody needs money. Baselines of comfort magically shift, and somehow people always need more of it." A deep sadness seemed to descend over him as he paused. "But you're right, of course. It helps me understand how to motivate people if I know their pressure points." His shoulders slumped slightly, and something about his demeanor softened, allowing me to relax enough to breathe. I couldn't detect any anger in him, and I felt confident that having me at a remote overlook point on a mountain was a strange tactic but not an intimidating one.

I envisioned my mother pretending that downsizing to a smaller home was a fun new adventure. I realized I hadn't gotten any calls in the past several years about the spoils of her shopping sprees. I had dismissed her not shopping as much, dining out as often, or attending as many fund-raisers in town as a function of my father's illness, but it occurred to me that perhaps she no longer had the means.

I swallowed hard, appreciating that this magnitude of opportunity to help her was something I might never have again, and said to Lenny, "Well, you know my pressure point now. You knew it was my mother even before I did. I didn't know about my father's will." I was embarrassed that a relative stranger had revealed a family matter to me. "I need to figure out a way for her to keep the house. I don't have time for different bank accounts and small deposits. I need to get her money."

Lenny nodded at whatever thought was forming in his head. "Chagall," he finally said.

"Chagall . . ." I repeated, though I had no idea what he meant.

"Marc Chagall and his first wife lived in my town house until she passed. When I bought the house—not from them but from the person they sold to—I knocked down a wall in the cellar to make more space for my wine collection and found dozens of paintings, which belong to me now. I'll give one to your mother, and she can do with it as she pleases."

My jaw dropped slightly, but he went on. "The provenance is legitimate, and she should have no trouble selling if she wishes. The one I have in mind was last appraised for seven hundred and fifty thousand dollars. It's good, but it was in the cellar awhile, and the condition is less than perfect." He sounded almost apologetic that it wasn't worth more.

I widened my eyes, trying to capture the fading light so I could see him more clearly, thinking of the painting on Jeremy's office wall. *It was a gift, Leonard . . .* I heard him say.

"Why would you do that for us?" I asked.

He shrugged. "I have plenty of art. And these works came to me as a bit of a windfall," he said. "To be clear, it's not a gift. I would expect you to copy for me in return."

I nodded slowly, not quite seeing the harm in being paid in kind for labor and trying not to flash-forward yet to my mother's tears of joy when I presented her with the work of a famous artist.

"For how long?" I asked. "I mean, how will I know when I've paid you back?"

Lenny thought for a moment. "Let's say five years? To make this a good deal for me. Consider it an advance for what will probably be anywhere from five to ten copies each year. I expect you to keep up your current level of quality. But you're welcome to live in the studio, if that sweetens the deal."

I couldn't believe he thought he needed to sweeten the deal. I nodded slowly, imagining the masterworks I'd see during that time, the sinking sun outside the balcony that I'd race in order to finish my last brushstrokes in natural light, the joy I'd take in the labor, knowing I was supporting my mother in the way my father never really had. My shoulders relaxed away from my ears, and the ever present knot at the base of my neck started to unwind. The sense of relief was so acute that a small tear of gratitude escaped out of the corner of my eye, and then another. I hoped the darkness would obscure them.

"Thank you," I said quietly, so overwhelmed I was unable to speak at full volume.

"Do we have a deal?" he asked.

"Before we shake on it . . . why are we up here, anyway?"

"Just wait a minute," he instructed, and looked out over the railing at the city in the distance.

As I did, dozens of buildings lining the harbor leaped to life with a symphony of dazzling lights and neon lasers dancing through the sky. The pinks, greens, and blues cut through the thick tropical air, leaving a hazy glow in their wake when they changed, as though my eyes were on time-lapse mode. I glanced over to the crowd to our right and noted all their cell phones were out, reminding me to scramble for mine; when the show stopped about fifteen minutes later, I quickly posted a clip to my story. The glittering lights of the skyline, impressive in themselves, returned. The crowd put away their phones and resumed their chatter as they backed away from the ledge.

"That was incredible," I said. "What's the occasion?"

"Eight o'clock. They do this every night. This is Hong Kong! Life is celebrated here—senses are meant to be tantalized. Stick with me, I'll show you the good life." He winked and started back toward the car.

I lingered for a moment, looking out over the city and realizing that I had spent so long trying to establish my independence from my father and run from my childhood that I had forgotten to actually live. I smiled and quickly turned, catching up to Lenny and matching his stride. Perhaps this was the good life I deserved.

"Yes to the painting. Yes to five years of work. Yes to the apartment," I said, causing him to slow down. "Your copies will be perfect."

He extended his massive hand to mine. "I've come to expect nothing less, Ms. Caan." We shook on it before getting back into the car.

A sign in English announced that we were making a left onto a street called Strawberry Hill, giving me the sensation that I was about to enter a fairy tale, and then we turned off the street onto a steep driveway cutting up through a thick set of woods. A light-studded horseshoe driveway came into view before I spotted two huge pillars flanking the door of a white mansion. The landscaping was lush and perfectly overgrown, a curated look of natural beauty.

"This is beautiful," I whispered, looking out the window.

"Yes," Lenny said, then chuckled. "But not worth three hundred million dollars, if you ask me."

I whipped my head around to see if he was joking about the price tag, but his disapproving expression indicated he was not. We stepped out of the car, aided by the driver, and a man walking a dog approached us. I bent down and extended my hand to allow the dog to smell me before petting it.

"No pet dog!" the man yelled.

I retracted my hand quickly as the German shepherd sniffed me, his fangs showing as his lips pulled back. Had I inadvertently come into contact with drugs in the past day or so? I couldn't imagine that I had. He moved on to Hank and Lenny before returning to the feet of the guard, who ushered us toward the front door. I tried to calm my nerves by reminding myself that this kind of people needed to take such precautions, but I couldn't fight the creeping feeling that along with a lot to protect, all of my recent acquaintances might have something to hide.

Before we could even ring the bell, a man in a suit opened the door. He gave a small nod and stepped backward, pointing us to

Yelena and Sergey waiting in the foyer with a dapper man who had pale, milky skin that I imagined made him appear much younger than he was. I presumed he was Curtis Tremblay. He was tall and broad, with a thick head of blond hair and clear-framed glasses. Curtis opened his arms to greet Lenny, while I hung back next to Yelena.

"Where's Micaela?" I whispered.

"She doesn't come here," Yelena said, then paused, barely trying to conceal whatever piece of information she was about to share. "Her parents were addicts . . .," she whispered, as though that had anything to do with why Micaela wouldn't attend a dinner party, and moved toward Sergey, who had called her over.

I watched Curtis hug Lenny as I stared off into the cool marble-floored living room, full of understated yet luxurious creamy beige furniture, whose back wall of windows looked out onto an illuminated swimming pool. I reminded myself of the price tag on the house and thought Lenny had been right, it wasn't beautiful *enough* to warrant that kind of money. Then again . . . what would be?

"This is Emma Caan," Lenny said, gesturing back to me. "She is representing Florence Wake at Basel, and we're delighted to have her with us tonight."

I took his gesture as a cue to step forward and smile, and Curtis shook my hand warmly. "Ah! Welcome! I was just at drinks with Florence last night. She told me all about you!" he boomed. "Let's head to the gallery for a toast before dinner!"

As we followed him down the grand hallway, I stepped as delicately as possible, putting pressure on the balls of my feet, trying to soften the click of my heel to harmonize with everybody else's muted footsteps, feeling as though I had missed the class all women take on how to walk properly in dress shoes. When we approached the end, Curtis switched on a light, illuminating a large room with a stone fireplace, wing-backed chairs with a marble chess set on a heavy wooden table, a tufted navy sofa, and art covering every inch of wall space.

I lingered behind the others as they took seats so I could glance up at the wall to my right. I was certain I saw a Renoir and a Monet, and what I thought was a Cézanne, and many others I couldn't quite place. They were all incredible impressionist works, all beautiful landscapes, but the sheer volume of the collection was overwhelming. I felt my jaw unhinge as I processed the fact that the value of the art in the room dwarfed that of the house itself.

I drifted along the wall, slowing to a stop in front of a hazy painting of a verdant wedge of land. Muddy river water collided at its tip, and lush forests filled the foreground with mountains off in the distance.

"What do you think?" I heard a voice say, and looked up to see Curtis watching me intently.

"It's very impressive," I managed. "Where is this?" I pointed to the painting.

"Ah, you do have a good eye," he said, a nostalgic smile playing on his lips. "Sun Tun Tai painted this for my grandfather. This place is called the Golden Triangle. It is where the borders of Thailand, Laos, and Myanmar meet. Our family business has been headquartered there for nearly a century."

I nodded, but before I could ask a follow-up question, Lenny called a toast from across the room. "Let's all raise our glasses and celebrate the newest addition to the collection," he said, and another member of the house staff appeared with a silver tray filled with glasses of golden champagne. We took them by the stems and extended them in the air, everybody looking to Curtis, who clinked Lenny's glass against his. "To my new Pissarro, with gratitude to my dear friend Lenny Sobetsky," he said, taking a sip of champagne as we all followed suit.

"Where will it go?" I asked, noting the lack of wall space.

"Certainly not in here," Curtis scoffed, as though I should have known as much. "They've just completed the photographs, so it will be on its way to Delaware now," he said, and called an iPad to life that I hadn't seen embedded in the wall. He stepped to one side and revealed a picture of the Pissarro on the screen. Squinting, I took a step toward the image and realized the copy of the Pissarro had to be done in a rush because Lenny wouldn't have the original for me to copy from. I furrowed my brow as I struggled to figure out why Lenny would have had me copy a work he was about to sell—would he hang my copy and pretend that it was the original? That seemed an uncharacteristically tacky move. And why had he brought a painting all the way to Hong Kong if the buyer was only going to ship it back to what I presumed was a freeport in Delaware?

I scanned the other walls for distraction from my muddled thoughts, worried that my expression might reveal my confusion, and quieted my brain with the impressionists' discreet moments of natural beauty, snapshots from before cameras were even invented. I found myself lost in the foaming sea waves and rivers flowing by lush banks. All at once I was struck by what all the paintings had in common. "There are no people in any of these," I remarked, not realizing I was speaking out loud.

"That's how I prefer it," Curtis said, and I noted that everybody else in the room was looking at me quizzically. "The people in paintings are so often sad. You're a painter, right? Why are artists so fascinated with pain?" he asked, elongating his spine as though he had just cracked some millennia-long case.

I stared back at him, wondering how the question had never come up in all my years of studying art. "There are paintings with so much joy in them," I said. "But you're right—many famous works do show pain, or at least solitude." I paused. "Maybe it's because life is hard, and seeing others in pain makes us feel less alone. Or maybe it's because joy is already beautiful, but paintings find the beauty in the uglier parts of life." My own analysis surprised me as I heard it for the first time.

"Well said, my dear!" Lenny cheered, raising his glass to me.

"Nice try, but they're depressing to me," Curtis said with a laugh. "I'm in the business of making people happy. Landscapes for me, then!"

I joined in the others' laughter but couldn't stop myself from studying Curtis. He must have been in his mid-fifties, with no wife or kids by his side, no photos of people to be found in his house—no signs of a personal life at all. I partly felt sorry for him, but I also envied how neat and tidy his life must be without the messiness of family life.

"Now, I know you've had a long day of travel, so please, follow me to dinner," Curtis said, ushering us out. I fell into step beside him and recalled Leah's email about the significant opportunity our host presented the gallery.

"Your collection is perfect, truly. But I'm surprised you don't play more in the modern and contemporary art space," I said, my tone neutral with an intentional hint of wonder. "A man with your exacting taste might find some worthy investments if you're willing to build out your collection in a new direction."

He chuckled. "Florence and I discussed something similar last night. I will be by the fair this week," he said dryly, knowing exactly where my pitch was going.

We turned right, into the dining room, and took our seats around the table, mine between Lenny and Yelena, as a server filled our glasses from a vodka bottle bearing the stag.

"Please, Curtis," Lenny said as he watched the waiter, "I know you're partial to wine. We don't need to drink vodka!"

"I insist," Curtis replied with a dismissive shake of his head.

"All right, then. To our most gracious host," Lenny said, gesturing to the bottle and holding up his glass.

Moments later, another server thrust between Lenny and me a sterling silver tray with five flat-bottomed serving spoons, each containing a small blue pill imprinted with a smiley face.

"Would anybody like to partake? Please." Curtis gestured in invitation. I was shocked at the offer of what I assumed to be ecstasy, but I also marveled that I was dining with a group of people to whom rules and even laws did not apply.

"I think not tonight," Sergey said, and I watched as Yelena's shoulders slumped in disappointment. The tray was removed and vodka was poured.

The hours passed, demarcated only by the courses of duck crepes, chili prawns, Mala beef, many more glasses of vodka, and an incredible dessert called an egg tart. In a quiet moment between courses, I glanced around at the opulent table covered in decadent dishes. *Is this my life now?* I wondered. More vodka was poured before glasses were emptied, so I never knew quite how much I was drinking. Eventually, we made our way outside, where Yelena fell flat on her face off the front step. While Sergey looked irate, Yelena couldn't stop laughing, in between pleas for Sergey to take her out dancing. When he refused for the third time, she unlinked her arm from his and looped it through mine.

"What did you think of the house?" she asked, her accent even thicker under the influence.

"Incredible. His art collection is amazing!" I gushed.

She let out a maniacal laugh. "The laundromat? Everything comes out of it clean as a whistle!"

"Enough!" Sergey said sternly, shaking his head while I took particular comfort in realizing that I was not nearly the drunkest person at dinner. A driver ushered me into the back of my own

Mercedes and whisked me away to the Hyatt, while the other three took off to their presumably much fancier hotel. I stared out the window at the blurry harbor lights through bleary eyes and felt the less photogenic parts of my former life slip away to make room for Florence Wake Gallery, the private plane, the spectacular dinner party.

The hotel was spectacular, too—a thick sheet of cool black marble spanned the floor of the lobby, which also featured tall pillars and an elegant black staircase. I found it difficult to imagine that Lenny was staying somewhere even more luxurious. I took out my phone and snapped a picture, which I posted to my story. I squinted to check my current number of followers and had to close one eye to confirm the number: 2,306. I looked at my alerts to see that Jules had reposted my photo from the plane and captioned it: *Can't wait for Basel with this one* ☺. I wondered if she realized that reposting made it seem like she was on the plane with me, but the spike in followers made me grateful for the misrepresentation either way. I felt that my Instagram persona was slowly taking on a life of her own, making friends without needing me as a gatekeeper now that she was public. I closed the app, eagerly awaiting what I would find the next time I checked.

The check-in line in the lobby was growing behind me even at the late hour, with people who I assumed were there for Basel. When I reached the front, I returned the smile of the petite woman behind the desk, handing her my passport.

"I just need a credit card for incidentals," she said, her fingers scurrying across her keyboard.

"Oh, but the room is covered by my company," I said, trying to hide the panic in my voice that my credit card was maxed out.

"Right. You won't be charged. Only for incidentals after your stay," she said kindly. I handed her an AmEx I was almost certain had been cut off the last time I'd been two months late in paying the minimum, and I hid my surprise when she handed it back to me with a room key.

I hurried toward the elevator, excited to see my room, and swayed slightly as I waited, the combination of vodka and jet lag throwing me off balance. The elevator doors opened, and I stepped into the glass case, pressing the button for the twentieth floor before turning my gaze back to the busy hotel lobby, where I spotted a familiar man in a suit. My eyes caught his hazel ones, and I coughed as I recognized him, as though choking on the information. *Why would he be here? The consultant from Gemini? Why would a management guy need to be at an art fair?* I blinked as the elevator doors closed. *Was I imagining it?* As I was whisked skyward, I put my face to the glass doors to continue looking at the man, but his features rapidly flew from my view.

I stepped back and stared at the two circular smudges of residue that my nose and forehead had left on the glass before the doors opened and I stepped out onto my floor. *Maybe I really should see a doctor.*

EMMA CAAN:	I honestly don't think Curtis Tremblay ever mentioned what he did for work, exactly. I do remember him saying something like he was in the "business of happiness," but I don't know what that means.
AGENT TILLWELL:	Now there's a euphemism I've never heard! Did you see any art change hands between Mr. Sobetsky and Mr. Tremblay?
EMMA CAAN:	[silence]
AGENT TILLWELL:	Ms. Caan?
EMMA CAAN:	No. I didn't see any art change hands.
AGENT GARRITT:	Are you sure? You look like maybe you want to say something further.
EMMA CAAN:	No, it's just that we drank a lot at dinner, so I'm trying to remember everything. But no, I am positive I didn't see any art physically change hands.
AGENT GARRITT:	While in Hong Kong, did you engage in any illegal activity whatsoever to your knowledge?
EMMA CAAN:	No, not to my knowledge.

I stared at the ceiling, replaying the dream sequence that had been the past twenty-four hours of my life, until sleep overtook me. At three o'clock in the morning, I woke to find myself slapping frantically at the sheets around me, desperate to suffocate the flames, before I opened my eyes and realized the fire was only in my head. I sighed at my own naive optimism. Had I really thought a new job and a few exciting new friends were going to make my nightmares disappear? I grabbed my phone, looking for a distraction.

"Hi, hon," my mother answered, sounding a bit low.

"Hey!" I tried to lift her spirits. "I'm calling from Hong Kong. It's three in the morning here, but I can't sleep. How are you?"

"I'm okay," she said, but her voice was shaking. "How's the trip?"

I told her a bit about the plane and the hotel, but I could tell she wasn't really listening. "What did you do today?" I asked.

"I just came from a meeting with the lawyer," she said quietly.

"How did that go?"

"It was . . . difficult," she said, seeming to choose the word carefully. "There's not quite as much left as we planned after medical bills."

I didn't know why she insisted on using the word "we," as though my father would be surprised that he'd left her with only a home she couldn't afford, then given the rest to his girlfriend. "I know you said you wanted to sell the house, Mom, but you love it so much. I just . . . I worry it's too much change for you—with Dad passing, and now moving. Maybe you should stay for a while," I suggested. "Even if there's not as much money as you planned on, I can help."

"Emma, thank you, but that's okay. You're just starting out . . ."

I knew she also didn't believe I was capable of helping her in any significant way. "Mom, listen to me. I have a painting by Marc Chagall. It's probably worth somewhere in the neighborhood of seven hundred and fifty thousand. I want you to have it—to sell, or whatever you'd like to do with it." I waited. "Mom?" I asked, checking the screen to confirm she was still on the line.

"Emma! How can you possibly?" Her voice rose an octave. "I cannot take your money," she said, but I knew from the giddiness in her voice that it was as good as done. Still, I indulged her in a little more back-and-forth, and when she finally agreed, there was a lightness to her tone that I hadn't heard in years. We hung up after promising to work out the details when I was back home, and I allowed myself a small smirk of satisfaction in the privacy of my hotel room. Could Lenny's painting possibly make my mother a happier version of herself?

I couldn't go back to sleep, so I opened my Florence Wake email and scrolled, catching up on the Fredrick Thomas sale Leah had made yesterday for full ask, the new artist Florence was going to meet, the emails to Optimum I'd been cc'd on because our Internet was out again. Then I looked at Instagram until the first rays of sunlight poked through the cracks in the heavy drapes. My video of the light show had gotten more than a thousand likes, and I'd since gotten seventy-two new followers, putting me almost at the three-thousand mark. I stretched my arms skyward and arched my back, then threw open the drapes, allowing daylight to flood in as the excitement of preparing for Art Basel Hong Kong propelled me into the shower and down to the lobby for coffee before I headed across the street to the Hong Kong Convention and Exhibition Centre, where I would spend the entire day setting up the Florence Wake booth.

The hall was full of people, but the first person who made eye contact with me was a tall, thin woman wearing a perfectly tailored pencil skirt and holding a clipboard, shouting in what I thought was German and pointing at three burly men pulling a cart filled with flat boxes, presumably containing art. I approached her cautiously, second-guessing my ripped jeans and T-shirt, which I'd specifically chosen for the day of manual labor ahead of me.

"Idiots," she said in thickly accented English, rolling her eyes and looking at me. "They don't know to use the service entrance for the art?"

I nodded, hoping my pieces were already waiting in the Florence Wake booth, as Leah had promised they would be. "I'm the gallerist for Florence Wake," I said, but the woman stared at me blankly and made no move to check her clipboard.

"Do I look like I work here?" she huffed as she turned on her heel.

Of course, I'd missed the check-in counter directly in front of me, which was staffed by two attractive women dressed in smart jeans and blazers, leaving me to wonder what exactly was insulting about looking like somebody who worked here.

I approached the desk. "I'm Emma Caan, with Florence Wake?" Though I cringed to hear myself say it as a question, the women both straightened when they heard the name of the gallery.

"Identification, please," one of them said in barely accented English while typing on an iPad. She then handed me a map of the convention center and a badge to get through security each morning of the fair. "Your delivery arrived yesterday, so it should be in your booth," she continued, handing me back my driver's license. "Love your jeans," she added. I tried not to smile as I realized Lenny might be right—the more you stood out with how you looked in the art world, the more people thought you mattered.

The convention center stretched out ahead of me. The size of an airplane hangar, it was filled with booths made from walls that stretched three quarters of the way up to the ceiling. The atmosphere felt like that of an ER, but the emergency was art, with people walking urgently in couture instead of scrubs, orders being shouted at deliverymen instead of orderlies, dragging carts brimming with packages instead of pushing gurneys. A variety of languages blended together in a frenetic hum, until a single voice hooked my attention from somewhere over my left shoulder. "Emma?"

I spun around. "Jeremy!" I said, more excited to see him than I'd ever thought I would be. We hugged warmly, allaying my fears that there was any friction between us, and made small talk about my new position at the gallery, what I thought of Hong Kong so far, and how his family was doing.

"Oh! You know who I saw in my hotel?" I asked.

"Who?" He leaned in close, and I knew he was expecting me to name a celebrity.

"That consultant you hired!"

I figured Jeremy would share my amusement or already know he was there, but he just blinked, blank-faced. "Who?"

"The youngest consultant! I forget his name. The one who did my exit interview."

Jeremy nodded slowly. "Small world. Look, I have to run. But," he said, placing a hand on each of my shoulders, "take care of yourself, Emma." He gave them a small squeeze and stepped to the side to keep going.

I bit my lip, realizing that it might have seemed insensitive to bring up the consultants called in to rescue Jeremy's company from crisis, and watched him weave through the packages marked FRAGILE, sidestepping a beautiful woman who strutted past him and nearly bowled him over, and dissolve into the crowd.

The woman seemed to be waving directly at me, though. "Your fucking phone has been off!" she shouted, and several people turned toward her.

As she approached, I could see Jules's broad, toothy smile. She wore a black jumpsuit with large cream-colored buttons, and white sneakers with a silver star on each side. It looked like she'd walked through mud in her shoes, a choice I assumed was intentional, and she'd slung a large slouchy bag over one shoulder. She kissed the air on either side of my cheeks, presumably in an attempt to preserve her shimmering makeup.

"What are you doing here?" I asked.

"I'm here to hang with you! Duh!" Jules still looked like the effervescent, striking creature I had admired on my phone, but in person, her manner seemed contrived—almost like a performance. Still, part of me was exhilarated to be seeing her show live. "I love your outfit. Cara Delevingne grunge vibes!" she said, linking her arm in mine. "I can help you set up the booth. It'll be fun!"

Unsure what I'd done to warrant her help but thrilled to have it, I checked the map, and we followed it to booth 442. There, we were met with three white walls surrounding a pile of boxes, all marked FRAGILE I understood why everybody in the convention center seemed to be barely holding it together. We had approximately twenty-seven hours to assemble a gallery from scratch. I snapped to action and grabbed the box cutter someone had left on the floor for me. "I'm so glad you're here to—" I began.

"Don't touch anything yet!" Jules warned, and pulled out a camera and tripod from her large bag and set them up toward the entrance of our area. "Look horrified!" she commanded, but before I had a chance to adjust my expression, there was a flash, and she was looking at her camera. "Perfect!"

"I don't have time for this!" I huffed, plunging the triangular razor of the box cutter into the first piece of cardboard, slicing carefully as not to damage the art. Jules stood over me, snapping pictures with her phone as I continued, and I found myself more annoyed than awed by her. "Can you help?" I finally asked.

"Florence didn't pay a boatload of money for only a pop-up. She invested in this fair to *sell* art. What you're doing is like . . . an eighth of the battle. I'm helping with the rest. But I don't need to post. I can help unpack instead," she said calmly, like I was an unreasonable child.

I shook my head in disbelief. How could she not appreciate how much work there was to be done?

"Relax, babe. I'll call my friend to hang everything once you decide where it all goes. That's the hard part, anyway."

I spent the next few hours carefully extricating paintings from layers of packaging and protection and leaning them against the walls where I thought they should hang. Jules had disappeared at some point, and while I relished the break from her chatter and camera flashes, I needed someone else there to tell me it would be fine. Though I had arranged my own art for final showings in college and had been in my fair share of galleries and museums, I had never been in charge of a project of this size. There was an undeniable therapy in creating something from nothing but an accompanying anxiety that I was getting it entirely wrong. I took a step back to view my progress.

Something felt off to me, so I shifted the works around until I was satisfied with the logical flow, then positioned a metal sculpture by one of our newer artists right off the center of the room, focusing the attention of any viewer toward the easternmost wall, where I had placed Fredrick Thomas's not-yet-sold paintings. I was crouching at the base of the sculpture when Jules returned.

"I come bearing lunch . . . and another set of hands," she announced proudly, holding up a large brown bag in each hand.

My breath caught as I stood and looked up to see Ryan Parker, just as handsome as he had been at the cocktail party, in a black crewneck sweater, fitted jeans, and black sneakers. "Ryan, Emma. Emma, Ryan," she said as she waved her finger in the air between us. I waited for him to mention that we had met, but he didn't.

"Thank you! I don't know how I would have hung all this myself!" I went to shake his hand, but he leaned in and hugged me, sending a small pulse of heat across my abdomen.

"Well, then, I'm going to be your new favorite person. As long as you know where you want everything, we'll have this done before you know it," he said, and winked, making my insides tighten. I expected somebody who looked like him to be somewhat aloof and withdrawn—but he was engaged and animated, with a certain magnetism drawing me toward him.

"Before we start hanging anything," Jules said, calling our attention back to her, "we need sustenance." She arranged a few of the empty boxes I hadn't yet cleared, forming a makeshift table, and laid out enough dim sum for ten people. Chili oil was poured in a shallow container, chopsticks were placed strategically, and spring rolls were misted with a spray bottle she had in her massive bag because it made them "glisten in the shot."

"Can you let me know if you're going to destroy any of the other food so I can taste it before you do?" I asked her, and Ryan snorted. I made a mental note to play up the sass.

By the time Jules commanded us to "dig in," I was salivating. I sat cross-legged on the floor and was shoving a room-temperature pan-fried dumpling in my mouth when I heard Jules pleading with Ryan to take her picture.

"Fine!" he said, sounding exasperated but good-natured, and grabbed the camera she held out to him. "I'm not eating this stuff anyway. My mother is doing keto, so now I am, too, because . . . I've let myself go," he said, slapping his rock-hard stomach.

"His mother is Sharon Parker," Jules said to me. "The fashion model," she elaborated, seeing my confusion. "The first-ever Black model to close the Dior show in Paris?"

I plastered an impressed look on my face. "So, you can't eat any of this?" I asked Ryan after I swallowed.

"Nope, it's all yours," Ryan said, shaking his head. "Jules only pretends to eat while people take pictures of her."

"I eat!" Jules protested with a pout that evaporated as soon as Ryan readied the camera. She threw her head toward the sky, taking large, slow, toothy bites of bao buns while he snapped away.

"Enough!" Ryan declared, taking a seat on the floor next to me. Jules had, as Ryan predicted, stopped eating and begun reviewing the pictures as soon as the camera stopped clicking.

I caught him looking longingly at the egg roll in front of me, so I picked it up, dipped it in duck sauce, and took an enormous bite. "So good," I moaned through a full mouth.

"I hate you," Ryan said plainly, our eyes locking in a way that made me find our interaction less funny and far more exciting.

"Get a room, you two," Jules said, and rolled her eyes. My cheeks reddened, but I felt exhilarated that she could also sense the taut air between me and Ryan. "He's the world's biggest flirt," she warned with a raised eyebrow. "Don't worry, I'm tagging you in everything," she added, looking back at her phone.

I took a large bite of something labeled *har gow*, then swallowed it. "Okay, seriously," I said, "I was sort of trying to mess with you, but this dumpling is incredible!"

"Oh, fuck it," he finally said, playfully grabbing for a *har gow* and shoving it in his mouth.

"Jesus Christ, Ryan. You have the self-control of a toddler," Jules snapped.

He looked quickly at her and then back to me, then shrugged and took an egg roll. "She's right. But you, Emma, are a bad influence," he said with a smirk before popping it in his mouth and rising to study the walls.

"How do you and Ryan know each other?" I asked Jules, worried that there might be more to her warning than I'd thought.

"Her older brother is my best friend from boarding school," he said before she could answer.

"Ryan is my honorary big bro." Jules smiled at him fondly, and I inwardly rejoiced at the platonic nature of their relationship. "He used to take care of me when I was studying at the Sorbonne, but he's still in Paris running a hedge fund and being an international playboy, and we never see him anymore except when he graces us with his presence in New York for work or Christmas."

I spent the next few hours yelling some iteration of "a little to the left" or "a quarter of an inch higher" at Ryan and Jules as they held the art up against the wall. Jules complained several times that she hadn't signed up for "manual labor," but she heeded my instructions nonetheless and even corrected some of the pictures unsolicited, which I found particularly endearing. With a few breaks to walk around and see how other people were progressing, we were done by six o'clock, and we stood back toward the entrance and assessed our work.

"It's good," I confirmed, wondering if I should ask Ryan to reverse the two paintings that I had switched four times already.

"I'm not moving those two paintings again," Ryan said, as if reading my mind. "This place looks great," he promised, then took my hand and squeezed it, his touch sending an electric shock up my arm.

"What the fuck? You have more than four thousand followers, Emma! You're blowing up," Jules said incredulously. She was laughing, but I heard a subtle bite to her tone. "And I'm losing followers every day since Instagram changed their algorithm. No offense, but it's sort of bullshit. Oh my God, I just had the most amazing idea!" She looked up from her phone. "I've never been able to get into the Down the Rabbit Hole party before . . ."

"My buddy from business school went two years ago and said it was the best party he's ever been to," Ryan said. "But I have no way in. I've been working so hard for the past few years that I'm completely out of the scene here in Hong Kong."

"Not you. Emma! Pleeeease? You owe us!" she wheedled, gesturing to the art on the walls. "It's an *Alice in Wonderland* party, and it's supposed to be a-maz-ing . . ."

I registered the practiced tone of her voice and knew she hadn't *just* had the idea. She had shown up that morning to help me with a goal of attending the party. I almost respected the long game, and I wouldn't have minded reciprocating the favor, but she had misjudged me if she thought I had any way to get us invited.

"I didn't even know about the party. I'm definitely not invited," I admitted sheepishly.

"Can't Leonard Sobetsky help?" she blurted out.

I narrowed my eyes, wondering how she even knew that I knew Lenny. Had she somehow recognized the inside of his plane from my post? I was growing increasingly cautious of her transactional nature, but I also knew that the party would create another opportunity to hang out with Ryan. "That doesn't sound like a party he'd go to. He's really very—"

"Oh my God, no, he'd never," Jules agreed. "But he can get us on the list, I'm sure."

"When is it?" I asked.

"Tomorrow," Jules and Ryan said in unison.

"I can ask . . ." I trailed off as I wondered if I should. Lenny had gotten me there physically, on his plane, and more broadly, with his connections, and it felt greedy to ask for more.

But Jules picked up my phone from atop one of the empty boxes and thrust it into my line of vision. I pulled up Lenny's number, my desire to spend more time with Ryan overriding my fear of overstepping with Lenny.

"Emma!" he answered on the second ring. "How is the setup going?"

"Oh, it, um, it's going well. We're pretty much done." I took a few steps away from Jules and Ryan. "Two of my friends came to hang out, and they were a huge help," I said at full volume, knowing they could still hear me.

"That's very generous," Lenny said, and I heard the flat skepticism in his tone. I had spent an entire day never questioning their motive, and he seemed to know in an instant. I couldn't ask him, then. It was too embarrassing. Too predictable. "Emma, my car is just pulling up to dinner," he announced. "Did you need something before I go?"

I turned back to Jules and Ryan, who watched me expectantly, and mentally weighed whether it would be worse to disappoint them or annoy Lenny. My relationship with them felt decidedly more tenuous.

"Have you ever heard of a party called Down the Rabbit Hole?" I began.

"Yes, would you and your friends like to go?" he asked plainly. I couldn't tell if I was imagining the judgment in his tone.

"Are you going?" I asked.

"No, but I think Yelena usually goes, so you'll see her there. How many tickets do you need?"

"Three," I said, feeling a bit childish.

"Sure. I'll have Micaela take care of it."

I winced at the idea of Micaela knowing I'd asked another favor from the man who freely gave so much, knowing she'd judge me for it. "How much are they? I'd be happy to . . ." I tried feebly, knowing nobody could purchase admission to these exclusive parties. The people who were invited were *somebodies*; their presence was their currency.

"Curtis is always trying to give me tickets to his party. Plus, he really enjoyed meeting you. He'll be thrilled to have you. I'll come by the booth tomorrow, but I have to run now." He hung up before I could thank him.

Curtis is the host of the Down the Rabbit Hole party? I recalled Curtis saying he was in the business of making people happy—I just hadn't figured him for an event planner.

I turned back to Ryan and Jules. "We're in," I told them.

"Emma, you're amazing!" Ryan said, and I knew I'd have asked a hundred more favors of Lenny if it meant hearing that again. Jules just pounced on me with an embrace before pulling back with a mischievous glint in her eye.

"Now the fun part. What are we going to wear?" she asked.

AGENT GARRITT:	Did you engage in any illegal activities in Hong Kong?
EMMA CAAN:	NO! Definitely not.
AGENT TILLWELL:	Do you think drug use is legal?
EMMA CAAN:	Do I need a lawyer? You said I wasn't in trouble. This is making me feel like I'm in trouble.
AGENT TILLWELL:	You have the right to have a lawyer present. You don't have to answer any of these questions, but again, you're not the one we're investigating here. We're just trying to get our facts straight. And you're certainly not in trouble for anything you did or did not do in Hong Kong.
EMMA CAAN:	Sorry, my reaction before was a bit of a knee-jerk one. Let me think. I took Ubers in Hong Kong. I think they're outlawed there. And . . . I might have taken drugs at a party. Honestly, I'm not even sure what's legal and not legal there.
AGENT GARRITT:	What drugs?
EMMA CAAN:	MDMA. At the Down the Rabbit Hole party. I'm guessing you're aware how prevalent drug use is there.
AGENT GARRITT:	Can you tell us a bit about the party?

A quick Uber ride down Queen's Road Central landed us at the mouth of a cobblestone staircase whose steps were so eroded by time and use that they now only formed a lumpy incline. I was first out of the car, stepping carefully onto the slick stones and venturing a few steps toward the market. The light was dimming from gold to burnt orange, bouncing off the glistening street and illuminating the long stretch of vendor stands.

"You're going to love it," Ryan whispered, standing close behind me and placing his hands on my hips for a moment before removing them. It was as though he was only flirting with the idea of flirting with me—but that made it so much more exhilarating. I basked in Ryan's attention, but simultaneously worried he would at any moment drift on to the next object to captivate him, the way he had that first night I met him at Lenny's party.

I shifted my focus from Ryan and looked out at the market, which Jules had called "Stone Slab Street," focusing on the electric blues and vibrant reds of the wigs in the shop to my right, and the orange Trump mask next to the jet-black Batman one in the stall to my left. There were Chinese lanterns and huge bows and greeting cards and sunglasses. Most signs were in English with Chinese characters below, but the people on the street were every color and shade you could imagine, haggling in more languages than I could count. I felt then exactly how I had imagined I might in a foreign country—deliciously lost, yet somehow more like myself, as though so many new things allowed me to take comfort in the familiarity of my own body.

I heard the snap of Jules's camera behind us, and was reminded to take a photo as well. I took out my phone and took a picture. I noticed that Micaela had already emailed me the Down the Rabbit Hole invitation. I opened Instagram and posted the photo with the caption: *It's amazing what you can find if you're willing to get lost in a new place*, as I noted a dozen or so new followers whose handles seemed to identify them as art enthusiasts.

We wandered from stand to stand, grabbing wigs, tutus, striped stockings, bunny ears, a blue French maid's outfit, and makeup palettes. Ryan and I laughed as we tried on masks, while Jules focused on capturing photos of the market in the waning light. I'd wandered off to pick out some candy when a man in a Joker mask popped up to my left, forcing a scream out of my mouth that made the group of young girls beside me jump. Ryan tore off the mask and threw his arm around me before leaning in and pressing his lips to mine. My breath caught, but he pulled away with a nonchalant expression, took my hand, and pulled me down the road. I followed him, gripping his hand to steady myself on the slippery cobblestones, trying desperately not to rejoice outwardly.

When Jules had filled two large shopping bags and declared that she had enough to bring her "vision" to life, we hopped in a cab for the Hyatt, where it turned out the two of them were staying. Ryan sat sandwiched between us, his long legs scrunched toward his chest. As I felt his arm against mine, I wondered if Jules could feel the current between us, too.

As she remained absorbed in reviewing her photos, Ryan handed me his phone and gestured to the screen, where he'd entered my name as "Emma (Beautiful)," and pointed for me to enter my number. It was a slightly cheesy move, but I was too flattered to care, so I entered my number and then hovered my thumb over the "Done" button. I stopped and wondered why Ryan was so interested in me now, and dimly recognized that I was somehow more accepted in this world—I had flown private to Hong Kong, I was able to get us into parties, and I worked for one of the preeminent contemporary art galleries. But rather than judge Ryan for that, I took pride in my newly carved space in the universe, realizing how much had changed in my life. I deleted the parenthetical next to my name and entered "Caan," then pressed Done and handed the phone back to him.

"Emma Caan," he said, and hearing him say my name gave me a chill. "But you are beautiful," he added, just as his phone dinged with a new text. I saw Jules roll her eyes, and I turned quickly toward the window so he wouldn't see the grin I couldn't suppress. Outside, throngs of people and neon street signs blended into brilliantly colored streaks. I fantasized about how Ryan would maneuver me away from Jules and invite me to his room for a drink and how I would pretend to be surprised when he kissed me again. At the Hyatt, Jules and I hopped out of the cab, but he stayed in the backseat. I turned back to the car as Ryan rolled down the window.

"I just got a text from a buddy. I'm gonna go meet up with him in Lan Kwai Fong. See you guys tomorrow!" He smiled broadly and waved, said something to the driver, and rolled his window back up as they pulled away. I stared at the car. Had I said something dumb? Started to emanate a strange body odor? Or had he simply changed his mind about me?

"Ryan Parker . . . always on to the next," Jules said, and shrugged. "He better show up tomorrow. He's the Joker, and our outfits depend on him. Whatever," she said, apparently deciding she no longer cared, and made her way into the hotel. I opted not to tell her that there was no Joker in *Alice in Wonderland*, unless she counted the one on a playing card, followed her into the lobby, and hugged her good night in the elevator. I got out on my floor and went into my room, which had felt luxurious the night before but seemed cold and lonely now.

The next morning, my alarm jolted me awake at seven o'clock. I checked my phone, noting nothing from Ryan but a long email from Leah with the price of every piece so I had it at the top of my inbox if anybody asked; a reminder to allow our art to speak for itself; and strict instructions not to panic if the foot traffic on the first day was slow (it always was, she assured me). I took a long shower, reminding myself that I needed to exude a positive attitude in order to sell. *Don't push. Speak to customers about themselves, like Leah said; the art can speak for itself.* I stepped out of the steamy bathroom feeling focused and refreshed, though I couldn't help checking my phone obsessively while getting ready. I promised myself that as soon as I got to the fair, my phone would go in my purse so I could focus on work, but when I got to the booth and still hadn't heard from Ryan, I decided to put it in my back pocket on vibrate just so I wouldn't be wondering if I'd missed a text.

The first day of the fair went better than I had hoped, thanks mostly to the steady flow of people following Jules's posts about #FlorenceWakeGallery #ArtBaselHK. The booth, crowded throughout the day with a young and glamorous throng who likely did not intend to buy, also drew the attention of more serious buyers, and I sold two of Fredrick's pieces as well as one by an artist named Merlin Breckman, all at full ask. When my phone vibrated in my pocket, I grabbed for it as soon as I finished explaining a piece to a customer, but it was only Jules telling me her day was "crazy" and she couldn't make it to my booth but would see me tonight. I thought it would have been nice to see a friendly face in person that day, but just then I looked up to see Lenny smiling broadly, a beautiful blonde on one arm and Curtis Tremblay at his side.

"Emma Caan, my girlfriend, Lori Tanner. And you know Curtis." Lenny introduced me to the blonde, whom I recognized from the pictures Sienna had scouted online.

"Pleasure to meet you," I said, smiling while attempting to study her. Her nose was impossibly delicate, and her skin was dewy and taut, without a single discernible pore. I couldn't decide if she looked incredible for mid-forties or just okay for mid-thirties. Either way, she was young for Lenny, but not nearly as young as she appeared in photographs.

Lori returned my greeting with a cool nod and announced, "I'm going to take a look around." Lenny took off after her, and I turned my attention to Curtis Tremblay.

"She pointed out an engagement ring as we walked through the mall on the way here. Needless to say, it turned into an argument,"

Curtis whispered, a mischievous look in his eye. I shifted my gaze from Curtis to Lenny as I pictured both men all alone in their enormous houses, with their vast amounts of money. Afraid my face would show the inexplicable sadness for them that I felt, I made myself smile.

"I'm starting to see why you prefer landscapes to humans," I joked. Curtis clapped his knee and laughed. I capitalized on the natural segue and waxed enthusiastic about contemporary art being a logical path for him to expand the breadth of his collection. It was fine if he wasn't a fan of the human form—we had tons of abstract pieces. He listened intently, and I maintained hope that I had laid the groundwork for a sale at some point in the future.

As I wrapped up, he looked around the booth and asked, "Which is the most expensive?"

I was taken aback by the question, but I tried not to let on. At Gemini, I had become well acquainted with the notion that some people were in the art market solely for speculation—the hope that their investment would appreciate in value—rather than any real love of art. Stating as much outright was considered gauche in most artistic circles, though, and clients at Gemini typically went into unnecessary detail to explain that their motive was to *protect* the art by placing it in a freeport while our copy hung on their wall. Of course, we were all aware that by stashing their art in a freeport, they were protecting *themselves* from taxes, biding their time in a free economic zone until they could trade it—without paying customs duties, because it technically never entered that country.

"This piece is five point five million," I said, pointing to the sculpture. "Actually, this one is five point five as well." I gestured to a painting.

He contemplated each of them for a few seconds, then said, "I'll take both." I quickly composed my facial expression and congratulated him on his new acquisitions, then drew up the paperwork just as Leah had trained me to do. The delivery address was in Geneva—a little odd, because we were only a few miles from his home—but I didn't dare ask about it. When we got to the payment section, he preempted my question before I could pose it, with a confident "I'd like to pay in cash."

I politely excused myself to make a phone call and told him I'd be right back. I knew Florence would be thrilled if I sold our two most expensive works, but the only reason I could imagine for spending cash on art worth $11 million was to launder it—and I thought not letting Florence know that beforehand would be a fireable offense, even if it meant calling her cell in the middle of the night.

She answered groggily after a couple of rings and listened to my anxious recounting of the situation.

"Yes, of course he can pay in cash. Lenny will keep it in the safe on the plane and courier it over to the gallery when you're back."

I was surprised by how unruffled she seemed, and I could tell she was preparing to hang up. "Oh, and . . ."

"Yes?" She sounded annoyed.

"He wants us to deliver the work to Geneva," I said as quietly as I could.

"Interesting. I'm glad you told me," Florence said after a long pause. "He must be afraid of Hong Kong's precarious freeport status when it comes to trade with the U.S., but I'd suggest Delaware over Geneva. I'm sure he's seen the latest on the Geneva freeport."

I furrowed my brow. "He had the work he bought from Lenny last night delivered to Delaware," I said, not really understanding why it was relevant but figuring it might be.

"Wonderful. He likely won't have an issue, then," she said. "Good job, Emma," she added before hanging up.

I plastered a smile on my face, headed back to Curtis's side, and suggested he consider taking delivery in Delaware if he had a facility there as well.

He seemed to think about it for an extended moment. "I appreciate that . . ." He trailed off, seemingly doing some mental calculations. "I miss the good old days, when being a Hong Kong resident came with freeport status," he lamented. "My Delaware unit is getting crowded. And I hate the idea of entrusting you Americans with my fortune." He laughed.

"Do you hate us enough to pay taxes?" I said with a smirk, and he let out a louder laugh. I updated the papers for shipment to Delaware, we signed on multiple dotted lines, shook hands, and assured each other what a pleasure it was to do business. I finally sat down for the first time all day and slipped off my shoes, no longer caring if a customer walked in and saw me. I crossed my right foot over my knee and pressed on the arch, closing my eyes to more acutely feel the delicious release of tension. It stayed quiet for a little bit, and I managed to take a few bites of the wrap Lenny had brought me, actually feeling the energy that came with sustenance.

As I closed up for the night, I forced myself to focus on the success of the day's sales rather than the deafening silence from Ryan, then headed back to the Hyatt with only thirty minutes to get ready for the party. As I ascended in the hotel elevator, I opened Instagram and reviewed Jules's stories, seeing snippets of the morning she had spent with Ryan on a boat out in Victoria Harbour, and videos of them checking out a booth at Basel that was just a few down from my own. So they'd been nearby but chosen not to say hello? The elevator doors opened again in the lobby, and I saw I had missed my floor and descended without realizing it. I sighed and pushed the button until it glowed again.

I slipped into the white spandex unitard Jules had chosen for me, grateful that I'd barely had time to eat all day, then wiggled my way into the white tutu, threw on the bunny ears and blond wig, pinned on the little cotton tail, and painted a black nose and whiskers on

my face with the eyeliner pencil she'd bought me. I took an extra
few minutes before leaving my room, thinking it wouldn't be bad
to make Ryan wonder where I was, but when I exited the elevator
in the lobby, I saw Jules alone, standing in the marble foyer in a
skimpy light blue French maid's uniform and a blond wig—a highly
sexualized version of young Alice, something I thought Lewis Carroll
would have appreciated.

"I'll have the hotel get us a car," she offered.

"Oh, um, should we wait for Ryan?" I asked, striving for a casual
tone but feeling a slight panic creeping in.

"I texted him, but he's all the way in Kowloon, so he's just going
to hang there for the night with his friends. Whatever! His loss,"
she said, and leaned in close to me and held her phone out for a sel-
fie. I felt self-conscious and uncomfortable from the elastic of the
tutu digging into my waist, like a sausage stuffed into a white casing, but I forced a smile as she snapped the picture and AirDropped
it to me. To my relief, I didn't look nearly as bad as I felt.

"You have to download Visco. V-S-C-O. They have the best
filters," Jules said knowingly before heading out to the car.

I trailed behind her as we exited the lobby, still staring at my clear
skin and highlighted cheekbones in the picture. I posted it along
with the caption—*Signing off for the night. Apparently, Wonderland
has crappy service. #DownTheRabbitHoleHK*—but not before noting
that at the end of my first day at Basel, I now had five thousand
followers.

"This picture is so cute!" Jules gushed, looking at her phone
as we climbed into the backseat. "What should I caption it?" she
asked me as the driver pulled out of the driveway.

"I just posted it and said, 'Signing off for the night . . .'"

"You already posted *my* picture?" Jules asked, shrillness in her
tone. "Did you tag me?"

I shook my head. "Just deleted it! Reposting now and tagging you," I assured her. As she nodded, looking reluctantly forgiving, I received a notification that @ItsRyanParker had begun following me and had commented a fire emoji on my picture. My breath caught. I was going to have to up my Insta game significantly if he was seeing my posts.

A new text tore me from my strategizing. "Yelena isn't going to make it," I told Jules.

"Who's Yelena?"

"She's Lenny's best friend's wife."

"Yelena Bartenev?" Jules asked, leaning toward me. "You know her?"

"Yeah, I flew over with her. How do *you* know her?" I asked.

"Yelena used to be at *every* art party before she got married. She was wild. It's so weird to see her now, playing the perfect wife and mother. She always pretends she doesn't know me, and I'm just like, I did coke with you before the MoMA garden party when you were still Renting the Runway while husband shopping, you know?" she said as our car pulled to a stop. I thought of how Yelena had leaned lovingly in to Sergey's side when she spoke but had drunk so much at Curtis's dinner that she couldn't stand and how furious Sergey had been. Jules opened her door, bringing me back to the present and reminding me to hop out of the car, too.

The entire facade of the Pedder Building was painted over with an enormous mural of the Cheshire Cat, his toothy grin making my stomach tighten uncomfortably. The door directly in the center of the cat's right eye opened and closed to absorb the leggy models wearing rabbit ears and striped tights and the men who followed them in, mostly in suits, some with top hats. I felt the excitement churning in my gut and looked to Jules to see the electricity of anticipation pass between us.

"This is going to be good," she announced, her eyes trained on the clusters of people walking the red carpet.

The concrete outside the gallery vibrated with the bass from inside, and I was posing for a photo with Jules when she shoved a shoulder forward at an awkward angle while cameras flashed in front of a step-and-repeat boasting "Art Basel" and "первая водка" with a rudimentary smiley face next to it on the backdrop.

"Curtis Tremblay owns that vodka company," Jules said, pointing to the words in Russian.

We approached the hulking bouncer, and I declared, "Emma Caan plus one," feeling delightfully important. He swiped his finger up his screen and furrowed his brow. "I have plus two, but I'm only plus one," I explained, my ego deflating, but he just nodded.

"Cell service is cut, so you'll have to come outside if you need to make a call. And of course, if we see you taking pictures, you're out," he said, and a doorman opened the cat's right eye to let us inside.

When the doors closed behind us, we stood in darkness until our eyes adjusted to identify an orange light glowing somewhere up ahead. The people who had entered ahead of us drifted toward the glow, which I realized was a metal and light installation of a Mad Hatter. I appreciated the very definite effect the theatrics were having on me and looked ahead at the spotlight, illuminating the white sign that said in black calligraphed letters: *"We're all mad here. I'm mad. You're mad."*

Two bouncers opened another set of large double doors, and deep thumping sounds and flashing colored lights spilled out into the dark hallway, sucking us in to a feast of color and music. Neon lasers sliced through the air in rapidly changing colors and patterns, and an enormous light installation of a blue caterpillar sitting atop a red-and-white-spotted mushroom sat in the middle of the room. Inside the mushroom was a small area where a DJ bopped his head and wiggled his fingers over a turntable. To our left, I saw a raw bar in the shape of an oyster, filled with actual ones, and a caviar bar made of ice. Large martini glasses filled with shrimp perched atop a table shaped like a foaming blue wave. To our right, gigantic chairs dotted a floor painted with huge playing cards. Men dressed as jesters passed champagne, and a woman dressed as the queen of hearts extended a tray with a small cardboard sign reading EAT ME. I peered down at a dozen appetizer spoons neatly arranged in a circle, each holding one blue pill with a smiley face etched into it. I looked up at her, a question on my face.

"E," she said plainly. "'Shrooms will be out in just a moment," she added, and I caught what I thought was an English accent. I held up my palm to pass, but Jules was already extending a tiny spoon to me.

"I've never done it," I said, slightly embarrassed.

"Oh my God, you'll love it. You feel totally the same, just super-happy and like you have this really intense connection to everybody around you. It's amazing," she promised.

I stared at the small pill, wondering how it would be to feel just like myself but super-happy. Jules placed the pill on the center of her tongue and tilted her head back, looking at me with a small smile. She looked so carefree and beautiful in that moment. I was reminded of how I used to watch her as the perfect creature. Without out another moment of deliberation, I took the pill from Jules and a small glass of water from the server and knocked it back, taking two big gulps to make certain I was past the point of no return.

As we swayed to the music along with the rest of the crowd over the next fifteen minutes, the only thing I felt was a bit of motion sickness. "I think I'm immune to ecstasy," I yelled into Jules's ear on the dance floor. "I just feel like I might puke."

"That happens to me sometimes," she assured me. "Just make yourself hydrate."

I forced the cool liquid down my throat, trying my best not to gag it up.

"Come on, let's find boys!" Jules exclaimed. I waited for the ecstasy to magically make me care less about Ryan, but the memory was still there—the electricity between us, his lips on mine. "He's cute!"

I looked where she was pointing and nearly dropped my water glass as I spotted the consultant from Gemini, looking very handsome in a perfectly tailored navy suit over a crisp white collared shirt, with a top hat—doing the bare minimum to follow the costume requirement. For a fleeting moment, I wondered if he had followed me around the world, and all those times I had been pining after him through the glass, he'd been returning my attraction from the opposite side. Then I thought it might have been reality softening into a porous haze that invited the possibility of such a thought.

Jules was studying me. "Do you know him?" she asked, running her fingers up and down her arm in a way that inspired me to do the same to my own. My forearm tingled beneath the white spandex and called every cell of my skin to life. I was suddenly blissfully aware of the contact the smooth unitard was making with every inch of me. I turned back to Jules and nodded.

"That's so random. Tell him to come hang out! I mean, what are the chances that you know the one guy I noticed at this party?" A radiant smile was spreading across her face.

"I was *just* thinking that!" I said, understanding that the entire purpose of my time at Gemini was to arrive at this moment, when I could introduce the consultant to Jules. It was why I'd never flirted with him or asked him out—I was supposed to be with Ryan, and the consultant was supposed to be with Jules. "I'm going to go get him," I announced as I pushed forward through the crowd. Now the lights were brighter, and the lasers left faint lingering streaks. I felt my heart racing so quickly that I had to pause and press my palm against it to keep it from flying out. Was it possible that I was allergic to ecstasy and I would very soon have a heart attack and die? Hadn't I watched a video about this in junior high health class? I forced myself to breathe deeply and realized I was standing right in front of the consultant.

"Hey!" I said, still kneading the skin above my heart. "Are you following me?" I forced a laugh to let him know I was kidding.

"Why do you say that?" he said, and smiled back, as though he knew a secret I didn't.

"I can't believe I'm bumping into you halfway around the world! I think you're in my hotel, too," I said, taking a bottle of water off a silver tray carried by a young man in a Mad Hatter ensemble.

"I had a mentor who used to say that one too many coincidences isn't a coincidence at all," the consultant yelled over the music. "Are you okay? You don't look great."

I'm dying. "I think I'm okay," I said, then inhaled slowly through my nose. And I was okay. The pins and needles were gone. I stared up at the magnificent blue lights on the ceiling that I knew were spheres of energy, calming my heart and coating my body in their warm glow. "I'm very okay. I think it's wild you're here and I'm here when we also spent so many days in the same building all the way on the other side of the earth! Have you ever even thought about how amazing it is that we're on a different side of the earth but with the same people, speaking the same language? Doesn't that just . . ." I put my fingers to my temples and them fanned them to mime my head exploding. "Oh! I forgot what I came to tell you! I'm here with a friend you should meet. I think you two would hit it off." I pulled at his arm giddily, realizing the fabric on his suit was almost electric.

"I'm actually okay," he said with a gentle smile.

"Welp! I'll see you around. Probably really soon, at the rate we're going!" I laughed and headed back to Jules, who was happily dancing by herself near the bar. She took my hand and pulled me toward her to dance, apparently having forgotten about the consultant.

"I'm just so glad I met you!" I shouted over the music. "Life before you was so boring!" Out of the corner of my eye, I saw a man wearing a scarf over his face.

"Fredrick!" I called, moving past Jules and pulling him in for a hug. "I'm the new assistant director at Florence Wake!"

"Hey! Oh yeah! Of course! Emma?" he said.

"Yes, and this is my friend Jules!" I shouted over the music. "Jules, Fredrick Thomas."

"We met at Leonard Sobetsky's Young Picasso event in February," she reminded him.

"Wait, you did? I was there, too!" I yelled, but they were no longer paying attention to me. Jules was speaking into his ear, and soon his hands were on her hips. They moved together to the music as I danced in place next to them at the bar, then they started kissing, and my brain began to spiral. Was it weird for me to be hanging out alone next to two people making out? Could everybody tell I had taken E? Did the consultant know? Why hadn't Ryan come, really? Instinctively, I checked my phone, but of course, I had no service.

I drifted toward the front of the room and climbed the wide wood steps to hoist myself onto an enormous purple armchair. I ran my hand over the luxurious velvet, watching the way my fingers left streaks of darker purple next to the light ones as they changed the direction of the fibers.

"Hey!" a voice yelled from below, and I saw Ryan standing below, staring up at me.

"You made it," I said, a sense of calm descending over me. I wanted to go down the stairs to greet him, but stroking the fabric felt too good to stop.

"Where's Jules?" he asked.

"Making out with Fredrick Thomas," I said, and Ryan climbed

the steps and lifted himself up next to me. There were feet between us, but I felt him on my skin, the energy from him floating
over and meeting mine. I knew he felt it, too—the electric tether
between us that only tightened as we drifted toward each other,
our fingers touching before our lips met. We didn't speak a single
word, but we kissed for what seemed like hours and a moment all
at once.

A tugging on my shoe pulled me out of the embrace, and I
looked down to see Jules standing below me. "Hey" was all she
said as she beckoned for us to dance with her. Ryan took my hand
and helped me down from the chair, then pulled me out onto the
dance floor. There, he draped his body over Jules, whose back
was to him, as I swayed behind him with my hand on his shoulder, dimly aware of a wish for him to face me but content to be
touching him at all. At some point, Fredrick joined us, and we
all danced together. It was four o'clock in the morning when we
flung ourselves into a car back to the hotel, silently watching the
headlights and city lights whiz by. When we got out of the car at
the Hyatt and into the elevator, Ryan pressed the button for his
floor and didn't stop me from pressing mine, then exited on his
floor with a casual wave that made me want to scream and cry all
at once. Once the doors closed, Fredrick handed me a broken-off
white pill.

"It's just a half, but it'll help you sleep. Which will help with the
hangover," he assured me as he threw one arm over Jules's shoulder
and exited the elevator with her. I climbed to my higher floor in the
glass case, feeling a hollow, pitted-out sense of loneliness.

When my room phone screamed with a wake-up call a few hours
later, I peeled my eyelids open to answer it. A chipper voice in-

formed me that it was seven a.m., but despite knowing that I needed to open the booth in an hour, I left the receiver off the cradle and closed my eyes to shut out the world yet again. When I reopened them twenty minutes later, I forced my legs over the edge of my bed and stumbled into the shower. After a hasty towel dry, a bit of makeup, and extra deodorant, I zippered my black cigarette pants, slipped a black turtleneck over my head, and took one final look in the mirror. I looked awful—a haggard, hollowed-out version of myself. The tiny crow's-feet sprouting out from the corners of my lids hadn't been there yesterday, I was certain. I paused, placing my hands on the sink for balance.

I poured myself two large cups of coffee in the lobby, documented the #doublefisting on Instagram as evidence of a fun night, and drank both before arriving at the exhibition center. Before I entered, I plastered a smile on my face because I had once read in a magazine outside my college therapist's office that smiling could boost your mood. I didn't think it worked, but I still made six sales, which Leah later told me was a gallery record. Right before the fair closed, I sold the last of Fredrick's pieces to a local couple, and I packed up the two unsold pieces to ship back to New York.

I stumbled onto Lenny's plane a little after eight o'clock that evening after retrieving the clothes strewn about my room and throwing them into my suitcase. I was somehow the first one to board even though I was ten minutes late, and I lay on the couch in the den as my head pounded from the drug-infused dance party, the nights of too little sleep, and the excessive caffeine. I closed my eyes and immediately felt Ryan's lips on mine, his hand on my leg, then realized it was the same hand that had casually dismissed me at the end of the night. I felt somebody fasten something around my waist, and I opened my eyes just wide enough to see Lenny draping a heavy blanket over me and tucking the corners under my feet. He whispered something soothing I couldn't quite make out and patted my head gently. I felt the pull of gravity as the plane fought against it, and my mind fluttered between thoughts and dreams until the dreams won out and I slipped into a suspended state of consciousness.

EMMA CAAN:	It was everywhere—served the same way all the other food and alcohol was. I just want to be clear that—
AGENT TILLWELL:	Ms. Caan, we have no interest in prosecuting your use of recreational drugs on foreign soil, I can assure you of that.
EMMA CAAN:	Then why does it matter? You keep saying you're not investigating me, but all your questions are about me.
AGENT GARRITT:	It matters because it speaks to your state of mind. It also gives us a sense of Mr. Tremblay's relationship with Mr. Sobetsky. And yes, your relationship with both of them.
EMMA CAAN:	They're just rich. They do rich-people things like exchange art.
AGENT TILLWELL:	They're not just rich.
AGENT GARRITT:	Nobody as rich as they are is just rich, Ms. Caan.
AGENT TILLWELL:	The Tremblays, for example, are the only non-Asian family to own a stake in the drug trade out of the Golden Triangle. Ever hear of it?
EMMA CAAN:	Yes. I think he had a painting of the area. But I didn't know what it was . . .
AGENT GARRITT:	Right. We're getting the impression that you didn't know much about the people you've been dealing with.
EMMA CAAN:	I'll try not to take offense to that in this scenario, I guess. If you're not investigating Curtis, who or what are you investigating?

I woke up with a jolt, searching for the flames all around me but seeing none. Instead, the lights inside the plane had been dimmed, and the world outside the small windows was dark. I looked around for any indication that I had been screaming, but there was none. I stood up slowly and shrugged off the thick blanket, then stumbled toward the front of the plane, passing the guest bedroom door with a "Do Not Disturb" sign; the theater, where Micaela slept curled up on the small couch next to another mass of a human whom I guessed was Yelena; the hallway bathroom; and then went into the lounge, where Lenny sat alone, poring over a stack of papers. He looked up when he felt my presence, his face brightening, and I gave him a small, sheepish smile just as a beautiful brunette popped in from the front of the plane.

"Ms. Caan, can I get you anything to drink? Or eat?" she asked. "We can prepare breakfast or lunch food."

"Can I just have water? Like a *huge* glass of water, please?" My mouth felt as dry as sandpaper. The attendant disappeared, and Lenny extended a hand toward the seat across from him. I slid myself onto it as a glass of water and a carafe for refills was placed before me.

"Nothing to eat?" the woman tried again.

"Bring her some breakfast, please," Lenny said, his eyes trained on me. The woman stood at attention, then hurried off again. "You're pale," he said. "How do you feel?"

"Tip-top!" I said with a laugh, then grabbed the water and gulped it down. I refilled it from the carafe, beginning to chug the second glass as well. "I think . . . I think I overdid it a bit at that Down the Rabbit Hole party," I said.

"I think that's the whole point of the party," Lenny said.

"I didn't see Curtis there," I said.

"He never goes," Lenny said. "He just makes certain everybody enjoys themselves from afar. Did your friends have fun, too?"

"They did. Actually, it turned out one of them used to know Yelena. And I realized I have no idea how you know Sergey." I knew I might be crossing a line by mentioning Yelena's past, but the traces of ecstasy in my system lowered my filter, and it made me uncomfortable that Jules knew more about my traveling companions than I did.

Lenny contemplated me, giving me the uncomfortable feeling that he was deciding which version of the truth to tell me. "We grew up together," he said. I said nothing, giving him space to elaborate. "We both grew up poor. One-room houses. Dirt floors. Never enough food. In the eighties, I was off mingling with artists, and he was telling me the country's wealth was about to be redistributed in perestroika and we needed to get involved in commerce. I never listened while he started his chemical business out of his apartment. When the Soviet Union collapsed, Sergey made billions, and I still lived modestly."

"Well, something changed," I said, gesturing around the jet with a short laugh.

"Yes. Something changed," he said pensively. "I needed money for . . . a medical procedure, and Sergey gave it to me. And I worked very hard to pay him back. But it is hard to pay back a debt like that. So Sergey gave me money to invest in art and told me when to buy and sell to make a profit. I got very good at it. Good enough that I paid him back and made money for myself—enough to invest in a few companies. I learned that all you really need to make money is money." Lenny shrugged. I nodded, struggling to see Lenny as anything but a billionaire. "What?" he asked.

"Maybe that's why you were so quick to help me?" I wondered aloud. "Because Sergey helped you." I paused. "I can't thank you enough for what you're doing for me."

Lenny shook his head as if to say it was nothing, but something somber passed across his eyes. I didn't know if it was some lingering effects of the ecstasy, but I watched as all the trappings of his world dissolved—he was no longer a Russian-billionaire client; I no longer saw the Rolex or the cashmere or the plane. I saw only Lenny, ruminating on his next words. Apparently to keep them from coming out, he tipped his glass of vodka back and opened his throat to receive it, then smiled softly with renewed control over his expression. What was he not saying?

"What was the first piece of art you bought with your own money?" I asked, wanting to fill the silence.

"A Rembrandt."

"Oh, that's nice that you started modestly," I said as I reached for a bowl of berries that had been brought out.

He placed his hands on his belly, leaned back, and laughed, and I felt a small victory in having lifted his mood. I devoured the brunch spread while Lenny sipped his vodka, telling me stories about his first art purchases after he moved to London, and the salty sustenance coupled with his deep voice cleared my mind further. I ordered a coffee, and he launched into telling me about a near-disaster of a deal with the royal family. I was completely enthralled.

"But enough about me," he said after he wrapped up his anecdote about the queen. "What was your favorite part of Hong Kong?"

I took a long sip of my coffee as I flipped through mental snapshots of visiting a world-class city for the first time, seeing Curtis Tremblay's collection, making deals at the fair, and Down the Rabbit Hole.

"People paying attention to me. People I don't even know," I said, instantly embarrassed that I'd said something so honest and so juvenile out loud. "I guess being the assistant director of Florence Wake means something. I haven't meant something in a while." I shrugged as Lenny stared at me just long enough to make me uncomfortable. "What?"

"Honesty," he said. "Refreshing."

I felt almost normal, with the food having magically absorbed my hangover. But when I took another sip of coffee, my stomach clenched, as though that final sip had upset whatever delicate balance I had created.

"Excuse me," I said, fearing that everything was about to come back up. I rose and made my way hastily to the bathroom just down the hall from the lounge, the gurgling in my stomach now audible, and then twisted the bathroom doorknob and shoved my shoulder into the door.

"Oh!" I yelled, covering my eyes, but not before seeing two figures—Micaela, her back up against the far mirrored wall and a man pressed up against her, her top off and his pants around his ankles. I could see his face in the mirror and didn't recognize it, but then I noted his entirely white outfit. *Fredrick Thomas.* I'd never seen him without the scarf. I stammered an apology, turned, and slammed the door behind me before running toward the back of the plane to the next bathroom. Thankfully, the nausea had passed, but I flopped down on the toilet seat and stared straight ahead. I had no idea Fredrick and Micaela even knew each other; I never would have introduced him to Jules if I had. I had already inadvertently taken Micaela's job—I didn't need ruining her relationship added to my list of transgressions.

"Good afternoon, all," a voice piped in from the speaker overhead. "We'll be beginning our initial descent into Teterboro. It's raining in New Jersey, and we do anticipate some turbulence. Please make your way to the front of the plane and secure yourself with a seat belt."

I teetered down the hallway and joined the other passengers in the lounge, where Fredrick and Micaela were now stationed, too, both staring out the window as the plane fought its way toward the ground. Lightning flashed just outside, and Yelena and Sergey held hands and said nothing while Sophie whispered what I thought was a prayer. Lori, in full makeup with her hair perfectly styled, emerged from the back of the plane and sat down next to Lenny, speaking to him in hushed tones. I folded my arms over my chest, realizing that everybody was worrying about somebody else—except me.

When we landed in Teterboro, thick sheets of rain coated the windows, and I called an Uber before we had even rolled to a stop. I wanted to process Hong Kong while curled up on my own bed, in my tiny unglamorous apartment, with nobody around. Still, I mustered the energy to thank Lenny profusely for the flight and decline a ride back to Manhattan.

"Micaela will be in touch with work," he promised with a wink.

After waving goodbye to the others, I ducked into my Uber and took out my phone. I had a slew of junk mail, an email from my landlord reminding me that my rent was due, and an email from Florence congratulating me on a job well done and suggesting I take Friday off and come back refreshed on Monday. It was exactly what I needed.

I rested my phone in my lap and stared out the window for the rest of the ride. When the car pulled up in front of my building, I marveled that it looked somehow smaller and dingier than when I had left. It might have been the gloomy weather, but I suspected it was more the juxtaposition of my real life with the private plane and plush pajamas, the sparking light show and collections of priceless art. The thud of the trunk closing snapped me back to reality, and I braced myself for the miserable dash into my apartment, but the driver had opened the umbrella to usher me to my door. I stepped out of the car into the small circle of shielded space and thanked him profusely, understanding that this was the last vestige of my week of extreme luxury and impeccable service before returning to taxicabs and subway cars.

"Door-to-door service," he said as he walked me to my door and stepped back. I thanked him again and went up the stairs, stopping for a moment at the threshold of my apartment before stepping inside. The far wall of windows was only paces from where I stood in the doorway, and my bed seemed close enough that I could touch it. I finally entered and cranked open my window to freshen the air, and paced around the room. The entire space was smaller than my hotel room in Hong Kong, and I felt restricted by it.

I made my way to the bathroom and turned on the sink to wash my face, realizing for the first time that the water in my apartment never got quite hot enough. How had I never noticed that before? I tried to recapture the feeling I had when my landlord first handed me the key to my studio, when I had been so overwhelmed to find a corner of the city all for myself that I had hugged him.

Impulsively, I reached for my phone to text my landlord. A sense of control calmed me. I had options now.

When Sienna buzzed from downstairs on Saturday, I held the apartment door open and watched her wind up the stairwell, huffing slightly before beginning the last flight. I was suddenly embarrassed that she had trekked all the way to Washington Heights for an update on Hong Kong, only to have to work even harder to get to my apartment. I hugged her close and followed her inside, where we plopped down on the couch that I only then realized was a love seat—as though it had shrunk since I had been to Asia, or perhaps my mind had expanded.

"Thank you for coming all the way up here. Well, thanks for coming . . . everywhere lately," I said.

She shooed away my gratitude with a flick of her wrist. "Tell me everything!"

I told her about Ryan Parker, my spandex tutu, the smiley-face pill, and all the paintings that I could remember from Curtis Tremblay's private collection.

"My brain is exploding!" she exclaimed. "And honestly, I can't get past the fact that the plane had five bathrooms and an office!"

"It was totally insane," I agreed as my mind flashed with the memory of the file I had found in the office. *All remaining proceeds . . .*

will go to Karen Simmons. I distracted myself by telling Sienna about Fredrick and Jules, then Fredrick and Micaela.

"What is it with men, you know? They feel like they're not living unless they're screwing somebody over by screwing somebody else," Sienna said, sounding a bit more negative than her usual sunny self. "But in your shoes, I'd just pretend I never saw anything."

"The thing about Fredrick is just . . . ugh! There's a part of me that wishes he wasn't a client so I could blow up his life. He's so full of it. His paintings are entirely mediocre, but because he walks around with a stupid scarf covering his face, he's the art world's it boy," I said, and rolled my eyes.

Sienna stared at me. "You should really give Florence your portfolio, you know?"

She didn't know that I'd already tried that years ago. *Technically superior. Emotionally detached.* But as she went on about her favorites of my paintings that she'd seen, my self-doubt was gradually replaced by a sense of possibility. There was a chance that Florence had never personally reviewed my portfolio and had only sent a form rejection, right? Maybe everything I had been through since college was all part of a cosmic plan to land me in front of one of the few people in the world who could single-handedly make an artist's career.

"Maybe I will," I said noncommittally. "But I'm not ready yet."

"Okay, okay. And what I really want to know: What's Lenny like?" Sienna asked.

"He's amazing," I said, putting my assessment of him into words for the first time. "He's nothing like I thought he'd be. He's really warm and so generous."

"It's easy to be generous when you have that kind of money," she pointed out.

"Right," I said, and shrugged. "But I've been freelancing for him from his studio in SoHo, and he offered to have me stay there because it's so much more convenient than commuting! I think I'm going to take him up on it," I added, as if I hadn't already told my landlord I was moving out.

"An apartment? Isn't that crossing a line?" Sienna said, looking incredulous.

"He's more like a father than anything," I said, trying to dispel whatever sordid scenario was brewing in her head.

"That's not what I meant," she said. "His being like a father is exactly what I'm worried about. When it comes to your father—"

"You don't know anything about my relationship with my father," I said softly but quickly, before she could finish. "Sorry. I appreciate the concern, but I *promise*, Lenny has nothing but the best intentions for me." The words coated my tongue in a bitter residue, making me feel further from her.

"Okay. I've never met the guy, so what do I know? Anyway," she said, brightening, "what are you doing the rest of the day? Do you want to get a drink?"

"Five years of friendship and you've never asked me to day-drink. Are you okay?" I asked.

"Totally! Yes! I don't know, your stories of debauchery from Hong Kong inspired a craving," she said, but she was picking at a cuticle nervously.

"It was pretty epic," I agreed. "But I am pooped, and my liver is pickled—can we take a rain check?"

"Of course," she said kindly, and took off soon after.

I spent the rest of the day on my laptop, reviewing my portfolio. I hadn't seen the paintings, which were in my parents' basement, in several years. The colors were bold and the people just imperfect enough to be fascinating. I had used real models and then made some of their features less attractive, googly eyes or a hook nose. *Technically superior. Emotionally detached.* I heard the words as

I clicked through the images, needing to stop and put a cool towel on the back of my neck to calm my nerves.

I reminded myself that Florence had sold far inferior pieces for millions. *Millions!* I tried not to think of the money, tried to pretend it would all be for the honor of my art hanging on collectors' walls, but I wanted both: acknowledgment of my talent *and* money in my pocket. I rifled through my nightstand for a flash drive and saved my portfolio to it before tossing it in my bag. The next time there was any opening to show Florence my art, I would seize it.

On Sunday, I completed the simultaneously exhilarating and depressing exercise of packing, which involved filling large trash bags with everything I would not be taking with me to the studio, including the cupboard's two plates, two bowls, and one cup (the other had cracked in the microwave; I had no silverware because I always used the plastic utensils that I stole from the supermarket salad bar), and I had no use for pans and other appliances now that I was moving to Lenny's. The box of Trojans that I had optimistically bought my first week in New York remained unopened. I had the disquieting sensation I had been living just the outer casing of a life. All my clothes that weren't already packed from Hong Kong fit into my largest suitcase, and I carefully laid out the microwave, toaster, and pans on the sidewalk next to a piece of cardboard reading FREE. From upstairs, I watched as people picked through the limited evidence that I had resided in my apartment, wincing slightly when a young woman inspected my one good pan and set it back on the concrete. Two hours later, I was done. I slipped my key under my landlord's door on the first floor and walked outside to hail a cab. It felt like a splurge, but I reminded myself that I wouldn't be paying rent for a while.

Once I arrived at the studio, I used my fingerprint to access the code and pushed through the front door into the open, airy space. I placed my phone on the cool gray marble of the kitchen island and uncorked a bottle of red wine off the rack in the corner and poured a portion into one of the delicate, long-stemmed glasses from the cupboard. Glass in hand, I paced my new home, which was even larger than I had remembered, and more beautiful. But for some reason, an uneasy feeling settled in my stomach. I double-checked that the door was locked, wondering if anyone else had access to the space. I looked at my phone to see an email from Micaela saying that we'd need to discuss delivery of the Chagall at my convenience, and that there would be three new works for copying dropped off by the week's end. I locked my phone without responding, suddenly needing air.

Not my apartment. Not my art. I couldn't even remember my thought process in accepting Lenny's offer to move in, which he'd made with such confidence that I'd accept. I didn't quite know how I had gotten there, and now it felt like he had somehow tricked me.

I pulled down the cool brass handle leading to the terrace and steadied my nerves by snapping a photo of the cityscape before me. *New digs. New views. New chapter.* I watched as the likes and hearts filled my phone, one from Ryan, whom I then requested to follow. The hearts and comments felt like a reminder from the world that I had made the right decision to move in. If all those people thought so, didn't it have to be true?

AGENT TILLWELL:	Did you ever try to sell your own art? Perhaps to Leonard Sobetsky?
EMMA CAAN:	Not to Lenny. But I've tried. Unsuccessfully.
AGENT TILLWELL:	That must be frustrating. You're very good. It must make you feel like the art world is rigged.
EMMA CAAN:	I guess. I think hitting it big as an artist takes talent but also luck. I haven't been lucky. Or maybe I'm not that talented.
AGENT TILLWELL:	That's a shame.
EMMA CAAN:	That's the art world.
AGENT GARRITT:	Hm. If the system is rigged anyway, have you ever tried to pass one of your copies off as an original? I could imagine—
EMMA CAAN:	No. I haven't.

I stepped onto the cool polished concrete floor of the gallery early on Monday with a renewed sense of purpose. The light in Florence's office wasn't on yet, which meant I had beat her in, thanks in part to my five-minute walk there. I logged onto my computer and sifted through a few of the emails I hadn't gotten to since Hong Kong, feeling proud of all the correspondence between Leah and new clients from the fair finalizing the transfer of payment and title and logistics of delivery. I looked up as I saw Leah burst through the door to the gallery backward, so she didn't spill the two coffees in her hand.

"Well, well, well, if it isn't 'at ecaanart' and her nine thousand followers," she teased, then handed me the larger of the two coffees. "Everybody needs a venti after Hong Kong."

"You're an angel. I so need this right now," I said, inhaling the classically burnt aroma of Starbucks coffee.

"Thank God you had the weekend to recover, amirite?" She widened her eyes knowingly.

"It was crazy," I agreed. "Happy to be back."

"I'd ask you how it was, but I think I know pretty much everything except what happened at Down the Rabbit Hole from Jules's Instagram," she said with a twinkle in her eyes that told me she wasn't judging my friendship or online persona too harshly. "You looked pretty cozy with Ryan Parker."

I gave a slight cough as my breath caught, jarred by hearing the name that had been echoing in my head uttered aloud. I wasn't certain how long I could withhold the information, so I was glad when she was distracted by the purple flash drive on the glass desk we shared. "What is that?"

"A flash drive," I said.

"Clearly. But what's *on* it?"

"My art portfolio. I was thinking of asking Florence to take a look," I said.

She sipped her coffee pensively for a moment. "I'd wait until she's in a good mood before you do that," she said, calling her computer to life and entering her password.

The door to the gallery swung open and Florence burst in, the red shawl draped over her shoulders fanning out behind her as she passed us. "Leah, to what do we owe the pleasure of your company so early?" she said without slowing, and then without waiting for an answer, "Welcome back, Emma. I'll need you with me at an auction next Tuesday."

"Great!" I said, but she'd already passed me.

"And today is *not* that day," Leah said.

The morning in the gallery felt frantic, and Leah told me it was one of the busiest Mondays she had ever seen. Almost every single guest was a young, fashionable woman who eagerly accepted the champagne I offered, but none of them bought a thing. When a gaggle of them departed around two o'clock, leaving only one man in the gallery who insisted twice he was just "browsing," I slumped down in my chair, kicked off my heels, and stretched out my toes on the cold floor. I really needed to invest in a pair of shoes rather than wearing Leah's hand-me-downs.

"Thanks for your help," I grunted sarcastically. Leah hadn't gotten out of her chair the entire morning and then had gone out for a lunch break, only to return with a small black-and-white-striped bag from Sephora while I had worked straight through.

"No amount of help was going to sell any art to those girls," Leah said, and I looked at her quizzically. "Oh, come on! They were only here to check out JustJules's new best friend! You must know that."

I rolled my eyes. "Yeah, right," I said, which Leah accepted as a challenge, scrolling through her phone and shoving it in my face.

I stared at a post of Jules's that I'd already seen: the two of us in costume in the lobby of the Hyatt, captioned, *Off to Wonderland with this wonder of a human #besties #alwayslate #ArtBaselHK*. The picture now had half a million likes.

"That's just creepy," I said, looking at the door to the gallery. I'd been trying to sell to young voyeurs all day.

Leah shrugged. "Maybe, but their posts are free marketing for the gallery. Somebody will buy something at some point. Oh, before I forget, Evelyn from Christie's called, and she is desperate for serious Cecily Brown buyers. Has anybody asked for works by Cecily Brown lately?"

I shook my head. "Isn't the point of the auction to attract buyers? Why does she need to find them before?"

"Honestly, it's a valid question. But there's too much to unpack here. Let's chat after your first auction. I promise it will make more sense after," she said.

I nodded, wondering if I'd ever have a command of the art world the way Leah did.

The afternoon was blessedly slow, and Florence left early to get changed for a charity event, while Leah followed at five on the dot, leaving me in the chilly space with only my thoughts for company. The familiar dread of evenings alone that I'd felt at Gemini lodged itself in my chest. I was now busy enough that I should have appreciated the downtime, but a solo evening still looked to me like a long, dark, lonely space filled with thoughts of what I wanted and did not have: furniture, an art career, a loving, functional family, a boyfriend.

I scanned my computer for missed emails, unsent invoices, anything. I thought about rearranging the southernmost wall of the gallery, but it was perfect just as it was. I stared out the glass door at the pedestrian traffic; in a city of four million males, there must be one with whom I could establish a relationship, and then the one I wanted rose again to the top of my mind.

I couldn't go home, so I texted Jules. She immediately responded that she was at a gallery exhibit on the Lower East Side for one of her best friends, Deepthi Madhavan, and that I should join her. Trying to delay my arrival as not to seem too eager, I walked the twenty or so minutes to the gallery and a space full of people and unremarkable clay sculptures of stretched-out people. However uninspiring the sculptures, the people were so effortlessly cool in their silver-studded leather booties and high-waisted jeans that the art also seemed more interesting, though I felt out of place in my business-casual outfit.

"Hi!" Jules ran up to me with a kiss on each cheek, linking her arm with mine and walking me into the crowd, explaining in a hushed tone that her ex-boyfriend was there so it was imperative that I never leave her side. I was fine with that, not wanting to leave the glow of her spotlight, either. I felt the crowd parting for us, and with every group we passed seeming to take more interest in us than the last, my mood improved. We stopped in front of a cast-bronze sculpture of a long, thin figure kneeling, her thighs folded back over her calves as she sat on her ankles, her hands covering her face so I couldn't tell if she was crying or praying. I looked around, wondering if the sculpture made anybody else in the room feel acutely depressed, but there was no sign of anything but contentment on people's faces. I shook off the feeling and plastered a smile on my face, falling in line. We took a few photos in front of it, the best of which I captioned *Funday Monday with this beauty* and posted it to Instagram.

A few minutes later, Fredrick waved at us from a few people away, and Jules slackened her arm so that mine naturally unlinked as she drifted away. I stood alone, waiting for her to look back at me, but she spent the remainder of the night with her lips pressed against his, directly in the center of the room beside the focal sculpture of the show. Without Jules next to me, I felt acutely alone—more so than during my first twenty minutes alone in the gallery. I made my way through the clusters of people, pretending to contemplate the sculptures when I couldn't have been less interested, and flashing a smile for selfies that I posted to my stories, before arriving at a small table holding wine bottles in the back right corner, its white paper covering stained with crimson rings. The photos garnered me floating hearts and *Where is this??* comments from total strangers, and a slew of messages from people asking if I wanted to "collab" with them on the rollout of a product, but not what I was looking for: any indication that Ryan had seen my post and was wondering where I was. I reached for a bottle of red and poured myself a large serving into a clear plastic cup.

"So, what do you think?" A petite, alluring woman had appeared next to me, her eyes large, soulful puddles and her long dark hair in a loose braid that ended just above her high-waisted pants as she made a Vanna White–style gesture across the room. I contemplated answering that Giacometti was doing in 1920 exactly what this artist was trying to do, and that he'd done it far better, but instead I said, "Exciting stuff."

"Thank you," she said, beaming, and I made a mental note to never say exactly what I thought of somebody else's art.

"You're Deepthi? Congrats on the show," I said, shaking her hand. "Emma Caan. I'm a friend of Jules's," I added.

"Who?" she asked.

"Jules Braun," I explained. *Your best friend.*

"I'm terrible with names," she said, laughing, but then her face brightened. "Oh! JustJules?" I nodded. "She's amazing, isn't she? We've never actually met, but we're *obsessed* with each other on Instagram. Is she here?" Deepthi looked around the room.

"She is something else," I said with a nod. "How's the show going?"

"We're sold out as of about two minutes ago!" She clenched her teeth as though attempting unsuccessfully to control her excitement.

My congratulations got stuck in my throat as I wondered how on earth it was possible that such an unoriginal sculptor could be more successful than I was. I resolved to show Florence my portfolio tomorrow and extended my glass. "That's incredible. Well deserved," I managed, then took a large gulp before drifting away from the table.

I circled the secondhand ideas throughout the room and stood in a daze before a sculpture of a man kneeling on the ground, almost an exact replica of a Giacometti. I took two more pictures of the art, both with hashtags complimenting Deepthi, followed her and immediately received a notification that she'd followed me back, and visited the wine station yet again. On my way back to the center of the room, I did a double take as I spotted Micaela standing beside an iron sculpture of a woman's legs twisted around a man, looking displeased as she kneaded her right thumb into her left palm. I wondered if she was in pain, but she wasn't looking at her hand or at the sculpture but through the triangle of negative space between the man's bent thigh and calf. I moved behind her to see what she saw: Fredrick and Jules, her thin neck stretched even longer as it craned up toward his, and his head bent low as she spoke into his ear.

"Fancy meeting you here," I said, sliding beside Micaela and contemplating the sculpture, hoping I could distract her from what I was sure was a painful scene. Micaela nodded but kept her gaze on the statue. I pushed on: "You know, I've been feeling really bad about something." She raised one eyebrow but didn't look at me. "I didn't know you and Fredrick . . . you know . . ." I trailed off. "I introduced them in Hong Kong. This is totally my fault." I gestured to him and Jules.

Micaela turned to me, her eyes sharp. "You must have a pretty inflated sense of power if you think you can cause two people to get together just by introducing them," she said dryly.

"That's not what I . . ." I should have known Micaela wasn't the type of girl who would welcome any words of comfort, however ungraceful, in the wake of rejection. "Enjoy the party," I said, turning back toward the bar for yet another refill.

"I've been encouraging him to go for her for months," Micaela said, stopping me in my tracks.

"Why?" I asked, rejoining her.

She shrugged. "Freddie is a good person," she said, as though that explained anything, her sharp edges softening into sadness. "I'm not good for his career. I'm not social like she is, and I have no public presence. I'm not going to help sales . . ."

I contemplated arguing with her, but I didn't think she was fishing for compliments, so I shrugged.

"Look, um . . ." Micaela shifted her weight. "Lenny mentioned that he's pulling a Chagall for you. For your mother," she corrected. I nodded, slightly embarrassed. "If she's looking to liquidate, she should do it privately."

I cocked my head to the side, giving her a puzzled look.

"Don't auction it," she rephrased. "Got it?" She gave me a curt nod and shoved her way through the crowd and out the door without looking back.

I contemplated her words as I bit at a loose piece of skin on my cuticle, prying until it came free in my teeth and left a bloody streak on my index finger. *Why shouldn't my mother sell the work however she wants to?* I searched the corners of my mind desperately for a logical explanation. More than likely, Lenny did not want it publicly known that he was in possession of unknown Chagalls, which might trigger a fight for ownership with the artist's heirs. That must have been the explanation, and while it didn't make Lenny seem totally aboveboard, it was one I could live with. That *needed* to be the explanation, because the only other plausible one I could think of for keeping a Chagall sale out of the auction houses and the ensuing press was that the painting Lenny was giving my mother was, in fact, a fake.

CHAPTER

16

AGENT GARRITT:	So, your work for Leonard Sobetsky was strictly as a copier?
EMMA CAAN:	Correct.
AGENT TILLWELL:	Do you think working as a copier made you more attuned to spotting fakes versus originals?
EMMA CAAN:	Maybe. I don't know. More attuned than whom?
AGENT TILLWELL:	Fair enough. While you were copying, did you ever try to sell your own works?
EMMA CAAN:	Yes.
AGENT TILLWELL:	And?
EMMA CAAN:	Let's just say it didn't quite go how I'd hoped.

I couldn't sleep that night, with Micaela's advice ringing in my ears, and at about three o'clock in the morning, I finally lifted my phone from the nightstand and googled Marc Chagall. I breathed a sigh of relief to see that he had actually lived at 4 East Seventy-Fourth Street with his first wife. Artists stored art all the time in their living/work spaces, and sometimes it came to light only years after their passing. I put my phone away and pounded my fists into the sides of my pillow to fluff it up, reminding myself that Micaela's advice might have been motivated by any number of things; but sleep still eluded me.

As my mind raced, it became occupied by visions of last night's sculptures and the obviously recycled ideas that were somehow garnering attention in the art world. When daylight overtook the last of the dark corners of my bedroom, I got up, showered, and headed to work with a new resolve. Once there, I grabbed the flash drive from my desk drawer, inhaled deeply, and knocked on Florence's door, my knuckles on the wood sending nervous shock waves up my arm. It seemed as though all my artistic pursuits—art classes, college, Gemini—had culminated in this moment, when a mega-gallerist would review my work. I couldn't stop my brain from barreling forward into million-dollar checks, getting my mother whatever she needed and wanted with no questions asked, buying my own apartment, a glowing review from Jerry Saltz and a full-page spread in the *Times* Arts & Leisure section . . .

"Florence?" I began. She looked up from her desk, seeming to expect something important. "I have learned so much in the short amount of time I've worked for you about what it takes to sell art. I don't think I quite understood the market before I went to Hong Kong and had the invaluable experience of interacting with customers." I slipped my fingers in my pocket and wrapped them around the small plastic rectangle, then took my hand out. "I was hoping you could take a look at my portfolio sometime. Whenever you have time. No rush. Of course."

Florence contemplated me with an inscrutable expression for what felt like an eternity. "Are you quitting?" she asked.

"No! No. Just looking for your opinion," I stammered. "I'd like to keep working here regardless . . ."

"Good. Glad to hear it. Sure," she said. Why did her response feel like a dismissal?

"Actually, I have it here," I offered, extending the flash drive to her.

"Great," she said, and though she seemed a little stressed, she uncapped the flash drive and shoved it into the port of her laptop.

"I didn't mean you need to look right this minute!" I said, realizing that until she evaluated it, I could hang on to the hope that she might be dazzled.

"Now is fine," she said, putting on glasses I'd never seen on her and leaning toward her screen. I swallowed so hard my ears popped, and I was hyperaware of the hiss of the air coming from the ceiling vent and the incessant ticking of the second hand on the clock above Florence's whiteboard. My eyes grazed every surface of the room to avoid the torturous exercise of attempting to discern her expression.

She finally looked up at me. "These are the same works you submitted a few years ago, are they not?"

Everything stopped.

I no longer heard the vent or the clock, only a faint buzzing in my ears, and I struggled to form words. "I didn't realize you actually reviewed it last time. I thought . . . I thought maybe you overlooked my submission because you never mentioned it to me," I managed, mortified.

Florence looked at me over her glasses for an uncomfortable moment before taking them off. "I try not to mention submissions I pass on because I figure it might be painful," she said evenly. "I give careful consideration to every single submission that comes across my desk. It's very brave for any artist to share their work. I've been in the business quite some time, and I still feel honored any time an artist asks for my opinion." She paused. It was the most empathetic, kindest version of Florence I had ever seen, and I resented her for it, as though her thinking I was weak made me so, her thinking she was crushing my dreams made it so.

"And it's important to remember that my opinion is just that—an opinion," she continued. "Everybody has one. I'm one of millions." I heard only a few of her words. "Brave . . . I would suggest . . . Perhaps a different medium . . . really advanced technically but somehow . . ." She trailed off there, searching for the word.

"Detached," I reluctantly finished her sentence for her.

"Yes. Exactly." She paused and furrowed her brow. "If you knew that these weren't quite there—"

I shrugged before she could finish. I didn't know why I had hoped she'd see the brilliance in what nobody else did.

"If you love painting, you should keep painting. And in the meantime, you've become an invaluable member of the Florence Wake team," she said, and I tuned out as she continued flattering my sales capabilities.

Eventually, I choked out a thank-you to her for taking the time to review my portfolio (again), apologized for wasting her time, and escaped out of the studio. I closed the door behind me and stared out into the gallery. One of the tiniest bones to be thrown from the universe: Leah still hadn't arrived at work, so at least I had a moment to myself.

I stood and considered my options. I could cry, or apply to other gallery jobs so I didn't have a daily reminder of my humiliation, or just suck it up. I chose the last option, spending the next few hours rearranging the wall abutting the Starbucks and making two sales in a manic, vibrating state. Leah sneaked in quietly around eleven, far too preoccupied with her own tardiness and the night before to ask any questions about my mood. The afternoon was busy with a steady flow of customers, and it was still light outside when Florence and Leah took off for the evening. It occurred to me that I didn't have a television or even a couch, and all there was for me to do in the enormous place where I now lived was contemplate my own inadequacies as an artist.

I pulled out my phone and texted Sienna to see if she wanted to get a drink, and then pinged Lenny to say that my night had freed up in case he had any work. I willed an ellipsis to appear beneath his name and then a project to fill my time—preferably something post-worthy. I opened Instagram to keep my brain occupied. My feed was filled with news sources and celebrities posting about the chemical plant explosion in Illinois that sparked a fire that was currently ravaging a small town. My heart rate quickened as I attempted to scroll past them. The art community had posted photos, sending well wishes and links for donations. I closed my eyes but still saw the flames, the scorched earth and devastation. Then I saw *her*, and I could practically feel the heat of the flames. I tore my eyes open, thinking that would be somehow better.

I looked down at my right hand as my left held my phone at my side, and I fanned my fingers apart, watching them shake and jump as though the concrete beneath me were vibrating. Suddenly, I saw a small spark of light appear on the nail of my right index finger. The spark ignited and traveled up my arm, bursting my sleeve into flames. I jumped backward and dropped my phone to the floor and swatted frantically at my forearm to suffocate the fire, but it was gone. I ran my hand over my forearm, and it was cool to the touch. I exhaled shakily. Memories of the fire always seemed to seep out of the cracks that formed when things fell apart.

I placed my palm over my heart, begging it not to pop through my ribs, and watched as my phone mercifully distracted me by glowing from the floor and dinging out into the empty gallery. Though the screen was now cracked, I could see that Lenny had responded, and I bent down and picked up the phone, blowing the sparkling shards into the air around me.

LENNY: Micaela will be in touch with a number of projects before the weekend. I will pull the Chagall ASAP. But if you're still free tonight, come to Balthazar. Sergey and I are here waiting for a buyer. We'd love you to join us for dinner.
EMMA: My plans just fell through and I'm right in the neighborhood.

Pretending I'd had plans that never came to fruition highlighted my pathetic social life in a way that remaining silent likely wouldn't have, but only until I saw a thumbs-up response from Lenny. I exhaled.

"We've just poured our first drink," Lenny said when I arrived. He rose to greet me with two cheek kisses, gesturing to the frosted bottle sitting in an ice bucket.

"So good to see you," Sergey said, smiling broadly as he stood by, making no motion to embrace me.

"Thank you for having me," I said as I pulled out one of the two remaining empty chairs, and we all sat.

"We're lucky to be your backups." Lenny bowed his head graciously and reached for the long neck of the clear glass bottle, raising his eyes to me in question as to whether I wanted a drink, to which I eagerly nodded.

I noted the stag on the bottle, thinking how it felt so long ago that I had borrowed the green dress from Sienna and drunk vodka for the first time with Lenny and Sergey. What would have happened if I had never gotten out of my Uber, never mentioned that I was looking for a gallery job, never met Florence? I'd still be painting copies for Jeremy and eating ramen, but I still would have had the delicate, sweet hope that I was a great talent, overlooked due to some back-office errors that caused my submissions to be lost in piles of paperwork.

Lenny handed me one of the glasses on the table and I blinked myself back into the bustling restaurant, watching escargot coated in melted herb and garlic butter pass on a waiter's tray. I said, "*Na zdorovye*," as I raised my glass to Lenny and Sergey, which they seemed surprised and pleased by, and I touched the freezing liquid to my lips. My first drink on an empty stomach always magically dissolved unpleasant thoughts, and I needed that tonight. Florence's careful words, my portfolio, my father's will all slipped away.

Just then a waiter passing our table did a double take and stopped.

"Excuse me, sir, this is not a BYO," he said, placing a protective hand on the sterling bucket of ice beside our table.

"Keith is always kind enough to make an exception for us," Lenny said.

The waiter's cheeks flushed. "Of course," he said with an apologetic bow of his head before turning quickly on his heel.

"Everybody works for somebody, yes?" Sergey commented as he lowered his menu just enough so he could see me over it.

"Who's—" I started.

"Keith McNally owns the place," Lenny explained sotto voce.

Waiters zipped by carrying woven baskets brimming with rustic brown bread and plates of steak next to glistening piles of french fries, while a group of impossibly attractive young women shouted to be heard over the raucous table of businessmen next to them. I sat and marveled at how exquisitely orchestrated the chaos seemed to be. I contemplated not doing it, but I couldn't resist—I took out my phone as surreptitiously as possible and filmed a video with my glass of vodka in the foreground and the bustling restaurant in the background and posted it to my Instagram story, keeping Lenny and Sergey out of the frame and my phone low toward the table, in the hope that the action would be less invasive to my dinner companions. Lenny and Sergey didn't seem to mind at all. There was something so satisfying about presenting this life to the world. Nobody needed to know a gallery had rejected my portfolio that day—and for the second time—or that my father had chosen his mistress over his family in his final days. Instead, they just saw me surrounded by beauty, luxury, and decadence.

"This place is great," I said just as my phone dinged. I checked it surreptitiously below the table to see that Sienna had texted to say she missed me and would meet me wherever I was. I'd started to type a response when I sensed a new presence behind me.

"Oh, look who's here—Ryan Parker," Sergey announced.

The clamor around me ceased completely, and I heard only a soft hum in my ears as I turned in my seat to see Ryan standing there. He shook Sergey's hand and flashed me a bright, easy smile—one that showed me just how little time he had spent thinking about me since Hong Kong. The outside world rushed back in on me.

"Emma and I actually met in Hong Kong," Ryan said, and winked. "Small world." As he kissed me on both cheeks, I struggled to remember who I'd been, how I'd acted, that day Ryan kissed me, in the hope that I could make him kiss me again, but that girl felt far away.

"How long are you in town for?" I asked Ryan, trying to sound casual.

"Couple of weeks. Unless I find a reason to stay longer," he said, shooting me a crooked smile and taking a sip of the drink Lenny poured him, and all the blood rushed to my head.

"Last time you said that, you stayed three years," Sergey reminded him. They all laughed, and I struggled not to get ahead of myself with the idea of him being here, with me, for the long haul. "Did Evelyn call you about attending the auction next week?" Sergey asked.

Lenny and Ryan both groaned and nodded. "She's relentless," Ryan said, and I felt a rush that I knew who Evelyn was and understood that she was packing the room with serious buyers.

The four of us drank more vodka and talked about art, and as we did, I found myself able to access the wit and sass that these men expected of me. Pretending that I was a cool gallerista and not a failure of an artist made the day's woes disappear. I wasn't just good at pretending nothing was wrong—doing so made me *feel* like nothing was wrong. I never stopped Lenny from refilling my glass, and by the time they ordered espressos and dessert, my head had begun to feel heavy on my neck.

After Lenny had paid the bill, we all stood to go. I wanted nothing more than for Ryan to ask me to join him for another drink, but I knew I had to play it cool. I held up my hand in a casual wave, but he spoke before I could. "I'm still jet-lagged," he announced, slapping his palm to the table. "I can't go to bed yet! One more drink?" Sergey and Lenny begged off with excuses of an early morning ahead, but Ryan's eyes had been trained on me anyway.

Without waiting for a response, Ryan took my hand and pulled me toward the bar. I followed, hating myself for having no backbone but surrendering to the warm comfort of his sturdy palm pressed to mine. There was only one seat left at the bar, so Ryan stood beside me and ordered us drinks. I glanced over his shoulder at the two women eyeing him, and instead of thinking that they didn't know why he'd be with someone like me, I decided to enjoy the evening as best as I could.

"Cheers!" Ryan effortlessly raised his glass, and I was instantly transported back to the charity event at Lenny's. I smiled inwardly, realizing how much had changed in just over a month. "I rushed us through dinner so I could be alone with you," he said after we clinked glasses.

"You did?"

"I wanted to," he said, and I wondered if that meant he had or he hadn't.

"I don't give partial credit for thought with no follow-through," I said, and smirked.

His eyes brightened, and I pretended not to notice him noticing me. "I should have never left you that first night in Hong Kong," he said. I looked up, and not only did I forgive him instantly, but I managed to forget that he had kissed me twice and not called me once.

We barely finished our drinks, and soon we were turning onto

Greene Street, my heels teetering on the cobblestones. At the building, I squinted to punch in the passcode, feeling him right behind me as we entered the foyer. The air between us in the elevator tightened as I fiddled with the fob to occupy my fingers, and as soon as we pushed through the door, his arms were around me and my shirt was off, his hands exploring my skin, bringing it to life.

I had slept with three guys in my life, two of them only once, and I worried for a second that he'd somehow be able to tell, but I forced myself back into the moment. We made our way up the stairs to the bedroom, and I attempted to gain control of my mind by moving my fingers underneath his sweater, feeling his rippled stomach and pulling his shirt over his head. Still, I could hear my breaths, pressured just as much from anxiety as from being turned on.

Ryan pulled away and took my face in his hands before cocking his head to the side and leaning in to kiss my neck. I exhaled, my brain finally quieting as I felt his curious, gentle exploration of the skin above my collarbone. The rest of our clothes came off, and we knotted into a mess of limbs.

He didn't kiss me again after we were naked, and his fluid movements turned spastic. I didn't know if it was my nerves or my anatomy or his failure to take his time with me, but I cried out in pain when he forced his way inside me, and he joined in my moan, mistaking it for pleasure. Since I'd first seen Ryan at Lenny's charity event, I had imagined what it would be like to sleep with him, but this was nothing like that. I figured it was my body that was somehow wrong for not feeling good, as he was clearly well practiced. So I bit my lower lip to keep from crying, matched my panting to his, and faked it.

After, we lay quietly with the sheets swirling around our legs, our heads at the foot of the bed and our feet propped on the pillows at the top. He kissed my forehead and sighed contentedly, and somehow the entire charade seemed worth it as I saw a small smile form on his lips. Though I knew that I'd never relax enough to sleep that night, we rearranged ourselves so our heads were on the pillows, then pulled up the covers.

"Get in here," Ryan whispered playfully, wrapping his arms around me and pulling me close. I placed my hand softly on his chest and rested my head on his broad shoulder, despite knowing that those words were well rehearsed. He'd obviously used that line on countless other women, pulling them in close. I remained still until Ryan's breaths deepened.

I grabbed at the pieces of space around me to make permanent a memory: the faintly almond scent of his shampoo, the stubble on his chin, the smooth skin of his chest under my fingertips. At some point in the middle of the night, Ryan eased me off his arm and turned over on his side. Even before the sun was entirely up, I felt him stand, and I opened one eye to see him stepping into the second of his pants legs. The memory of him had already gone fuzzy even before he was out of my presence. When I saw him pat his backside in search of his wallet and take his cell phone off the nightstand, I closed my eyes again and pretended to sleep, curious whether he would sneak out or wake me. It felt like a small victory when he sat down beside me and placed a palm over my hair. I opened my eyes and saw him in hazy silhouette as the sunlight filtered in through the window.

"I had a great time last night," he said. "I gotta get going."

I nodded and he leaned down and kissed my cheek, then stood and left without hesitation, without any further words—as though it were the easiest thing in the world for him to leave my side.

I stared up at the ceiling. I could focus on my disappointment that the night and morning hadn't gone just as I wanted, or I could appreciate that I somehow had the life now that so many young women in New York coveted. I had the SoHo loft, the gallery job, the supplemental income, and the devastatingly handsome man visiting from Paris who spent time in my bed. It was time to retire my dream of being an artist and start living the incredible life I'd been taking for granted. My lids grew heavy, and sleep overtook me.

AGENT GARRITT:	You mentioned a freeport—what is your understanding of why collectors utilize freeports?
EMMA CAAN:	First, simply to keep works safe. Freeports are like vaults particularly suited for art because they're humidity-controlled, climate-controlled, fireproof . . . all that good stuff. Second, people avoid taxes by placing expensive items in these tax-free zones so they can avoid taxes when they offload works because the individual is considered to never really take delivery of an item even though they have registered ownership if it goes into a freeport. The art can also be sold overseas again without any taxes at all, so this can save tens of millions of dollars for serious art collectors. Last, they're private. Nobody knows what is in them, at least in the U.S. Because it's believed lots of stolen goods—including items looted during World War II—are in there, lots of European countries have passed laws infringing on the secrecy surrounding freeports. But not in the U.S.
AGENT GARRITT:	Did you ever see art owned by Mr. Sobetsky that wasn't on popular display? Say, a private collection he wasn't hanging on walls?
EMMA CAAN:	I had to visit Leonard's freeport unit in Delaware to appraise three works he was consigning to our gallery.
AGENT TILLWELL:	He let you see all the works in the freeport? Did you notice anything suspicious about the works?
EMMA CAAN:	We only entered his short-term unit, so I only saw those paintings. And no, I didn't notice anything suspicious at that time.

*   *   *

My phone alarm woke me in what felt like moments after I had
fallen back asleep. When I saw I had a text, I held my breath for a
second before realizing it wasn't from Ryan.

MICAELA: When can the next two works be dropped off? Today?
EMMA: Sure. Any time after 6.

I lay back down and looked at the lingering indentation of Ryan
in my bed and smelled the fading scent of his aftershave on my
sheets, then peeled myself out from under the covers and stared at
the clothes in my closet, dissatisfied with every option. After set-
tling on the black pants and a black blazer I always wore and Leah's
pumps, just for some color, I turned to the safe in the far corner of
my closet, punched in the code, and took out the envelope. I felt
the heft of the bills and reminded myself that I wasn't paying rent,
my mother was being taken care of, and I'd soon be getting my
next paycheck from the gallery.

With my guilt assuaged, I shoved the envelope in my purse and
locked it tightly under my armpit as I walked to work. Florence
was visiting an artist in Malibu through the following day, and I
convinced Leah to lock up the gallery and duck out of work for an
hour to take me shopping.

"I seriously thought you'd never ask to do this," Leah said, taking me by the arm giddily as she made a sharp right into Intermix.
"Spending other people's money might actually be my greatest skill."

"Okay, but I want to look like me. I can't pull off the stuff you
wear!" I said, gesturing to her cuffed harem pants, which made her
look like some impossibly chic Bedouin. "I'd look like . . . an oversize toddler wearing a tapered diaper."

"First of all, everybody looks ridiculous in these pants, but tapered
diapers are weirdly in style right now, so I don't ask questions. Second

of all, I get it! You are this hipster artist, and we're absolutely going to keep that vibe," she said, flipping through the items on the rack.

Could that really be the *vibe* I was giving off by not trying? "Am I?" I asked, looking down at my stolen pumps and plain top.

"That's your brand. On Instagram. Do you not know this? Ripped jeans. Baggy tees." Leah paused and laughed. "Whether intentional or not, when you roll with people like JustJules and attend Basel Hong Kong while working at Florence Wake, people assume whatever look you have is a curated one," she said as though acknowledging that she understood I simply didn't know how to dress. "I'm going to help you incorporate it into your professional clothes." She gestured to my uninspired black ensemble. "Though I must say, my red shoes spice it up. We're going to get you looking hot, though. Just browsing," she said—confusing me because there'd been no change of intonation in her voice—to an approaching saleswoman who turned on her heel.

Leah took my phone and snapped pictures of me in each outfit even though there was a mirror in the dressing room. "If you want to engage users, you can create polls asking them what to buy."

"I have no idea how to do that," I admitted, turning to the side to look at my butt in the leather leggings she'd forced on me.

"That's why you have me," Leah said, her thumbs already gliding over my screen.

"You could seriously be like an influencer," I said.

"Easy with the insults," Leah said sarcastically, her lips flattened out as her eyes lifted from the phone, as though following her train of thought. "I was sort of on the way to being one. Only a few thousand followers, but I was pretty good at connecting with people. I used to be obsessed. I'm pretty sure it ruined my relationship with my ex-boyfriend. He used to say we were a throuple. Me, him, and my phone." She finally looked up at me and handed my phone back. "He's engaged now, and while I have a pretty amazing-looking online dating profile . . . I guess he wins," she said sadly. My phone began to glow as Instagram notifications flooded in. "That shit is the devil," she warned me with a sad chuckle. I looked up at her, wondering whether I should put my phone away. "Refresh it!" she yelled, sliding up beside me to view my feed.

Moments later, I had thousands of people weighing in on which outfits looked best. It felt surreal to imagine complete strangers caring enough to voice their opinions and, even more bizarrely, believing I'd care what they thought.

"You're so good at this!" I said to Leah, and she nodded knowingly.

I received one direct message informing me it was insensitive to post pictures of me "easily fitting into off-the-rack sizes when so many people struggled with their weight," immediately followed by an offer from a personal trainer to train me at a discount because she, too, "used to struggle with stubborn belly fat." I went to delete the post before it invited any more comments, but I saw ItsRyanParker had viewed it, and a few minutes later, my cell phone buzzed with a message.

MAYBE: RYAN: Hey, it's Ryan. Thinking of you. When can I see you again?

"Oh my God!" Leah said, pointing at my face with an accusing finger. "Is that Ryan Parker? Look at your face!" I blushed and shoved my phone in my pocket without responding and headed to the register. "Tell me!" she pleaded, following me.

I couldn't help myself. "I've been seeing him," I whispered, somehow feeling like the sales assistant at Intermix would know him and not wanting her to hear.

Her eyes grew wide, but she was smiling. "I hate you," she said. "I can't seem to match with anybody who is not an actual hobbit, and here you are, dating a guy who passed up a career in modeling to start his own hedge fund! I'm taking full credit if it works out, and completely attributing it to your new wardrobe!" I laughed, but she contemplated me more seriously. "Just kidding, obviously. You deserve somebody just as fabulous as you are," she said.

I lifted my gaze to hers, prepared to graciously accept the compliment, but all I could think about was what she didn't know about me. *I'm a bad person.* I coughed to distract from whatever expression had plagued my face, and gave her a small, uncomfortable nod as I dug into my purse and peeled several bills out of the envelope. In all, I bought four new tops, one pair of leather pants, and two new jumpsuits, and was astonished at how quickly money could be spent in a store like Intermix. I couldn't make a habit of shopping there, but the trip was entirely worth it because it had made Ryan reach out. I texted him on our way back to the gallery, relieved that I didn't have to lie about being busy—most of my free time this week would be spent copying for Lenny.

EMMA: Hey! Uh, this week is crazy busy. Around Friday and Saturday night though!
RYAN: ☹. I am excellent company after a long day.

I stared at my phone as it sat on my desk. It felt slightly insulting that Ryan hadn't asked me on a date or even really responded to my response, but I also felt elated that he was showing interest in me, and I eagerly accepted the challenge to work my way up on his list of priorities. As I stared at my phone, it lit up with a new call from Florence.

"Hi!" I answered on the first ring.

"I think this guy I'm meeting with is the real deal," Florence announced with no preamble before launching into background on the new Australian artist who was in Malibu for the month. I wondered what she saw in "this guy" that she hadn't seen in me, but I resolved to focus on the positive. "I was supposed to go with

Lenny to his Delaware freeport tomorrow to look at three pieces I'm thinking of taking on consignment from him, so I need you to go in my place." I grabbed a pen and pad from my desk and began to write. "Take pictures if the facility allows it, but I doubt they will. Take notes if not."

"Notes on what, exactly?" I asked.

Through her pause, I could tell Florence was annoyed by the question. "The pieces. I need you to do what I would do if I were there. Evaluate the work. Report back to me on quality, tone, color, and your recommendation on pricing." There was another pause, and I heard the clicking of her phone as she typed a text to somebody else. "Jesus Christ," she said as she continued to type. "One second." I waited. "Evelyn Radler sat next to me on the way to L.A. and had absolutely no idea who I was, and now she won't stop texting to try to make it up to me." There was more clicking.

"Who is Evelyn Radler?" I asked.

"Exactly!" Florence said, as though my question were rhetorical. *Oh, right, co-chair of contemporary art at Christie's—the one always trying to pack the room with serious buyers.* "Maybe that's why she put me toward the back of the room last time . . ." Florence thought out loud. "Anyway, back to Lenny's collection. I've been given a photo and size specifications of all the works, so no need to measure," she continued. "But I need your opinion on all the subjective aspects of the work, whatever you need in order to give me that. The chopper is leaving from Thirtieth Street on the Hudson River at eight o'clock tomorrow morning. I'll let him know I can't make it but you can."

"Okay," I said, even though there was no question in her tone, and the line went dead. "Bye," I said to nobody, and put the phone down.

The rest of the afternoon moved at a feverish pace with customers, some seeming keenly interested but, frustratingly, none of them buying, and I returned home wanting nothing more than to flop down on a sofa and watch bad television. But I had no sofa or television and nothing to copy until Micaela delivered the next pieces, so I explored the walk-in closet by the front door, sifting through thousands of dollars' worth of art supplies: Phosphos acrylic paints, linen canvases, Mimik Hog brushes, all the things I would have given a right arm to be able to afford while in school. I took a new easel out of the closet, too afraid I'd set off some alarm if I used the ones with sensors in the pressurized chamber, and set it up by the balcony windows. I felt a rush of possibility as the canvas settled into the ridge of the small horizonal wooden lip and I could release it from my hands, yet it remained at eye level. There was a soothing weight to the air as the heat from the warm day remained trapped in the apartment, and I closed my eyes and stretched out my neck.

There is no pressure. This is just for me. Not for sale. That ship has sailed.

I stood up, I walked around, I rocked my hips forward and then back. Nothing. I reminded myself that inspiration couldn't be hurried. The sun dipped below the buildings, and the white clouds turned purple and pink with burning orange outlines. I stared out past my canvas at the stunning scene and impulsively kicked the leg of the easel so the whole thing crashed to the ground. I stormed up the stairs, furious at myself, at my mother, at Jeremy for giving me a job that had suffocated my ability to think creatively, and wiggled between the top sheet and comforter, squirming to get comfortable to no avail.

Why can't I paint? And why does it even matter if no one wants my work, anyway? Under the covers, I didn't feel like I slept a wink as I circled the questions, but I woke up to a screaming alarm and sheets soaked through with sweat at eight o'clock the next day. I sat up in bed as I recalled my dream—she was burning, rolling around on the cold grass to suffocate the flames, while my father stared at me. I could only scream, but I did it with such force that the noise shattered all the teeth in my mouth, blowing them out onto the lawn in jagged white pieces.

I ran my tongue across my teeth, breathed a sigh of relief that they were all intact, and wiped the sweat from my torso. I pressed on my temples before realizing I had forgotten to set an earlier alarm so I could meet Lenny. I grabbed my phone off the night-stand and ordered an Uber, then launched myself out of bed to splash water on my face.

At seventeen minutes past eight o'clock, my Uber driver turned off the West Side Highway and drove through a high black fence, obviously designed to keep out prying eyes, onto a nondescript concrete slab containing two black helicopters at the far end, one with the top blades just beginning to churn. I had expected an airport of sorts, but a small box of a building with a sign of a pair of angel wings was the only structure in sight at what seemed to be just a large parking lot off the river. We pulled up next to an empty Porsche and a Rolls-Royce SUV with impossibly dark tinted windows.

A man wearing aviator glasses and large headphones opened my door and ushered me toward a matte black helicopter whose ro-tor was now chopping through the air with a chuff that vibrated throughout my body. I instinctively copied the man and bent for-ward as we neared the door. He closed it behind me and placed sturdy cushioned headphones over my ears, which blocked out the powerful thumping noise, leaving only a peaceful quiet. Lenny was already buckled in, sipping a bottle of water, smiling brightly at me, and gestured to the seat across from him.

"So sorry I'm late," I began. "I—"

"No trouble, my dear," Lenny said, and I heard him through my headphones. He winked for a fraction of a second, as though to sig-nal that he wasn't mad, but he also needed to make up the time I'd cost him. "Let's go!" he shouted to the pilot, who gave him a thumbs-up. As soon as the words were out, we lurched forward and then sideways, flying low over the river before gliding up into the air.

"Quite a life you lead, Mr. Sobetsky," I said, and shook my head, and he just laughed. There was a serenity to the city from above, and a contentment that came with navigating the world as easily as Lenny did. I leaned out over the window, instinctively took a video of us careening over the placid water, and posted it to my Instagram stories.

Thirty minutes later, we touched down in the parking lot of an inconspicuous dark gray rectangular building. The doors to the helicopter were pulled open, and there was Hank, who extended his enormous hand to help me out. Steve helped Lenny out, and as soon as we were far enough from the chopper to hear one another, I looked at them. "What are you guys doing here?"

"They work here," Lenny answered. That surprised me—I'd always assumed Hank and Steve were on Lenny's payroll, given how diligently they followed his orders, but I supposed they had always been with his art in every situation I had seen them in.

In any place I'd gone with Lenny thus far, I'd felt as though I was being ushered in simply by being connected to him, but the freeport was the opposite. We entered through a sleek gray-tiled foyer, and I noted at least a dozen security cameras capturing every nook and cranny of the space. A tall older man in a double-breasted suit greeted Lenny as I was patted down by a female security guard.

"Emma Caan, Mr. Marc Neilson," Lenny said in a way that let me know I was supposed to address him as Mr. Neilson, not that I planned on addressing him at all. We nodded politely at each other.

I showed identification, gave a fingerprint, then handed them my purse, as no personal belongings were allowed.

"Oh!" I said, extending my hand to the woman as I remembered my phone was in my purse. "I'm supposed to document some of the specifics of a piece of art."

"There's a pen and paper available in the room. And a tape measure," the woman added, pointing to what looked to be a large pair of goggles embedded in the wall. "Place your eyes in the retina scan, please," she said, her voice completely monotone. I tried my best not to laugh. I had never "placed" my eyes anywhere, because they were attached to my head, but a diagram on the wall assured me I was supposed to lean my entire head forward as a small blue light scanned my retina. Lenny jumped through the same security hoops without protest.

"Which room will we be visiting today?" Mr. Neilson asked.

"Short-term," Lenny said. As we walked down a long cement-floored corridor toward Lenny's unit, Mr. Neilson told me about the seventy-degree temperature-controlled chambers, the consistently maintained 50 percent humidity, how they used gas to remove all oxygen and choke out a fire rather than sprinklers—which would damage the art—and the armed guards on standby "in the occurrence of a breach."

"Have you ever had a fire?" I asked, my heart racing as I realized I'd never remember how to get out of here in the event of one.

"Never," the man said. "In fact . . ." He continued, but, relieved, I didn't hear anything further. We turned left down a long hallway with glass rooms on either side, tinted to obscure their contents, and I could feel the power of whatever was inside. I knew what people kept in freeports—gold bars, precious jewels, coronation crowns, and priceless masterpieces—and my mind raced with the possibilities of what was housed behind each wall. There was a certain energy to the still air, as though the contents of each room were vibrating, struggling to break free.

Lenny and Mr. Neilson slowed down, and Lenny extended his palm and pushed it against a black glass square on the wall to the right of the door we had come to. As it scanned his hand, a glowing blue line started down at the wrist and up through the fingers, and then a mechanical click sounded. The man in the suit departed without another word, and Lenny pushed through the glass door into his chamber. As the fluorescent lights overhead slowly built to full capacity, I saw that every inch of the twelve-hundred-square-foot room was covered with art on racks, none of it touching but all of it stacked closely together. Hundreds of works.

"Holy shit," I whispered, my eyes grazing over David Hockneys, Robert Rauschenbergs, Edward Hoppers, and Marc Chagalls, the last of which I paused on the longest, wondering which one might be earmarked for my mother. Some works I had seen in textbooks and some I'd read about, and I knew that others had never seen the light of day. Each was more spectacular than the next.

"And the long-term chamber is right through there," he said, pointing at the wall to my right. "Those are works that are going to be stored for thirty years or more without being moved." I looked over, but the wall was entirely dark. I turned back to the room, overwhelmed by the artistic feast.

"What?" Lenny asked.

"It's incredible," I said quietly, wiping a tear as it spilled down my cheek.

"Is there something else?" he said, studying me.

I shook my head, but his silence coaxed it out of me. "It's just . . . so sad," I said. The warmth in his eyes invited me to continue. "I understand why you keep these here, I do. But nobody will see them. These paintings are meant to be marveled at by the masses."

Lenny smiled softly. "You are a true lover of art, my dear. That is why I have you! I keep these safe here, and you let the world see them exactly as they are, without the risk. Your copies are every bit as good. Don't be upset!" He let out a small laugh.

Self-conscious about my display of emotion, I continued to scan the room while Lenny began to sift through paintings on the wall farthest from me. I saw a light switch on the wall beside me and flipped it curiously. The black glass wall bordering the long-term room faded to a steamy opaque gray and then turned completely clear so that I could see inside.

I peered in and saw *Te Fare* in all its vibrant glory, flanked by two stunning Monets that I had never seen before, and beyond, hundreds of other works. The room went dark, and I looked back at Lenny, who had flipped the switch off. He stared at me, and I worried that I had overstepped disastrously, but the sharp look of anger I thought I'd seen on his face passed.

"Okay, then!" he exclaimed, giving one short clap and putting on cotton gloves before shifting the racks to expose three more works. I swallowed hard and pulled on my own gloves, shifting from Lenny's flash of anger to the symphony of color. I had never seen the artist, but they were breathtaking, each more so than the next. The first was a series of shapes in tender yet vibrant hues— imperfect pinkish circles and squares atop blue triangles with a black-and-white-checkerboard bottom. I leaned back to see the whole painting at once, and I knew the figures created abstract dancers, and the colors created buzz and excitement to the dancers bouncing off one another. The tag on the frame read: *Junior Prom*. It was perfect. I leaned forward to get a better view of the piece behind it: six white figures with hazy yellow rings around them and a deep, textured navy background. The title of the work was *Those Who Came Before*. I got lost in the dark blue, knowing I was far too excited by the artist's unique use of negative space to re-member exactly how the paintings looked, and just as I wished they had allowed me to bring a camera in, Lenny handed me a pad and paper from a cubby by the door. I flipped back to the first painting to make notes in order, and meticulously wrote down every detail, making a few sketches of each piece, and finally nodded at Lenny to let him know I had finished.

"We'll take this one with us for your mother," he said, winking as he pulled a small, dreamy Chagall of a woman cradling a baby in her arms as she floated over a sleepy town at dusk.

"What's it called?" I asked.

"*L'Attrape-Rêves. The Dream Catchers*," Lenny translated. "I almost wonder if Marc forgot about those six paintings, since they've never been on the market. It's possible they got lost in the shuffle of moving after his wife passed away."

He placed it on the aluminum tabletop and pressed a small button on the far wall. A few minutes later, there was a knock on the door and Lenny opened it. Hank entered and they exchanged a few words before Hank began wrapping the painting carefully in what looked like cheesecloth. I couldn't formulate the appropriate response—what could I possibly say to the man affording my mother this kind of happiness after so many years of misery? I didn't know what else to do, so I took a step toward Lenny and wrapped my arms around his neck.

"It's nothing," he said, giving me a small and slightly awkward pat on the back, and pulled away from me. "Let's get you back to the office, shall we?"

Forty-five minutes after landing, we were headed home in the helicopter. I opened Instagram to see how my first helicopter video had been received, and then I leaned in close to confirm my eyes.

"I just hit ten thousand followers on Instagram!" I said before I could think better of it.

"Do you stop trying to get more now?" Lenny asked.

I shook my head. "Well, you still try to get more, but it's just way easier now."

"Higher number indicating increased value is just a trick of capitalism, my dear," he said, his tone wry.

"Spoken by the man who is stockpiling hundreds of priceless works of art. Maybe you should just pick one and sell the rest," I said, and rolled my eyes, but Lenny didn't laugh this time.

"The real secret nobody tells you is that anything worth having is better in small quantities. The art in those rooms is the same as a stock or a bond for me. I *wish* it moved me like it moves you," Lenny said. "Nobody brags about finding the love of his life fifty times, being married a dozen, having thirty kids with thirty different women, having true faith in six different religions." He shrugged. "Just be careful wherever people positively correlate quantity with quality. It's a trap."

I stared at him, annoyed. Easy for a billionaire to say. Why was he trying to dampen my excitement over one of the few things moving in the right direction in my life? "So it's better to have none than tons? Is your way better? No love, no wife, no kids, and I'm guessing no religion?" I took a sip of my water just as the chopper pulled west, making my stomach flip. When I met Lenny's eyes again, I saw sadness in them where the frost used to be, and where a powerful man once sat, there was just a slightly broken one. I swallowed hard, waiting for him to speak.

"One love. One wife. One daughter," he said softly. "One religion, but I lost faith."

"I didn't know. I'm sorry," I said. "You have a daughter?"

He rearranged his feet beneath him, looking ill at ease in a way I'd never seen.

"Had," he said softly. "She passed. When she was very young. And my wife had passed giving birth to her. If I had faith, I'd say they were in heaven now," he added. He turned and stared out the window at the dark smoke billowing up from the refineries in New Jersey.

"I'm so sorry," I repeated, and opted to leave it at that, because I always wished people would stop asking questions when they found out my father had died, but he continued.

"She got sick as a child. Leukemia. We were still in the Soviet Union," he said, wincing ever so slightly. "I got her the best doctors, but it wasn't enough. I never had the privilege of knowing her as an adult." He paused. "But I think she'd have been a lot like you."

"Chances are, with a father like you, she'd be a lot less screwed up than I am," I said. "It sounds like a terrible loss."

"You're not screwed up," Lenny protested, and I looked out the window because I was afraid my expression might reveal too much. "Everybody has things that keep them up at night. And wake them up with a start after they've fallen asleep. That's not being screwed up. That's being human."

I spun my attention back to him. Were there cameras in the studio watching my every move, including my sleep?

"The flight attendant asked me if she should wake you when she heard. That's how I know," he said. "But it's okay, I promise." Lenny watched me for a moment and then nodded, a mutual understanding of painful pasts that we didn't wish to discuss further passing between us. I understood then that he also perceived pain as a choice, something you could choose not to experience.

"What will you recommend to Florence for pricing the works?" he asked, calling my attention back to the pad in my hand.

I launched into a hedged estimate of the works, with the caveat that Florence would have final approval on everything. We sailed forward smoothly through the blue sky, the smut and smog of industrial New Jersey fading into the distance as we made our way back to Manhattan.

I texted my mother to let her know that Hank was heading to Ardmore with her Chagall, and I was back at Florence Wake by noon, counting down the hours until I could pour my body into bed. I typed up a detailed report of the works and my pricing analysis, along with iPhone shots of my sketches, and emailed it all to Florence, then headed home at six. I took a long shower, luxuriating in the hot droplets that fell from the large square showerhead and the steam locked in the glass case coaxing my reluctant pores open.

I stepped out onto the cool tile and wrapped a towel around myself, folding one end into my cleavage to keep the towel under my arms, and swiped my hand across the mirror over the sink, prepared to look at myself just as my phone rang out from my nightstand. I rushed out into the comparatively frigid bedroom and grabbed it.

"Oh my God. It's here!" my mother sang giddily, her voice lifting me rather than pulling me down the way it had during every one of our conversations in recent memory.

"What do you think?" I asked, smiling broadly into the bedroom at nobody, a small puddle from my wet hair forming under my feet.

"It's stunning! The blues in the . . ." I sat down on the corner of the bed and pulled my sopping hair forward over my shoulder so it wouldn't drip on the comforter and listened as my mother went on about the painting with an exuberance that I hadn't heard in years, if ever. I chimed in every so often with further prodding, just because I didn't want the conversation to end. When we finally said our goodbyes, I exhaled slowly, satisfied, though I knew I hadn't done much to allow my mother this happiness. I savored the moment and felt the anxiety that had been rolling up on itself since I had read my file on Lenny's plane suddenly disappear. My mother was going to be okay. We were going to be okay.

AGENT TILLWELL: When you say that you didn't find anything suspicious at the time you went to the freeport, did anything become suspicious to you after?

EMMA CAAN: No. I don't know why I said that.

AGENT TILLWELL: A few of the pieces we believe were held in Mr. Sobetsky's freeport unit were later auctioned off at Christie's. Did you attend that auction?

EMMA CAAN: I did. Yes. With Florence.

AGENT GARRITT: Do you know who the seller was at that auction?

EMMA CAAN: He was anonymous to the public. I think the buyers might know from the provenance.

AGENT GARRITT: He? How do you know the seller was male?

EMMA CAAN: I don't. The proverbial "he." Also, the pieces seemed masculine to me. But you're right. I don't know for certain that the seller was male.

After I hung up with my mother, I looked around the room for any activity to prolong my good mood. I composed and deleted a text to Ryan at least a dozen times, then finally put my phone down, unable to find the right tone, and slipped into the pajamas I'd taken from Lenny's plane. As I got into bed and pulled the smooth cotton duvet up toward my chin, I registered the glow of my phone screen in my peripheral vision.

A smile crept across my face as I saw a text from Ryan asking me what I was doing.

EMMA: Just back from a big dinner and already in pajamas.
RYAN: I bet they're sexy. Want company?
EMMA: Sure ☺

I immediately peeled off the pajamas and hopped back in the shower, careful not to dampen my hair as I scrubbed my body and shaved my legs. I was back in my pajamas just in time to answer the buzzer. When I opened the door for Ryan, he scanned me up and down, and I could tell that he'd been expecting something far sexier.

"What have you been up to tonight?" I asked, but he just started nuzzling my neck. I wondered whether my skin was still damp from my shower and if he'd mistake it for sweat, then panicked when I remembered that I hadn't put on deodorant. Rather than let on that I was spiraling, I closed my eyes and made small noises the way I imagined the other women Ryan dated did.

I spent another night pretending to sleep on his chest and stumbled into the gallery the next morning feeling like an empty shell, but just behind the exhaustion was the buzzing excitement that I was on my way to having a boyfriend—the first real one I'd ever had.

"Emma!" Florence called as soon as I entered. "Your mother is on line one."

I winced. Had my mother called this early for a chance to chat with Florence when I wasn't there? Despite being slightly annoyed and a bit embarrassed, those feelings were tempered by the image of my mother so giddy with her new piece of art that she simply needed a new person to talk to.

"Sorry! I've told her not to call here—" I began.

"That's okay," Florence said, ducking back into her office. "I like her. I invited her to the next Christie's auction! It's during the day for a private collection."

I imagined my mother attending the next auction with me and my boss, trying to sound like she had any idea what she was talking about when she commented on the art. Could Florence have invited her just to spite me—some retribution for wasting her time and asking her to look at my portfolio twice? She couldn't possibly have done it sincerely.

"Aren't seats already assigned?" I asked in a last-ditch effort to keep my professional and private lives separate.

"Evelyn will just have to figure it out. I'm sure she won't be forgetting my face again any time soon." Florence winked. "It's no trouble," she assured me with a wave, as though doing me a favor. *For me and Evelyn, it is!* I thought as she turned away from me.

"Hi, Mom," I said, cradling the phone under my ear as I called my computer screen to life.

"Hi!" She sounded perkier than I'd expected.

"Look, can you please just call my cell phone? It makes me seem unprofessional when you call my office."

"I *tried* to call you. Your phone is off," she said. I dug into my purse and saw that she was right. I'd forgotten to charge it in the excitement of last night. "Florence is just so lovely," my mother gushed as I plugged my cell into the charger Leah kept next to her monitor. "She invited me to a Christie's auction at the end of the week!"

"That's so nice. But we're usually just in and out, and I have to go back to the office right after. Are you sure you want to drive all that way for a quick visit?" I asked, then softened my tone. "I want you to come, I just don't know if it will be worth it."

"You usually get out at a decent hour on Fridays, don't you? I can keep myself busy in the city until you're finished with work, and then I was thinking we could go furniture shopping."

I searched for an excuse, other than I wanted to avoid spending that much time alone with my mother, but came up short. "I don't see why that wouldn't work," I told her.

When we hung up, I rested my cheeks in my hands and leaned my elbows on the desk, not knowing how my day had gone sideways before I'd even finished my coffee.

Almost as a gift, serious buyers swarmed the gallery for the remainder of the week. I returned home each night and copied for Lenny, nearly completing both works, and Ryan came by both Tuesday and Thursday evenings. Each morning we'd get there early, even Leah, and she and I could barely fill out the purchase orders before one of us would need to attend to the newest walk-in customer, while Florence flitted in and out of her office with quick words of praise for us.

"You're crushing it," Leah said to me on Friday morning as she entered the latest delivery details in the system, and I realized how familiar and comfortable it felt to be good at something I had never really put any value on being good at.

Just before ten o'clock, Florence said from her office, "Emma! I trust you've called us a car," and I gave her a thumbs-up even though I hadn't yet. "Will your mother be meeting us there?" she asked. I nodded as she answered a call on her cell.

Leah raised an eyebrow at me. "My mother called the office looking for me the other day, and Florence invited her to the Christie's auction," I explained as I ordered an Uber. "Kill me."

"Who knows, it might be fun," Leah said.

"You don't know my mother," I said.

The closest Uber was ten minutes away, seven minutes longer than any car had ever taken to get to the gallery, and when it finally arrived, Florence let out a small puff of air through her lips and muttered, "It's about time."

She said nothing to me on the way up to Rockefeller Center, occupied by her phone and with requests for the driver to unlock her window so she could put it down, turn on the heat because she was "freezing," and "go easy" on the brakes. The incessant clicking of her texting and the constant swooshing of sent messages and dinging of responses grated harshly on my ears. I pulled up my Instagram to try to tune it out.

"I just reached fifteen thousand followers!" I announced, hoping she'd make the connection that the gallery's increased foot traffic and sales numbers had some connection to my social media.

"Is that a lot?" she asked flatly.

"Compared to some, yes. I suppose not compared to others," I admitted, slightly annoyed by the question.

"Does that mean you're a leader?" She raised her right eyebrow. "How many followers do you need to be a leader?"

"Following just means you keep track of another person's posts," I said.

"So everybody's a follower?" Florence asked with a bemused expression.

"I guess," I said, not sure if she really wanted an explanation of how Instagram worked.

"And everybody is okay with that?" she asked rhetorically, turning her gaze out the window as we crossed Forty-Second Street. "This is the way I'd have gone if I didn't want to get where I was going," she grumbled, just loudly enough for the driver to hear.

When we stopped outside Christie's and exited the car, I recognized the reporter who'd asked her about Jane Kantrowitz and braced myself for another encounter, but Florence just walked past without so much as a nod. She stopped a few feet later to field questions from a reporter from a B-list online publication, who looked just as surprised that she was speaking to Florence Wake as everybody else.

"Emma!" I heard a high-pitched voice call my name as small arms wrapped themselves around my waist.

"Alexei!" I bent down and hugged him. Sophie came sprinting through the crowd after him, laughing apologetically when she saw he was with me. "What are you doing here?" I said, taking his rosy cheeks in my palms, careful not to knock off his magician's top hat.

"My mom and dad let me come to the auction," he said, fanning out his black cape and spinning around.

"I didn't know they allowed magicians in auctions! What if you make all the art disappear?" I said.

"I don't think I can do that," he said with a pout.

I looked over his shoulder and saw my own mother approaching. She was wearing tailored black tuxedo pants and a white turtle-neck. Despite barely leaving the suburbs and having no under-standing of the art about to be auctioned, she'd come up with a perfect outfit for the event. I would have been more impressed had I not been worried that she was spending money she didn't have yet on new clothes. *It's none of my business*, I reminded myself. And she did look wonderful.

I waved her down and embraced her. "Mom, this is my friend Alexei. Alexei, this is Barbara, my mother."

"Your *mom*?" Alexei laughed as though he couldn't quite imagine that I had one of my own.

My mother, always charmed by children, bent over to introduce herself to Alexei, and a mere moment later, he was performing a magic trick for her. After Florence finished speaking to the reporter and Sophie steered Alexei away, I introduced my boss to my mother. They kissed once on each cheek while my mother said predictably that it was "so nice to put a face to the voice." I made my way into the auction house after them as they chatted like old friends about my mother's drive in, leaving me to wonder if the universe had taken mercy on me today.

As Florence and I filed into our row, my mother behind us, I scanned the room for familiar faces, picking out a few that I had seen in the gallery and at Lenny's party. I hadn't expected a daytime auction from a private collection to draw such a crowd, but word must have gotten out that it would be worthwhile, because every seat was full. Florence chatted with a woman in the row ahead, so I felt obligated to fill the silence between my mother and me. We'd spoken more in the past few weeks than we had in years, so I was somewhat at a loss for new material. I decided to regale her with tales of my day at the freeport—the helicopter, the retina scan, the art. My mother leaned in, practically salivating at the details.

"I got to see *Te Fare* by Paul Gauguin again in person. I copied it for Lenny when I worked at Gemini, but it was even more impressive than I remembered," I told her. "But the public won't see the original for like thirty years, which makes me sad. It's really stunning, I mean, jaw-dropping . . ."

Just then the auctioneer stepped to the microphone and greeted the audience. My mother turned toward the stage, as giddy as a kid on Christmas morning.

"Hi!" Jules whispered, appearing in the aisle beside me, her hair perfect and her makeup flawless as she bent down to hug me. "This is me!" she said excitedly, pointing at the empty seat beside my mother.

"Hi!" I whispered back, thinking that I couldn't have asked for a more perfect opportunity to hear what Ryan might have told her about our burgeoning relationship. I introduced her to my mom in a hushed tone as the auctioneer opened the bidding at $5 million for a beautiful Manet, and then I made my mother switch seats with me. We sat in four chairs—Jules, me, my mother, then Florence in the aisle.

My mother patted my leg excitedly as the auction began, but for me, there was less of a sheen this time around since I understood the weeks of negotiations and phone calls between collectors that went on in private before they bid in public. Understanding the elaborate charade to establish demand, while my mother's eyes widened at the superficial bidding, made me feel a wider gulf between us. The painting went for $12 million to a bidder via phone, and my mother looked gleeful as Florence and I shot sideways glances at each other, tacitly agreeing the buyer had overpaid.

"You look beautiful," I said to Jules when there was a break in the action.

"Ugh! I wish it were for a better reason. Fredrick broke up with me and said something on Instagram about how he only wants to be with people who 'connect deeply,' which obviously makes everyone think I'm superficial. Anyway, I've been stressed, so I haven't really been eating. But don't I look good?"

"Oh, shit, Jules. I'm sorry."

"I couldn't care less about him. I just can't believe he had the balls to do public shit-talking!" she said, which I thought was an enviably detached reaction. "I'm even losing followers because of it. Such a disaster." She looked up at the auctioneer as the bidding resumed.

When a man with gelled hair wearing a Patagonia vest over a purple-checked collared shirt spent $15 million on a Monet, Florence rolled her eyes. "New private-equity money," she whispered over my mother. I nodded, having figured as much.

"How's Ryan?" I asked Jules while the next piece was being brought out.

"Ryan who?" she asked, turning her entire body toward me. "Oh, my Ryan?" she said, her eyes meeting mine, and I stiffened.

"Ryan Parker," I clarified, feeling a crushing pressure on my chest. He clearly hadn't mentioned me to her, but we weren't keeping it secret, so I figured I could. "We've been hanging out a bunch." As soon as the words left my mouth, I regretted them. Jules's entire body went rigid before she plastered a smile on her face.

"Then you know better than me, because I haven't seen him since Hong Kong," she said, turning back to the stage even though nothing was happening up there. "It's weird, because I didn't think you were really his type. But I'm so happy for you," she added with a tight smile. What *was* his type? Why wasn't I it?

"And now a very special piece. Paul Gauguin's *Te Fare*," the auctioneer announced, blessedly distracting me from the conversation. I looked up at the piece that I knew so intimately, and in that moment, I stopped hearing the auctioneer, his voice replaced by a slight buzzing in the air. I saw nothing but the painting. I blinked twice and it was still there, the extra shrub I had so impulsively dabbed on the canvas that night at Gemini. I felt the bile rising into my throat as I recalled the original piece in the long-term unit of the freeport.

I snapped back into the moment as the auction buzzed around me.

"Do I hear twenty-five million dollars? Twenty-five million to the bidder on the phone. Do I hear twenty-six million dollars?"

I leaned across my mother to Florence. "Are all of these pieces from Lenny Sobetsky's private collection?" I whispered.

My boss nodded and shushed me.

I sat there with pure terror coursing through my body, as though I were free-falling right there in my seat. I stared straight ahead at the room, wondering whom I should tell that my name would be on the back if they looked. My mother looked at me, and I knew what she was thinking, though I willed her not to say it out loud.

"Isn't that the piece you just told me was going to be in storage for thirty years?"

"Shhh," I hissed at her, cursing her inability to receive the tacit message not to speak that I was sending her through the air.

"Yes, it is! You said you were sad it wasn't going to see the light of day," she said, not keeping her voice low enough. I saw Jules's back straighten, and though she stared straight ahead, I could feel her listening to us.

"Thirty-one million to the gentleman in the front . . ." the auctioneer continued. I blinked twice, commanding it to disappear from my vision, but the shrub disobeyed me and remained. I didn't understand. I had signed that work as a copy. Hadn't I?

"Sold! For thirty-three million dollars to our bidder on the phone," the auctioneer shouted.

"Your copy was just as good, I bet," my mother said, and I wondered if she knew how she always managed to make every bad situation worse.

Jules slowly picked up the auction booklet from the floor and leafed through it, narrowing her eyes at the photo of the original *Te Fare*, her gaze oscillating between it and the piece up on the stage. She pursed her lips and surreptitiously fiddled on her phone inside her purse. I couldn't see her screen, but I knew she was looking up photographs of the original painting to compare with the one onstage and in the catalog.

In that moment, I felt the dark, misshapen energy that had been conspiring against me all day coalesce. I understood that I was in trouble, though I didn't know exactly what kind or how much. I squinted, trying to see all the parts that I'd stored into the far corners of my brain, all the little things in the past few months that didn't quite add up that I had foolishly dismissed as irrelevant. I saw the original *Te Fare* in the long-term storage unit at the freeport. I furrowed my brow, wondering why he'd have the painting in the long-term unit eight days before he was about to sell it.

I dimly registered the outside world—my mother bragging about the work I had done, Jules taking her phone out of her bag and holding it next to the catalog, and Florence contemplating my expression, wondering what was plaguing me. And I began to see the nature of my predicament clearly.

My copy of *Te Fare* was just sold at auction as the original. I had forged a masterpiece. My breath grew pressured. *Did he sell all of my copies as originals?* I had completed dozens of copies for Lenny over the years—potentially hundreds of millions of dollars' worth of forgeries. But I had always signed my name . . . hadn't I? *Is Sienna in trouble, too?* I racked my brain for any work I knew Sienna had done for Lenny but couldn't recall any. *Is Gemini in trouble? Could Jeremy have known about this? Could he have been in on it?* Then my brain circled around the next question, one that I'd dismissed before. But I slowly settled down into it. *Was the Chagall Lenny gave my mother real or fake?*

"Are you okay, Emma?" Florence was reaching across my mother's lap and gripping my forearm. "What's wrong?"

"I think . . ." I met her eyes and had the inclination to tell her everything, but when I opened my mouth to speak, I saw the next piece being wheeled out onto the stage.

"Miss, you can't have your phone out," said a man in a black suit as he appeared in the aisle next to Florence. We turned to follow his eyes to Jules, who had her phone pulled in close to her face to examine it. She lifted her head and nodded, putting her phone away, then avoided eye contact with me as she turned her gaze back to the podium.

Shit.

"And now the final piece in today's auction," the auctioneer began, his voice taking on a new level of excitement.

I closed my eyes, wishing I could go back to that morning, wondering if I simply hadn't gotten out of bed, would the day have just reabsorbed back into the cosmos, and I could have kept living my life in some parallel universe where everything was not falling apart. The auctioneer's numbers climbed, and I heard Florence ask again if I was okay as applause sounded out and the auction concluded. I had missed the sale entirely.

"You're pale," Florence said, looking around the room as though trying to figure out a way to usher me safely through the crowd, now filing out in a less than orderly fashion.

I shook my head. "I think I must have eaten something weird," I said, placing my palm to my stomach for dramatic effect. Even if the truth could absolve me from blame, even if people were to believe me that in all the years I copied works for Lenny—more works than any one person would ever be able to display—I never knew that he was selling my copies as forgeries and I always signed my name, the truth would bring about an investigation. If my mother had been given a Chagall forgery, it would be worthless, and if she'd been given the original, it would likely be confiscated and given to the heirs or tied up in a legal battle. Either way, she'd lose the precarious balance she'd attained.

The sounds of the auction rushed back in on me as the crowd oozed out from the rows into the aisle.

"So sorry," Jules whispered as she turned sideways and shuffled past us, even though we were all headed in the same direction. Florence stepped back dramatically to make space for her and let her know how rude it was to push by us. "It's an emergency. So sorry," Jules said again, never meeting my eyes.

"Hi! Oh my gosh, I follow you on Instagram. Is there any way I can just . . . ?" A young girl in a skirt and blazer stepped in front of her, blocking her path into the aisle.

"Of course!" Jules said, a large smile I now knew to be disingenuous spreading across her face as she pulled her hair forward and draped it over her shoulders.

"Thank you!" the girl said, handing her phone to Jules and leaning over the back of the aisle in front of me, wrapping her arm around my shoulder. She looked at Jules and smiled expectantly, and I watched

Jules's eyes narrow with a flicker of fury before she took a shot of me and the girl. The flash brightened and then faded. "Thank you! My friends and I are *obsessed* with you. We love the inside view of the art world you give us," she said to me as Jules handed the girl her phone, turned on her heel, and disappeared into the departing crowd.

I forced a smile at the girl, at a complete loss for words, and shuffled in a haze toward the street behind Florence and my mother, who was chatting animatedly about how she had no idea I was famous and how she needed to download Instagram immediately. Once outside in the bright sunlight, I managed to wiggle out of my mother's arm lock and tell her I'd be in touch as soon as I could scoot out of work.

"I won't keep her late," Florence assured her as we hopped into an Uber.

I rolled down the window on my side of the car and told Florence that I felt nauseated, trying to further the groundwork for an early exit. There was no way I could work, with all these questions racing through my mind. *What is the jail sentence for art forgery? What if I had no intent? What the hell happened to my signature on the back?* I expected her to suggest I take the afternoon off, but instead she asked me to get out at a red light and take a separate cab back to the gallery, because she *really* couldn't afford to get sick.

I welcomed the opportunity to google the questions ricocheting in my mind, away from Florence's prying eyes. I drifted toward the R station while looking at the sale history of every piece I could recall copying for Lenny. Not surprisingly, there were few records, and he wasn't even listed as the title holder to most of them—that was the benefit of buying and selling privately and storing in a freeport, of course. I descended into the subway station, trying to remember any piece Sienna had done for him, and as the train screeched to a stop before me, I thankfully couldn't think of a single one. I exhaled in relief.

When we screeched to a halt in the Prince Street station and the bars on my phone jumped from one to four, I googled *"L'Attrape-Rêves"* as I exited the train. There wasn't much. I tried *"The Dream Catchers"* and "Chagall" while approaching the gallery, growing more confident with every step that my mother's painting was real. I knew it wouldn't be of much help to her if Lenny were caught up in an investigation, but it gave me peace nonetheless to know that he hadn't defrauded my mother. I was just about to put my phone away when I saw a link to an Instagram account for @KikiKraft. I clicked on the link to a girl named Kayley Kraft, and a picture of a beautiful blond woman snuggled up to a dashing dark-haired man popped up. They wore cable-knit sweaters, and a happy bouquet of white flowers poked their petals in from the side of the shot. I checked the location—Copenhagen. The caption was in what I presumed to be Danish. I had no idea why Instagram had pointed me to the photo. I clicked "See Translation" under the caption. *Happy to catch my dream and spend this first Valentine's Day as a married woman with my husband in our family home.* My shoulders relaxed as I noted her post had nothing to do with my mother's painting, and I opened the door to Florence Wake. But then I read the hashtags: *#TheDreamCatchers #Chagall.* I furrowed my brow and zoomed in on the wall just behind the couple. I swallowed hard, seeing the exact painting that Lenny had just given my mother.

"The auction was that good?" Leah asked sarcastically. I looked up from my phone, startled, not knowing how I had gotten to the seat beside her. I rechecked the date on the post. It was from *this past* Valentine's Day. But Lenny had said he'd found the painting years ago. "Earth to Emma," Leah said, waving her hand in front of my face.

I blinked twice. "You know Florence's friend, the one who got caught up in the forgery scandal?"

"She whose name we do not speak?" Leah asked with a short laugh.

"She sold impressionist art?" I asked. Leah nodded. I went on, "Why impressionist? I mean, if you're forging, why pick that era? It's so much harder to copy than abstract and modern art."

"First of all, it's not like Jane actually forged them herself. But she did help Lenny Sobetsky off-load them. She claims she didn't know they were fake, but she's not dumb enough to believe some bullshit story that he found these priceless works of art in his basement or whatever the story was," Leah said. I felt my eyes widen. "I mean, he sold the works through a million other conduits—people, companies, et cetera—so his name hasn't been anywhere in the press, but everybody in the art world sort of knows it was him."

"*I* didn't know that! *I'm* in the art world!" I was practically yelling.

"I mean, well, whatever! Most people know . . ." She rolled her eyes. "Florence won't do business with him anymore because of it. And obviously, she doesn't talk to Jane."

"But Florence *does* do business with him. She sent me to Hong Kong with him. And then she sent me to look at pieces in his freeport," I said, totally confused.

"Yeah, but did you ever report back to her on those pieces?" Leah asked, as though it were the most obvious thing in the world. I had, of course, but she'd never responded to the email I'd spent hours crafting. "She always comes up with an excuse not to go herself. I went last time. And when Lenny asks, she'll pretend your notes were insufficient. He's bound to catch on soon. It's just a formality. A courtesy. A way not to insult him. He's not really somebody you want to insult. He's made mistakes, but he still has enough money and powerful friends to shift the market to or away from a gallery or an artist if he wants to. Your friend is a pretty powerful guy."

"I guess she never did acknowledge my notes from last week," I said, still lagging a few steps behind.

"Second of all," she went on, "it's beyond dumb to forge paintings by artists who are still alive. They'd just show up and call you on it." She shrugged as though it were obvious. "The impressionists painted recently enough that it's pretty easy to match the paints most of the time but long enough ago that all the artists are dead. Monet's not showing up at Sotheby's shaking his fist."

"Got it," I said, processing just how screwed I was. Nobody would believe I had no idea what I was doing, especially once I'd left Gemini.

"But proving provenance is a bitch for the same reason it's easy to match paints—because they were done fairly recently, so provenance is usually pretty clearly articulated. Not too much room for large holes in the time line," she added, just as Florence burst through the door and raced past us into her office with only a small nod of acknowledgment.

"But if you own the original, your provenance is bulletproof," I said, almost to myself.

"Yeah, I mean, you legitimately could never get caught," Leah said, and laughed. "But if somebody owns the original, what's the point of selling a forgery?"

"I have no idea," I said. But then I did. He was doubling his investments. He'd been more than clear with me that he didn't care about the art. He was in it for the money, and he had found a way to make twice as much.

I felt Leah staring at me.

"Are you okay?" she asked. "You're like . . . sweating."

I wiped at the perspiration forming on my upper lip. "I actually don't feel well," I said, touching my stomach again, but this time it was true. The anxiety had tied it into knots.

"Go home! I got this," Leah said, gesturing around the gallery. "I'll tell Florence you were about to puke on her precious refinished floors." I nodded in gratitude and headed out the door.

The noise of the city crashed in on me as soon as I reached the sidewalk, making my problems feel even more pressing and less solvable. I didn't really want to spend time with my mother, but I also did not want to be alone with my thoughts, and none of my problems would get solved by sitting in Lenny's studio apartment and thinking. I stared at my shoes as I shuffled across Prince Street.

"Emma Caan?" a deep voice said. I squinted, knowing I had heard the voice before and trying to place it, then raised my eyes to see two men in suits standing outside a hulking black Escalade: one young and trim, with sandy hair and a toned build, and the other short and stout, with a mop of gray hair.

"Yes?" I answered their question and asked my own at the same time.

"I'm Agent Garritt with the FBI," the young one said. "This is my partner, Agent Tillwell. We were hoping we could ask you some questions."

"You're with the FBI?" I asked, staring at the sandy-haired consultant from Gemini. "Are you joking?" This felt like a really dumb episode of *Candid Camera*.

"Only a few questions," he promised, and I recalled the flash cards in my exit interview. His partner flipped open what looked like a black leather wallet, the top of which held an ID with his picture and the bottom a gold badge. I glanced at it before returning to studying the other man's face. I remembered him watching me at Gemini and seeing him at the club in Hong Kong. Where else had he followed me?

"Didn't you need to disclose that when you met me?" I turned to his partner. "And I love how you show me a badge, like I have *any* idea what an official FBI badge is supposed to look like. That could be fake, for all I know."

"It isn't," he assured me, turning the leather case over on itself and returning it to his breast pocket.

"We were hoping you could tell us a bit more about the art you've been copying," said the guy I still thought of as the consultant, and I prayed they hadn't noticed me choke back a rush of vomit.

"Sure," I finally said, wanting to appear as casual and cooperative as possible. "Here?"

"We can go to our offices," Agent Garritt offered. "It might be more private."

"Okay," I told them, and Agent Tillwell opened the back door of the Escalade. My legs shook so violently that I needed to use the handle to hoist myself up into it. When he shut the door after me, I allowed my eyes to close. I cycled through what they must know (that I copied for Lenny while at Gemini, that I now knew Lenny personally) and what they might not know (that I was still copying for Lenny, that I was aware he was selling my copies as originals, that he had given my mother a potentially valuable or potentially fake piece).

Shit. I stared out the window at a young girl wearing baggy jeans and a Hanes V-neck and gagged, not able to comprehend how I had gone from the person I was three months ago to the person in the backseat of an FBI vehicle.

EMMA CAAN:	I don't know anything about art forgery. I'm sorry, but I was supposed to meet my mother two hours ago to go furniture shopping.
AGENT TILLWELL:	We understand. Just a few more questions.
EMMA CAAN:	Look, I've answered every question you've asked me. I really don't know anything more than what I told you. If I think of anything, I can be in touch.
AGENT GARRITT:	We appreciate your cooperation. Do you need a ride home?
EMMA CAAN:	I'll get a cab.
AGENT GARRITT:	One last thing, Ms. Caan.
EMMA CAAN:	Yes?
AGENT GARRITT:	It's critical to our investigation that you don't discuss the fact of our meeting or its contents with anybody. Do you understand? You must continue to act normally, even continue to paint for Mr. Sobetsky if requested.
EMMA CAAN:	I'm supposed to just act like I don't know any of this? How?
AGENT TILLWELL:	Fake it. Do you understand? It's critical.
EMMA CAAN:	I understand.
AGENT GARRITT:	Thank you for your time. We'll be in touch.

In a daze, I hailed a cab outside Tribeca's Federal Plaza, staring out the window as I contemplated my next steps. I understood only the basics of what I had become involved with in the past few months. These men who had welcomed me into their homes, who had given me jobs, food, a social life, were bad men. Criminals, in fact. I didn't know where Sergey fit into the mix, but I was certain he was aware of how his friends made their money. Curtis Tremblay was apparently an international drug trafficker who cleaned his money by buying ridiculously expensive art. In retrospect, being sniffed by dogs prior to entering and being offered ecstasy at a dinner party had been red flags, but everything about the trip to Asia had been so foreign, literally and figuratively, that nothing had stood out to me as strange. Though I didn't know Curtis well, I still felt somehow betrayed by his hospitality—as though he should have had a disclaimer on his door: "Drug Lord Lives Here."

As the gray grit of the city kicked up around the cab wheels, my brain clouded over with the realization that Lenny was not the man I'd thought he was. He hadn't thought I was a talented artist—he had thought I was a good forger and stupid enough not to ask too many questions. He was right. I looked down at my black pants and red pumps in disbelief, feeling as though at least a week had passed since I'd gotten dressed that morning.

The cab pulled up outside the Greene Street apartment, and I stepped out, instinctively looking over my shoulder, though I didn't know for whom or what. The bustling metropolis that had always made me feel anonymous seemed to be thinning out around me, leaving me exposed.

"Where have you been?" my mother asked, stepping down off the one step up into the entrance of the building, opening new channels of unease throughout my body. "I called the gallery an hour ago, and they said you went home sick, so I came here. But clearly, you had other plans!"

I closed my eyes for a moment as I brushed by her, using the fob to enter the building. "Mom, stop calling the gallery" was all I said in response.

"If you didn't want to go furniture shopping, you should have told me. I wouldn't have spent this whole time wandering—"

"I do want to go furniture shopping," I said quickly, realizing that I couldn't be alone in the apartment or have her in it for an extended period. "I just need to get out of these shoes."

I entered the code on the pad by the door and pushed through into the studio, holding the door open for my mother. She exclaimed in awe, taking a tape measure out of her purse before she realized that it didn't come close to measuring the full length of the room. She drifted toward me, looking up to the ceiling to assess its height.

"Honey, you have arrived," she gushed. "I'm so proud of you. Is this where you paint?" She pointed to the pressurized glass case. My chest tightened as I noted the two works I had been asked to copy for Lenny, which I hadn't started, and recalled the years of work I had promised him in exchange for the Chagall, which I obviously couldn't perform.

I nodded, taking in a deep breath.

"Are you okay?" my mother said. "Do you want to lie down?"

I shook my head but took her upstairs so she could giddily explore the bedroom, fluffing my pillow and fixing the corner of my sheet. I grew more and more annoyed at how concerned she was with appearances.

She stopped and cocked her head to one side. "You're pale. We don't have to go today, if you'd rather just rest."

"Nope, I'd love to. Let's go," I said, wanting to be anywhere other than the apartment provided to me by the man who'd masterfully backed me into a corner I couldn't see any way out of.

We walked to ABC Carpet, the afternoon sun bestowing a quiet calm on the downtown residents running errands or meeting for drinks. I felt like an interloper in their well-adjusted world. All the while, my mother prattled on about her vision for my new space, barely navigating through the crowds in Union Square because she was gesticulating so wildly. Mercifully, ABC sprang up ahead of us before I could snap at her.

I'd never been inside. We entered from the street into a room of chandeliers, the delicate crystals choreographing a dance of rainbow prisms across the ceiling, then into a large room bursting with color, its displays layered with linen, velvet, brushed brass, and porcelain, and enhanced with the smells of honeysuckle and vetiver from the shelves of candles and diffusers.

My mother found a salesperson while I stood still, overwhelmed by the sensory feast. She explained loudly to the poor salesman that she hadn't "been in the store since we redid my husband's study ten years ago" and asked for help selecting a couch for "my daughter's new SoHo loft." I could feel my amusement over her transparent self-aggrandizing slipping slowly down toward irritation. *I have far bigger things to worry about*, I reminded myself. Still, her voice started to grate on my already frayed nerves. To steady myself, I placed my hand on the sturdy piece of furniture next to me.

"Oh my gosh, no! Not *that* credenza!" My mother chuckled, leaning toward the salesman, whose name tag read "Rafael," like they were old friends. I raised my hand from the wood, making eye contact with Rafael, who'd already picked up on the fact that Barbara Caan was going to be a difficult customer. "Let's start with a sectional as a focal point and go from there. Hm?" My mother pushed me into the depths of the store, past rugs with fifteen-thousand-dollar price tags and couches with seven-thousand-dollar ones.

"We can either meander, and you can point out anything you like," Rafael kindly suggested, "or you can let me know what you're looking for, and I'll try to direct you."

"I think we're just browsing today, to get some inspiration," I said, to which my mother let out a nervous burst of laughter, as though I had just said the most ridiculous thing she had ever heard. She extended her hand into the air and pressed it toward the floor, like she'd done when I was a kid to tell me to calm down.

"This is her first *real* apartment," she explained to Rafael, "and it's spectacular! But she's never decorated, so I'm thinking a dramatic green or blue velvet sofa with . . ." I stopped hearing her, zoning out entirely as I ran my hand over the silk pillows on display, trying to grab on to something in the room to stay in the present. I was brought back to my teenage years, when I'd detested the way my mother floated from room to room when she had company, pointing at new drapes or the reupholstered wingback chair. It occurred to me that the only reason I'd gotten myself into this situation with Lenny was that my mother was incapable of handling anything that life threw her way, and the only things that seemed to make her happy were absurdly expensive material ones. Why did I need to support her? Why did she *need* that house? Why couldn't she downsize to a small condo? As I followed my mother and Rafael, trying to tune her out, I caught a glimpse of myself in the brass circular mirror on sale for the bargain price of ten thousand dollars.

My cheekbones protruded a bit more than they had when I'd left Gemini, probably from the constant activity and lack of sleep, and my hair looked somehow shinier, maybe a result of the superior products I'd been using in Lenny's studio. My eyes were still large and sad, though, and I had a disquieting sensation that I was looking at my mother wearing a blond wig. *I'm turning into her. The studio, the new clothes . . .*

"Emma?" my mother said. "Rafael asked you a question!"

"Hm? Sorry." I looked back at them.

"Do you entertain much?" he repeated. "Because if so, I think we could go with an L-shape—"

"Not really," I said, his benign question turning malignant as it reminded me just how few real friends I had.

"You will now that you have space," my mother assured me. I stared at her and felt the horrible thoughts rush in on me. I saw

her running out to the backyard, her white robe billowing out behind her. She hadn't been the one to pull me away from the fire,
she hadn't tried to help my father put out the flames on *her* clothes
as she writhed on the ground in agony. I hadn't thought about my
mother on that night often or possibly ever—it was always memories
of myself, my father, and *her*—but it all came rushing back in
on me. I remembered my mother offering to get the policemen
coffee while the firemen finished their job, ever the consummate
hostess, and I remembered her holding my shoulders, my back
flush against her stomach, as she explained that her husband was
a workaholic and took meetings in the shed at night with his secretary so "he doesn't keep my daughter and me awake," as if there
weren't a study and a basement and a number of other rooms in
our big house that he could have used.

"I don't think I really like anything," I said now, trying and
failing to steady my voice, staring out over the room of furniture,
knowing the tears were about to come.

"You haven't even looked, Emma," my mother said incredulously.

"I'll give you two a minute," Rafael offered politely as he faded
out of our presence and toward the back wall.

"It's hard to see in the showroom, but just try to picture this
couch in your gorgeous apartment," my mother said, sitting down
on a velvet hunter-green sectional and extending her arms across
the back cushions. I shifted my weight to my left foot, my legs
suddenly jumpy, but I inhaled deeply and stood my ground. My
mother patted the cushion next to her, and feeling calmer, I took a
seat beside her, thinking that I had just gained control of my emotions for the first time I could remember.

"Just imagine hosting a dinner party . . ." my mother started,
beginning to paint a picture of an evening around the couch.

I cleared my throat. "Mom, I've been thinking a lot about the
Chagall, and I think we should give it back. Like you said, down-

sizing would actually be great for you. That painting came from the man I work for, and I don't think we should be taking handouts—"

"Emma! Keep your voice down!" my mother said, a sternness to her voice that I hadn't heard since I was a child. "What a time to bring this up! Let's talk about it when we're in a more . . . private setting," though I was certain no one was paying attention to our conversation.

"Why? What's wrong with here? It's not like you'll ever see these people again! Who cares what they think?" I said, gesturing wildly to the handful of other people in the room, a few of whom were actually starting to pay us attention.

"Well, I sold it already," she said, her voice quiet and tight. "Privately, as you instructed."

"What? Already? How did you find a buyer? For how much? You could not *possibly* have gotten fair market . . ." I heard myself yelling.

"For Christ's sake, Emma. You are always overreacting to every little—"

"*You* never react at all! To anything! Ever!" I could see Rafael approaching, presumably to ask us to keep our voices down, but I was past caring. "Daddy cheated on you, gambled away our money when he was healthy, and gave the remainder to his mistress when he was dead. And you do *nothing*."

"How do you know that?" she said, her eyes wide and her breath labored. Once she realized I had no intention of responding, she took a step toward me, her voice coming at me in a low growl this time. "What did you want me to do, Emma? Burn her alive? Well, I didn't have to. You did that for me!"

Out of the corner of my eye, I saw Rafael back away slowly as I stared at my mother, dumbfounded. On some level, I'd always understood that I had set the fire, but I'd been able to blame my father for it—they were his matches, it was his affair—and I'd never allowed myself to see the entirety of the event. I'd operated under the assumption that my mother was blissfully unaware. My father had known, of course, because he had seen the matchbook in my hand, but I'd supposed he had kept that to himself, to protect me or my mother or both of us.

I saw the whole night at once, sitting there on the green couch in ABC. I saw him intertwined with his mistress and heard them grunting as I peered through the window, and I only wanted to make it stop before my mother came out and saw them, before they broke her heart. I looked down on the bench beside the shed and saw the matches from my father's local bar and his pack of cigarettes, even though he maintained that he'd quit. I took a match and lit it, dropping it into the dried and browned leaves that had blown up against the shed, and there was a soft, calming crackle and a bit of smoke before I heard the whooshing sound of the flames devouring the air and the hissing and popping of the cans of spray paint in the shed. I backed away slowly. And then there was nothing but her screams.

I started to cough, feeling the smoke in my lungs as I rose from my seat on the green sofa. I looked around, my eyes wide as the flames licked at the carpets and the couches. I began to back away from my mother as she extended her hand toward me and said something I couldn't hear over that whooshing of the flames. I shook my head, but the flames only grew, and I turned and ran, pushing past Rafael and the gawking shoppers who pretended to be concerned but secretly delighting in the spectacle of the girl they'd seen having a nervous breakdown in the trendy downtown furniture store.

I burst out onto the street and continued to run, hot tears streaming down my face as strangers turned to stare. I made it a few blocks and through Union Square before I slowed, gasping for air. I noticed a man holding up his phone toward me and cringed at the text I imagined him sending to his friend. *And I thought I was having a bad day* or something equally callous. I pulled my hair over my cheeks to hide my face and continued down the strip of paved sidewalk lining University Place, eyes glued to the ground, walking with my shoulder flush against the buildings to draw as little attention as possible until I reached the Greene Street apartment. I lay down in the middle of the empty floor, my arms and legs stretched as far away from the core of my body as I could manage, trying to take up as much space as possible in the universe that seemed to be too easily devouring me.

My instinct was to grab for my phone, to open Instagram and find something to distract myself, but I was aware I was beyond that point. I tried to meditate, as my college therapist had taught me, but no matter how hard I tried to focus on the floorboards under my back and the pink setting sunlight streaming in on the ceiling, my mind retreated into a fiery past or lurched into a nightmarishly uncertain future. The strange part of my mother's declaration was that it somehow felt like new information—like I had woken up with a dead body in my house only to discover I was the murderer. In all my memories, I'd been holding matches that night, and I could recall the horrified look in my father's eyes as he saw what I had done. But somehow I'd distanced myself from culpability. I felt it all now.

I rolled uncomfortably to one side, wondering if the beds in prison were as hard as the wood floor, wondering what the punishment was for forgery and too scared to google its actual definition to see if I'd committed it. *Did I need to know what I was doing to be guilty? Would anybody really believe I had no idea what was going on?* I pictured myself in an orange jumpsuit, then the jumpsuit going up in flames.

I pulled myself upright, bringing my head over my outstretched legs, and bent down toward the floor. When I looked up, the blank canvas on the easel where I had tried to paint so many times was in my line of vision. I limped over to turn on the light and then walked more easily over to the canvas as the blood circulated through my limbs. I squeezed a few colors out of the aluminum tubes and grabbed for a brush. My hands moved quickly, dipping the brushes in and out of the thick paint. I heard the slop and crack as I mixed the colors, finding peace in the act of allowing the images in my mind to escape. I cried as I painted, large hot tears spilling down my cheeks so quickly that I stopped trying to catch them before they hit my chest.

I made two more trips to the supply closet for new canvases. Now on my third, I improved with each new canvas I turned to. I had spent so long painting like the people I was supposed to copy that I had almost forgotten my own strokes. It was like trying to sing a song I hadn't heard in years, slow to start before the memory of the melody came back all at once. I stared at the sketch I had done of my younger self, and every single detail of that night returned to me in sharp relief. I grabbed the paint to fill her in with the colors in my mind, and I shivered as I felt the chill through the bare trees in the yard, heard the leaves crunching under my feet. I painted the pack of cigarettes and matches on the bench, and suddenly, I was climbing off the bench and taking the matches, the crackle of the leaves now seemingly goading me on. I lit the match and dropped it. The girl in the painting's fingers were still extended, the match suspended inches from them on its way to greet the leaves, my burden transferred to the canvas. I moved on to the next blank one.

I sketched my father smoking outside the hospital where he'd been diagnosed with lung cancer. He couldn't "see the point in stopping now," despite the doctors repeatedly informing him it was necessary for his treatment and that he still had a chance. I sketched more from my memory, snippets of the life I hadn't allowed myself to think about, even in therapy.

My hand shook violently as I painted myself sleeping in the chair in my father's hospital room, my fingers interlaced with his even though we weren't on speaking terms, and the IV lines that ran from his crepey forearm into the bag of fluid that hung from the pole between us. The colors were complicated and conflicting, clashing without blending, reflecting my complicated emotions. When I finished the painting, I wept again, grateful to feel the pain of the full memory of losing my father.

Eleven canvases in, I dropped my brushes to the floor. The sun was just rising, and I realized I'd been painting for the entire night. The paint on the first palette I had used was already cracked and dried. I had lost track of time and my phone was dead. Over my right shoulder, I looked at the steps leading upstairs, feeling tempted to crawl into bed, but then turned back to the paintings spread out before me. I felt protective of them, a maternal instinct not to leave them even to sleep until they were fully dried kicking in, and so I curled up at the feet of my easels in a pool of warm sunlight on the wood floor.

I woke up in a puddle of drool, my cheek resting on my hands and a terrible kink in my neck. I sat up on the floor, closed one eye, and grabbed for my cell phone to stop the incessant ringing that had woken me, but realized it was still dead. The intercom on the wall was signaling that somebody was at the door. My mind raced. Was Lenny somehow aware I had been questioned by the FBI? Had he come to ask me what had been discussed or to make sure it never happened again? I thought about ignoring the buzzing, but it was his apartment, after all. And regardless, a man like Lenny could always find me if he wanted to.

My knees buckled in relief when I heard Sienna's voice through the intercom. I buzzed her up and stood at the door, and when she stepped out of the elevator, she practically lunged at me.

"Are you okay? I've been texting and calling, but your phone has been going straight to voicemail for twenty-four hours! You scared me." She pulled away from me and held my shoulders at arm's length, her eyes locked with mine. "Are you okay?" she repeated.

I didn't know how she always knew when I wasn't okay, but I was too groggy to care and too glad to be the subject of somebody's concern. I was about to explain to her the auction and the forgeries and the FBI, but instead, I paused and asked, "How do you even know where I live?"

Sienna cracked a smile. "You're still sharing your location with me from the night you went to Lenny's party. And I didn't find you in the Louis Vuitton store downstairs, and this is the only other unit in this building. Thank God I didn't have to go to every door." She gave a short laugh, though I knew she wasn't kidding, she really would have done it, and looked past me and into the studio for the first time, her lips parting in wonder. "You live here?" I nodded. "Then what on earth is there to cry about? Aside from the fact that you have nowhere to sit."

"Cry?" I asked, touching my cheeks and finding them to be dry.

"I'm sorry, that's not funny. That was really insensitive, I'm sorry."

"I'm confused. What are you talking about?" I asked, wondering just how long I had been asleep. "I mean, I'm glad you're here, but . . ." I stopped there, knowing from Sienna's reluctance to speak that I wasn't going to like the answer.

She sighed. "One of your followers saw you running through Union Square yesterday and posted it. And now it's sort of a meme." She paused and waited. I grabbed my phone from the floor, but of course it was still dead.

"Show me," I demanded, pointing to her bag. She reached in and pulled out her phone, unlocking it with her thumb and opening Instagram.

"Nobody will remember this tomorrow," she assured me, wincing as she handed it to me. I gasped and covered my mouth at the two-second video of me shoving through a crowd in Union Square, tears streaming down my face, my mouth twisted like an Edvard Munch subject. The caption read *Influencers React to Instagram Changing the Algorithm.*

"On the upside, they called you an influencer," Sienna said, trying to get me to laugh.

"I look like I'm having a nervous breakdown!" I groaned. I leaped up and plugged in my phone on the kitchen island, needing to get on my account, wondering whether Ryan had seen it and reached out, a whole new set of concerns plaguing me in addition to my legal worries.

"Are you?" Sienna asked, approaching my side.

"Am I what?" I asked, willing my phone to charge faster.

"Having a . . . nervous breakdown?" she asked quietly.

I met her eyes, and there was no humor in them, only concern. My impulse was to laugh, to shake my head, but I was honest. "I don't know," I said. "What's the definition of a nervous breakdown? My life is sort of falling apart, and I'm having really intense hallucinations and the usual nightmares . . ."

"That was one stupid meme, Em. Honestly, nobody will remember it tomorrow. Your life is *not* falling apart!"

I looked at her seriously. "The meme is the least of my problems."

I led her out onto the balcony and told her everything—the fight with my mother that sent me running from ABC in tears, how I had seen actual flames sprouting up throughout the store, the consultants who were really FBI agents, Curtis Tremblay, the Chagall for my mother, my father's will . . . everything. "I can't think of a single copy you did for Lenny. You never forged for him, right?" I asked, turning to her. She shook her head, and I breathed a sigh of relief that she hadn't gotten mixed up in the madness.

Sienna was quiet for a long moment as she looked out over the city streets, but I could tell she was seeing nothing. "Jesus. I mean . . . Jesus! The consultants are from the FBI?" she finally asked.

"I really think you are safe. You never copied—"

"I'm not worried about me!" she explained. "I'm worried about you! More worried than when I got here, if that's possible. I don't understand. Didn't you sign your copies?"

"Of course," I said, but my mind was circling around something I couldn't quite put my finger on. I had signed every copy, never forgotten. Except when I'd gone to sign *Te Fare* and my signature was already there. But no matter who signed it, shouldn't my name on the back have kept it from being sold at auction?

"Do you think Jeremy knew?" she asked.

I shook my head. "He basically invited the FBI in to investigate," I reminded her. "Just my luck that my crush turns out to be trying to lock me up."

"What are you going to do?" she asked softly.

"I don't know. Literally, I don't even understand how this happened. I signed everything. I need more information," I said. "The FBI kept saying I wasn't in trouble, but I need to figure out *how* Lenny is doing it—taking my copies and wiping the signatures off them. Then I can know how much trouble I'm in. And believe it or not, I don't think the FBI knows, either, so maybe I can at least get brownie points by helping them out."

"You don't need to *help them out.* They're the FBI! They can handle it. Are you crazy? It's dangerous to go poking around in the criminal activity of billionaires just to see the mechanics of it all. Also"—she breathed, trying to center herself—"I can't believe you spoke to them without a lawyer." She shook her head. "I mean, I get it, but—"

"It's the FBI! I wanted to cooperate! And I've done nothing wrong!" I said defensively. "I really feel like I'm screwed here. I need to talk to Lenny."

"Emma—"

"The agents told me to act normal. They told me to fake it. I'm going to do just that." I didn't leave Sienna any room to respond as I turned and guided her back into the studio from the balcony. "It'll be easy enough. Everything I do is fake already . . ."

"What are you talking about? You're the most genuine . . ." she said as we entered the main room.

"This apartment isn't mine. I've built this following on Instagram who think I live this fabulous life. Or at least they thought that before that post. I am still seeing fires. And having nightmares. I gotta get my shit together."

Sienna looked around the room, her eyes stopping on my paintings. She moved closer, carefully digesting my brushstrokes, and stopped in front of the one of me with the matchbook in my hand in front of the fire.

"You set that fire in the toolshed," she stated without judgment. I nodded, even though it wasn't a question. "Somebody got hurt," she whispered. I nodded again, my vision growing blurry. "You were just a kid," she said, turning to me. I blinked and allowed the tears to spill out.

"I was old enough to know better," I said, unable to look at her.

"You were just a kid," she repeated. "An angry kid, from the looks of this painting," she said, gesturing to my wild eyes, the flames reflected in them.

"I don't deserve a friend like you. You've shown up, literally, everywhere the past year," I said.

Sienna shook her head. "You lied to let me keep my job, so call it even," she said with a small laugh.

"Seriously," I said. "Nothing in my life is real except for you."

Her face fell. "Well, now I feel really bad," she said. "I think I've been such a great friend lately because it's been a great distraction from the fact that Michael and I broke up."

"What? I had no idea."

"He was cheating on me with his coworker. I moved out last week, but it's been months since I found out. The visits up to Washington Heights, the trip to Pennsylvania . . . I mean, I was glad to do all of it, but it was a bit disingenuous, too. I needed not to think about my own stuff."

Sienna told me how she had gone to surprise Michael for a drink the night my mother had taken us to Giorgio's, but when she'd called to tell him she was outside his office, he hadn't answered. She had ducked into a nearby bar to wait, only to spot Michael and his associate sitting on the same side of a small booth, far too cozy to be discussing work. His cell phone was out on the glossy wood table, so she called him again. Sienna watched as he saw her name on his phone, sent it to voicemail, and kissed his coworker.

"Gross," I said, curling my lip. "I'm sorry." I wondered how I could have missed all this. I replayed the conversations we'd had about Michael—her warning me not to date a banker, her saying he was always working. "I seriously had no idea."

"How could you have? I never said anything. I preferred to focus on your life, your problems," Sienna said. "Sometimes it's just easier to pretend everything is rolling right along, but the truth always catches up to you, I guess. I'll be okay, though. So will you."

We heard the ding of a text come through on my phone and stared at each other for a pregnant minute. I walked slowly over to my phone and saw I had 63 voicemails, 123 text messages, and 747 direct messages on Instagram. None of them from Ryan. I also had forty-nine thousand followers now. I thought for a moment, then searched my followers for Ryan's handle, but it didn't come up. He had unfollowed me. I swallowed down a large lump in my throat.

"I guess the good news is, I doubled my following," I said. "But I don't know how I'm going to deal with all these messages."

"Don't do it now. It'll blow over," Sienna said. She was right—the good thing about the number of messages was that it was too overwhelming to even put a dent in. "And you have bigger things to worry about, unfortunately," she added. "What can I do to help you figure things out?"

"Nothing," I said honestly. "I just need to figure out how my mother sold a piece Lenny gave her. And whether we can unwind the sale quietly. Then I need to figure out how exactly he's been selling my copies as originals if I always sign the back. I think I just need to get into his house, which shouldn't be too hard. He prints absolutely everything. The man hates computers. I'm sure there's some sort of ledger of the sales—even if it's well hidden."

"Are you kidding me? Tell me you're kidding!" Sienna said. "*That* is your plan for figuring things out? You are told by the FBI—the FBI!—that Leonard Sobetsky is dealing in forged art and knowingly does business with drug lords, and your plan is to go poking around in his house? You are joking, right?"

"Lenny doesn't know I know any of that!" I insisted, though I wasn't certain that he didn't. "I just want to know if my mother's painting is real and how much trouble I'm in. I can find this out quickly, I think." I paused. "And to be honest, I'm holding on to this small hope that the FBI is somehow wrong about Lenny. I need to figure it out if they are. I really don't want to be disappointed by another man in my life . . ."

Sienna nodded. "I do get that. But I'm going on record that this is a terrible idea. Be careful."

I nodded at her, knowing she was right but not seeing another option.

When she left, after making me promise many times that I'd keep myself safe, I held my cell phone and inhaled and exhaled deeply ten times before dialing the number on the screen.

"My dear!" Lenny said after picking up on the second ring, and I could tell from his tone that he knew nothing of the meme.

Everything I had learned in the past forty-eight hours melted into the background, and I heard only his voice and thought of how large a role he had come to play in my life. He asked how my mother was and how I'd enjoyed the auction. He let me know Micaela would be arranging delivery of two works in the next few days even though I hadn't finished the previous ones. I let him know his copies would be flawless. Then, before I needed to come up with an excuse to stop by, he invited me to a small dinner party at his home the following night, an invitation I graciously accepted.

I hung up, shocked by how easy it was for me to pretend things were okay before realizing that I had spent my entire youth compartmentalizing difficult emotions and storing them away from present interactions. I paced my apartment, empty besides the memories that I'd flung onto canvases, and exhaustion hit me hard. I checked my phone to confirm it was Sunday and ignored the slew of calls and texts that continued to roll in, mostly from my mother back in Ardmore and supposedly worried about me, and I put myself to bed.

When my alarm sounded the next morning, I winced at the thought of a Monday morning in the gallery, full of nosy Instagram followers who would try to follow me in real life only to get a shot of something they could turn into a meme. And God only knew what Leah and Florence would think. I fought every impulse I had to call in sick and forced myself into the gallery, prepared to prove that I was very much sane and employable.

When I got there at 8:45, Leah was already seated at her computer.

"Hey!" she said cheerfully, still looking at her screen. I wondered for a moment if she hadn't seen the video. "Want to talk about it?" she asked, looking up at me. *No such luck.*

"I really don't," I said.

"Great. We're too busy today, anyway. Also, Florence won't ever know about it, so don't worry about that," she said, which I appreciated. "We actually had four calls on Saturday about the new Marjorie Mejia painting," and she launched into work talk and didn't mention the meme again. She did, however, come up with reasons for me to leave the room—an inventory check or a coffee run—whenever a pair of young girls entered in search of a view of me. I happily obliged.

At midday, I looked out the gallery door and saw a black Escalade parked out front. I immediately began to sweat, wondering if the FBI had found out something else, if they knew about my mother's Chagall, if they were going to come in and arrest me right in my place of work. I watched as an older man climbed into the backseat before the vehicle pulled away, and realized it was just an Uber XL. I breathed a sigh of relief.

After work, I downloaded a calming meditation and listened to it on the subway uptown to Lenny's. It did absolutely nothing to calm me, and I exited the 6 train at Seventy-Seventh Street still listening in the hope that my heart rate would slow as I walked west. It only quickened. I was wearing one of my new tops from Intermix with black cigarette pants and Leah's red pumps. I had no bulky brown coat to stash in the bushes this time—in fact, I'd given away that old coat when I'd moved. I'd just come from my job at arguably the most well-known art gallery in the world. But curiously enough, I found myself nostalgic for my former self—the girl I'd barely taken the time to know and couldn't wait to get away from. I missed her sense of wonder, her awe at the world around her. I stood outside the concrete and brick town house and steeled myself.

As predicted, Lenny greeted me warmly at the door and proceeded to introduce me to a board member from MoMA PS1, two aspiring artists, and a Russian friend who was in New York for just one night from Monaco, on his way to L.A. to attend the third wedding of his stepson from his second marriage. I smiled obsequiously and accepted a glass of vodka off the silver tray, taking my first sip slowly, careful not to spill any from the brimming glass on the glossy marble entryway. Just as I pulled it from my lips, I felt Alexei's small arms wrap around my waist. I bent low and hugged him close, certain to keep my glass level, and stood to greet Yelena and Sergey, with a polite nod to Sophie.

"Want to see another magic trick?" Alexei asked.

"I do. I really do. But in just a bit. I want to get something to eat first," I said.

"Okaaaaaay," Alexei said. "But I'm warning you, Mom and Dad said I have to go home and go to bed soon, so if you wait too long, you're going to miss your chance." He looked serious.

"Oh, then I'll be quick for sure!" I said as I headed off toward the back of the living room. I drifted amid the bleached-white furniture, my heels clicking softly against the glossy dark wood floors. I took an oyster off a passing tray and leaned in close to a Hockney on the far wall. I had no real evidence, just my gut instinct, but I was almost certain it was real. I slurped down the oyster and moved on to the next painting, uncertain what I was looking for, and regardless, I wasn't going to find anything on display that told me how Lenny ran a forgery ring. I leaned back and glanced into the dining room, where servers dressed in all black were placing baskets of bread, napkins folded over to keep it warm, at evenly spaced increments throughout the table. Given that bread was out, I figured I didn't have more than fifteen minutes before people were seated for dinner and my absence would be noticed.

"Now can I show you a trick?" Alexei asked, appearing at my side.

I was briefly frustrated by the interruption, but then realized it could be an opportunity. "I have a better idea," I said, making my eyes wide with excitement. "Want to play hide-and-seek?"

"Oh, yes. Yes yes yes!" Alexei said as he began to jump around.

"I think there are better spots to hide upstairs," I whispered, and he nodded eagerly. I watched Sophie slip into the kitchen, probably to grab dinner for him before taking him home. "Do you want to hide first?" I asked, checking to confirm that no guests were looking in our direction. "Go!" I whispered. "You have one minute before I come—" He had already taken off up the stairs.

No one was paying attention, instead popping bite-size delicacies into their mouths and laughing easily as the alcohol entered their bloodstream. I took a moment to look around the room, understanding for the first time that I would never be one of them. I would never laugh that easily, with no painful past, no easy present. Or maybe they were all pretending, too. I shook my head, dismissing the thought, and slipped up the stairs.

"Ready or not . . . here I come!" I yelled, in case anyone was watching or listening. I stole a quick glance at the ceiling for security cameras, and though I didn't see any, I was certain they were there. I turned the knob of every door I could find and peeked in every room. The second floor had only two bedrooms and a small den, so I took another flight of stairs. The first door I opened on the third floor was a billiards room, where I spotted two small sneakers poking out from beneath the thick sage-colored drapes. Alexei needed a little more practice at this game. Pretending I hadn't seen

him, I continued down the hall, and the next door I opened was
an office.

Bingo.

As on the plane, the desk was piled high with stacks of paper.
I called Alexei's name a few times for dramatic effect, just quietly
enough to make sure he couldn't hear me, then placed my hand on
the table while pretending to look under it, knocking over a stack
of papers in the process.

I sifted through the papers as quickly as possible, but they contained only pictures of art and spreadsheets with numbers I couldn't
possibly digest in the moment. Realizing I wouldn't have enough
time, I took my phone out of my bag to video the papers as I sifted
through them, but just as I began to film, my phone died. I stared
at it, not believing my stupidity, but I grabbed a pen from Lenny's
desk and a piece of paper out of the printer. Just as I turned back to
the papers on the floor, I noticed a manila folder labeled "Gemini."

I lunged for it and opened it. The file contained lists of works,
over half of which I'd copied for Lenny, the date on which each had
been put in the Delaware freeport, as well as the date and price at
which the piece was sold and the buyer's name. My eyes bulged. My
Cézanne was in the freeport and had been sold to Curtis Tremblay.
A Monet copied by a Gemini colleague had gone into the freeport
last June but had also been sold to a buyer in South Africa for
$7 million. I knew there was only one way a painting could be in
two places at once. I uncapped the pen and began to scribble down
what I could.

"Emma! You're supposed to be looking for me!" yelled a voice
from the far corner of the study.

"Holy shit!" I yelled, grabbing my heart and dropping the paper
and pen. "Where did you come from? You scared me!" I looked
down at Alexei's feet. He was wearing only socks, no shoes.

"Did you fall for the decoy?" he asked, wiggling his toes and laughing. He was apparently better at the game than I had given him credit for.

My gaze caught on the pen on the cream-colored Oriental carpet beneath my feet, its black ink in a large streak where it had hit the floor.

"Fuck," I whispered under my breath. They were the same pens we used at Gemini, and those marks were permanent. There was no way I could cover my tracks now.

Alexei grabbed his stomach as he doubled over laughing. "That's the second time you cursed! That's ten dollars in the swear jar! Five for each!"

"Okay," I said, nodding, "okay," talking more to myself than to Alexei. "Ten dollars. You got it." I was staring at the marker smudge as I spoke, full-blown panic radiating through my body. There was no way to explain why I'd taken a pen while playing hide-and-seek with a kid, even if Lenny were to believe the story of why I was in his office.

"Ten dollars!" Alexei demanded. I reached into my purse, hoping he would leave if I paid him, but stole another glance at the carpet.

"Don't worry about that," he said, following my eyes to the black smudge. He picked up the signature pen and handed it to me. I placed the cap on it and threw it in my bag, then fished out a ten-dollar bill from my wallet and handed it to him. He nodded, then pulled from his pocket a small black pouch imprinted with a white rabbit. *More magic tricks*, I thought, inwardly rolling my eyes, but as I feigned interest, he filled the rubber top of a dropper from a small vial of clear liquid. He squeezed the top and picked it up out of the liquid and carefully let out droplets over the black smudge in the carpet. Immediately, the ink disappeared. I leaned in closer to inspect it. It hadn't just faded, it had evaporated, as though it never had existed.

"I make messes with marker all the time," Alexei assured me.

"But my dad makes me use his magic markers." He refilled the dropper and continued until there was no evidence whatsoever that there had been a stain. "See? Don't be sad," he said as he put the pouch back in his pocket and wrapped his arms around my waist. "I know a magician never tells, but I didn't want you to be sad."

I stared at the pristine carpet, understanding that my former colleagues and I had been forging for Lenny for years—probably over $500 million worth of art. That was why the type of paint I used mattered, why Sergey's company supplied all the paints, canvases, and pens, why Lenny was so particular about the borders and having me copy off the original. It was why Micaela had sneaked into the studio the day we started using the new signature pens and signed *Te Fare* in my name before I ever had a chance to do so.

"Holy shit," I whispered, and Alexei whipped his head around, ready to ask me for another five-dollar bill, but we both heard a floorboard creak and turned toward the door.

Lenny's hulking frame took up the doorway as he stood, his ice-blue eyes absorbing the papers spread out on the floor and Alexei and me standing over them. I froze, a slight buzzing in my ears, like an internal alarm to signal danger. I did a quick survey of the room and a mental calculation of what Lenny knew.

"We were playing hide-and-seek," I said, ruffling Alexei's hair as he stood at my side.

Lenny didn't respond at all, just looked down at the papers on the floor again. "It's the second time you've spilled papers off my desk," he said slowly. The calmness in his tone felt like added torture. "Once is an accident. Twice is—"

"She also dropped a pen, but I showed her the disappearing-ink trick, Uncle Lenny!" Alexei chimed in giddily.

I closed my eyes. *Shit.*

When I opened them, Lenny was watching me intently, an amused twinkle in his eye. I heard Leah's voice in my head telling

FAKE   291

me Lenny wasn't a man to be messed with, and Sienna formally registering her opinion that snooping was a terrible idea. I tried to swallow, but my throat was so dry I couldn't manage it.

"Alexei, you mother and father say it's time for Sophie to take you home," Lenny said, the glint in his eye now gone, and the child scooted out of the room without protest.

Lenny was watching me with the most horrifying expression—no discernible one at all. His lips were in a thin, straight line, and his eyes were calm and motionless.

I contemplated apologizing profusely, but I stopped myself. Instead, I asked, "Is the Chagall you gave my mother real?"

Something shifted in his eyes, and I could tell he was caught off guard by my refusal to grovel.

"Yes," he said, and I felt my body release a bit. At least my mother wouldn't be in trouble for selling fake art, if he was telling the truth.

I looked around at the papers on the floor and the square of carpet where the ink stain used to be. "I think I'm up to speed on the rest," I said, and Lenny nodded. "So of course, I can't paint for you anymore," I managed.

"Why?" he asked, his calm continuing to unsettle me.

"Because . . ." I gestured to the floor. "I know what you're doing."

"Oh, really? You just discovered what I was doing, Emma?" he said, his voice incredulous. "You knew all along. You're too smart to think you were getting all those somethings for nothing." I opened my mouth to defend myself, but he continued. "Plus, what am I doing? Taking advantage of the stupidity of purchasers who buy an artist rather than art? What's so wrong with that? Their idiocy gave you an amazing life. It gives me one!"

"You do business with drug kingpins! Who knows what other . . . industries . . . you're promoting!"

"Fakes, Emma. I sold Curtis a fake. And generations from now, when the original is out of the freeport and his family tries to un-load the fake, it will be worth nothing. And *I* will be dead, with no offspring to suffer for my sins," Lenny said. "I'm screwing bad people."

I shook my head. "You don't sell only to bad people," I said, but I could see the logic in his argument. "And I *had* a good life before I met you."

"Did you?" Lenny asked, cocking his head to the side. He was right again, of course, but it made me angry to admit it. "I insulated you entirely from any risk. I've paid you in cash. I've paid you in kind—with a real Chagall. There is no paper trail to you. Nothing with your name on it. I've taken care of you."

His paternal tone sent me into a rage. "If you've insulated me so well, why did the FBI haul me in for questioning?" I asked, my voice shrill, then immediately covered my mouth. I couldn't believe I'd made such an enormous misstep.

Lenny's eyes widened before he regained composure. "What did you tell them?"

"Nothing. They knew a lot already. I don't think they know ex-actly which pieces have been forged, and I don't think they can wrap their mind around all the buyers, because you're smart enough to sell most privately. But that auction . . ."

"I have to sometimes sell publicly to maintain legitimacy," he said, looking away from me.

"They know you've sold to Curtis, though. I don't think they know how you're doing it," I said, my eyes drifting back down to where the stain had been. "But if they can't figure it out, I'm wor-ried they'll try to punish me just to punish *somebody*."

"They won't be able to. You didn't know anything," Lenny said, in direct opposition to his earlier statement.

As we stared at each other, we both understood the exchange. I'd likely risked an obstruction charge by not ratting him out, and it was an enormous favor to him. "We are square," he said, and I understood he was simultaneously giving me the Chagall as payment for what he'd put me through, while also saying goodbye to me. He was dismissing me from the life he had given me just as quickly as he had welcomed me into it.

I nodded and walked out of the room, half elated that he was letting me leave so easily and half devastated. He stayed behind in his office as I made my way down the stairs and exited the beautiful town house onto the quiet city street—I was certain a few around the table had seen me leave, but none of them cared. I looked down the tree-lined block, at the perfect gated entryways, the manicured trees, and wondered what really went on behind each imposing exterior.

I walked all the way back downtown to the studio, reminding myself that as tough as it had felt, the night had been a success. I had cut ties with Lenny, I had made certain my mother would be okay. Though I hadn't planned to reveal to him that he was the subject of an ongoing investigation, it had worked in my favor, as he knew I owed him one. And I didn't need to worry about him: Lenny had the ability to leave the country and billions of dollars to live off without ever selling another piece of art.

I had somehow untwisted myself from the life that I had gotten tied into, but rather than feeling relieved, I felt deeply, mercilessly sad.

The life I had been leading since that first night at Lenny's was not my own. I couldn't afford it if I worked one hundred lifetimes. It was pretend, make-believe. Fake. But that was precisely why I'd miss it so much. Without the planes and helicopters, dinner parties and priceless works of art, I was left with just myself. Ryan had clearly lost interest in me after seeing the meme. Jules hadn't reached out to me, either. When I turned onto Greene Street an hour and a half later, I almost expected the fob to be deactivated, or to see some bulky men waiting to ask if I really thought it would be so easy to stop working for Lenny, but everything was normal. I took the small elevator up to the apartment I knew I'd need to vacate, and soon.

"Jesus!" I said after opening my door and grabbing for my heart. "How did you get in here?"

Out of all the things I had imagined waiting for me inside, I hadn't predicted Micaela standing with her back to me, her long dark hair covering most of her back as she looked at my paintings perched on their easels.

"Hi . . . ," I said cautiously, not sure what she knew or whose team she was on.

"Who delivered these?" she yelled over to me, an accusatory nature to her tone. "I mean, what the fuck? You fuck up the business, *and* you arrange deliveries behind my back? Are you trying to set Lenny up? It won't work. He'll get out of this."

"What?" I whispered, shaking my head, too confused to react appropriately.

"Who delivered these?" she repeated.

"Nobody. They're mine," I said.

She whipped her head back toward me before turning to my paintings again.

"What do you mean, 'I fucked up the business?'" I asked, but Micaela ignored me completely. I knew I had missed something yet again. I grabbed for my phone and opened it. "What the . . . ?" I whispered in disbelief.

I had more than fifty new missed calls from numbers I didn't know and a dozen more from contacts stored in my phone, plus a full voicemail box. I skimmed my texts and found that most linked to an Instagram post by Jules. I clicked through to see the picture of us just before the Down the Rabbit Hole party in Hong Kong, which she'd posted at the time, but the caption was new.

One of the hardest lessons to learn in life is that people are not always what they seem. Many wolves wear sheep's clothing. All of you have come to know Emma Caan as my new bestie. We were attached at the hip. I never wanted anything from Emma except friendship, and I never imagined she wanted anything else from me but the same. I recently attended an auction with her, and let's just say I discovered she is not a person I should be friends with. Link in bio for the full story of what I learned and how friends can break your heart way worse than lovers can. Xx, JustJules

"Wow," I whispered, looking down at the marble island, tracing my finger over the gray swirl in the stone.

"Are you just seeing this shit for the first time?" Micaela asked, walking over to me.

I nodded. "What does the article say?" I asked her, not wanting to—not even sure I'd be able to—read it myself.

Micaela's eyes softened slightly. "Apparently, she noticed an inconsistency in the painting sold at auction and the photographs of it. *You* added a little something extra. A hill or something."

"A shrub," I corrected her. "An extra shrub."

"Why?" Micaela asked.

"I don't know," I told her. It was the truth.

"Right," she said, but she meant that she didn't believe me. "Well, the FBI has Lenny in custody now . . . and I'm now out of a job," she added.

Though I knew he probably deserved to be punished for swindling people, I felt only sorry to hear the news. I felt bad that Micaela was out of work. I worried that my mother's nest egg would need to be relinquished, that I would still be somehow liable for fraud or perhaps obstruction for telling Lenny about my encounter with the FBI. But most of all, I was sad for Lenny—and despite the fact that he had used me, I wanted him to be okay.

"I'm going to get going," Micaela said. "You'll need to move out," she added carefully, as if that hadn't been clear. "You're going to be okay." She touched my shoulder, not quite gently, even though I thought she was trying for that.

After she showed herself out, I stared at my phone, not knowing if I should read Jules's article, and it glowed with an incoming call. *Leah.* I contemplated ignoring it, but I thought she might be able to summarize the article so I didn't have to.

I picked up to a barrage of questions, first about how I was and then about what happened.

"It's pretty wild that somebody on Instagram had enough influence to sway an active FBI investigation. They had to arrest him after Jules's story went viral," Leah said after I assured her I was okay.

"I haven't read anything except Jules's Instagram post," I told her.

"Don't!" she commanded. "I can give you the CliffsNotes if it's helpful."

"So helpful."

She started in on the headlines coming through. "Over five hundred million dollars of forged art . . . Spurring questions about the legality of freeport secrecy policies . . . Case cracked by Instagram influencer @JustJules . . . Gemini's Jeremy Jacobsen dutifully allowed the FBI to monitor Leonard Sobetsky from the Gemini offices, where he commissioned many of his forgeries."

I knew Jeremy would never want Gemini mentioned in the same sentence as "forgeries," but this was probably the best way to have it done. At least Gemini would be legally insulated, though it was doubtful they'd weather the PR battle.

"Also, I broke my one-hour rule for this, and I've been on Instagram.

Jules has seven million followers now," Leah said, then she paused. "You have almost two."

"Million?" I asked.

"Yep. So, that's good. You can, like, do that as a career," Leah said. Whatever wavelength we were speaking over seemed to tighten, and I braced myself for what she was about to say. "Look, um . . ." she hesitated. "Florence heard about the post and . . . well . . . she thinks it best if you don't come into the gallery anymore." Though she couldn't see me, I nodded slowly, understanding that I was officially out of work, with no prospects for employment, no health insurance, a potential obstruction charge lingering over me, and no place to call home.

I finally convinced Leah I would be okay, and we hung up. For a few moments after the line went dead, I just stood there, almost convinced I was okay. Then suddenly, I knew with certainty I would not be. My hands shook violently, and my lungs seemed to expand in my chest, desperate for air as though there were none in the room. The lights over this city streamed out in small wavy ribbons as the outline of the world went fuzzy. I grabbed my phone.

"Hi," I said. It had been so long since I'd asked somebody for help—so long since I'd trusted somebody enough to come when I needed them. "Can you come over?"

Sienna stayed with me for three nights, sleeping in my bed with me, gently taking my hand when I screamed in my sleep. I had never had another human being in my presence long enough to see the extent of my anxiety, night terror, and pyrophobia. She didn't make me feel bad that I sweated through the sheets every night, and she read out on the balcony for hours while I painted. She was mostly quiet but listened when I had anything to share, and I found that having another living being in the large, open studio space slowed my heart rate when the memories became too much.

When I finished the painting of *her* on the ground, flames nipping at her flesh, I dropped my brush and turned to Sienna. "I have to go back home and set some things straight," I said, releasing my brain from the memory. "And I have to tell my mom she's on her own."

Despite Sienna's diplomatically worded suggestion that the stress of being with my mother might not be the best thing at that time, I knew I had to speak to her in person about my past, my father, her finances, and our future. I packed my new clothes, took my suitcase in my hand, and looked back at the apartment I had never really moved into.

"You're leaving your paintings?" Sienna asked.

"What am I supposed to do with them? I see them all the time in my mind anyway. Whoever is showing the apartment to buyers will toss them, I'm sure. They were just therapy. There will be a lot more of them," I promised her.

At the Ardmore house, my mother listened as I explained the forgery scheme I had gotten tied up in. When I told her we needed to alert the buyer of the Chagall that it had been double-sold to a couple in Denmark, and warned her we might need to return the money from the sale, I braced myself for a meltdown, but instead she nodded sadly and took my hand.

"I don't know how I could have been so stupid," I admitted.

"I know what it's like to want to believe in something because it feels good to, despite all the signs that it's too good to be true."

I knew she was talking about my father, though I failed to see the parallel. In all my memories of my parents together, they were either shouting and tense, or the atmosphere was still and heavy. My mother had known about my father's affair. I couldn't see how it had felt good to continue living with him.

I noticed her studying my expression. "My marriage to your father was complicated," she continued. "I loved your father and he loved me. He wasn't perfect. He drank too much and smoked too much and used to take the money he earned for us and risk it all on bets in an attempt to make more. And he had other . . . indiscretions. But he loved me."

I thought for a moment and opened my mouth to tell her that he didn't love us—that we deserved better than all of that—but she spoke again before I could.

"Or at least that's what I choose to tell myself." She peeled herself out of her chair without another word and made her way to the kitchen, where I heard the water run and the stove click on as she prepared herself a cup of tea. I sat alone in the den, running my finger over the plush cream-colored arm of the chair, and understood then that my mother knew the truth but chose the delusion. I couldn't stop her from it, but I couldn't do the same any longer myself.

The next morning, I opened my eyes and looked around my childhood bedroom for the first time in almost a decade. My T-shirt was soaked through with sweat and my throat was dry. I took my glass of water off the nightstand and sipped, the water stinging on its way down. I closed my eyes, wanting desperately to back out of the arrangements I had made for the day, but forcing myself into the shower and then driving my mother's old car to the coffee shop in town.

"What can I get you?" asked the young barista behind the marble counter. I'd been too focused on biting my nail off to realize it was my turn to order.

"Just a water for now," I said. "Actually—a tea. Or should I wait?" I shifted my weight uncomfortably.

"First date?" she asked with a smile.

"I wish," I told her. "Just a glass of water for now, please." For what felt like the millionth time, I scanned the interior of Coffee Bar, one of the trendy artisanal cafés that had sprouted up in Ardmore since I'd left for college.

I sat at one of the small marble-topped circular tables and saw her open the door out of the corner of my eye. As she approached, I heard my heart beating in small thuds as I asked myself what good the meeting would do, whether it was necessary, whether it would do anything to ease the guilt that plagued my dreams. When she got to me, I took a long sip of water before looking up and making eye contact.

"Thank you for coming," I said, trying to look at her without focusing on the burn running up the side of her neck as she sat opposite me.

"I'm glad you asked," she said, clearing her throat and looking just as nervous as I was.

We both ordered tea instead of coffee, which provided two minutes of empty conversation about how we were each trying without much luck to cut back on caffeine after our first morning cup. I wondered if I had the nerve to say what I'd planned to, but then she wrapped her reddened and scarred fingers around her paper cup and raised it to her lips to blow on her tea. A cloud of steam drifted from the top of the cup toward me in the air-conditioned restaurant, and all I could see was her writhing on the ground to try to stop the flames from swallowing her whole.

"I asked you here so I could apologize," I started, which felt completely insufficient.

She put down her cup without taking a sip and looked at me. "I think we both have some apologizing to do," she said softly.

"I set that fire," I said through tears, as the thing I had never said out loud, the thing I had tried to bury impossibly deep, finally surfaced. "I'm so sorry. I'm sorry I burned you. And hurt you. I didn't mean to. I just wanted to stop you guys from . . ."

She reached across the table and took my hand to stop me, tears welling in her eyes. She said nothing, only nodded to accept my apology, and I exhaled a shaky breath. I looked down at my hand in hers, and I cried harder to see her red and wrinkled skin against mine.

"You were just a child," she said, holding my gaze until I had to look away. "You saw your father with another woman, and you wanted to stop it."

She was right, but it was no excuse.

She let go of my hand and leaned back. "For what it's worth, I tried to stop seeing him. To send him back to his family. To you. But . . . I loved him," she said, a deep sadness in her eyes. I stared at her, wondering how my cheating, gambling, drinking father had managed to make two women so attached to him and tacitly agree to share him. Part of me had always assumed she was in it for the money—a young woman who wanted to live a certain lifestyle—but I cringed at my own projection. She'd really loved him.

We sat and talked about my father, the graduate school my father put her through, her work as a history teacher, and my art, until our second cups of tea had grown tepid. She left before I did, and I sat, small tears escaping from the corners of my eyes. I had thought the process of catharsis would be more pleasurable than painful, but it hurt. A lot. I inhaled deeply, digesting the pain, preparing to return home to my mother, and paused. I felt it then, the extra space left in my chest for a deep breath after our conversation. As I exhaled, I realized, for the first time in as long as I could remember, that I was okay. I had faked being okay with distance and sarcasm, coffee to perk me up in the morning and pills to put me to sleep, Instagram, texting. Noise. I didn't reach in my bag to check my phone before I stood and left the coffee shop, knowing that regardless of how the trial turned out, I would keep painting, and I would be fine. Really fine.

Three months later, my mother and I had settled into a routine. We power walked three miles each morning and came home for coffee together. I'd head into the garage to paint while my mother busied herself cleaning out the house, meeting with Realtors, and preparing for the sale. We never mentioned Lenny's name until after dinner, when we watched *Jeopardy!*, followed by the news, and sometimes shared a bottle of wine. All commentary around the trial indicated that Lenny would be going to jail, as would Sergey, but I still envisioned a world where Lenny slipped out of the country on a private plane. On some nights when I missed him so much it kept me awake, I almost wished for that freedom for him.

Lenny's was one of the most highly publicized art forgery cases in recent history, primarily because he had sold forgeries to some very important people who were not keen on being publicly embarrassed, and while my name constantly popped up in the media coverage of the trial, it didn't bother me. I felt like I was watching the trial of some stranger, hearing somebody else's name mentioned as his "primary forger." Every so often, I found myself curbing the smile on my lips when I'd see experts poring over my forgeries, trying to determine whether they were originals. The FBI had asked me to cooperate fully in exchange for immunity from any obstruction charge resulting from tipping Lenny off or withholding information, so I had already identified all my forgeries on the record. Still, experts needed to corroborate everything I said. I wasn't to be trusted, which was strange to think, because I was sitting on a beige Pottery Barn sofa in Ardmore, Pennsylvania, drinking pinot grigio with my mother. I wasn't an international impressionist forger. Not anymore, at least.

Sienna had visited for a day the prior weekend, if only to assure me in person that Gemini was doing fine: "You didn't ruin anybody's life!" In fact, she was busier than ever; the company was busier than ever. "I guess what they say is true, all press really is good press!" she had said, laughing, as my mother poured her more tea on our front porch. Sienna and I went to the farmers' market without my mother for a late lunch. She was taking a break from dating, and I wouldn't have known how to date then if I'd wanted to, which I didn't, so we happily found ourselves speaking about art: the Basel Miami sale that broke records for a decomposing horse carcass, the gallery owner who churned out mediocre lithographs but understood marketing, supply, and demand so well that they were selling for $2 million a pop.

I wasn't jealous of these people any longer; I was content to paint and not sell. Sienna and I laughed and joked about the absurd and nonsensical world we worked in with an appreciation behind our eye rolls. When we finished lunch, I hugged Sienna close and breathed a sigh of relief that my mistakes hadn't had consequences for her. I stood on the platform and waved as her train pulled out of the station, the pang of missing her already in my chest.

This was my home now—my home again. I couldn't afford to live in the city even if I wanted to; nobody was hiring the girl associated with the Leonard Sobetsky scandal. My daily routine was the quiet suburban life with my mother that I had spent the past decade getting as far away from as possible. Shockingly, I was enjoying it.

On Sunday, my mother and I were returning from our morning power walk when she stopped to fix the "For Sale" sign on our property that had been made crooked by the wind, and I spotted a silver Mercedes SUV with tinted windows in the driveway. My stomach knotted up immediately. Fearful it was the FBI or worse, I couldn't decide whether we should keep walking at our quick clip past the house.

"Whom do we have here?" my mother asked me curiously, turning toward the driveway as though it were a pleasant surprise.

"Stop! Stay here," I commanded her at the base of the long driveway. There was a slight ringing in my ears. *I'm safe. Lenny is in custody. The FBI has assured me they're watching Sergey.* Still, my lunch lurched up into my throat as the driver's side door opened.

I saw a woman's tan loafer first, and then Florence emerged from the car wearing light jeans, a pale yellow sweater, and not a stitch of makeup, her pixie cut grown out enough to be tucked behind her ears.

"Hi!" I said, holding my chest as I bent over slightly in relief. "What are you doing here?"

"I was hoping we could talk," she said.

"Of course," I said. "Do you want to come inside?"

"It's beautiful out, do you want to take a walk?"

I nodded. "Actually, there's a trail just past our yard." I told my mother we'd be back in a bit.

As Florence and I approached the path, I rubbed nervously at my forearm. She walked quietly beside me, saying nothing for a few minutes.

"I'm so glad you're here, because I want to apologize," I said, mostly because I couldn't take the silence any longer. "You took a chance on me when you hired me, and I totally squandered it. I'm sure the gallery's name has come up in articles alongside my name, and I am truly sorry for any trouble that has caused you and any negative effect it's had on the business. I'm sorry," I repeated.

"Thank you for that," she said, meeting my eyes.

I wondered if there would ever be a day I could stop apologizing, but it felt better to have the words out.

We went a bit farther, and I told her how the towering pine trees marking the end of our property had been only up to my knees when my parents bought the house. We both shielded our eyes to the sun and stared up to their tops before continuing. I couldn't imagine that Florence had driven two hours just to hear my apology, and so I waited to hear what else she would say.

"So, Emma. I have some good news," she finally said.

"Oh, God, Florence, if you could give me one more chance, I promise I will be the best assistant director—"

"God, no!" She burst out laughing. "You're entangled in an FBI investigation of art forgery, for Christ's sake!"

I stared at her, wide-eyed. I had never heard her laugh that freely before. "Right, of course."

"So, no, I'm not rehiring you," she said, though her tone was kind. "But I'm hoping you will hire me." I forced a smile, not understanding the joke this time. "Micaela dropped off your new paintings for me to look at. She said she was cleaning out Lenny's studio because it was being sold, and you were going to throw them out, but . . . she thought I would want to see them." My jaw slackened as I tried to process. "They're sensational. Your use of color . . . mesmerizing. Your command of pain . . . it's a revelation." I stopped in my tracks. "It would be an honor to sell your work and to help you navigate this process."

"Really, Florence? Are you sure?" I remembered her reaction to my portfolio and didn't understand how she'd seen something so different this time. "And you don't think there's too much of a bad association with Lenny?"

"Oh, no," she said. "I doubt it was her intention, but your *influencer* friend already created quite a buzz around you with that post about the forgeries. I'm told you have millions of followers. It will make my job that much easier. But I wouldn't take you on if I didn't love your work."

"Thank you, Florence. And of course, of course, I'll sign with you," I said, unable to believe the words coming out of my mouth.

"We'll make the girl in the hospital room piece the focal point."

I bit my lower lip. "I used to visit my dad while he was dying. But only while he was sleeping, because I hated him so much that I didn't want him to know I still loved him."

"Life's complicated," she said. "That's why we have art. To help us make sense of it."

I nodded, allowing my gaze to drift up and the nape of my neck to bend back so I could see the tops of the trees lining the yard. I felt overwhelmed. I had been going about it all wrong my entire life. The reason to make art wasn't the recognition or even the therapy of putting my feelings down on the canvas. People had been widely recognized for any number of ridiculous things since the advent of social media, and anybody could pay somebody to help them work out their feelings. The real reason for art—the honor in it—was inspiring a stranger to recognize herself in my paintings and perhaps, if I was doing it right, make her feel a bit less alone.

ACKNOWLEDGMENTS

To my parents, siblings, and extended family, who tell everybody they know—and even some people they don't—to buy my books. None of this could be without you.

To Sujean, who has mastered the subtle art of truly listening in a way I only aspire to. Thank you for forever receiving my ideas and deftly guiding them to elevated spaces.

To Phoebe Mendelow, may you never lose your creativity and passion. I only hope that I can afford your book cover art one day!

To Emily Griffin, for being so darn good at her job and for leading the amazing team at HarperCollins to do theirs so well. You are a master. To Leslie Cohen and Becca Putman, who work tirelessly to get people who would never otherwise see my books to actually purchase them. Thank you.

To Allison Hunter, for expertly steering me through this process (which I continue to know very little about) with incomprehensible honesty, compassion, and grace. Having you in my corner makes it a very cushy place to be and I am so grateful for you here.

To Jason Richman for all you do without ever telling me you're doing it. One day, after this pandemic, I will buy you a drink and thank you to your face.

To my friends, who constantly ask how the writing is going and to read my drafts, I appreciate this more than you know.

To everybody who reached out to say they saw bits of their own lives in *The Boys' Club*—I wrote this for you.

ABOUT THE AUTHOR

ERICA KATZ is the author of *The Boys' Club*. A native of New Jersey and a graduate of the University of Michigan and Columbia Law School, she works at a large law firm in New York City.